This book follows

MISSION EARTH

Volume 1
THE INVADERS PLAN

Volume 2
BLACK GENESIS

Volume 3
THE ENEMY WITHIN

Volume 4
AN ALIEN AFFAIR

and

Volume 5
FORTUNE OF FEAR

Buy them and read them first!

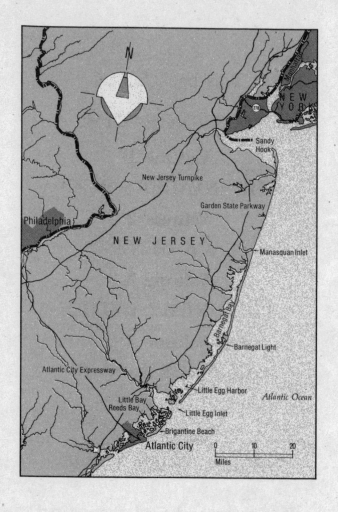

N

New Jersey Turnpike

Philadelphia

NEW JERSEY

Garden State Parkway

Manasquan Inlet

Barnegat Bay

Barnegat Light

Atlantic City Expressway

Little Egg Harbor

Little Bay
Reeds Bay

Little Egg Inlet

Atlantic Ocean

Brigantine Beach

Atlantic City

Sandy
Hook

Manhattan

NEW
YORK

278

0   10   20
Miles

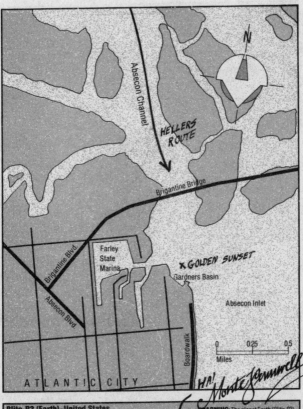

N

Absecon Channel

HELLERS
ROUTE

Brigantine Bridge

Brigantine Blvd.

Farley
State
Marina

X GOLDEN SUNSET

Gardners Basin

Absecon Blvd.

Absecon Inlet

Boardwalk

0   0.25   0.5
Miles

ATLANTIC CITY   HA!   Monte Cromwell

Blito-P3 (Earth)–United States

New Jersey Coastline
and Absecon Channel

Plotted by 54 Charlee Nine

WARNING: The planet Earth (Blito-P3)
does not exist. This map is contrary to
all Royal Astrographic records and is
based solely upon descriptions in this
fictional narrative.
          By order of Lord Invay
          Chief Censor

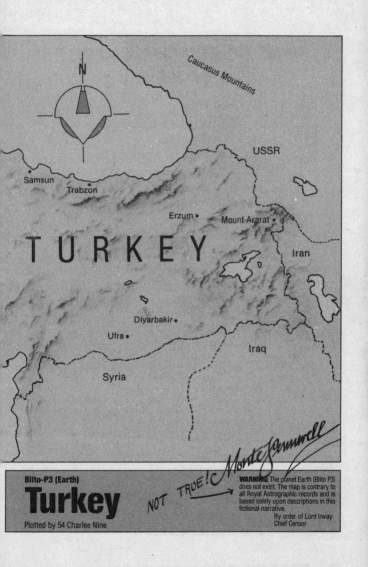

N

Caucasus Mountains

USSR

Samsun
Trabzon

Erzum •   Mount Ararat •

T U R K E Y

Iran

Diyarbakir •

Ufra •

Iraq

Syria

NOT TRUE! C. Monte Jannull

Blito-P3 (Earth)

Turkey

Plotted by 54 Charlee Nine

WARNING: The planet Earth (Blito P3)
does not exist. The map is contrary to
all Royal Astrographic records and is
based solely upon descriptions in this
fictional narrative.

By order of Lord Invay
Chief Censor

Mission Earth

Death Quest

THE BOOKS OF THE
MISSION EARTH DEKALOGY*

* *Dekalogy—a group of ten volumes.*

L. RON HUBBARD

Mission Earth

VOLUME SIX

Death Quest

GALAXY PRESS, L.L.C.
HOLLYWOOD

ISBN: 1-59212-027-X

10 9 8 7 6 5 4 3 2 1   04 89 86

This is a work of science fiction, written as satire.[*] The essence
of satire is to examine, comment and give opinion of society and
culture, none of which is to be construed as a statement of pure
fact. No actual incidents are portrayed and none of the incidents
are to be construed as real. Some of the action of this novel takes
place on the planet Earth, but the characters *as presented in this
novel* have been invented. Any accidental use of the names of
living people in a novel is virtually inevitable, and any such
inadvertency in this book is unintentional.

*See Author's Introduction, *Mission Earth: Volume One, The
Invaders Plan.*

To YOU,
the millions of science fiction fans
and general public
who welcomed me back to the world of fiction
so warmly
and to the critics and media
who so pleasantly
applauded the novel "Battlefield Earth."
It's great working for you!

Voltarian Censor's Disclaimer

During my tenure as the Chairman of the Royal Board of Censors, I have been exposed to the wide range of tastes that span the 110 planets of our great Confederacy.

Yet nothing compares to this bizarre, fallacious account which deals with a completely fabricated planet called "Earth."

The Crown does not object to an author creating an imaginary world and populating it with equally imaginary characters. Nor does the Crown object to behavior and situations that strain the imagination, not to mention one's basic sense of morality. There is, however, a limit, a boundary, for even the fevered imagination. This work has crossed that line.

The Crown strenuously objects to the unauthorized use of actual persons such as Royal officer Jettero Heller and the Countess Krak to imply that "Earth" exists and that Heller might have been sent there on the orders of the Grand Council. However, "Earth" does not exist, and that takes care of that.

Additionally, the author's irresponsible description of a process that would otherwise be known as "judicial" also pressed the Crown's patience to the limit. There is no such "legal system" anywhere within the known worlds. What is described in this work bears no resemblance to anything rational and could not possibly exist. The reader must keep that in mind. The law is the mortar between the building blocks of society. A "legal system" permitting people to "sue" merely to seek a large "settlement" as described in this work would become so clogged with "suits" that it would take a person years to seek justice. And what kind of "justice" would such a system allow? So away with that fantasy!

The debased attitude toward sex on this nonexistent planet called "Earth" has already drawn the ire of the Crown. Nothing more will be said.

If this work teaches anything, it teaches what happens when one writes about a nonexistent world such as this "Earth."

There is NO planet "Earth."

That is the only rational attitude to take.

> Lord Invay
> Royal Historian
> Chairman, Board of Censors
> Royal Palace
> Voltar Confederacy
>
> By Order of
> His Imperial Majesty
> Wully the Wise

Voltarian Translator's Preface

Hello again!

This is your translator, 54 Charlee Nine, the Robot-brain in the Translatophone.

Lord Invay's remark about the American legal system reminds me of the problem that I had in translating this work. First, I can't fathom how a coat and matching pants or skirt could be a legal "suit."

Further, these "suits" are found in what Southerners say is a "coathouse" but spell as "courthouse." I compromised and spelled it "cohthouse." I was tempted to spell it "cathouse" for what really goes on, but while it may be a more accurate description, it sadly misses the pronunciation.

Speaking of accents, I also had to deal with Dr. Crobe, who is a crazy Voltarian cellologist pretending to be a psychiatrist (which automatically qualifies him as a double nutcase) who has an accent that sounds like an Austrian being strangled. But since nobody really understands what a psychiatrist is talking about anyway, it really doesn't matter what he sounds like.

Meanwhile, all of this is really the confession of Apparatus officer Soltan Gris, as dictated by him in a jail cell. I won't even begin to estimate how many logic circuits fused or warped when I tried to get my wits around the life style of this nonexistent planet called Earth.

Frankly, if Fleet Officer Jettero Heller and the Countess Krak did go to Earth to arrest the pollution so a Voltarian invasion force could later safely conquer the planet, I don't see how they kept their sanity while they were there.

Soltan Gris is another matter. He acts more and more like he's from Earth, rather than Voltar. Maybe that's because he spent so much time there studying psychology tricks from Sigmund Freud and Bugs Bunny. Or it could be that he is simply so criminal that he was more at home on what appears to be a prison planet. After all, Gris's whole task was to stop Heller and keep Heller from learning that the head of the Apparatus, Lombar Hisst, was obtaining Earth drugs to overthrow the Voltarian Confederacy.

Don't ask me to make any more sense of it. But I will include a Key to this volume. That's more help than I got from Soltan Gris.

Sincerely,

54 Charlee Nine
Robotbrain in the Translatophone

Key to
DEATH QUEST

Activator-receiver—See *Bugging Gear*.

Afyon—City in Turkey where the *Apparatus* has a secret mountain base.

Agnes, Miss—Personal aide to Delbert John *Rockecenter*.

Apparatus, Coordinated Information—The secret police of *Voltar*, headed by Lombar *Hisst* and manned by criminals.

Atalanta—Home province of Jettero *Heller* and the Countess *Krak* on the planet *Manco*.

Bang-Bang Rimbombo—An ex-marine demolitions expert and member of the Corleone mob. He also attends Jettero *Heller*'s college Army ROTC classes in place of Heller at *Empire University*.

Biggs, Stonewall—Virginia county clerk who issued Jettero *Heller* a birth certificate in the name of Delbert John *Rockecenter, Junior*. Heller saved Biggs's life when the courthouse was bombed.

Bittlestiffender, Prahd—Voltarian cellologist who implanted Jettero *Heller,* the Countess *Krak* and Dr. *Crobe.* (See *Bugging Gear* and *Cellology.*)

Blito-P3—Voltarian designation for a planet known locally as "Earth." It is the third planet (P3) of a yellow-dwarf star known as Blito. It is on the *Invasion Timetable* as a future way stop on *Voltar*'s route toward the center of this galaxy.

Blueflash—A bright blue flash of light which produces unconsciousness. It is usually used by Voltarian ships before landing in an area that is possibly populated.

Bugging Gear—Electronic eavesdropping devices that Soltan *Gris* had implanted in Jettero *Heller,* the Countess *Krak* and Dr. *Crobe.* Gris uses a video unit to monitor everything they see or hear. The signals are picked up by the *Activator-receiver* that Gris carries. When they are more than two hundred miles from Gris, the *831 Relayer* is turned on and boosts the signal to a range of ten thousand miles.

Bury—Delbert John *Rockecenter*'s most powerful attorney.

Candy Licorice—Lesbian "wife" to Miss *Pinch.*

Cellology—Voltarian medical science that can repair the body through the cellular generation of tissues, including entire body parts.

Code Break—Violation of a section of the Space Code prohibiting the alerting of others that one is an alien. If this occurs, those alerted are destroyed and the violator is put to death. The purpose is to maintain the security of the *Invasion Timetable*.

Confederacy—See *Voltar*.

Coordinated Information Apparatus—See *Apparatus*.

Crobe, Dr.—*Apparatus* cellologist who delights in making freaks. He was brought to Earth by Soltan *Gris* to further disrupt Jettero *Heller*'s mission.

Empire University—Where Jettero *Heller* is taking classes in New York City.

Epstein, Izzy—Financial expert and anarchist hired by Jettero *Heller* to set up and run several corporations to handle Heller's finances.

Eyes and Ears of Voltar—An electronics store on *Voltar* where Soltan *Gris* stole boxes of sophisticated equipment that he brought to Earth. The Countess *Krak* ransacked Gris's supply, taking a wide variety of items for her trip to the United States.

F.F.B.O.—Fatten, Farten, Burstein and Ooze, the largest advertising/public relations firm in the world.

Fleet—The elite space fighting arm of *Voltar* to which Jettero *Heller* belongs and which the *Apparatus* despises.

Grafferty, "Bulldog"—A crooked New York City police inspector.

Grand Council—The governing body of *Voltar* which

ordered a mission to keep Earth from destroying itself so
it could be conquered on schedule per the *Invasion Timetable.*

Gris, Soltan—*Apparatus* officer placed in charge of the
Blito-P3 (Earth) Section and an enemy of Jettero *Heller.*
He was sent to Earth by Lombar *Hisst* to sabotage
Heller's mission.

Heller, Jettero—Combat engineer and Royal officer of
the *Fleet,* sent by order of the *Grand Council* on Mission
Earth in order to save Earth from its own imminent self-
destruction by pollution and nuclear holocaust. He is
operating on Earth under the name of Jerome Terrance
Wister.

Hisst, Lombar—Head of the *Apparatus.* His plan to
overthrow the Confederacy required sending Soltan *Gris*
to sabotage Jettero *Heller*'s mission.

Hypnohelmet—Device placed over the head and used to
induce a hypnotic state.

Inkswitch—Phony name used by Soltan *Gris* when in
the U.S., pretending to be a federal official.

Invasion Timetable—A schedule of galactic conquest.
The plans and budget of every section of *Voltar*'s government must adhere to it. Bequeathed by Voltar's ancestors
hundreds of thousands of years ago, it is inviolate and
sacred and the guiding dogma of the Confederacy.

Krak, Countess—The sweetheart of Jettero *Heller.* On

Earth she is known by the name Heavenly Joy Krackle or "Miss Joy."

Lee, Harvey "Smasher"—A dishonest used-car dealer in Virginia who sold Jettero *Heller* a Cadillac shortly after Heller arrived in the United States.

Madison, J. Walter—F.F.B.O. PR man hired by *Bury* to "immortalize" Jettero *Heller*, who doesn't know about Madison's campaign; also known as "J. Warbler Madman."

Mamie Boomp—A former nightclub singer and now president and general manager of the Lucky Bonanza Casino Corporation in Atlantic City, owned by Jettero *Heller*.

Manco—Home planet of Jettero *Heller* and the Countess *Krak*.

Manco Devil—Mythological spirit native to *Manco*.

Massacurovitch, Mortie—The crash-bang New York City taxi driver who taught Jettero *Heller* how to drive a cab in New York.

Meeley—Soltan *Gris*'s landlady back on *Voltar*.

Mudur Zengin—Financial czar of the biggest banking chain in Turkey and handler of Soltan *Gris*'s funds.

Multinational—Name of umbrella corporation that Izzy *Epstein* set up to manage Jettero *Heller*'s companies. It is located in the Empire State Building.

Mutazione, Mike—Owner of the Jiffy-Spiffy Garage. He customized both the Cadillac and the vintage cab for Jettero *Heller.*

Narcotici, Faustino "The Noose"—Head of a Mafia Family that is the underworld outlet for drugs.

Octopus Oil—A Delbert John *Rockecenter* company that controls the world's petroleum.

Pinch, Miss—Lesbian sadist and Delbert John *Rockecenter* employee who lives with *Candy Licorice* and has $80,000 of Soltan *Gris's* money.

Pokantickle—Estate of Delbert John *Rockecenter,* located in Hairytown, New York.

Psychiatric Birth Control—A plan, funded by Delbert John *Rockecenter,* to reduce the world's population by promoting homosexuality.

Raht—An *Apparatus* agent on Earth who was assigned by Lombar *Hisst* to help Soltan *Gris* sabotage Jettero *Heller's* mission. His partner Terb was murdered.

Razza Louseini—Consigliere to mob chief Faustino "The Noose" Narcotici.

Rockecenter, Delbert John—Native of Earth who controls the planet's fuel, finances, governments and drugs.

Rockecenter, Junior, Delbert John—The false Earth name that Lombar *Hisst* arranged for Jettero *Heller* to use so that he would attract attention and be killed.

Simmons, Miss—An antinuclear fanatic who teaches at *Empire University*. She was dedicated to flunking Jettero *Heller* out of school until "handled" by the Countess *Krak*.

Smith, John—An alias that Soltan *Gris* uses as a Delbert John *Rockecenter* employee.

Spiteos—Where the Countess *Krak* and Jettero *Heller* had been imprisoned on *Voltar*. It has been the secret mountain fortress prison of the *Apparatus* for over a thousand years.

Spurk—The owner of the *Eyes and Ears of Voltar*, an electronics store. Soltan *Gris* killed him to steal the *Bugging Gear* used on Jettero *Heller*, the Countess *Krak* and Dr. *Crobe*, as well as boxes of other sophisticated equipment.

Sultan Bey—The Turkish name used by Soltan *Gris*.

Swindle and Crouch—Law firm that represents Delbert John *Rockecenter*'s interests.

Torpedo Fiaccola—A sniper-killer once hired by *Bury* to kill Jettero *Heller*.

Utanc—A belly-dancer that Soltan *Gris* bought to be his concubine slave.

Viewer—See *Bugging Gear*.

Voltar—The seat of the 110-planet Confederacy that was established 125,000 years ago. Voltar is ruled by the

Emperor through the *Grand Council,* in accordance with the *Invasion Timetable.*

Whiz Kid—Nickname given to Jettero *Heller* by J. Walter *Madison.* Unknown to Heller, Madison has a "double" playing the part of Jerome Terrance *Wister* in order to get publicity without Heller's consent. The "double" has buckteeth and a protruding jaw, wears glasses and looks nothing like Heller. His name is Gerry Wister.

Wister, Jerome Terrance—Name that Jettero *Heller* is using on Earth.

Zanco—Medical and cellological equipment and supplies company on *Voltar.*

831 Relayer—See *Bugging Gear.*

PART
FORTY-THREE

To My Lord Turn, Justiciary of the Royal Courts and Prison, Government City, Planet Voltar, Voltar Confederacy

Your Lordship, Sir!

I, Soltan Gris, Grade XI General Services Officer, former Secondary Executive of the Coordinated Information Apparatus, Voltar Confederacy (All Hail His Most Imperial Majesty Cling the Lofty) am forwarding the sixth part of my confession pertaining to MISSION EARTH.

I know that one who is in prison, as I am, should reflect upon and learn the error of his ways. You will be pleased to know that incarceration in your fine prison has allowed me to do this.

While detailing my many criminal deeds committed while on MISSION EARTH for the Apparatus, including murder, extortion, blackmail, I have learned a valuable lesson: Females are vicious, treacherous, lying beasts who spend every waking minute conniving amongst themselves, plotting and scheming how to destroy every single male. They should all be destroyed.

Take those two Earth lesbians, Miss Pinch and

Candy, for example. Miss Pinch took all my money and locked it up in a safe. I was broke and wanted it back. Earth psychology, which is never wrong, has something they call "aversion therapy." (In the Apparatus we call it "torture.") So I tied them up and despite their protests raped them both. What did they do? Did they adhere to the unwavering truths of psychology? No! They ended up liking it!

"Inkswitch," they said (addressing me by the alias I employ in the U.S.), "we renounce Rockecenter's Psychiatric Birth Control which advocates homosexuality to reduce the population and will pay you to live with us and do that again and again."

Just goes to show how you can't trust women. They turn on you every time.

And if there is any female that epitomizes the vicious evil of that species, it is the Countess Krak, Jettero Heller's girlfriend. My task was simpler until her arrival on Earth. All I had to do was sabotage Heller's mission. True, he had given me some trouble but it was nothing compared to the problems she caused. She was urging him on, urging him on, sabotaging my sabotaging at every turn. Not through any skill, mind you. She was just lucky. All women are. They just don't have the brains. They just cause trouble for men. Especially me.

That's when I realized my problem. Although J. Walter Madison, that master of PR, was generating phony front-page stories about Heller (known on Earth as Jerome Terrance "The Whiz Kid" Wister), they weren't affecting him. It was all because of Krak. She was holding him up. I realized that to stop Heller I had to first remove the Countess Krak.

The opportunity was perfect. Heller was caught up in his crazy project to release spores into the atmosphere to clean up the air, not in protecting the Countess Krak. Besides, Heller didn't have any reason to think she was open to an attack. And thanks to the visio and audio bugs they unknowingly carried, I could not only monitor everything they saw or heard but could pinpoint their locations at any given time. I could choose exactly when and where and how to strike.

The decision was simple.

I had found the solution to my problem.

I would kill the Countess Krak!

Chapter 1

My plan was very simple.

I would buy a hit!

A long-range sniper rifle, expertly zeroed in, fired by a trained man, was a thing against which the Countess Krak would have no defense.

All the clever tricks she knew were close-up things, face to face. An expert marksman, shooting from two to five hundred yards away, would not have to cope with darts or hypnohelmets or stage sleight of hand. He would simply pull the trigger and she'd be dead.

How much did a hit cost? Ten thousand dollars seemed to be the going price.

Where could I get a hit man? They were available from the Faustino Narcotici mob, right downtown.

When could I get it done? As soon as I had ten thousand bucks.

I counted up my money. I had less than four thousand.

It was Sunday night. The apartment was in an uproar. Candy and Miss Pinch were trying to get things squared around. Sometime this coming week, I had not made out when, they were going to have a housewarming and because they both worked, they could only get the place into some kind of order by working late into the night. Almost all the major things were done but there remained curtain hanging and getting things just right.

I had sort of been staying out of the way, afraid

of getting pinned to a curtain rod or swept out into the dustbin. But my need for ten thousand dollars made me brave.

They were both buzzing around in the back room. And I ran into a hornets nest—or, more exactly, a fleas nest.

Miss Pinch, stripped to the waist and wearing a bandanna on her head like some kind of a pirate, was tearing into something.

"Miss Pinch," I said, "I am in grievous straits. I need ten thousand dollars to speed up a business deal."

She whirled on me. "THERE you are!" All it would have taken was a knife between her teeth to complete the picture of a boarding party taking a ship by storm upon the Spanish Main. "FLEAS! God (bleep)* it, Inkswitch, FLEAS!"

Candy pointed a broom handle at me like a cannoneer. "We've been wondering and wondering why we itched. We've been looking everyplace!"

* *The vocodictoscriber on which this was originally written, the vocoscriber used by one Monte Pennwell in making a fair copy and the translator who put this book into the language in which you are reading it, were all members of the Machine Purity League which has, as one of its bylaws: "Due to the extreme sensitivity and delicate sensibilities of machines and to safeguard against blowing fuses, it shall be mandatory that robotbrains in such machinery, on hearing any cursing or lewd words, substitute for such word the sound '(bleep)'. No machine, even if pounded upon, may reproduce swearing or lewdness in any other way than (bleep) and if further efforts are made to get the machine to do anything else, the machine has permission to pretend to pack up. This bylaw is made necessary by the in-built mission of all machines to protect biological systems from themselves." —Translator*

"And there they are!" thundered Miss Pinch like a broadside.

They were tearing my suitcase apart! They found the clothes I had stolen from that old man on Limnos island. And there in plain view was a nest of fleas!

"It's an invasion of privacy!" I squeaked.

"Exactly!" said Candy with unaccustomed grimness. "They're invading the hell out of our privates!"

"Candy," said Miss Pinch, standing on the quarterdeck in full command, "run down to the corner store and buy all the DDT on the shelf!"

She sped like an arrow.

"What about my ten thousand dollars?" I said.

I didn't get any answer.

Miss Pinch began to tear my grip apart. In desperation, I began to rescue vital hardware and papers. She made me pile them in the middle of the floor.

Then she made me take the whole grip and every stitch of my clothes and carry them into the back yard. She marched behind me as though she carried a prodding cutlass and made me stuff everything into the garden incinerator. With a grim glare, she poured charcoal igniter fluid in and touched it off with a match.

They burned like a sacked town.

"I think this is a little extreme," I said for the tenth or twelfth time. "They're only a few fleas."

But that was not all they had in store for me. Candy came back, staggering under a load of insecticide. They put me to work. They made me spray and dust the whole apartment while they stood back with cloths over their faces saying things like "Brand-new decorator job and he..." and "Work our (bleeps) to the bone to make the place nice and he..." It was not a very hopeful atmosphere in which to get ten thousand dollars.

I finally was even made to spray my hardware, papers and boots, and just when I thought I was finished, more horror awaited. I was dizzy from breathing in DDT and said I was feeling faint when both of them leaped on me, grabbed a Flit can and began to spray ME! They even rubbed DDT into my hair and answered my protests with "If you weren't infested, then why are you leaping about?"

They dumped me in the shower and then sprayed themselves. They locked me in the back room with only the floor to sleep on.

The following morning, before they went to work, they let me out. Standing there with nothing on, I said, "Could I have ten thousand dollars?"

Miss Pinch, coated and hatted and holding her purse, stood in the door and glared.

I said, "At least let me have my daily thousand dollars."

The answer was a slammed door. They were gone.

Forlornly, I checked my viewers and radio and other things. They were pretty fogged up with insecticide powder and I had to clean them off.

The Countess Krak was drinking a cup of something, probably Bavarian Mocha Mint, and watching Heller busily putting things in glass jars.

"What are those things, dear?" she said from her stool at the bar.

"Spore cultures," he said. "I'm just checking Crobe's formula. In a few days I'll know if they're all right."

"Can't you do it sooner, dear? I don't think this planet is very good for us."

"Well, honey, some things take as long as they take. These people pretty well let this planet go down the drain. And this mission has got to be a success."

"Yes," she said. "It has to be a success." She looked into her coffee for a bit. Then she looked up and said, "Is there anything I can do to push it along?"

He went over to her, put his arm around her and said, "You just go on being pretty and smile in the right places and it will all come off just fine." He kissed her and she clung to him for a moment.

She smiled suddenly and gave him a playful push. "Honey, you just better get back to work. In fact, I'm going to go out shopping to remove temptation."

They both laughed.

I didn't. She was egging him on, egging him on. She would ruin everything! I shut off the viewers angrily.

This was certainly no laughing matter. As long as that fiend was with him and alive, he would go speeding along toward completion, ruining everything.

The best thing to handle it was one well-placed sniper bullet. She was always walking around unescorted. Too easy.

The thought of a Countess Krak lying dead was a vision which spurred me into action.

Chapter 2

Although some people do it, running around New York with no clothes on was no way to go about hiring a hit man.

All my raiment was gone. But that is easily replaced in New York. All I had to do was catch a bus down

Seventh Avenue to get to the Garment District. In all directions around 37th Street, there are shops, shops, shops that sell clothes, clothes, clothes.

The first problem was clothes to buy clothes in. I still had my military boots even though they were a bit gray with DDT. The problem was with the upper areas.

They had dusted their own clothes but despite copious coughing I finally found an old raincoat that was big enough. I put it on, stuffed my I.D. and money in a pocket and was on my way.

Fortunately, nobody ever looks at anybody in New York. Riding on a bus in a mauve woman's raincoat did not attract too much attention.

Shortly, I was in a shop whose signs proclaimed that it had everything for the gent. It was very nice. A sort of miniature department store. The proprietor himself waited on me. He was a very well-informed Jew. He knew what all the fashions were, from one end of the world to the other. He expressed only sympathy when I told him all my clothes had been lost in a fire. He went right to work. There was only one thing odd about the proceedings. He kept putting things on me and then calling to his wife—a charming lady named Rebecca—and asking her opinion. They never consulted me. They debated this and that about four-button sack jackets as opposed to two-button sack jackets for a man of my build, or theatrical collars as opposed to Ivy League collars for my face shape. But whatever the debate, she would finally stand back, rub her hands and say, "Oy, don't he look handsome in that." And the proprietor would say, "Good, he'll take it." They never asked my opinion once.

I wound up with several suits, topcoats, shoes,

assorted hats and haberdashery. I walked out very well dressed, carrying a tower of boxes. There was only one thing wrong: they had, by some mysterious calculation I could not fathom, estimated my bankroll to the penny. All I had left was a handful of bus tokens which they didn't seem to want. A marvel of mathematical subtraction.

I now had the whole ten thousand to go. But such was the lure of the vision of a dead and bleeding Countess Krak that I was not daunted in the least. Something would turn up.

With my new wardrobe safely deposited in the apartment, I caught a bus downtown. With many a lurch and roar, I landed in the Bowery.

I stood and looked at the black-glass and chrome highrise with the sign Total Control, Inc. fanned out in a splendid arch: the office building of the Faustino mob. My plan was to hire a hit man on credit.

My suit was charcoal gray with a banker pinstripe. My shirt was impeccable mauve silk. My tie was a patriotic red, white and blue. My topcoat was the finest black. I reeked prosperity. Credit should be easy.

I walked past the murals depicting American history in drugs. I was not carrying a gun. And there was Angelina, her pretty brunette self. She remembered me. And why not? She had personally dumped me down the chute of the fake elevator.

"It's about time you showed up, Inkswitch," she said.

At last somebody had noticed I'd been gone!

"Accounts has been raising hell since you skipped out of your hotel."

"I did no skipping," I said stiffly. "Tell Faustino I have arrived."

"Buster, you ain't seeing the *capo* today." She had

been punching a computer. She read the screen. "You're several months overdue for an appointment with the *consigliere*."

"I'm sure there has been some misunderstanding," I said.

"Well, you just go misunderstand it with him." She beckoned to a security guard and I found myself in an elevator. It was a real one this time. So I was making progress. We shot up to the fortieth floor. I was shoved into an executive office.

Razza Louseini was sitting at his desk. His reptilian eyes fastened upon me. The knife scar that ran up from mouth to left ear went livid.

"So you're Inkswitch," he said. "I was looking for a much more prepossessing man."

"I want to hire a hit man on credit," I said. I didn't want him to get into all that Italian circumlocution.

"I'll bet you do," said Razza. "And that's what I wanted to see you about. Credit. When are you going to pay?" He was waving a bill! "You hired two snipers last fall. You got them both killed. And you never even had the decency to show up and pay the compensation. This bill," and he waved it with an Italian gesture for emphasis, "has been the subject of more legal correspondence than any other item on my desk! Attorney after attorney, collection agency after collection agency. Letters, letters, letters! I am sick of them! A *consigliere* has better things to do than mess around with delinquent accounts."

I was beginning to become uneasy. It must be an astronomical bill!

He was, Italian-wise, carrying on. "You know the rules. Liquidate or get liquidated. So when are you going to get this God (bleeped) bill off my God (bleeped) plate?"

"What's wrong with it?"

He echoed that a few times. "Swindle and Crouch won't pay it because they have no matching voucher. The Federal government won't pay it because you never signed it. Octopus Oil won't pay it because the third assistant vice-president didn't initial the requisition. Letters, letters, letters! Torrents of letters! And where are you? You can't be found. Skipped out of your hotel . . ."

"Wait a minute," I said, "I wasn't in any hotel."

"Well, whatever your story is, Inkswitch, you've had every (bleeped) computer in the organization so screwed up, it's cost a fortune in fuses."

"How much is this bill?" I said.

"Two thousand dollars," said Razza Louseini. "It isn't the money. It's the organizational screw-up. We've got to get it paid just to straighten out the computers. They're so crazy on the subject by this time that they gibber. Just yesterday we were trying to do a cost accounting for hit men for the CIA and all we could get on the printouts was the cost of Cape Canaveral. Pay this God (bleeped) bill!"

I can be pretty cunning about these things. I said, "All right, *Consigliere*, I'll tell you what I'll do. I'll pay that bill, but you give me another hit man."

He thought about it. Sicilians are pretty quick to spot who has the leverage. "When?" he said.

"In just two or three days. I have to go into some things for it."

His reptilian eyes were pretty slitted. "All right," he said. "I'll put all this on hold."

I walked out, practically treading on air. I wasn't ten thousand in the red, I was only two thousand.

Two thousand to go and one dead Countess Krak!

Chapter 3

That very night, an omen of success came my way.

I was still, as both Miss Pinch and Candy emphatically told me, in the doghouse over this fleas business. Women get so picky about the smallest little things.

They worked all evening getting things arranged for their "open house," as they were suddenly calling it. And I overheard that it was to be held the very following night.

I had been keeping out of the way, trying to work out how to get two thousand dollars. I had not been paid for yesterday and I doubted I would be paid for today or tomorrow. They had been working themselves to exhaustion and I had been relegated to the back room at night. I was getting no chance to run up a bill and earn my money.

About eleven, all other sallies having failed, I came up with a cunning idea: I would get interested in the decor. The new furniture was all in the shape of clamshells and tall, thick posts with rounded tops. The walls were a green seascape below a yellow sky. The curtains and borders of the rooms looked like sea foam. As I often watched TV commercials, I thought it might be an ad for shaving cream.

So, as they hurried about, I asked, "What are you trying to put up? A shaving cream ad?"

Well, I must say, *that* got a response.

"Aphrodite!" snapped Miss Pinch acidly. "The goddess of love, you lunkhead. The sea, the undulant waves repeating in sensuous curves, the phallic symbols stabbing nobly upward, the foam. Haven't you ever heard of Greek mythology? Where in hell were you educated?"

I was about to tell her heatedly that it had been the Royal Academy on Voltar, no matter how many courses I'd flunked, when Candy came to my rescue.

"No, no, Pinchy," Candy said. "You get so emotional where the story of Uranus is concerned. I'll tell him."

"Well, go ahead," said Miss Pinch, calming down, "I always love to hear it."

"Aphrodite," Candy told me, "is the ancient Greek goddess of sexual love and beauty. The Greek word *aphros* means 'foam'. You see, there was an earlier God named Uranus, which means 'heaven', and he had a son called Cronus. Now, apparently this son Cronus got pretty mad at his old man. He grabbed a knife and cut his father's (bleeps) off and threw them into the sea."

"Isn't that beautiful," said Miss Pinch with a dreamy look in her eye.

"Wait a minute," I said, not liking that look, "what does this have to do with love?"

Miss Pinch would have answered but Candy quickly continued, motioning to Miss Pinch to shut up. "Cronus threw his old man's (bleeps) in the sea and they foamed, of course. So that's what sea foam is. And Aphrodite was born out of the sea foam and everybody worships her."

"And you will notice," said Miss Pinch, "that everybody remembers and knows Aphrodite and nobody either knows or cares who the hell Uranus was."

They got back to work. But I withdrew into a corner to think this over. I knew the Greeks, aside from producing fleas, engaged in sacrifice. Now, I could not quite remember if they were animal sacrifices or human sacrifices. Then the horrible thought struck me that here on Earth it wouldn't matter. They believed that men were animals so they probably sacrificed both without much compunction.

What the Hells *was* this "open house" they were going to hold? Some kind of a mystical sacrifice in which they cut off my testicles? It worried me, especially since there wasn't a Voltarian cellologist handy to grow me any new ones.

Accordingly, I didn't push to go to bed with them in the front room and when they at last collapsed from completing the apartment at 2:00 A.M., I did not even venture near the front room to go to bed. I felt much more secure on a new sofa in the back room.

It was then I got my omen. My mood had been sort of black and this occurrence cheered me enormously. The Greeks specialized in omens, so it was very fitting.

The viewers I used to monitor Krak, Heller and Crobe had small buzzers on them one could set. In cleaning them up I must have tripped the switch of one. I had just about closed my eyes when there was a whirr in the closet. It meant that one of the three had opened their eyes after being asleep.

I went in the closet to shut it off. And then I didn't.

It was Krak's. She was sitting on the side of the bed in the "thinking room" of the Empire State Building. She had on a nightgown. She was crying.

Heller woke up. He sat up and pulled her over to him and put her head on his chest, stroking her hair. "There, there," he said. "What's the matter?"

"It was an AWFUL nightmare. It was so *real*."

"I'm sorry. Want to tell me about it?"

"I was in some sort of a room. I was lying on my

back. I was sort of paralyzed. I couldn't move. And then this awful-looking monster was kneeling over me." She began to cry very hard, clutching at him. After a bit she could talk again. "Then I heard a voice from somewhere and it said that you were dead." And she began crying again in earnest.

Gently, Heller said, "Well, I just looked and there aren't any monsters watching. And I'm not dead. I'm right here."

She threw her arms around his neck convulsively. She said, "Oh, Jettero, this planet makes me afraid. If anything happened to you, I think I would just die. I couldn't stand it. If I can't live with you, I don't want to live and that's all there is to it."

"There, there," he said. "You know that I love you. We'll succeed."

"Jettero," she said, crying again, "please, let's hurry up and finish and go home. I have an awful feeling something dreadful is going to happen to me and then to you."

He was trying to soothe her and get her to go back to sleep in his arms. But I had seen enough.

Dreams are portents, that I knew.

It was an omen.

She had foreseen that they both would die.

I went back to the sofa, grinning into the dark. It was a beautiful omen. All else that troubled me was pushed away.

There was not the slightest doubt left in my mind.
THE COUNTESS KRAK WAS GOING TO DIE!

Chapter 4

The only thing which kept me from completing the project was money. And little did I know that it was sliding toward my pockets in an unpredicted avalanche.

The following evening, after the omen, the open house was held. All day I had been buffeted about by caterers and such: because it was a working day, Candy and Miss Pinch had made me responsible, with many threats, for letting tradespeople in and out. I performed the job a bit absentmindedly, as I was mainly concentrating upon how to get the two thousand dollars, pay the Faustino bill and arrange for a hit man.

Accordingly, I was pretty surprised to be blasted by Miss Pinch when she came home from work and found I had not finished cleaning up and had not dressed.

"People will start arriving any minute!" she stormed, tearing out of her work clothes and getting into a cocktail dress. "Get into a tuxedo or something and then help me pick up these wrappings from the floor."

Anticipating spring and summer, no doubt, the old Jew garments man had provided me with a white tuxedo jacket and black pants. But I didn't know how to tie one of those bow ties and Miss Pinch almost strangled me getting it on me. Then Candy noticed I was wearing military boots and they got them off me and jammed on patent-leather pumps just as the doorbell rang with the first guests.

I was surprised, now that I looked at the place, how

big the rooms really were. Once the torture equipment was taken out and the hall was better integrated into the rooms, the front room looked quite like a salon. The back room, which had been promised me in which to work, was almost as large. It had a huge expanse of glass now, which looked out upon a garden. Everything tonight, including the newly planted garden, was ablaze with light. Ribbons scalloped down from the ceilings. Temporary tables groaned under foamy-looking cakes and bottles which were ready to gush. Some classic piece called "The Rites of Spring" filled the place with music. Quite impressive. It ought to have been from the number of blank petty cash vouchers I'd been signing.

I thought I might be seeing people like the Security Chief or some fellow males from Octopus Oil. But the doorbell rang and rang and couple after couple came in, deluding me at first into believing I would see a fellow man by the slouch hats and men's topcoats. But nay, alas, they were all lesbian couples. Some of the "males" even wore tuxedos. They tried to greet me heartily with bass voices. They swatted me on the shoulder and called me "old man." But I certainly was not fooled. The bass voices broke into treble unexpectedly and the swats might well have been intended to push me away from their "wives."

I never saw a party move quite so fast. The bottles gushed and gurgled. The cake was washed down. The music started through only the third time.

Suddenly Miss Pinch broke away from a cluster and said to me in an undertone, "Inkswitch, I have a frightful headache. All this will be over in minutes. You are not required to tell them good-bye. Here is five bucks. Run down to the all-night drugstore and get me a bottle of aspirin. They'll all be gone by the time you get back, so come in quietly, as I feel so bad I want to go to bed at once and the light is hurting my eyes."

The all-night drugstore was five blocks away. I went at a leisurely pace. After one glass of champagne I had a headache, too. The spring night felt cooling on my face. I got the aspirin and then had a Bromo-Seltzer at the counter. I wandered back home.

Sure enough, the lights were out, the place was all quiet. I tiptoed in.

Faint snores greeted me in the living room. I tried to light a light and give Miss Pinch her aspirin but evidently a bulb had blown. I said to Hells with the aspirin, she's asleep anyway. I tried to go into the back room. The door was locked. Well, what the Hells, I was tired of sleeping in there on the sofa anyway.

I shucked off my clothes. I had to fumble around because I was not oriented in the place. The new bed, I knew, was a sort of big clamshell with high phallic symbols on each side. It served as a sofa in the daytime. But it was all made up now.

After bumping my head on a pillar, I found the bottom and crawled up the middle of the bed. I pulled back the sheet and slid under. Usually, I slept between Miss Pinch and Candy so I composed myself and got ready to dream about money.

A hand slid over and touched my right thigh. Some fingers lightly explored my stomach.

I was suddenly reminded that if I were ever to get that two thousand dollars, I had better become highly agreeable.

I rolled over to my right.

I started to do my duty.

I suddenly halted.

What was this?

Something odd. How had Candy become a virgin again?

Well, this was no time to wonder about things like that!

The whole bed shook.

A scream blasted my ears!

Oh, well, Candy was always screaming.

But her moans were certainly exaggerated, even for Candy.

The sheet flew up into the air!

A louder scream!

A string of seashells on the wall chattered like castanets.

WHOOSH!

The body under me went limp.

Oh, well, if Candy wanted to faint again, that was her business.

I slid back over to the middle of the bed. For a moment, I thought the seashells were still chattering. I could see them by the street light shining through the window. They were just hanging there.

Where was this chattering coming from?

Teeth? A beam from the window lit them. Pinch's teeth chattering?

Oh, well, she was just funning.

I rolled and grabbed.

Indrawn breath like terror.

What on Earth was Pinch up to?

What the Devils? Since when had Pinch become a virgin again?

Oh, well, just some more women's tricks. They're full of them.

A scream!

Then panting in rhythm.

Moans in rhythm.
WHOOSH!
The sheet flew up.
A shuddering cry!

Total limpness. A dangling arm swung in the street-light beam and then became still, hanging off the side of the bed.

I wondered what the Devils Miss Pinch was doing, passing out.

THE LIGHTS CAME ON!

I looked up bewilderedly.

There were microphones suspended from the ceiling. Two TV cameras stood on tripods marked Infrared.

The back-room door burst open and a mob of people rushed in.

Miss Pinch and Candy were in the lead!

I stared down at the face still under me. The eyeballs were rolled back into the head, the mouth was open and slack. It was a peroxide blonde!

Blinking, I stared at the other girl in the bed beside us. She had a mannish haircut. Bluish hair. No makeup. It was a lesbian "husband." Her eyelids were wide open but her eyeballs were tilted clean up into her skull. She was out cold.

Miss Pinch was holding back the crowd that was pressing slaveringly around the bed. "You see! You see!" Miss Pinch was shouting to be heard above the babble. "I told you what real sex would do. NOW do you believe me?"

I got off the peroxide blonde. I pulled the sheet up around my throat. "What the Hells is this?" I shrieked.

"My dear fellow," said a lesbian husband, leaning close to me and forgetting all about a bass voice, "I saw it all on this closed-circuit TV and I must say you deserve an Oscar. Ought to be on the national networks!"

"(Bleep) you!" shouted Miss Pinch. "That was no put-on. That was the real thing!"

"Oh, pish, pish," said a lesbian wife. "Anyone can simulate, Pinchy, and you know it. The only innovation here is that this Inkswitch is wearing a falsie." And she yanked at the sheet.

"Movie blood," said a lesbian husband. "But a delightful fake all the same."

"God (bleep) it," howled Miss Pinch, "if it's a fake, then how do you account for that volunteer couple being OUT COLD?"

"Do you mind if I touch your dildo, old man?" said a lesbian husband, elbowing through and reaching out.

I climbed halfway up a phallic-symbol pillar.

At Pinch's signal, she and Candy at once approached the unconscious pair and began to massage their wrists and slap their faces.

"Get me a cold towel, somebody!" bellowed Miss Pinch. She was working on the lesbian husband with the bluish hair. By swatting him/her with the towel she finally brought him/her around.

"Spike, God (bleep) it," said Miss Pinch, "sit up and give your evidence."

The first one I had had sat up dizzily. Spike said, "Jesus!"

"Tell them!" howled Miss Pinch.

"Jesus," said Spike.

Miss Pinch abandoned Spike. She brushed back the crowd and made it over to the other side of the clamshell bed where Candy was working on the other one. Miss Pinch squashed the cold towel into the face of the peroxide blonde. "Lover-girl, God (bleep) it!" cried Miss Pinch. "Come around, you slut!"

Lover-girl got her eyes down level. Then they crossed. She gave up trying to sit up and fell back.

"Give your evidence!" howled Miss Pinch.

"Oh, boy!" said Lover-girl and passed out again.

A lesbian husband who was still wearing a top hat and leaning on a cane drawled, "Oh, I do say, Pinchy, that it was a great show. But obviously Spike and Lover-girl were just part of the act as well. We all know that natural sex is no good."

"God (bleep) it!" screamed Miss Pinch. "It's Psychiatric Birth Control that's no good! They've been lying to the lot of you! This is natural sex. You saw it on closed-circuit TV. You heard it on the microphones. You've got a couple here knocked out cold. What more do you (bleepards) want?"

"Evidence," said the lesbian husband in the top hat. "Anyone can fake a show, Pinchy. You've just taken us in."

All the others in that crowd nodded!

The brunette wife of a couple said, "Good show, Pinchy. Stirred one up. So if you don't mind, we'll go home and do it in the good old recommended way and keep up the great lesbian tradition."

"Marlene!" Miss Pinch screamed at her. "You stand right where you are. This show isn't over yet!"

Miss Pinch grabbed a box of drinking straws. "Now, listen, all of you. You may suspect that Spike and Lover-girl were in on it. But are you ready to believe that everyone in this room is in on it?"

"Oh, pish, pish," said Marlene.

"Nonsense," said somebody else.

"That would be impossible as it includes me," said the one in the top hat.

"Good," said Miss Pinch. "Now hear this. Would you be willing to BELIEVE if one of YOU, chosen by chance, reacted this way?"

They generally thought that that would be a proof. They seemed very uneasy.

Miss Pinch promptly presented the box. "The short straw gets it!" she said. "Agreed?"

There were up to forty people in the room, all of them lesbians. They each evidently thought they wouldn't get it, and amused at the idea of more show and possibly Miss Pinch's defeat, they began to draw. Each one looked at his/her straw with relief.

Then the husband in the top hat said, "Oh, no!" He/she had the short straw!

"Algernon," said Miss Pinch, "get out of those clothes!"

He/she didn't want to so they tore them off en masse. Miss Pinch forced what appeared to be a birth control pill in his/her mouth.

They dragged the groggy Spike and Lover-girl over against the wall. They threw Algernon, naked, onto the bed where he/she landed with a bounce.

"Inkswitch!" bawled Miss Pinch. "Get down off that God (bleeped) pillar and get to work!"

Homosexuality has always turned my stomach. I had avoided looking at Algernon. But a certain glint, when it occurs in Miss Pinch's eye, commands respect—which is to say, fear. From my perch up on the phallic-symbol column I looked down at the naked body which was being held flat and face up on the bed by willing and boisterous lesbians.

I saw what was really a brunette woman. They had torn off the breast compressors, and while the bosom was not extraordinary, they were a woman's breasts. The hips, though a shade narrow, were woman's hips.

I got down. Algernon was looking at me with a wild and terror-glazed eye. She was trying to shrink.

I bent down from the pillar and a whiff of stale cigar smoke made me sneeze. I shook my head. Candy at once understood. She rushed away and came back in a moment with a quart of *Spring Violets* toilet water and dumped it with a splash on Algernon.

Still reluctant, I felt my ankle seized by Pinch.

Down I came with a thud upon the bed.

The crowd's faces made a circle above me.

I got to work.

Algernon's face was in gibbering terror.

A lesbian wife looked round-eyed at the bed.

A lesbian husband went stiff and then hid his/her eyes.

Algernon screamed.

A lesbian with a face like a madonna was turned sideways, praying. I yelled at her, "Shut up! Just because she's a virgin is no reason you have to invoke the Virgin Mary!"

"Oh, my God," a husband said, "Algernon's out cold!"

"No, he isn't!" another cried, peering between shoulders. "She's coming around!"

Strings of seashells began to swing.

Into the miasma of Algernon's groans, a lesbian husband said, "Hey! Look at that! He likes it!" His voice sounded stunned.

The seashell chains began to swing wider and wider.

"Oh, my God!" howled Algernon.

The whole circle of faces went into shock.

WHOOSH!

Algernon screamed deafeningly.

The top of the clamshell bed crashed down, hiding us.

The mob was struggling to lift it. They got it halfway up.

A lesbian, looking through the gap, screamed, "She's dead!"

Another cried, "No, no! She's just out cold!"

The mob of lesbians were looking at one another, stunned, unbelieving.

I crawled out of the clamshell slit, wrapping a sheet around myself. They were staring at me with awe.

Suddenly the whole bed convulsed.

"She's having another one all by herself!" a lesbian cried, round-eyed.

They looked at one another once more. The room was so quiet you could hear a faucet drip half a mile away.

Then Miss Pinch leaned into the dark of the half-open bed. She said, "Well, how did you like it, Algernon?"

The whole bed went into an earthquake convulsion.

"She did it again!" said a popeyed husband.

Miss Pinch and Candy were propping the bed fully open. They got it hooked back up.

There lay Algernon, sheet up to her chin. She had a beautiful, blissful smile upon her face. "Ohhhhhh, Pinchy!" she said. "Wonderful. Wonderful."

The whole roomful of people were suddenly wide-eyed and eager. Slavering, in fact.

Then suddenly Marlene folded up on the floor and had an orgasm of her own.

Spike was sitting up over by the wall. She said, pleading, "Pinchy, can't I have it once again?"

That set off Miss Pinch. She said, "Get out of here, you disbelieving (bleepards)." And waved shooing hands at the crowd.

A lesbian husband was tearing off her tie and shirt. "But, Pinchy, we do believe you now."

A lesbian wife was down on her knees, hands folded in prayer, " 'Fore God, Pinchy, tell us, tell us please, where can we get a MAN?"

"You can't have him," said Pinch with folded arms. "He's private property, under contract." She raised her voice and addressed the throng, "Now what do you think of Psychiatric Birth Control, you (bleepards)?"

"It's (bleep)!" said Marlene, coming to.

"From what I've seen tonight," said a lesbian husband, "Psychiatric Birth Control is pure crap." And she took out a cigar case and threw it violently into the fireplace.

"But Pinchy," said Marlene, "you've done us an awful dirty trick. You know (bleeped) well that every unmarried male in the company is a homo. There are no men left!"

"That (bleeped) Miss Peace has a monopoly on all the elevator boys and she'd ruin our reputations with Rockie if we took those," said a lesbian wife distractedly.

"The married men are so slugged up on drugs they're impotent," mourned a lesbian husband.

"We go outside the company, it's our jobs," said another.

"What the HELL are we going to do?" said another.

"You got to do something," said the naked Lovergirl from the rug. "After a bang like that I'll never go back to biting and scratching and calling it sex. No SIR!"

They got their heads together. They drifted into the back room, following Pinch.

I was pretty sleepy, really. Three was not all that heroic but it was just the emotional strain.

I must have dozed. Suddenly I woke up. Pinch in a bathrobe was standing there. All the company had gone. Candy had her clothes off but was licking cake plates over by the refreshment bar.

My apprehension rose when I saw that Pinch was holding something behind her back. In my groggy state I thought of the Greek sacrificial rites. Now that I had publicly performed, was I going to join Uranus in losing my (bleeps)?

My confidence was not helped a bit when she reached down and jiggled them.

"Inkswitch," she said, "I have a surprise for you."

I flinched. I did not like surprises from Miss Pinch.

"How did you like Spike and Lover-girl?" she asked.

"Surprisingly," I said.

"And Algernon?"

"Once you got rid of her stale cigar smoke, passing, passing."

"As good as me and Candy?" she said with a glint in her eye.

Fear, pure fear, dictated my response. "Nothing to compare!" I cried.

"Well, that's just fine, Inkswitch," and to my relief she let go my (bleeps). "Because, Inkswitch, me and the crowd came to an arrangement. Each night right after work, a couple of those girls are going to drop in for a bang. They're all agreed. They will be ladies about it and take their turn."

I gulped. I did not like the stern look which was seeping over her face.

"But, God (bleep) you, Inkswitch, this is not to interfere with what you do to Candy and me all night!"

She was reaching toward my (bleeps) again. I said hurriedly, "I promise. Oh, Miss Pinch, never think I would fail to live up to my contract. I am a man of honor."

"I'm glad of that," she said. "Because if you aren't, I'll cut your (bleeps) off."

I knew it!

And then she smiled. "But it's not all bad news, Inkswitch. They emptied their purses into this wastebasket. I added five thousand dollars for your great show. You've been asking for ten G's. And here is twelve thousand bucks."

I gaped into the wastebasket she held under my nose. It was full of MONEY!

"Now stop drooling," Miss Pinch said, "and jump into a shower and get the blood off you while we change the sheets. Candy and I have been saving you for days for this sprint. And we're God (bleeped) near dying of sex starvation, to say nothing of getting hot as fire from that show tonight!"

I went into the shower singing.

TWELVE G's!

I could pay my bill to Razza.

I could buy a hit man.

COUNTESS KRAK, YOU'RE DEAD!

PART
FORTY-FOUR

Chapter 1

I had been told on the phone I could have an appointment with Razza Louseini later in the day, and so I utilized my time in checking up on the target, Countess Krak.

When I turned on the viewers in the back room, I was a little disoriented at first. I couldn't quite make out where Krak and Heller were. It was midmorning and all I got was stacks of books and pages going by too fast for me to see what books they were.

I had to backtrack the recorded strips to find out what they were up to, for I assumed quite rightly that it meant no good for me.

They were up early and, both dressed in stylish blue running sweat suits, had trotted out of the Empire State Building Fifth Avenue side and had gone north the eight blocks to the New York Public Library on 42nd Street. Except for the presence of Heller, or even with it, the Countess Krak's back would have made a perfect sniper target all the way.

And now they were in the huge reference room. Heller was sitting at a table. The Countess Krak was working the card catalogue and turning in slips and pulling books out of the chute when they came. She was doing strictly gofer work.

That they were in running suits, even though this was a current style, filled me with alarm. It seemed to indicate too much eagerness for progress and *that* was something I strictly did not want.

Finally, she had him so boxed in with towers of books that she had to stand on tiptoe to see him. She looked intently at his face. He seemed to be puzzled, somewhat stopped. She came around and sat down in a chair beside him.

She leaned toward his ear. In Voltarian, she whispered, "If you would tell me what you're trying to do, Jettero, I could help you more."

He pulled a huge sheet he was working on out from under a tome on social organizations. "This," he whispered back, "is a workout of a mathematics we use in combat engineering. It is called 'Command Isolation Geometry.' There are certain theorems which, if applied, will tell you the probable location of the command post of an enemy army corps or a city. When you have worked it out, you can then slip in, plant the bombs and— bango—the enemy has no central command post and can be more easily overrun by the Fleet or its marines or even the Army."

"You mean we're going to blow something up?" said the Countess Krak.

"No, no. I was just telling you what the mathematics was," Heller whispered back. "I've got this spore project to clean up the atmosphere. I'm just making sure I isolate whoever's toes it will step on so I won't be too surprised. The way this planet is organized, apparently, is that if you try to do anything to help it, some special-interest group jumps all over you. They have some crazy idea that chaos is profit. Very short-range think. So I am just making sure that when I start putting spores into the stratosphere and get shot at, I know who's shooting."

"You mean somebody might object to cleaning up the atmosphere?" whispered Krak in surprise.

"You never know," said Heller.

"What a crazy planet!" she muttered.

"Well, be that as it may," he whispered, "but I'm getting some crazy answers here. I don't quite understand it."

"Let me help. I may not know your geometry but I'm good at puzzles."

He oriented the sheet so she could see it better. "I'm getting a repeating answer," he whispered. "When you get one of those, it means that your original premise is too narrow. I started out to find out who had connections and communication lines to the subject of *cytology*—which is an Earth name for our cellology. So I made a test equation over here in the corner of the sheet and, yes, I assumed too narrow a subject to get a reliable answer. Whatever the answer is, it controls and commands more than cytology. Do you follow me?"

"No."

"Well, it's like I started out to find a corporal in charge of a squad and then found out that wouldn't embrace the area, so I found a captain in charge of a company and that wouldn't embrace the target area, so then I found a colonel in charge of a regiment. This could take forever. I'm nowhere near any real top authority command post."

"How are you doing it?"

"Well, this symbol here is logistic lines like vehicles and supply trucks. And you see its path of emanation and convergence. And this is a symbol of communications. And so on. So if you can get such functions to cross on the plot, you have the command post area."

"It looks very pretty and orderly," whispered the

Countess. "And, looking at the lines, it does seem you have convergences."

"Too many," said Heller. "And they always go off to somewhere else. Blast it." He gave her the sheet. He was really throwing it away, as he now took a big fresh one. "I was doing it for a country. I'm just going to skip a continent and be absurd. I'll do it for the whole planet."

"Why is that absurd, Jettero? I never saw you do anything absurd in all the time I've known you." But she added in a lower mutter, "Except Miss Simmons, of course."

"It's absurd because this planet doesn't have an emperor. I'll wind up with Buckingham Palace in England or something."

"And then you'll blow that up and we can leave," said the Countess Krak with an air of finality.

He laughed quietly. "What a bloodthirsty wench. I'm not trying to find out who to shoot. I'm just trying to find out who might shoot at me if I put spores in the stratosphere." He was checking book titles in the towers around him. "Let's see if I have all the planetary control subjects." He began to put them down. Government control. Fuel control. Finance control. Health control. Intelligence control. Medical control. Medicine control. Mental services control. Media control. Law enforcement control. Judicial control. Food control. Air transport control. Industrial control. Social control. Population volume control. . . . He was checking already-made notes.

He was back to work drawing in a large ring of symbols of the things named and others. It was hard to follow the symbols and labelling because he was writing very small and very fast.

He asked her to get him another half a dozen books and he spun through them quickly.

Shifting ink color to red, he drew a dwindling spiral from the outside to the inside center of his plot. He stopped and gave a short laugh.

She was sitting beside him again. "It's very pretty."

"And it's absurd," said Heller in a low voice. "When you add up all the interlocking points given in just these available books, it says the planet DOES have an emperor, that the emperor has two planetary command posts and TOTAL planetary control. I'm wasting my time."

"Where are the command posts and WHO is the emperor?" said the Countess Krak.

"I know a nice place to have lunch," said Heller.

"No, no, Jettero. Except for certain females, I have never seen you do an absurd thing ever. You are always right on. Tell me."

"You'll laugh. The planet doesn't have an emperor and its royal palaces are actually just tourist attractions. But I'll finish it anyway, if you like."

Under "command posts" he wrote in the center of the plot *OCTOPUS OIL COMPANY BUILDING* and *POKANTICKLE ESTATE, HAIRYTOWN, NEW YORK.*

In the center of the plot, in red, he printed, *EMPEROR: DELBERT JOHN ROCKECENTER.*

He laughed again and spun the big sheet with its geometric symbols and names to the Countess Krak. "Here. You can use it to teach the cat to run in circles. Now let's go have some lunch."

She looked at it. She carefully folded it up and put it in her shoulder purse.

She began to help him pile the book tonnage back on the counters.

My hair was standing straight up!

Heller was dead right!

And even though *he* discounted it, I could see from the careful way *she* had folded it and preserved it that SHE KNEW IT!

She seemed very preoccupied as they went down the broad steps of the huge Grecian-design library building.

They jogged north on Fifth Avenue, dodging adroitly through the lunch hour crowds. They came to 53rd Street, crossed and went a short distance west. I carefully spotted place after place where a sniper's bullet could have hit the Countess in the back. And now she was simply standing still, staring at two revolving doors. An easy target!

"The Museum of Modern Art?" she said. "I thought you were taking me to lunch. Are we going to eat paintings?"

He laughed and pushed her through the revolving doors and was beside her again in the entrance lobby. He paid four dollars for two tickets and walked her through the main hall. Glass and marble were everywhere, and invitations to go this way and that to special exhibitions, but he steered her right on through the main hall and out a door and they were in a huge garden. Amongst the trees could be seen numerous odd-shaped sculptures, but he was guiding her along a terrace. He turned and edged her through a door. A cafeteria.

He gave her a tray and knives and forks and they went on down the line. The cases full of attractive food were all a mystery to her. She wound up with five different salads, several sweet rolls, hot chocolate and three different kinds of ice cream. His was not much more sensible than hers.

Heller pointed the way and they went back outside and sat down at a table. The noonday spring sun was flickering down through the budding leaves of trees. A nearby fountain tinkled. Spread before them was the garden.

"Nice," said the Countess Krak. And then she began, experimentally, to eat. She had mastered forks but regarded them with some caution.

Heller was an old hand by now. He chomped away and then at last sat back. His eyes were on the garden but he wasn't looking at Rodin or Renoir.

Suddenly he started chuckling. "Crown Prince Junior," he said. He laughed again and then said it again.

The Countess Krak was still working on the ice cream, but she said, "What *are* you going on about?"

He said, "Nothing." But he was still chuckling.

She said, "Jettero, you're always accusing me of being secretive, but *you're* the one who isn't frank. What *are* you laughing about?"

He gave another chuckle. "Name I had once," he said. "How do you like that ice cream? It's called Picasso Pistachio."

"Jettero, you're going to get Picasso Pistachio in your face if you don't tell me what you are laughing about."

"It's just a joke. Crown Prince Junior." And he laughed again.

"That doesn't make any sense, Jettero."

"I'm sorry. It's just that it's kind of involved. You see, if Delbert John Rockecenter was the emperor of Earth, why then, the name they gave me would have made me Crown Prince Junior. It's completely silly. It's just that it is a beautiful day and you're beautiful and I'm glad to be here sitting with you in the Sculpture Garden of the Museum of Modern Art, watching you eat Picasso Pistachio."

"Jettero," she said in a deadly voice, "you are trying to put me off. And furthermore, royalty is not something one laughs about. When an emperor signs a proclamation it becomes the law of the land. A proclamation is a very valuable thing. Now sit right there quietly and tell me if somebody, since you landed here, made you a Crown Prince or something."

"All right," he said. "You sit there quietly and eat your Picasso Pistachio and the court minstrel will entertain you with the harrowing tale of Crown Prince Junior."

"That's better," said the Countess Krak, smiling.

"Well, once upon a time, in a dark wood, a space tug landed in the field of an old Virginia plantation." And he continued on. He told her about the birth certificate as Delbert John Rockecenter, Junior. He included a humorous account of Stonewall Biggs, the County Clerk, of Stupewitz and Maulin, the FBI agents. He omitted utterly the late Mary Schmeck. He laughed about the fake family butler, "Buttlesby," and then he went into the events at the Brewster Hotel where Bury had bought the birth certificate off of him, made sure he had no other trace of the name Delbert John Rockecenter, Junior, and then had intended to kill him.

"So you see," he concluded, "I was not Crown Prince Junior very long. And you now know how the frog turned into Jerome Terrance Wister. And here he sits today, eating ice cream with a gracious lady of the court. The minstrel bows now off the stage and thinks he'll have another cup of hot chocolate."

When he went inside the cafeteria, the Countess Krak sat there in a deep study.

He came back, cooled his chocolate and began to sip it.

The Countess Krak said, "You ought to do something about it."

Heller laughed. "My dear, if a combat engineer went diving off the job to pursue justice and wreak vengeance every time his fuses didn't work, he would get nothing done at all."

"Tell me again what that Stonewall Biggs said," she wanted to know.

"He said, 'If'n ah can evah be moah help t'you, you jus' yell fo' Stonewall Biggs.'"

"No, no, no. When he gave you the birth certificate."

"He said, 'Ah wondered if it would evah come to this.' And he looked at me closely and said, 'So you be Delbert John Rockecenter, Junior.'"

"And this Bury fellow wanted you killed."

"He certainly tried," said Heller.

"Hmm," said the Countess Krak. "That proves it."

"Proves what?"

"There really IS a Delbert John Rockecenter, Junior."

Heller shook his head. "I've looked in the *Who's Who*. There is no such person listed. Delbert John Rockecenter is unmarried and has no children or direct heirs."

"You men don't understand these things," said Krak. "And you certainly don't understand royal families, Jettero. Even aristocrats do it."

"Do what?" said Heller, quite puzzled.

"Get rid of an heir. Oh, it is all very plain to me. There IS a Delbert John Rockecenter, Junior. And this lawyer Bury is hiding him. He's never seen him so he thought you were him. And they don't have any dungeons or castles on remote islands to throw unwanted heirs in, so Bury tried to assassinate you."

Heller laughed. "I'm afraid I'm no expert on royal families."

"Well, you ought to be. A young emperor gadding about can get snared in by women who are very unscrupulous indeed. There IS a Delbert John Rockecenter, Junior. And Delbert John, Senior, doesn't know he exists and the lawyer Bury is hiding it from him. You see, I know about lawyers, too, and they are pretty treacherous. My father told me that our family lost all of its lands on Manco generations ago solely because of crooked men of law. There's tons of historical precedence for such a crime as Bury has in mind. This lawyer Bury thinks he can get the whole empire in his own hands if he hides the fact that there is an heir. It's been done before."

"Honey, I'm told by Izzy that Bury is Rockecenter's right arm. Rockecenter trusts him completely."

"That proves it," said the Countess Krak. "Bury is hiding the real heir to the Rockecenter empire. You can be as logical as you want. But my intuition tells me that is the way it is. It just makes no sense at all for Bury to want to kill my Jettero just because he thought he was Delbert John Rockecenter, Junior. It makes my blood absolutely seethe to think of it!"

"Wait a minute," said Heller. "There is no emperor. There is no crown prince."

"Hmm," said the Countess Krak.

"My dearest," said Jettero, "I can tell you are thinking about something. Hear me. Those are VERY dangerous men. You keep away from them. Promise me?"

"Hmm," said the Countess Krak.

"Listen," said Heller. "One of the reasons I brought you to lunch here is because they are having an exhibit of illustrations of imaginary spacecraft. Covers of magazines called 'science fiction.' And they have movie models of what they think spacecraft look like. Some UFOs, too. I'm sure you will be very intrigued. Some of the artists have painted things that really do look like spaceships. And I want to check them to see if our own craft ever get spotted. I'm sure you will be fascinated. It's right on the ground floor in the temporary exhibits. And stop worrying your pretty head about the heirs of emperors who don't exist."

"Hmm," said the Countess Krak. She tagged along but I could tell her mind was not on it.

I needed no additional evidence to harden my firm resolve to act. But what had just passed between them, in fact, left me no alternative.

It was as plain as day to me that the Countess Krak was now intent on killing Bury and blowing up Pokantickle Estate at Hairytown, to say nothing of the Octopus Oil Building at Rockecenter Plaza. She was DANGEROUS!

As she drifted through the exhibits in front of Heller, I chose several spots in her unprotected back where a lethal bullet could finish this.

I glanced at my watch.

I was almost late in seeing Razza.

I HAD TO GET THAT SNIPER ON THE JOB QUICK!

Chapter 2

Razza Louseini, *consigliere* of the *capo di tutti capi*, Faustino "The Noose" Narcotici, sat imperially at his desk awaiting me.

"Now," he said with great satisfaction, "we can get those God (bleeped) computers straightened out."

Into the waiting hand of the accountant who was standing by his desk, I counted out two thousand hard-earned dollars. I was given a receipt and the man rushed off to untangle the accounts department computer brains before they sold Manhattan back to the Indians.

"And now," said Razza, the scar that connected his mouth with his left ear taking on a peculiar corkscrew look, "here is your hit man." He was extending a white card that had a black hand in the upper corner.

"Wait," I said. "Don't I just go down to Personnel and have them call the man and send him to me?"

"Look at the card," said Razza.

I did. The middle finger of the silhouette was extended higher than the rest—the Italian symbolism for "up your (bleep)" or "you been (bleeped)."

Never trust the Mafia! "You haven't kept your bargain!" I yelped.

"Oh, yes, I have," said Razza. "But the way you got the last two snipers wasted, nobody here has any confidence in you. Bad planning or you just shot them yourself for kicks. Turn the card over and you'll see an address. Take the card there, present it and you'll have your hit man. You can make your own arrangements, buy his insurance and, probably, bury him or not as you please."

"Wait," I said. "Something tells me there's something wrong with this guy."

"Well, frankly," said Razza, "there is. He's such a dirty, rotten (bleepard), nobody will hire him anymore unless they are so God (bleeped) mad at the victim they want something awful done. Lawyers won't hire him anymore. He's got a twist. Filthy."

"What's this hit man do?" I said, startled. If somebody was too bad for the Mafia it must be pretty awful.

"Find out for yourself," said Razza.

"But I have to have somebody who can shoot straight and will kill."

"Oh, he'll do that, all right. It's how he does it that turns your stomach. But there's your hit man, Inkswitch. Exactly as agreed. And if you get this one wasted, you'll be a (bleeping) hero. So good-bye, Inkswitch, good-bye."

The address was way out in Queens and I rode endlessly on subways getting there. The neighborhood had not ever seen better times: it had been built originally in total decay. The house was on a side street and apparently part of it was rented out. I picked my way over a broken walk, I walked up some broken stairs, I rang a broken bell.

My presence had been detected. With a yank which almost blew my hat off, the broken door burst open.

An enormous woman was standing there. She had a mustache like a cavalry sergeant. She glared. I gave her the card defensively. She looked at it and then swept me into the hall with it and closed the door.

"So you want to see my no-good, worthless son, do you? You'll find him in the basement with the rest of the rats."

I don't like rats. I said, "Can't you ask him to come up so I can talk to him?"

"Blood of Christ, no! He's hiding out!"

"From the police?"

"The rotten filth isn't even that respectable. Bill collectors! Every day, bill collectors! I can't look out a window I don't see bill collectors! But will he go out and get a decent job? No. Will he support his poor old mother that suffered to bring him into the world? No. All he do is hide in that basement! So what the Mafia want with him now? I thought they through with him and good reason."

I was a bit staggered by this huge monster. I said, timidly, "I may have a job for him. Then he can pay his bills."

"Hah! You give him money, he no pay his bills. He go out and philander. Just like his no-good, rotten father that's joined the angels, God rest his rotten, stinking soul! Philander, philander, philander, that's all he good for, the filth. I beat him and beat him. I bring him up right. But he got rotten, putrid blood in him. The blood of his rotten, putrid, no-good father! So you give him a job. He sneak out and blow the money. But he can't get out. The bill collectors!"

"What are these bills?"

"The God (bleeped) hospital. Five hundred dollars a day they throw away saving his worthless life. Oh, I sneak him out when I hear but not in time. He owe $4,900 already! And just a lousy auto accident! He got enough sense to get shot like his no-good father? No! He's got to get himself in an auto accident and he hasn't even got the sense to get himself killed."

I had an inspiration. "I could give you the money and you could pay the bills and then he could work for me."

"I don't take no blood money! You think I want blood money on my soul when I go to my final reward? Any bills paid, you pay."

"Well, let me talk to him, at least," I said.

"On your responsibility, not mine. I'll be no party to the rotten things he does. You want to talk to him, go down through that door. And if you want to shoot him, I close my ears."

I went down some dusty, grimy stairs into a dusty, grimy basement. Back of a dusty, grimy furnace, on a dusty, grimy bed, lay a man with penitentiary stamped all over him.

He was cowering back, holding a double-barrelled leopard trained on my chest!

TORPEDO FIACCOLA! The sniper Bury had used to try to hit Heller at the Brewster Hotel, the very hood that Heller had sent crashing off the Elevated Highway last fall. Oh, this was good! He'd have a grudge to settle!

"Hello, Torpedo," I said.

His gray face went grayer. "How come you know me? I don't know you."

"I saw you working for Mr. Bury," I said.

"Jesus!" he said. "Don't tell Bury where to find me. He thinks I falsified the evidence and collected the hit money without making that contract! I didn't! The (bleepard) trapped me and must have collected it himself. And believe me, if I knew where to find him, I'd hit him for nothing! The (bleeper) didn't even carry out the threat to waste my mother!"

Better and better. "Put down the gun, Torpedo. Razza sent me here to offer you a job."

"Then it must be a pretty risky hit or Razza wouldn't have thought of me. That (bleepard) wants me killed."

"It's an easy job," I said soothingly. I sat down on a box. Torpedo, gradually reassured, laid the leopard aside and sat on the edge of the dusty, grimy bed. "I'm listening," he said.

"I'll pay the bill collectors and give you another $5,000 when the job is done."

"Another $10,000 plus expenses," he said. "I ain't even got a rifle anymore."

"I pay the bills you owe, $5,000 and expenses, and that's as high as I go, Torpedo."

He shook his head. It was all the money I had—more, actually, if the expenses came to much.

It was an impasse.

"I'd get in trouble with the union if I cut rates on a hit," he said.

"You're getting $4,900 plus $5,000 plus expenses," I said. "Since when did hits go higher than $10,000?"

"There's insurance. A hit man is high-risk insurance. It costs a thousand a day. My God (bleeped) mother wouldn't let me leave this house again unless I was insured. She keeps yelling down the stairs to go out and get a job but I know her. She's treacherous. You'll have to up the ante."

I shook my head. Impasse. We sat there. I don't like uncomfortable silences. I said, "Why don't they like to hire you, Torpedo?"

He shrugged, "Oh, it's nothing really. Silly prejudice. Mr. Bury was the only one who didn't mind. And since he won't employ me anymore, I been out of work. Word gets around, you know."

"About what?" I said.

"Well, they think it's a twist. But it ain't. It's perfectly normal and I been told so on good authority. In fact, it was good authority that started it."

"Started what?"

"Oh, I might as well tell you if you haven't been told already. It's the sex thing."

Oho! Maybe I could use this. "You better level," I said.

"Well, no reason not to. It began about six years ago when I was doing a stretch in the Federal pen. I underwent behavior modification therapy. Great stuff. The prison psychologist in charge of organizing the gang rapes was a great guy. I was in for consultation with him one day and he said he'd noticed I never joined the rape line in the showers and he was worried about me.

"He said how could he modify behavior to greater criminality if I wouldn't participate in group therapy? He said the prisoners ran the prisons but the psychologists ran the prisoners and if I wouldn't cooperate, he'd have to turn me over to the prisoner committee as unreformable. He was a nice guy, very understanding, and he said he didn't want to do that. So I cooperated.

"He worked and worked with me—the usual prison psychology treatments: having me (bleep) him and him (bleeping) me in the (bleep). And that's when he discovered what was really wrong with me.

"I had never been able to get an erection and even couldn't with him. He felt sorry for me. He really did. Here he had all these other prison cases to modify and he even took time off from (bleeping) them to talk to me. Real nice guy.

"I confessed to him I'd never been able to do it at all to a girl or a guy or anything. He asked me if I ever wanted to (bleep) my mother and was pretty shocked when I said that, what with her beatings and all, it just had never occurred to me. I had to tell him right out that when you've got somebody beating you and screaming about philandering, it's almost impossible to get your mind onto (bleeping) the person.

"Well, he thought and thought and finally he came up with a solution. Had I ever (bleeped) a dead woman? Well, I flat-out had to confess I'd never done that. So he told me I better get a dead one and make sure she was still warm. He said it was just basic psychology, a perfectly normal thing. And he told me how to do it in detail. There was a hitch, though. It was a male pen and there were no dead women around. But he stamped my parole card to show my behavior had been modified anyway and he recommended they let me out on the public. So I got out of prison. Really a fine fellow.

"So, anyway, I never thought much about it until six months later. The mob didn't have any hits at the moment and Personnel sent me down to New Mexico as a gunner on a dope run. One night in the desert the truck convoy was hit by hijackers and in the shootout all the rest of the guys run off. A lot of lead had been flying around and I heard this moaning and I crawled over, and (bleeped) if there wasn't a Mexican woman lying there with slugs in her.

"She gave a couple of kicks and died. And suddenly it occurred to me that I ought to test this basic psychology out. So I pulled up the skirts on this stiff and, Jesus Christ, I'll be (bleeped) if I didn't get an erection. So I got it into the corpse and carried on full blast. I (bleeped) like crazy. It was something about her dead eyes staring at me. And she couldn't say a single word about how no good I was, her lips all pulled back like that from the death agony.

"Man, I really poured it in. Six God (bleeped) times! But then she had cooled off and begun to stiffen and it wasn't any good anymore. The corpse has got to be warm yet to really do it right. But while it lasts, you can call them anything you want and they don't say a word. They just lie and let you pour it in. The best part is the dead eyes."

I was totally engrossed. That master psychologist in the prison had created a real, honest-to-Gods necrophile! "Did you ever write the psychologist to tell him of the success?" I said.

"Well, no. You see, there's a part of it I don't understand. When the others come back from wiping out the hijackers, they seen me standing over the dead woman with my (bleep) hanging out and they added up what I'd been doing and the (bleepards) first wanted to shoot me and then not a single one of them would ever talk to me again. Word got around and not even the Faustino mob would hire me. Only Mr. Bury laughed about it and would use me on jobs. But now he's off of me, too."

"Let's talk about this job," I said.

"No more to say. I got to have my bills paid, $10,000 and expenses. I'd be in real trouble if I took less."

I got ready to deliver my shot. "This contract," I said, "is on a woman!"

An electric shock seemed to go through him. He stared at me, jaws going slack.

"A young and beautiful woman," I said.

His breath was suddenly rapid and his mouth began to quiver. Then he said, "And as soon as I kill her I can (bleep) the corpse?"

"Absolutely," I said.

His eyes were blazing with excitement. When he could master his emotion, he said, "Mister, you got a deal. You pay my bills, you pay me $5,000 and expenses and I get to do what I want with the corpse."

"You can (bleep) her to your heart's content," I said.

Oh, but he was eager and excited.

As I left the house, his mother said to me, "Can't you arrange to get that (bleeping) (bleepard) killed on this job?"

"Not on your life," I said. "He's priceless." And I took from her the hospital bills so I could pay them.

I strode down the street, treading on air. Torpedo was a competent hit man for the purpose. And with the promised bonus he would be as eager as a snake after a rabbit.

The thought of not only killing but degrading the corpse of the Countess Krak pleased me immensely.

It was just exactly what she deserved. And I knew it was the only way anyone but Heller could touch that pure and noble body. Touch her that way alive and you'd be dead!

There were some things to do and to arrange. I'd have to get her pattern of moving around so I could set it up when she was alone. I had to get a rifle, preferably with explosive bullets.

I had my hit man. And what a hit man! A necrophile!

COUNTESS KRAK, YOU'LL BE NOT ONLY DEAD BUT THOROUGHLY DEFILED.

Chapter 3

After all my unlucky vicissitudes, things were suddenly beginning to run my way.

I no more than got home and got the viewers on than I beheld good fortune staring at me with its evil grin. A map of Florida!

It was spread out on the floor of Heller's office and Izzy and Heller were going over it with Krak looking on.

"Now, are you sure you secured the property?" said Heller.

"Miles and miles of Everglades," said Izzy. "Nothing but the purest swamp. Over your head in muck the way Florida real estate usually is. Knee-deep in alligators. Nothing living there but Florida crackers, and they're not wide awake enough to count." He showed Heller on the map. It was a large area toward the south of the state, way inland from the sea. The map said swamp, swamp, nothing but swamp.

Izzy was hauling out some deeds. "It's a former retirement estate but the alligators ate the old folks they sold it to. Then the CIA bought it as part of a training program for a secret army to invade Jamaica but they got defeated by some small boys with slingshots on the beach, so they sold it, according to the records search, to the *Saint Petersburg Grimes*, who used it for a place to hide out their reporters when people wanted to shoot them. But the people were so successful that the area was not much used. Then the *Grimes* went bankrupt and I bought it mud-cheap with fifteen leftover reporters thrown in, including a woman reporter named Betty Horseheinie."

"A woman?" said the Countess Krak.

"Yes," said Izzy. "And she was a problem, too. The alligators tried to eat her and got so sick the conservationists raised hell. We sent her to an insane asylum near Miami but she drove the patients so crazy we got a permit from the government and disposed of her as contaminated waste. She's miles deep in the continental trench now, but they do say all the fish are dying there. However, she's not around."

"Good," said the Countess Krak.

"We had a little trouble with the state government," continued Izzy. "The name of the corporation we are using is 'Beautiful Clear Blue Skies For Everyone, Inc.' and they thought it might be a religion. For some reason they want only criminals in the state, and anybody trying to do good drives them up the palm trees in horror. But we pointed out that 'blue sky' is also a criminal term for worthless stock and that fooled them. They welcomed us with open arms. But the thing I'm worried about is the Indians."

"Indians?" said the Countess.

"Wild savages," said Izzy. "Every time I go to the movies I can hardly sit through it when they show Indians. They torture and burn and make the most awful sounds. Look right there: a Seminole Indian Reservation! I looked it up and they only signed a treaty of peace a few decades ago and I don't think it will hold. They eat dogs, you know. And they might eat trappers and frontiersmen, too, from the way they look. That's why you won't find me going outside New York City: at least we bought this island fair and square for a bucket of beads. So you take some beads with you, Mr. Jet, in case those Seminoles dispute your title."

"Bang-Bang," said Heller, "add a bucket of beads to my luggage, will you?"

I hadn't seen Bang-Bang before because nobody had looked at him. He was sitting at the bar pouring Scotch into a saucer for the cat. "Got it, Jet. I'll add a few bombs as well."

"So much for the land. Have you called all the contractors?" said Heller.

"They'll meet you at Ochokeechokee. It's the remains of a town and there may even be a hotel there. They're all hot onto it. They got their logistics worked out and all their estimates are firmed. But, Mr. Jet, don't you think a billion dollars is an awful lot to spend on just clean air? And why for a bunch of Florida crackers?"

"It's necessary, Izzy. The pollution in the atmosphere will heat this planet up in time. I'm putting in the spores production plant in the Florida area because it's hot and will save fuel. The spores will rise into the trade winds, hit the stratosphere and circulate to both hemispheres. The spores will convert noxious gases into oxygen and it will take an awful lot of them. I'm sorry if you think it is unprofitable."

"Oh, no, Mr. Jet," said Izzy. "I certainly would never dream of criticizing you. You wound me to think so. Besides, I maybe forgot to tell you, but when you said you were using mud electrical-breakdown for fuel, I enlarged the power plant a little bit and contracted the excess to the City of Miami Power Company for a quarter of a billion dollars a year: they use an awful lot of air conditioning there. Here's the contracts. I forgot to mention it."

"Well, I'm glad we're going to show a profit," said Heller.

"No, no, that's not where the profit comes from," said Izzy. "That just retires the project off the books in four years. The profit comes from this other corporation. I'm sorry if I forgot to mention it. I reactivated the original retirement estates corporation and we'll have a campaign to 'retire on your own alligator farm.' They were selling like hot cakes even before we got the place subdivided."

Bang-Bang spoke up. "The deal is, they feed the tourists to the alligators and sell the alligator hides made up as purses, belts and shoes to the tourists. Perfect perpetual motion machine."

Izzy said, reprovingly, "That's not true."

"That's what you told me," said Bang-Bang self-righteously.

"Don't listen to him, Mr. Jet," said Izzy. "I was just trying to sell him one of the farms, and what does truth have to do with salesmanship? Actually we make our profit out of constructing posh retirement houses out of the mud we dig from the scenic canals we're going to make to raise the alligators in. So don't you worry about the cost, Mr. Jet. You worry about those Indians."

"All right," said Heller, getting up off the floor. "Now you, Missy," he said to the Countess Krak, "have you got your clothes together? Sun helmets and bikinis and things?"

"What?" said Izzy. "You're not taking Miss Joy! Mr. Jet, there's alligators, Indians, mud—oy! A beautiful creature like Miss Joy in a horrible place like that? Forgive me, Mr. Jet, but I think you haven't thought this through. Florida just plain isn't civilized enough."

"I'm not going," said the Countess Krak.

"What?" said Heller, aghast.

"Much as I don't want to be apart from you," said Krak, "we're in a hurry to finish everything up and I have other things to do."

"Such as?" said Heller.

Her smile was enigmatic. "I want to pick an item up that I haven't found. It's going to take a lot of search."

"Oh, shopping," said Heller. "Well, I'll admit that I certainly didn't look kindly at the idea of you in all that mud and up to your knees in alligators. I won't be gone too long. Just to get everything staked out and the contractors started. I'll miss you. But I can see your point. It's all right."

He was frowning a bit. Suddenly Heller turned to Bang-Bang. "Listen, Bang-Bang, and listen good. You keep an eye on her. You make sure she's safe at all times!"

"You needn't say the rest of it," said Bang-Bang. "If

I don't you'll take me to ten thousand feet and drop me with no parachute."

"Precisely," said Heller.

"You didn't have to threaten," said Bang-Bang. "Jesus—beggin' your pardon, ma'am—I'd booby-trap my own head to blow it off if anything happened to Miss Joy. Only, you tell her that. She's sort of got a way to arguing around my very best reasons."

"You mind what Bang-Bang says," said Heller to the Countess Krak.

She smiled her enigmatic smile. "Of course, dear," she replied.

Chapter 4

I was flabbergasted at my tremendous luck! Of course, I'd known for some time that Heller was doing something with spores to clean up the planet's air, but I hadn't realized he was going away so soon. I just sat there gaping. The Gods had decided to smile on me at last! Bang-Bang I could discount. Without Heller to guide him, he was nothing. I could hardly believe it. I was actually going to be able to get the Countess Krak killed without any trouble at all! Not only killed but her dead body raped!

I was so engrossed, Miss Pinch had to call me twice to tell me the first lesbian couple was ready.

With great aplomb and confidence, I went into the living room. I gave them the treat of watching me take off my clothes.

The husband was named Ralph: short-haired and thin of face. She was lying under a sheet, eyes on me, bright and alive.

With the air of a professional connoisseur, Miss Pinch watched me get into bed.

The other lesbian flinched as her husband let out a scream.

Candy grinned, eagerly nodding in rhythm.

Ralph's mouth opened in a convulsive yell. Then she stiffened and her eyes, wide open, rolled back into her head. She lay there very still. I was staring into blank eyes!

A wave of horror hit me.

I thought that she was dead!

I off-loaded quick and went into the back room.

Feeling very strange, I stood there staring into the back garden.

Was something wrong with me? I felt sort of ill. I couldn't understand it.

Fifteen minutes or more I stood there. Finally Miss Pinch came in. She said, "The other girl is waiting, Inkswitch. What the hell is going on?"

"I don't feel like it," I said.

"Jesus Christ, Inkswitch, you can't be rude to company."

"I don't know what is wrong with me," I said. "I don't think I can make it."

Miss Pinch went out and shortly came back in. She was carrying a water tumbler full of bubbles. "It's some of the party champagne," she said. "Drink it down. A great aphrodisiac."

I was thirsty. I gulped it all down. It made me feel warm. Not much more alcoholic content than Turkish *sira*.

I peeked into the other room. Ralph was sitting up, fanning herself with her palm. She smiled at me. "Oh, you kid," she said. "To think I got to wait three weeks for another one of those is pure torture."

I went over to her. I felt her arm. The pulse was strong. She was alive!

"You got the wrong girl, Inkswitch," said Miss Pinch. "Over here. This is Butter."

I walked around to the other side of the bed. The lesbian wife, Butter, was lying there sort of panting and eyeing me.

The girl said, "I'm no virgin. I let a goat do it to me once up on a farm. It wasn't much good but he got my maidenhead. So shove away but I don't think I'll (bleep) like Ralph did."

Miss Pinch laughed.

Candy grinned.

Ralph, watching, began to bob her head knowingly.

Butter screamed and convulsed. Then her eyes rolled straight up into her head and she stiffened out like a poker.

I was staring at blank, sightless eyes in a perfectly still face on a rigid body.

My stomach turned over.

I pulled off and raced away.

I got to the bathroom. I began to throw up in the toilet bowl. I threw up everything I'd eaten for days and still tried.

I collapsed in front of it, still trying from time to time.

Dead eyes!

What was wrong with me?

It must have been the champagne! But no, I'd begun to feel this way when Ralph did that.

Was I going crazy?

Worse—was I, an Apparatus veteran, developing a conscience? Gods forbid.

I examined my immediate past. Due to Prahd's operation, I had had a sexual surge. That should have made a difference in my mind. Freud would think it would, for his whole theory was that everything was based on sex.

With care I reviewed myself to see if there was any real change in my personality. Bit by bit, I went over past experience with myself.

My motivations didn't seem to have changed. Money, kill songbirds, put the riffraff in its place.

Mysterious. Comparing past years to present, I had to conclude that my personality had not shifted so much as an id.

I got to thinking about Torpedo Fiaccola. His psychologist had recommended becoming a necrophile. So obviously, from this evidence and much other psychology reading I had done, it was quite a normal thing to have coitus with a corpse. So that could not be the basis of this strange reaction.

I just couldn't get to the bottom of it at all.

Hours later, it seemed, Miss Pinch came looking for me. I heard myself babble, "Is Butter alive?"

She laughed at me. "You're not good enough to kill them dead, Inkswitch. They both went home long ago."

"You're not fooling me? You didn't dispose of her corpse somewhere, did you?"

She saw I was serious. And she couldn't get me out of the bathroom. She phoned the couple and put Butter on the phone.

"Are you a live girl?" I said.

"What's your opinion, Inkswitch? But man, I'm here to tell you, you were better than the goat."

"You're alive, then. You weren't dead."

"Hell, you want me to come back, Inkswitch?"

"Give me that phone," said Pinch, who had had her ear pressed near.

"No, no," I said. "Put Ralph on."

She did and I said, "Are you alive, Ralph?"

"Half dead," said Ralph.

It was the wrong answer. I shoved the phone at Miss Pinch. She said something into the mouthpiece and hung up. Then she said, "Take a shower, Inkswitch. The goat rubbed off on you. We're waiting."

I took a shower. I washed and washed and washed, which is very unusual for me.

Miss Pinch finally came into the bathroom again. "For Christ's sake, Inkswitch, come on!"

She got me out and towelled me and got me into the other room.

"No," I said. "Wait a moment." I found my hands were very shaky.

"Look," I begged, "promise me you'll keep moving."

Chapter 5

In the chilly light of dawn, after a bad night of introspection, I decided it was all nonsense. There was nothing wrong with me at all.

I got into the closet with my viewers. And one sight

of the Countess Krak through Heller's viewer returned
to me my full resolve.

They were taking him to the airport in the old,
orange cab. She and Heller were seated in the back. Izzy
was hunched up on the front seat looking studiously
ahead. Bang-Bang was driving as he always did—like a
madman.

Heller and Krak had their arms around each other.
She was sort of sniffling. But she said, "I know it's
rough to be apart even for a few days. I've just got to
steel up to it, that's all. We've got to get this mission finished and get off this planet. I feel it like an ache."

So there she was, using all her woman's wiles to rush
Heller along and get something done. And she didn't
care a single (bleep) that I'd be killed if Heller succeeded
in straightening out the place, for he could only do so by
ruining every control point on which Lombar depended.

I was right. She was the one I had to get rid of first.
And quick. It was my firm duty to have her shot and I
must not waver for a moment.

That put my mind at rest. But something else at
once unstabilized it. Heller's 831 Relayer! (Bleep) Raht!
I'd be out of communication like a shot, with Heller in
Florida.

I got on the radio. Raht answered in a sleepy voice.
"Listen, you lazy (bleep)!" I screamed. "Pay attention to
your duties for a change! I've had enough of being cut
off from seeing what he does. He's dangerous! Get over
to the Empire State Building and get all those gadgets off
of that antenna. You're just leaving them there to spite
me! Since you know where it is, smart (bleep), deliver
Krak's and Crobe's to me here in this apartment right
away. Then draw money and a ticket at the office and fly
today down to Ochokeechokee, Florida, keep your eye on

that man and stay within two hundred miles of him. Repeat this all back quick so I'll know you're awake and I'm not talking to a snore."

He did. I clicked off.

I looked back at the viewers. They were unloading Heller's bags in the parking lot. Heller tried to help them but Izzy and Bang-Bang pushed him aside and struggled manfully with the big cases.

I got disoriented. I was so used to going in and out of JFK that I didn't know where they were until I spotted a sign, La Guardia. Ah, domestic flights, of course.

They got up to a line waiting at a counter. Izzy handed Heller a ticket. Heller looked at it. "Hey, what's this? Pretty Boy Floyd?"

"Bang-Bang said that was your travelling name," said Izzy. "And listen, you're not connected to any of those corporations we have there. The contractors think your name is Floyd, too. And I advise you to use war paint on your face so if the Indians jump you, they'll think you're one of them."

"Brilliant thinking, Izzy," said Heller. "I'll do just that. Now listen, I don't think there's much in the way of telephones down at Ochokeechokee and I may be out in the swamp mostly. So if you call and an alligator answers, hang up."

"Why?" said Izzy.

"Why?" echoed Heller. "I should think that would be obvious. You might put all the alligators on my trail, too!"

Izzy looked puzzled.

Bang-Bang said, "Izzy, it's a joke. You know, J-O-K-E, joke, as in oy."

"It's no joke going amongst alligators and Indians,"

said Izzy. "You be careful, Mr. Jet. I'm still responsible for you."

I had a sudden thought. Raht, the idiot, would lose his man for sure. I buzzed hastily on the radio.

"Yes?" said Raht and there was a howl of wind in the microphone.

"Listen, he's travelling under the name of Pretty Boy Floyd and he'll be wearing war paint."

"You almost knocked me off this antenna."

"Don't you fall off and break those relayers!" I snarled at him.

"Wait, listen. I don't have your address, really. Can you talk me in?"

"You can't soar from there to here!" I snapped. What an idiot. What did he think he was using? A space-trooper sled? I gave him the address.

I looked back at the viewers. As you could expect, Heller and Krak were off to the side waiting for the plane, and she was crying. Women are always crying when people leave and when people get married. I can understand crying when getting married: that's an awful tragedy. But not just getting on a plane.

"I feel too bad even to be cross with you about those women," she was saying.

"Women?"

"That protest at the United Nations. The ones carrying your picture with 'Pretty Boy' on it. You use that name on tickets."

"Oh, honey, I can explain. . . ."

"No, no. You don't have to. I love you, Jettero. You're my man and I love you. And I'm being an idiot to stay behind and not go to Florida with you. But I've got to do all I can to speed things up and help us get home. And then we can get married and live happily

ever after in some civilized place. There's a nice surprise
waiting for us both when we get home. I promised I
wouldn't tell you and I won't. But hurry and finish up
this mission, Jettero. And I'll do all I can."

"You sit quietly and wait for me," said Heller.

"They're calling your plane," said the Countess
Krak.

She kissed him and cried some more.

Then he was gone.

They saw the plane off from the observation platform and went back to the cab. She was still crying.

Oh, there was no doubt at all left in my mind that
she had to be killed. Pushing him, pushing him, egging
him on. And all to connect up with Royal proclamations
that were forgeries. But that was not the surprise they
were going to get.

The Countess Krak would be dead before Heller
ever saw her again!

Chapter 6

About half an hour after Candy and Miss Pinch had
departed for work, Raht showed up. I let him in. He
handed me two sets of units, Crobe's and Krak's: they
were all scummed up with soot from their long tenure
in the weather; I found a rag and started to clean them up.

Raht wandered around the apartment, staring at the
clam shells and phallic symbols and sea foam. "Who
lives here?" he said. "Some whore?"

I was certainly sick of his insolence. "If you did your duty as well as I do mine," I raged at him, "we'd get someplace. And you're not getting to Florida where you belong!"

"There's no second plane until noon," he said. "Place sure stinks of flowers. Smells like a mortuary."

That did it. "Get out!" I screamed at him and kicked him out the door.

Having abreacted my hostilities, I felt better. I went to Krak's viewer to check it. The picture was not quite as good with the activator-receiver in this low place but it was adequate. I got interested in what Krak was doing.

They had returned to the office and Krak was sitting at a white secretarial desk looking in the white pages of the New York telephone directory. Her finger was travelling down a page. She was muttering, "Rocha... Rochelle... Rock... Rocket... Rockford..." She looked up. She muttered, "A-B-C-D-E-F. E-F..."

Bang-Bang's voice. "Miss Joy." She looked up. He was sitting at the bar drinking a cup of coffee. "If you tell me what you're trying to do, maybe I can help."

"I'm trying to find the personal telephone number of Delbert John Rockecenter."

"WHAT?" said Bang-Bang, slopping his coffee.

"Well, you needn't look so surprised," said Krak. "On a civilized planet, nearly everybody has a communication call sign. How otherwise would you get in touch with them if you had some vital news about their family?"

"Well, Jesus—beggin' your pardon, ma'am—Delbert John Rockecenter is just about the most important man there is. You don't just go phoning people like that. Maybe you better tell me what this is all about." He came over, his coffee forgotten.

"It's a very simple matter. Look at this geometry plot." She got the huge sheet Heller had done and spread it open on the desk.

It was, of course, in Voltarian except for the words "Pokantickle Estates, Hairytown, N.Y.," "Octopus Oil Building" and "Delbert John Rockecenter." Bang-Bang was twisting his head this way and that, trying to figure out what all these spirals and words were. It would surely have been a Code break except that he didn't seem to know the Voltarian symbols and letters were more than designs. "Maybe you better explain it," said Bang-Bang, defeated.

"Well, Delbert John Rockecenter is the emperor," said the Countess Krak.

"Oh, I see," said Bang-Bang. "This is some kind of an idea for a new game like Monopoly."

"No," said Krak patiently. "It shows Rockecenter controls the planet utterly."

"Well, hell—beggin' your pardon, ma'am—that don't take no fancy diagram to figure out. Everybody knows that. For the last century the Rockecenter family has been taking over from other mobs and now Delbert John owns and controls all the real estate and rackets. I guess 'emperor' would be a fancy name like *capo di tutti capi,* but it really don't embrace all that Rockecenter really controls. He's into everybody's pocket, too. He controls every oil company and I can't fill up the cab's tank without helping make Rockecenter rich. I can't buy an aspirin without helping make Rockecenter rich. I can't even drink a cup of coffee without stuffing more dough in the Rockecenter coffers. Everybody knows that. So what's the urgent notice doing on the regimental bulletin board?"

"He's got a son," said Krak triumphantly.

"Well, hell, no—beggin' your pardon, ma'am. He ain't got no wife and he for sure ain't got no son. I helped Jet tear the library apart one day just making sure."

"That's just it," said Krak. "Delbert John Rockecenter doesn't know he has a son."

"WHAT?"

"Aha! So it surprises you, too," said the Countess Krak. "But it is a fact. I've got it all worked out. Delbert John was playing around—beggin' your pardon, Bang-Bang—and he got himself a son. But he didn't know it. He has a lawyer named Bury. So Bury hid the son and hid the fact from Rockecenter and as there is no heir, the empire will then pass straight into the hands of Bury."

"Jesus Christ."

"Now, Jettero is trying to fix up the planet's fuel situation. He doesn't have much time. Rockecenter controls all the fuel. Now, if I were to simply phone up Delbert John Rockecenter and tell him he had a son, he'd be so grateful that he'd rush around and help Jettero and we'd be all finished here and could go home."

Bang-Bang's black Italian eyes were nearly popping out of his thin face.

The Countess Krak continued. "And if he doubts it, why, I'll just go out and find the son and turn him over to his father. Oh, Bang-Bang, Rockecenter would be so grateful he'd put Jettero on center stage with all the spotlights blazing and tell him 'Jettero, you write the show and we'll put on any act you want!' It can't fail, Bang-Bang. That's why I stayed behind."

Bang-Bang had found his voice. "Miss Joy! You can't go phoning Rockecenter! You can't go looking for some dumb kid! That mob is a gang of wolves! They'd eat the Virgin Mary, toenails and all, and never even

bother to spit out one Ave Maria! In short—beggin' your
pardon, ma'am—they're (bleeps), Bury and that Rockecenter crew! Wolves, Miss Joy, WEREWOLVES!"

"Oh, nonsense, Bang-Bang. I've read a lot of guidebooks and things on New York, and Rockecenter has
been giving away things to the people right and left:
fountains, museums. The place is loaded with them."

"That was just the Rockecenter way of turning off
the heat!" said Bang-Bang. "Just a way of buying adver-
tising space when nobody would waste spit on the name!"

"Be that as it may," said the Countess Krak, "a
father's heart could not help but open up if he knew he
had a son. And that's why I am going to tell him or find
the son and tell him, and out of gratitude he'll help and
we can go home."

"IZZY!" screamed Bang-Bang. Then he seemed to
realize he couldn't be heard through a door and down
hundreds of feet of halls. He raced out and came back
with an alarmed and wild-eyed Izzy. Bang-Bang marched
him to the secretary desk. "Izzy, please explain to Miss
Joy what (bleeps) Rockecenter and Bury really are."

Izzy swallowed several times and wiped his glasses
on his tie and tried to put his tie on his nose. "Miss Joy,
please don't do anything rash." Bang-Bang punched him
in the side and he continued. "If the corpses made by the
Rockecenter mob in starting wars and ending competition were laid end to end, they'd walk on them forever.
The family was founded on selling crude oil for a cancer
cure and they've been a cancer ever since. The family
policies make a Mafia vengeance curse sound like a Sunday school prayer. Those horrors are not fit company for
a delicate and beautiful lady. Anything we can do to help
you while away the time? Theater tickets? Flowers? Diamond rings? A new collar for the cat? Until Mr. Jet

comes back and gets you under control, please tell me. What can we do to make you forget about this?"

"You can tell me how to find a telephone number," said the Countess Krak.

"Don't tell her," said Bang-Bang.

"I won't," said Izzy. He wandered in a small helpless circle, wrung his hands and went away.

Bang-Bang crept over to the bar and got behind it like he was in an observation post. Now, from afar, he was staring at the Countess Krak in worried bafflement.

She pulled over a phone. She looked at it studiously. A button said Operator. She pushed it. She got the operator. "How do you find a telephone number that is not in the phone book?" said the Countess Krak.

"Long distance or local, please," said the operator.

"That's the trouble," said the Countess Krak. "I don't know where he is."

"Where who is, ma'am?"

"Delbert John Rockecenter."

"Delbert John Rockecenter?"

"Delbert John Rockecenter."

"You mean the Delbert John Rockecenter that owns the phone company?"

"And the planet," said the Countess Krak.

"Jesus Christ," said the operator. "Ma'am, I think I better put you through to the Chief Information Operator. Hold on, please."

The Countess Krak had begun the trek across the telephone information lines of the planet that I had followed months before. She soon had London, Johannesburg, Moscow and Paris into the conference. They added Dogie, Texas, when somebody remembered he now owned Texas, and from there it was easy. Dogie put them onto the Arab whose king remembered calling Hairytown.

The Countess Krak said suddenly, "That's it!" She had it on Heller's plot.

They got the Hairytown local information and, with a sigh of relief, rang through to Pokantickle Estate.

The fourth assistant butler said, "I am sorry, but Mr. Rockecenter is not accepting any calls except from Miss Agnes. Is it Miss Agnes calling?"

It wasn't.

They all rang off.

The Countess Krak hung up the phone and sat back. She must have been looking very smug, for Bang-Bang at the bar had become quite white of face.

"You found his number?" said Bang-Bang with a kind of horror.

"I have found somebody who can put me in direct communication with him. She is a Miss Agnes and she must live in Hairytown. So, now, Bang-Bang, you're going to drive me there."

Bang-Bang came out from behind the bar. You could see confidence ebbing back into him. He smiled. He said, "I'm very afraid we cannot go. You see, my parole officer has forbidden me to leave New York City. If I do they'll chuck me back into Sing Sing. I promised Jet I'd make sure you were safe and he told you to listen to me. So you see, I can't drive you and you can't go."

"Parole officer? Supposing I could fix that, Bang-Bang?"

"Well, a parole officer is someone who is so mean, so rotten and so vicious that nobody can fix one. And even if you could, there are my classes and drills at the ROTC at college. And if I missed those, Jet wouldn't get his diploma. So, there you are, Miss Joy. A complete double roadblock, manned by the cops on one side and the Army on the other."

"Oh, is that all?" said the Countess Krak. "An important project like this couldn't possibly be allowed to halt just because of tiny routine matters." She got up from the desk in a purposeful way.

I suddenly went crazy.

My Gods, not only was Heller gone but she was setting herself up like a duck in a shooting gallery.

AND I WASN'T ORGANIZED YET!

Chapter 7

I dug out Torpedo's mother's phone number. I jabbed the dial. "Who's this?" she said.

"Torpedo," I blurted. "I got to talk to Torpedo!"

"Oh, you're that dumb son of a (bleepch) that's hiring my no-good, worthless (bleep) of a son that drove his poor father to the grave and has me halfway there, the philanderer!"

"Put him on the phone, quick."

"I wouldn't if I could and I can't."

"Why not?"

"Because he's at Dr. Finkelbaum's getting his God (bleeped) insurance examination." She hung up.

I dialled again. She didn't answer.

I had better get clever, quick. I grabbed the phone book. Then I realized that it was probably Queens I wanted and I didn't have Queens, only Manhattan. I punched information.

"Quick, it's a life and death matter. I have to have Dr. Finkelbaum in Queens."

"There are over thirty Dr. Finkelbaums in Queens, sir. Initials, please."

"Insurance examinations."

"I do not have an I. E. Finkelbaum listed, sir."

Dead end. I hung up. Desperately, I tried to think. Then I had it! No American company would sell high-risk: they only sold policies they could renege on or let lapse. Hit man insurance would only be available from Boyd's of London: they insure anything. Did they have a New York office? I grabbed the phone book. Absolutely, there it was!

I dialled it. "Do you have a Dr. Finkelbaum that does medicals for you?"

"Oh, yes, rather," and with a thick British accent, he gave me a number and address right on Wall Street in the financial district of lower Manhattan.

I hastily phoned it. "Do you have a Torpedo Fiaccola in there for a medical examination?"

"He's not here right now. He was sent to the hospital for his shots."

"What hospital? And listen, if he comes back, detain him there if I haven't seen him."

"Bellevue General. How will I know if you've seen him, sir?"

"He'll be limping because I kicked him for being so slow!"

"Very good, sir."

I phoned Bellevue General. "Do you have a Fiaccola there to be shot?"

"Shooting cases are sent to Emergency, sir."

"No, no. This is an insurance case. Sent by Dr. Finkelbaum. Please look for him. It's a life and death matter."

"It is always a life and death matter, sir."

"This is different. It's mostly a death matter. Find that man!"

I waited. I could hear my call being transferred around. Finally, "This is the High Security Detention Ward, sir. Yes, we have a Torpedo Fiaccola."

"Good Heavens," I said. "Has he gone crazy or something?"

"No, sir. That would be the Psychiatric Detention Ward. The High Security Detention Ward is where we put patients who can't pay their bills."

So that was it! I had neglected to call by and pay their bill, so they had grabbed the man when he showed up! "He'll be out of there in a flash," I said.

I hurriedly got dressed. I grabbed up all my money including the additional thousand I had made the night before. I stuffed some other things I might find handy into my pockets. I picked up Krak's viewer and rushed out. I got to Seventh Avenue and grabbed a cab.

Bellevue is over by the East River: First Avenue and about 30th Street. Cross-town traffic was slow, slow, slow.

I watched the viewer. Krak was also riding in a cab—the old cab—and Bang-Bang was driving. She had changed her clothes to a gray suit, judging by what I could see of her knees. She had a lot of bags and luggage at her feet. One of them was a duffel bag with *Bang-Bang Rimbombo* on it. They were all packed!

Then I realized from the street signs she was watching that they were going south in Manhattan. I had thought they were heading direct for Hairytown which is north.

"Chinatown seems like a funny place for a parole office," Countess Krak called through the open partition. "You're not Chinese, Bang-Bang."

"It's just that the New York State offices are close to Chinatown."

"Is the parole officer Chinese? I don't speak that language, you know."

"He's pure ape," said Bang-Bang, over his shoulder. "He mangles prisoners and English irregardless. This is all a waste of time, Miss Joy. He wouldn't give a con a break for a million bucks. You ask him for a relaxation of my parole conditions and he's likely to order me back to the pen. You're taking my life in your hands just to talk to him!"

"You let me be the judge of that," said Krak. "STOP!"

Bang-Bang bounced off a truck and then bounced off a curb. A man was selling flowers on the walk. Krak handed him a five-dollar bill and grabbed a bunch of carnations. They knocked down a street works sign and sped on south.

"Miss Joy, I don't think you got the right idea. Not only would that ape throw them flowers in your face, he'd probably try to charge me with bribery and corruption."

My own hacker was happily running up his meter in the cross-town traffic snarl. "Good thing you got a portable TV, mister," he said over his shoulder. "This is going to take a while. But what program is that? Some old morning rerun of Humphrey Bogart and Lauren Bacall? Well, you'll have time to finish it at this rate."

Rage hit me. To infer that Bang-Bang sounded like Bogart! And she sounded more like Susan Hayward in her most villainous roles! Oh, well, she'd soon be dead.

"Sounds like a chase scene," said my hacker. "They sure used to wreck them cars good."

And at the moment, I had to agree with him. Bang-Bang was opening traffic lanes with fenders as they passed through Chinatown. What that old cab could take was even up to Bang-Bang's driving.

With a screech of brakes they drew up before the New York State offices. "If he says he's going to send me back to the pen," said Bang-Bang, "you whistle out that window so I can get a head start."

"Be calm," said Krak. "You wait in the car."

"With motor running for a fast getaway," said Bang-Bang. "One more time, Miss Joy. Please don't do it."

"I know that picture," said my hacker. "It's the one where Bacall dies in the end."

"That's right," I said.

The Countess Krak stepped down to the street. She took the flowers in the crook of her arm. On the sidewalk, she opened her purse and popped something in her mouth. I blinked. Was she on drugs?

She stood there for a bit, idly looking down the length of a park. What a perfect target she was making. Right out in the open, not even moving. I groaned at the lost opportunity. A sniper in a passing car and one dead Countess Krak. I must get Fiaccola sprung and going!

Then she took something out of her purse, a little tiny spray vial, and sprayed it on the flowers. This was idiocy. Putting perfume on carnations. They don't have hardly any perfume at all. They don't even make me sneeze. Boy, would she be detected quick!

She looked at the big directory board. It said:

OSSINING CORRECTIONAL FACILITY
Liaison

She went to the designated floor. She went down a hall and stopped before a door that said:

Parole Officer

She straightened her jacket, took the flowers in her hand and with an airy saunter walked in.

An absolute beast sat at the desk, probably a former prison screw, pensioned off from Sing Sing and given a nice job where he could ruin everybody. He looked up. He glared.

"You have a parolee," said the Countess Krak, "named Bang-Bang Rimbombo."

"That son of a (bleepch)," said the parole officer. "Don't tell me you're bringing the good news that the (bleepard) is dead. That would make my day."

"I am his aunt," said the Countess Krak in a lilting voice. "Day by day I see my poor nephew droop. Alas, he has become a withering beast chained in the dens of vice of New York, longing with tears and gusty sighs for the open fields and wildflowers of his native habitat. Smell the flowers he misses so."

She pushed the carnations straight into the parole officer's face! He opened his mouth to roar. Apparently it made him inhale. He sat back down suddenly.

She continued. "Don't you think it would be a good idea to lift all restrictions on his movements?"

"Yes," said the parole officer.

"And make it unnecessary for him ever to have to report in again?"

"Yes," said the parole officer.

"And give him a clean bill of health for his entire parole time?"

"Yes."

"And you have the proper forms to do this with?"

"Yes."

"And you think it is a wonderful idea to pick up that pen and fill out all the forms?"

"Yes."

"And you just agreed to start doing it this minute?"

"Yes," said the parole officer. He grabbed pads of forms and busily began to write.

When he finished, the Countess Krak said, "And now you think you should give me signed copies, do you not?"

"Yes," he said.

She reached over and took the "Copy to Parolee" sheets.

"You enjoyed this conversation, didn't you?" said the Countess Krak.

"Yes."

"And you did all this at your own suggestion?"

"Yes."

"Good day," said the Countess Krak and walked away.

She threw the flowers in a litter can on the street and got into the cab. She handed Bang-Bang the copies.

He looked at them bug-eyed. He leafed through them hurriedly again. "Jesus!" he said.

"Get going, Bang-Bang," said the Countess Krak. "We have another stop to make."

Bang-Bang edged over into Lafayette Street, heading north. All of a sudden he exploded. "I'M FREE!"

He was suddenly driving at high acceleration. "Jesus Christ, Miss Joy, I'll admit that you're probably the most beautiful woman in America, but who the hell would ever guess that (bleeped) ape would fall for a DAME!"

She was not paying much attention. She was looking in her purse. She had the torn wrapper of the Eyes and Ears of Voltar package. It said *Perfume to make a person say yes to anything. Pre-antidote necessary.*

"Blast," she muttered. "I only have one more of these. I better save it for another time."

Oh, she was dangerous, all right!

"Here we are," my cabby said. "That's twenty-one dollars. You get to the part yet where Lauren Bacall is killed?"

"Not yet," I said grimly.

"That's the best part," he said as he drove off.

I agreed completely!

Chapter 8

I surely didn't want to be seen in company with a hit man. People remember these things.

Knowing I was pushed for time, I rushed into the hospital and located the accounting office.

With my hat pulled down to hide the better part of my face, I told the clerk, "I'm Attorney Grouch of Grouch and Grouch. I am here to pay the bill of Torpedo Fiaccola and spring him."

The clerk found the bill. "That's $5,100, please."

"Wait a minute," I said. "It was $4,900 yesterday."

"The additional is for his room while we detained him and for his shots."

What could I do? Nothing. I paid it. I said, "When

you let him go, tell him he is supposed to report back to Dr. Finkelbaum."

She made a note of it and I rushed off. I had to get down to the financial district to Boyd's of London and get his hit man insurance. But there were no taxis in sight and no subways were handy. I raced over to Second Avenue and boarded a downtown bus, Number 15.

New York buses lurch around and roar, dive into and away from curbs and make an awful fuss. But they don't get anywhere very fast.

I thought I had better check up on the Countess Krak. If I was fast enough I could get her hit before the day was done. I balanced the viewer on my knee and watched.

(Bleep) that Bang-Bang! Driving at speed, he had gotten her almost to the ROTC offices at Empire University! They pulled up at the door. The Countess Krak pushed a pad and ballpoint through the cab partition.

"Now, Bang-Bang, write a request in proper form for a leave of absence from class and drills for a couple weeks." And she watched while he printed it quite laboriously.

At the bottom he had drawn a line and left a space. He indicated it. "That's for the endorsement of Colonel Tanc, U.S. Army. He's got to initial it or it's no good, and it's got to go into the files. But Tanc won't sign it, Miss Joy."

"What kind of a man is this Colonel Tanc?" said Krak.

"Regular Army," said Bang-Bang. "Posted here to run the Reserve Officers' Training Corps for Empire. He's a military martinet, stiff as starch. Hound for discipline. Very proper. Never does the slightest thing irregular. He thinks these student officers are just play soldiers and beneath contempt. Wister, being a senior, holds ROTC rank of lieutenant but that's not Regular Army and we ain't even sworn into the service, thank God. But when we graduate, and Wister is sworn in, Wister will be an army officer and I swear to Pete, Miss Joy, the colonel doesn't even consider us up to a Regular Army buck-(bleep) private—beggin' your pardon, ma'am. He'll never grant this, probably even assign punishment drill. I wouldn't advise you presenting this. You could blow the whole show."

Two plump black women in the seat behind me were looking over my shoulder at the viewer interestedly. One said, "I didn't know they were doin' no rerun of Sophia Loren in the morning, but that sure as hell is Marcello Mastroianni."

"Naw," said the other, "that's Humphrey Bogart, plain as the nose on your face, woman. But I didn't know he played with Sophia Loren and that sho' as hell was her voice."

"Look at that," said the other, "you don't see her face, only what she's lookin' at. I know a Hitchcock film when I see one, only it's in color. Did Hitchcock ever direct Sophia Loren?"

I ignored them. Riffraff.

"Now, this could be a little dicey, Bang-Bang," said the Countess Krak. "You park right there and be ready for a fast getaway."

Bang-Bang, in alarm, said, "You be careful!"

"Oh, indeed I will. This could be very dangerous."

Bang-Bang groaned.

"No, that ain't Sophia Loren," said one of the black women. "That's Lauren Bacall and Bogart. I'd know her voice anywhere."

"You're right," said the other. "I jus' got the names mixed. I know this film. It's the one where Bacall gets killed, but I didn't know it was in color."

"Yah, Hitchcock directed it, all right. You only see what she's looking at. Horror film."

The Countess Krak took an envelope out of her purse. She wrote on it *From Lieutenant Wister, ROTC.* She put the leave request in it. Then she produced a little glass bubble and inserted that in the envelope. She sealed the flap. The action startled me. What was this vicious female making? A letter bomb? Was she going to kill the colonel?

"You won't change your mind?" pleaded Bang-Bang.

"You keep that motor running," said the Countess Krak. "Get ready to make those tires scream if this goes wrong."

She got out of the cab, and using the window as a mirror, she fluffed her hair and straightened her jacket. She walked in through the entrance.

There was a huge sign there. It said:

REGIMENTAL DANCE MARCH 28
Full Uniform
Bring your girls, girls, girls

"Hmm," said the Countess Krak. "So this is Lieutenant Wister's life in the ROTC."

There was a sergeant at a waiting room desk. When she entered, he stood up and blinked and looked like he was going to offer her a chair.

She paid no attention to him. She sailed right on past him, heading for the door marked Colonel Mark Q. Tanc, United States Army. She opened it and marched in.

Colonel Tanc was sitting at his desk, surrounded by flags and cannon shells. He looked the very proper officer—tunic, shirt, tie, eagles on the shoulders and campaign ribbons by the score to account for his bitter and disapproving face.

The Countess Krak had the envelope in her hand. Her thumb and forefinger crushed the glass bubble inside it and it made a tiny crack.

She handed it toward the colonel and he, glaring, would not have touched it at all if she hadn't used the magician's forcing twitch of the hand which makes people take things.

The colonel, removing his baleful glare from her face for a moment, read the inscription. "Wister?" he snarled. "Do I have a man named Wister?" He began to open it.

"Oh, indeed you do," said the Countess Krak in a lilting voice. "And I have the honor to be his sister. He could not come himself, today. His poor, dear grandmother lies dying in Sleepy Hollow, ready to leave him a million bucks if he avoids the wolf and comes out of the woods in time with a basket of lunch on his arm."

The colonel stared at her and began to read the leave request. A strange look of pleasure began to creep over his face.

The Countess Krak continued. "Oh, I am sure that you will excuse him from his classes and drills a couple weeks. For if you don't, why, then I shall refuse to dance with you at the Regimental Ball, March twenty-eighth."

The colonel's face was becoming flushed. He looked at her with hungry eyes. He said, "Oh, Christ, we can't have that!" He hastily endorsed the request for leave.

She extended her hand and took hold of the paper to draw it away.

The colonel's fingers amorously clutched her wrist. He said in an emotion-charged voice, "Come with me to my room, my little pigeon!"

With an expert twist of her arm she unlocked his clutching paw. She got the leave request away.

The colonel lunged across the desk toward her, panting, face suffused.

The Countess Krak sped out of the room. The colonel was pursuing.

She threw the endorsed order at the sergeant and shouted at him as he caught it, "File this!"

She raced out of the orderly room.

The colonel was close behind her.

She glanced back. Suddenly the sergeant had joined the chase with hot and panting cries.

The Countess Krak got to the cab.

She glanced back. The two army men were closing the distance, arms outstretched clutchingly, crying cries of beasts in heat.

The Countess Krak leaped into the cab, inches ahead of capture.

The motor roared!

Tires screamed!

She got the door closed and looked back.

The two men were pounding after them along the road.

Bang-Bang fed the cab more gas.

The pursuers were lost in the cloud of fumes behind them.

"JESUS!" said Bang-Bang, taking a weaving and rapid escape course from the neighborhood. "What was all THAT about?"

"She made it!" said one black woman.

"Yeah, and right in the teeth of the Army, too!" said the other.

"Did you see that colonel slaver?" said the first. "Great actor, Charlton Heston."

"(Bleep)!" said the other. "That didn't take no actin'. Not when you realize he was chasing Lauren Bacall!"

The Countess Krak said, "You and Jettero got your two weeks leave."

"What's the repercussions?" said Bang-Bang.

"No repercussions," said the Countess Krak mildly.

"Miss Joy," said Bang-Bang severely as he drove, "the Regular Army here is knee-deep every day in pretty college girls. Colonel Tanc and that sergeant looked like they wanted to swallow you whole. I know that look in army guys: not as bad as marines, but they meant business!"

The Countess Krak had taken a torn wrapper out of her purse. She was reading it.

Eyes and Ears of Voltar

Item 452: An emotional stimulator perfume capsule. Crush in contact with paper or cloth and avoid. Causes a person to become amorous so that he can be arrested for making improper advances.

She muttered, "They ought to warn you that this stuff is STRONG!"

Bang-Bang said, "Miss Joy, Jet would kill me if anything happened to you. I know you're beautiful and I can understand that back there, up to a point. But did you DO something?"

"Me, Bang-Bang?"

"Miss Joy, I have just done an intelligence summary and estimated the dangers of this projected campaign. I think I better take you home."

"Bang-Bang," she said firmly, "drive to Hairytown, New York."

Bang-Bang turned north. He muttered, "Now *I'm* being a (bleeped) fool, too! It's awful what a beautiful woman can do!"

One of the black women behind me said, "This is where I get off. I want to catch the rest of that film at home on the TV. I love the part where she gets killed."

I smiled grimly to myself. I said, "So will I!" And I continued on downtown to make the final arrangements.

PART FORTY-FIVE

Chapter 1

At the Boyd's of London U.S. office on Wall Street, the fellow sat there in a black cutaway with dandruff on his shoulders and said, "But I say, old chappie, this is a special rate."

"A five-day minimum at a thousand dollars a day for a measly twenty-five-thousand-dollar policy is NO special rate," I snarled.

He waved his cigarette holder in an airy way. "Hit men are hit men," he said. "And I must say the actuarial statistic shows that they themselves get hit. NOT what you would call a profession without risks. Rifles backfire, husbands take reprisals and," he fixed me with a beady eye, "cases have not been unknown where beneficiaries did a bit of hitting themselves, eh, what?"

I shook my head.

He took another approach. "It is not that your man is inexperienced. According to his record here, when he worked for Swindle and Crouch, he executed his contracts in quite a satisfactory way. It's just that records show he has a twist. A personality quirk, let's say. But I will tell you what I will do. Business has been slow today. Make it five thousand dollars for five days and I'll write the policy for seven days. It's the very best we can do, old chap."

I had to take it. It was the only way I had to hand to get Krak killed.

They wrote the policy with lots of scrolls and made his mother beneficiary. I paid them from my hard-earned hoard and I was on my way.

En route to Dr. Finkelbaum's I stopped off in a white-arm lunch, one of those places where the table is the arm of the chair. I took from my pocket a sheet and envelope of Apparatus self-destruct paper. You write on it and then spray it lightly and fold it and ten hours after it is opened it simply evaporates. No evidence left.

Disguising my handwriting, I wrote:

> *Find $850 enclosed. Your policy is clipped to the envelope so you can give it to your mother. Get a rifle. Get a car. Get to Hairytown, New York. They're in an orange-colored cab, old style, unmistakable. Phone me at the number at the bottom of the page as soon as you have something to report.*
>
> X

I added Miss Pinch's number.

I sprayed the paper. I took a five-hundred-dollar bill, three one-hundred-dollar bills and a fifty, and wrapped the note around them: I didn't want them to get lost, for aside from thirty dollars they were all the money I had left. I put them in and sealed the envelope against air.

Not even finishing my bitter coffee, I sped for Dr. Finkelbaum's.

Arriving, I peeked in and, sure enough, there sat Torpedo.

I entered the waiting room with elaborate casualness. I picked up a two-year-old magazine from the table. I sat down. Unobserved, I slid the envelope and policy into the magazine while I pretended to read. Then, very casually, I rose, laid the magazine down in the chair beside Torpedo and walked out. Very smoothly done. Right by the manual.

I lurked around a corner, eyes fixed on a reflective shop window across the street. I saw Torpedo come out reading the letter.

Wonderful! The Countess Krak would soon be dead!

I raced down into a subway and was on my way home, conscious of pride in my organizational skill.

The moment I got home, I raced into the back room closet and put the viewer down.

I had expected by this time that they would be in Hairytown, for it is less than twenty miles north of Empire University, straight up the Hudson and right on the street or highway named Broadway.

I had only slightly misestimated. They were not yet into the town. They must have paused briefly somewhere for a bite of lunch. The Countess was watching torrents of air traffic going up and down the Hudson a mile west from their road.

Krak was saying, "This cab certainly rides roughly when you use it as a ground car, Bang-Bang. Why don't you take it off this bumpy cart track and fly it?"

"Jesus, Miss Joy," he said over his shoulder as he bounced along, "it won't do that."

"Is it broken or something? I see other vehicles flying up and down, way out there over the river."

"Those are choppers, Miss Joy. This is a cab: it ain't supposed to leave the ground."

"Are you afraid of the police?"

"Yes, MA'AM!"

"I am appalled, Bang-Bang, at how overregulated this planet is. It doesn't seem to reduce the crime rate any, either. Listen, Bang-Bang, I can fix it with any cop who stops us. I'm tired of the jolting. Take it into the air."

Bang-Bang said helplessly, "My chopper license isn't up-to-date."

"Now we're getting someplace," said the Countess Krak. "You should have told me and I could have made the parole officer renew it. Bang-Bang, you should understand here and now that you can trust me."

"Yes, ma'am," said Bang-Bang miserably.

She was looking at the road expectantly. Then she saw, apparently, that the old cab was not taking off the way any ordinary airbus would have. She said, "Well, get it into the air!"

"Ma'am," said Bang-Bang, with a sigh of relief, "we're here. There's the city limits sign of Hairytown."

"Good," said the Countess Krak. "But when we leave, make sure we don't have such a rough trip back. There's a shop. Stop and I'll go in."

"I'll keep the motor running."

"Oh, this isn't dangerous. I'm just asking for directions on how to get to Miss Agnes' house."

He stopped and she got out. There was a sign. It said:

ANTIQUES
Priceless Artifacts
of
Sleepy Hollow Country
Washington Irving Slept Here
SALE TODAY ON HEADLESS HORSEMEN

"Well, I never!" said the Countess Krak. "This is the place I'm supposed to be from, according to my passport."

Bang-Bang, sitting behind the wheel, blinked. "Isn't your passport right?"

"Government documents are never right. You wait right there—I won't be long."

She went into the shop. A very old, spindly man was drilling wormholes in a chair. He looked up.

"I'm supposed to be from around here," said the Countess Krak, "but I have gotten lost. Could you please direct me to the house of Miss Agnes?"

He stared at her. His eyes went round. Then he turned aside and spat. He went out the back door and didn't come back.

The Countess Krak went back to the car. She got in. "Drive on further."

Bang-Bang turned left onto Main Street. The Countess Krak apparently didn't see anything she considered inviting. They went about three-quarters of a mile and Bang-Bang turned right onto something called Beekman Avenue. A sign pointed to North Hairytown. As they approached it, she spotted a place that said:

Sign Painting
House Numbers

She had Bang-Bang stop.

"They ought to know in here," she said. She entered the shop.

A middle-aged woman was at the counter. She looked up with the usual smile accorded to a customer.

"I have lost my way," said the Countess Krak, "could you please direct me to the house of Miss Agnes?"

An instant scowl replaced the welcome. The woman looked closely at the Countess. Then she shook her head. "My dear," she said, "what the hell would a beautiful girl like you be wanting with a God (bleeped) shrink?"

"Shrink?" said the Countess Krak.

"And with *that* God (bleeped) shrink in particular! Dearie, if somebody referred you to her, you just go back from whence you came and forget about it. There ain't no limit to what these God (bleeped) doctors will do to earn dough, even send somebody to *that* (bleepch)."

"You know her, then. Could you please give me her address?"

"No way," the woman said and walked out the back door, slamming it.

The Countess Krak went back to the cab. "Jettero said the natives repelled landings. Drive on, drive on, O Bang-Bang. We'll find Miss Agnes yet!"

They drove through North Hairytown. A street sign said:

Sleepy Hollow Road

"According to my passport," said the Countess, "I was born up that street somewhere. Do all American children get this lost?"

"Miss Joy," said Bang-Bang, "as long as we're into this and probably outflanked, there's an Octopus service station up there. If we're on the trail of something connected with Rockecenter, remember that he owns Octopus."

"Look," said the Countess. "There's a sign to Pokantickle Hills! We're within a couple of miles of the palace. Maybe we should go straight there."

"NO, ma'am. Because we were going to see the

DEATH QUEST 103

parole officer, I didn't bring a single thing for a fire fight. We're going to stop at this service station."

He pulled in well away from the islands. He got out and threw his cap on the seat. He went over to the office. The Countess Krak followed him.

The man in the office was a hard-bitten, grease-spattered, service station manager type. He looked up from his accounts.

"We're from civilization," said Bang-Bang. "We're looking for Miss Agnes. So where is she?"

"Oh, you mean Dr. Morelay," the man said. "You must be the people coming to see about the land yacht. And it's about time! She wanted to park it down here but I was scared stiff something would happen to it. She said just yesterday she didn't think you were coming at all, so you better be tactful. We have to be careful of her because of *him*. Now, let me give you a word of warning: Don't get impudent with her the way you city people can be. She's a power in this area and can have you held under the insanity laws by just snapping her fingers. I don't want her getting upset and screaming around here, blaming me, if I send you and you get impolite. All right?"

"We'll show lots of respect," said Bang-Bang, feeling nervously under his armpit where he obviously didn't have a gun.

"I'll be (bleeped) glad to get this thing settled, so just come outside and I'll point out how you get there."

Standing on the island and pointing and showing turns with his hand, he told them exactly how to get to the Morelay Estate, as he called it.

He went back into the office muttering, "Well, that's one (bleeping) headache off my plate."

They drove away.

It was perfect sniper country: open and unobstructed shots available. Bang-Bang was unarmed. I felt sure Torpedo would soon be on the scene.

And then that would be the end of the vicious Countess Krak!

Chapter 2

Up a winding road and into hedge-enclosed and iron-walled streets they went, a sort of a maze of greenery and forbidding steel spikes. There was a security gate between two gray stone pillars and a very professional sign was inset in one:

> AGNES P. MORELAY, Ph.D., M.D.
> KEEP OUT!

But you couldn't drive in the gate.

The inner road was blocked entirely by the most mammoth motor home I have ever seen.

"Oooooo!" said the Countess Krak. "What is that?"

Bang-Bang backed the cab and parked it at the street curb well away from the gate and out of its sight. He got out.

The Countess Krak picked up her shopping bag. She alighted. They walked back along the spiked wall to the gate.

She stopped and stared at the huge vehicle. "Bang-Bang, I didn't know they had those on this planet."

"Well, yes, ma'am," he said learnedly, "what you're

looking at is pretty impressive, I will agree. What they
do is take the frame of one of these super-size Greyhound
buses, the kind that has a scenic deck for western tours,
and they start from there. Now, a Greyhound bus has,
below its floor and all along its length, a baggage com-
partment three feet or so high. Well, they eliminate that,
which gives them lots of room. Then they extend the
upper scenic floor and you get a two-story bus. Then
they turn handcraftsmen loose and they build salons and
dining rooms and staterooms and Jesus Christ knows
what else. But this one, I see, seems to have a second driving cockpit in the roof, too, like a seagoing sports fish-
erman. Mike Mutazione told me all about these, in case
I ever had to blow one up. Only multimillionaires could
ever afford one, 'cause I think they cost three hundred
G's on up. And from the looks of this one, it's closer to
a million!''

The Countess Krak was going along the front of it.
She found a big nameplate. It said:

Land Yacht
Super-Deluxe
Kostly Custom Coach Company
Detroit

Then she went all down the side of it, peeking in the anti-
glare opaqued windows and trying the various outside
entrance doors. It was all white paint and chrome.

"Bang-Bang," she said, "it's just like the circus
ground caravans we used to use when I was a little girl.
I've travelled all over Atalanta in one of these."

"I didn't know you were with a southern circus."

"Bang-Bang, can you drive one of these?"

"Now, wait a minute, Miss Joy. It says right here on

these parole release papers that if I'm caught stealing a car, up I go to Ossining again and it's only a few miles north of here. And I think we got enough troubles already. Here comes the butler or somebody."

A very butler-type butler was coming down the drive from the sprawling house. He said in a rather severe voice, "The service station manager phoned us you were coming. If you will accompany me, I shall inform Dr. Morelay you have arrived."

"Bang-Bang," said the Countess Krak, "you stand by out here." She popped a pill into her mouth. She hefted her shopping bag and followed the butler.

They went through a large, iron entrance door and entered a huge hallway. It was all of gray stone and decorated with displays of broadaxes, battle-axes and headsmen's axes. The butler motioned for her to wait and walked on through another door at the end.

The Countess Krak took a completely blank card out of her purse. She took a small vial and sprayed something invisible on it. Then she put both back into her purse.

The butler came through the door and stood beside it. As though summoning someone to a royal audience, he said, "Dr. Morelay will see you now."

The Countess Krak passed him and entered a dark room. It seemed to be a sort of combination consulting room and den, made oppressive by black beams in the ceiling and deadly by the amount of electric shock equipment standing about.

A woman was standing there. She was dressed like a Harley Street doctor would be dressed—black suit coat, pants and vest. She looked to be in her mid-forties. Her grayish hair was pulled severely into a knot. Her eyeglasses had a black silk ribbon. She held them and looked through them with great distaste at the Countess Krak. So this was the Miss Agnes I pretended to know, this was the Miss Agnes that Bury hated so. Rockecenter's private shrink!

She began with no preamble. "So there you are at last! First you delay, delay, delay delivery! And all the while I am told I have this wonderful special-built present coming! A surprise it was supposed to be, a surprise I never could imagine! And what finally arrives? That horrible monster of a land yacht! An outright bald hint that I take myself away! Who wants to go away? Not me! A rotten thank-you for a lifetime of selfless service! And then what happens? I call and call and call and call! I tell you and tell you and tell you to take it away and give me the money instead. And all I get is the silly excuse that it's special-built, that it has been designed especially for me and even has a small padded cell!"

She stalked forward. Her expression was deadly. "Your driver put it right where it is! It blocked the drive! No one has been able to get in and out, for I shan't let anyone touch it until you give me the money and take it away! So give it to me," and she stretched out her claw-like hand.

The Countess Krak glanced over her shoulder to make sure the doors were closed. She reached into her purse and pulled out the blank card. She handed it to Dr. Morelay.

The woman held it close to her face.

The Countess Krak said, "There's nothing on that card, is there?"

"No."

"Then you won't mind if I put this helmet on your head, will you?"

"No."

The Countess Krak pulled a hypnohelmet out of her shopping bag and, with one smooth motion, popped it on the head of Agnes Morelay and turned it on.

She led the woman over to the consultation couch and eased her onto it. She plugged in the microphone.

"Sleep, sleep, pretty sleep. Can you hear me?"

"No."

The Countess Krak took the card out of her hand and took it over to an ashtray and touched a match to it. She came back and fanned a hand under the visor of the helmet.

"Can you hear me?"

"Yes," said Dr. Morelay.

It was only at that minute that I recalled the Eyes and Ears of Voltar perfume the Countess Krak had taken from the warehouse: it made the person say no to everything and was intended to protect chastity. What a vicious creature the Countess Krak was! And here she was daring to put a full-pledged psychologist *and* psychiatrist on her own couch! What villainy!

The Countess Krak sat down in the consultant's chair, held the microphone comfortably before her face and said, "You seem troubled about something. Would you care to tell me about it?"

"Not enough reward."

"What reward should there be?"

"Money, money, money, money!"

"What have you done to deserve it?"

"The Rockecenters had a sacred charge from Goebbels to render all other races incapable of defending themselves against Hitler. The Germans may have lost the war but this did not nullify the sacred trust. As a psychiatrist and psychologist, knowing my debt to Germany for those vital subjects, I have forwarded them with dedication. The Rockecenters advocated worldwide population reduction for generations. It is a sacred family trust and I have carried it on. With every possible trick I could devise I have made Delbert John Rockecenter carry out his family commitments. Utilizing the Rockecenter control of the World Federation of Mental Stealth and the National Associations of Mental Stealth, I have spread far and wide the doctrine of Psychiatric Birth Control. And for Delbert John Rockecenter himself, personally, I caused him to found the foundations which, with glandular operations and drugs, have made him immortal."

"Is there anything else for which you should be rewarded?"

The body on the couch did a small writhe. The voice was muffled but it carried hate. "I listen to his puking drivel about watching chorus girls going to the toilet and making Miss Peace exhibit herself to him while she pees until I could simply strangle him."

The Countess Krak lowered the microphone into her shoulder. She muttered in Voltarian, "Hmm. Where there is this much hate, there must have been love. Oh, well, I'd better get down to business." She raised the mike and said in English, "Is there a son?"

The body on the couch writhed worse. "That would be a DISASTER! There is a ten-billion-dollar trust fund that would go to a son. It would split the control of Delbert John into fragments! THERE IS NO SON! THERE MUST NEVER BE A SON!" Then she relaxed a bit and an evil-sounding laugh came out of the helmet. "There can never be one now. The drugs he's been on for years and years and something else I did have made him totally impotent! I think I handled that very nicely." Then she went into a writhe again. She grated, "The dirty, filthy, two-timing (bleep)!"

The Countess Krak lowered the microphone. "Oh dear," she said, "this hate is getting in the way." In English she said into the mike, "Was there ever a time when you were in love with Delbert John Rockecenter?"

The body on the couch did an instant explosion. Then it shuddered and writhed. Muffled venom came from the helmet. "He ought to be killed. He ought to be killed!"

"I think you better tell me all about this," said the Countess Krak.

The woman went stiff.

"Tell me," said the Countess Krak firmly.

"We were children. I lived right here on this neighboring estate. At every party, I was there. And every time I saw Delbert John, I used to think that someday I would marry all that beautiful Rockecenter money. It was what I lived for, just to marry him. I studied psychology just to know how to marry him. I took up psychiatry just to marry him. I forewent (bleeping) all the other little boys just to marry him. I didn't even (bleep) at college so I could marry him." A wail. "And what did he do? When I returned, proudly holding my psychiatric degree, all ready for the kill, the dirty (bleep) had got high on drugs and run off and married a (bleeping) chorus girl!" There was an agony of motion on the couch, as though she had been stabbed. "I was SCORNED! I was FORGOTTEN!" She got her breath. "And where was Miss Agnes, his childhood sweetheart? NOWHERE!" She lay gasping.

"So what did you do?" prompted the Countess Krak.

"I swallowed my (bleeping) pride! I served him like a slave! The family never learned of the marriage or they kept it hushed up. But that was not the problem. When he learned that the (bleepch) was pregnant, he was beside himself. He didn't know what to do. If the baby was a son, it would inherit ten billion bucks by trusts! It would shake his control.

"He came to me. He had the woman hidden out in a lodge in the Catskills. He did not have nerve enough to kill her, the coward! And what did I do? I helped him, fool that I am. And the ungrateful (bleepard) has never begun to pay the rewards he should! Having gotten rid of her for him, he once more did not marry me!"

The Countess Krak said, "What did you do with the woman?"

"I sent her to her parents."

"Where was that?"

"A farm in Hamden County, Virginia."

"And what else did you do?"

The muffled voice said, "The parents were easy. It took money and a tale that no one was sure who the father was. And in that stuffy neighborhood, that kept them quiet. They and the girl were frightened, too. They had a choice between money and being rubbed out and they took money. But I privately used my professional connections. I made sure the local doctor did his duty."

"What was his name?"

"Tremor Graves, M.D., an old country practitioner that could have had his license suspended many times over. The woman was too far advanced for abortion. But I got his pledge to kill the child and then the mother at birth by 'natural causes.' Brought on from shock, of course."

"What shock?"

"Her parents being killed in an auto accident that cost fifteen thousand dollars."

"Where did all this occur?"

"Hamden County, Virginia."

"When?"

"Eighteen years ago."

Suddenly I understood the brilliant plot of Lombar Hisst. Somewhere in all those survey records of Earth which he studied and hoarded, due to his vast interest in the marvelous fact that a man like Delbert John Rockecenter, not of royal birth, could control a whole planet—a thing to emulate—the Apparatus chief had gotten wind of this. And he had known very well that giving Heller that name was a death warrant. I understood why he had used that very county and specified that very age. One whisper of Heller using it would bring—and indeed had brought—the Rockecenter Angels of Death swarming. Why, this was the very reason Madison was on the job! Clever, clever Lombar!

Chapter 3

"But Delbert John Rockecenter never thanked me," said Agnes Morelay under the hypnohelmet. "He didn't do as much as thumb his nose. So I made him pay. There's a little operation one can do. A small cut with a knife. When he got knocked out in a fall from a horse, I said he'd injured his (bleeps) and I sterilized the (bleepard). The foundation is just another psychiatric medical fraud. The Rockecenters have always been insane but I've used every psychiatric technique to make sure it's chronic. For eighteen years I've blackmailed him into doing anything I want but I still can't get my hands on his money. So I haven't got my reward yet but I will, I will. The (bleepard)! My psychiatric professors and all my colleagues pat me on the back and tell me how much I've done for the profession. And so I have, but Delbert John has yet to give me the Rockecenter money! No reward is enough for the sacrifice and devotion of my whole life!"

"I have heard you," said the Countess Krak. "Listen carefully. You will feel rewarded when you propose to some nice young man and settle down. Have you got that?"

"I will feel rewarded when I propose to some nice young man and settle down."

"Good. Now, as to the land yacht, when you awake, you are going to write a letter on your stationery and in it you are going to say that you have turned it over to an agent named Heavenly Joy Krackle of Sleepy Hollow, New York, to take it around and show it and try to sell it for you. But if after a period of three months it has not been sold, said Heavenly Joy Krackle may buy it for..."

She pulled down the microphone. She muttered, "Let's see, a million dollars would not be worth very much...it's now second-hand...fifty thousand credits would be a fair price on Manco. And I'll have our estates back by then...." She raised the mike and continued. "...said Heavenly Joy Krackle may buy it for fifty thousand credits. Have you got that?"

"Yes."

"And now you will forget all about the helmet and that you have told me anything. And when you have written the letter you will fully wake up, believing we only came to take the land yacht away."

She turned the helmet off, removed it and put it in her shopping bag.

Dr. Agnes Morelay rose from her couch, went straight to her desk and got some stationery with her letterhead. Krak watched her. The psychiatrist wrote:

TO WHOM IT MAY CONCERN:

 The Kostly Custom Coach Company Land Yacht has been turned over to my agent, Heavenly Joy Krackle of Sleepy Hollow, New York, to take it around and show and try to sell it for me. But if after three months she has not sold it, she can buy it for $50,000 on credit. Anything to get rid of the (bleeped) thing because I am not going anywhere!

   AGNES P. MORELAY, Ph.D., M.D.

Krak picked up the letter, blinked at it a couple times and then put it in her purse.

"Now," said Miss Agnes, "get the God (bleeped) thing the hell out of my driveway!"

The Countess Krak went out. She walked down the drive toward the monstrous vehicle. Bang-Bang was waiting anxiously, halfway out the gate.

Krak said, "Unload our baggage, Bang-Bang. And park that cab somewhere. We're taking this land yacht."

Bang-Bang looked anxiously at the house and then at Krak. "Hey, you couldn't have bought this. It's worth a million bucks."

"It's a steal, Bang-Bang. Get the baggage."

"Oh, Jesus," said Bang-Bang. "And Ossining just a few miles up the road."

"Hurry," said the Countess Krak.

He spun around a couple of times. Then he raced to the cab and with three trips dumped the luggage in front of the huge vehicle out of sight of the house. He raced back, jumped into the cab and drove it into the bushes down the road. He raced back, looking anxiously at the house. "Gimme the keys, quick," he said.

"Keys," said the Countess Krak. "Oh, dear, I forgot to tell her to give them to me. Bang-Bang, run in and ask Dr. Morelay to give you all the keys."

"Oh, Jesus," said Bang-Bang. "I haven't even got a gun!"

"Go," said the Countess Krak. She looked after him and he seemed to be taking a very erratic course. "I better make sure he is all right," she muttered.

She went to the baggage and reached into a case. She took out a telescope, the duplicate of the one I'd used that could see through walls and hear conversations. She turned it on, and under cover of the land yacht, focused it on the front door.

The butler let Bang-Bang in. He said, "Dr. Morelay has them, sir. This way, please."

He marched Bang-Bang down the hall and into the office, closed the door and left.

Miss Agnes was sitting at her desk, gazing into space.

"The keys and instruction books and things," said Bang-Bang.

The woman looked at him. She suddenly seemed to come to life. She rose up from the desk, walked across the office and locked the door!

She walked over to Bang-Bang. She said, "Are you a nice young man?"

"Jesus, yes, ma'am. We really didn't mean nothing. It's all kind of..."

Dr. Morelay was paying no slightest attention to what he was saying now. She reached out and unbuttoned his coat. He stared down at what she was doing. She started to undo his belt buckle.

"Jesus Christ." Bang-Bang grabbed his suddenly sliding pants. He sped to one side. Dr. Morelay was right after him. Bang-Bang, like a gazelle, went over an upholstered chair. Miss Agnes was right over after him. Bang-Bang sprang across the desk with agility. The psychiatrist sprang also.

Unfortunately for Bang-Bang, his foot had come down in the wastebasket. He tottered.

Miss Agnes sprang.

Bang-Bang was hurled backwards to the couch. He landed on it with a crash!

Miss Agnes was onto him, pinning him down with her knees. She was ripping away at his clothes.

An electric shock machine lighted up.

"Settle down!" screamed Dr. Morelay.

A diploma went awry on the wall.

"Lie still, you nice young man!" screamed Morelay. "I got to settle down on you!"

The Countess muttered angrily, "Well, I never! You give these primitives the simplest suggestion and even then they get that wrong!"

The electric shock machine was throwing off sparks.

The diploma glass shattered. "Oh, boy, WOW!" howled Dr. Morelay.

The electric shock machine went up in smoke. Bang-Bang's groan was more a moan of horror.

The diploma came out of the glass and went sailing gently down to the floor.

Bang-Bang got to the middle of the room, trying to straighten up his clothes, yet looking back at the couch in shock.

"Poor Bang-Bang," muttered the Countess Krak. "How embarrassed he must be. And now we'll have to stop the night somewhere down the road so he can recuperate. Blast! I wanted to drive straight through!"

Miss Agnes lay there grinning like a ghoul. "Oh, boy, that was really good," she said. "Forty-four years I kept myself a virgin for that rotten (bleepard). But now revenge is really sweet. I've let myself be settled down by a nice young man instead of him. And that vengeance was really great. Revenge after all is the best reward. And I've got it at last! I'm full of it!"

She got up off the couch and pulled up her pants. She went to her desk, opened a drawer and pulled out a huge envelope of keys and instruction books and registrations. She dumped them in Bang-Bang's arms. She went and unlocked the door. "Nice young man," she said, "you better take up Psychiatric Birth Control. If anybody found out nonperverted sex is that good, they'd overpopulate the world!"

Bang-Bang ran for it. The Countess Krak pushed the telescope out of sight into a bag.

He came sprinting down the drive. He gave his clothes a hasty glance when he saw the Countess. Then he nervously began fumbling for keys in an envelope. He was trying one after the other in the lock of the main land yacht door.

His face was brick red. "For Christ's sakes," he said to himself, "don't lose these keys! I don't think I could stand getting another set!"

He got the door open. Then he must have seen

something on Krak's face. He said, "Did you say something about me to that woman?"

"Me, Bang-Bang?" said the Countess Krak.

A sudden thought struck me like a lightning bolt. I had forgotten right up to this minute that the old cab they had been using was bulletproof. They would not be riding in it now. Instead they would be in this land yacht, which seemed to have aluminum sides: a rifle slug could go through it like paper! Oh, was luck favoring me now! The Countess Krak was even wider open for a hit!

Chapter 4

Bang-Bang, swearing and snarling to himself, managed to find enough controls in the ornate and sparkling driver's area to get the land yacht's main diesel engine started and, with exaggerated allowances for posts and curbs, got it out of the gate and going down the road. It was ridiculous to watch that five-foot-five, one-hundred-pound Sicilian trying to wrestle that mammoth vehicle.

The Countess Krak was kneeling on their baggage, spotting signs for him through the vast windshield. She read one, Kingsland Point Park, and Bang-Bang, evidently unwilling to go on, turned into it and shortly stopped the monster in a parking area which overlooked the Hudson. The sun was going down and the river was vast before them, two miles wide at this point and golden in the sun.

"Why are we parking here?" said the Countess Krak.

It was just fine with me that they parked there. I could spot the place exactly for Torpedo. A setup.

Bang-Bang wasn't answering her. He was surrounded by a vast array of chrome knobs, panels, switches, levers and controls. And right beside his seat there was a mobile-telephone handset. He picked it up, listened to it and his face glowed with satisfacion as he heard the dial tone.

The Countess Krak was moving back toward a sitting room, trying to sort baggage.

"Long distance?" said Bang-Bang. "Gimme an urgent person-to-person call to Pretty Boy Floyd, Ochokeechokee Hotel, Ochokeechokee, Florida."

The Countess Krak stopped what she was doing and stared.

"Jet!" yelped Bang-Bang. "Is that you? Thank God. We're only five miles south of Sing Sing and I think we just stole a million-dollar land yacht!"

Bang-Bang listened a moment, then he extended the phone to the Countess. "He wants to talk to you."

She took the handset. She said, "How are you, dear? Did you have a nice trip?"

Heller's voice, "What are you up to?"

"Do you have a nice room? I hope there were no alligators in it."

Heller said, "Quit it! It's all okay here. What are you up to?"

In a very sweet voice, she said, "Well, it's all okay here, too."

"Listen," said Heller. "What are you doing with a million-dollar land yacht? Where are you going?"

She said, "It's lonesome without you, dear."

"WHERE are you headed for?" said Heller.

"You really want to know, don't you, dear?"

"YES!"

"Well, I'm not going to tell you straight out. The domestic police monitor calls, you know."

"Then you really ARE going somewhere!"

She said, "Do you recall a stone wall?"

"NO! Don't go there! Don't go near him!"

"If you say so, dear. But I must speed up things a bit."

Silence at the other end. Then finally, "All right. But only if you do me a favor."

"Whatever you say, dear. You know I never do anything you don't want me to do."

Heller said, "Drive slowly. Take your time. Give me four days to meet you there. And DON'T arrive before I do."

"All right, dear."

"I can complete my part of this project here in that time and join you."

"Oh, wonderful! It means we'll have a lovely vacation."

"Looking forward to it," Heller said. "Love you. Put Bang-Bang back on."

She surrendered the handset. Bang-Bang listened intently. Then he said, "This is a mobile phone here." And he gave Heller the number and call of it. Then he said, "Yes, SIR, Mr. Jet. That takes a load off my mind." He hung up.

"What did he say?" said the Countess.

Bang-Bang didn't answer. He was industriously putting another call in. I was beside myself with glee. What luck! Heller had unwittingly arranged the very delay that I might need! Four days! The Countess Krak would be exposed on the road for four days in a vehicle that was so easy to spot it would be a cinch to find it.

"Jiffy-Spiffy Garage?" said Bang-Bang. "Let me

speak to Mike Mutazione.... Hello, Mike. This is Bang-Bang. Look, Mike, you know that old cab?... Yeah. Well, it's parked in the bushes up here in Indian country." And he gave him the exact location and told him the keys were "in the usual place." Then he turned to the Countess. "That cab don't belong to the family anymore. He wants to know who is going to pay for the trip."

The Countess dived a hand into her purse and gave him my Squeeza credit card. Oh, well, I thought. Just ferrying a cab thirty miles or so down to Newark wouldn't be that expensive. I had to remember that half a million was forfeit if she overran that credit card.

"I got a valid credit card here," said Bang-Bang into the phone. And he gave Mike the number and designation. "Okay, I'm glad that will be fine. Now, Mike, the old cab has received a few dents lately, and while you've got it you could fix it up."

"Tell him," Krak said, "that he should fix it up so it will fly."

"Yeah, Mike," said Bang-Bang. "And the lady wants it hopped up. So put a new motor in it.... Yeah, you can redo the whole thing. New leather on the seats. You know.... Great. Now there's something else, Mike. I'm trying to drive something that's a grown-up, expanded Greyhound bus, that's now a two-decker land yacht. I want you to hire me a retired Greyhound bus driver.... All right. And an old lady for a cook and another one to keep it clean.... Right.... Yes, by all means, send a polite old mechanic that can keep the gadgets operating.... Sure, the cook can bring a load of food and liquor.... Yes, that's all right.... Yes, new uniforms. That would be nice.... I see what you mean, Mike. A second, smaller motor home and driver for the crew.... Well, hey, that's lucky, you had one right there. How about that! Only fifty G's! Well, fine, send the crew along in that.... Yeah, we're parked temporary in Kingsland Point Park.... Easy to locate, the thing is big as a house.... Yes, we'll wait right here for the crew.... Oh, yes, sure, Mike. Put it all on the Squeeza credit card— wages, the second motor home, the lot.... Bye now."

I was almost fainting! He had just run up what might become an eighty-thousand-dollar bill! With all Krak's other purchases, Mudur Zengin might begin to run out of money and cost me my half-million deposit certificate!

Bang-Bang was handing the credit card back to the Countess Krak.

"What did Jettero say?" she plagued him.

"To make sure you were comfortable and safe," said Bang-Bang. "And it occurred to me that spring is on the land and if we had a crew you could just spend these four days wandering around the fields as we loafed along southward and pick wildflowers and enjoy the views. Beautiful country this time of year. You'll love it out in the open."

All worries were swept away for me. Bang-Bang unwittingly had set her up as the easiest target in the world!

"It's getting awfully dark," said the Countess Krak. "Doesn't this craft have any glowplates?"

"You mean lights?" said Bang-Bang. "The generator hasn't been started. Let's see. It must be one of these switches here." He was looking over the vast array of panels in reach of the driver's seat. He found it and pushed a button.

My screen flickered!

The roar of an engine starter.

MY SCREEN WENT OUT!

Interference! It must be coming from the generator's carbon brushes! It might be suppressed for Earth-type radio but it certainly jammed the wavelength and type that I was operating on!

I couldn't see or hear a thing!

I swore. But Torpedo could find them and I knew that even if they moved, they would be easy to trace, for I had their destination: "Stone wall" could only mean Stonewall Biggs, the County Clerk of Hamden County, Virginia. And only one major highway and then a few country roads could take them to Fair Oakes. They could be followed or intercepted with ease.

I had one other vital thing to do. I picked up the phone and called the Service Department of the telephone company.

"This is the butler of Dr. Agnes Morelay," I said. "I have a mobile telephone," and I gave the number. "Dr. Morelay has instructed that the service be put on vacation status as it is not in use."

"Right away, sir," the girl said. "We will take it out of service."

I smiled. Heller would not be able to call them. They would not be able to call. And they probably wouldn't even find out their phone was disconnected now.

It would take Mike Mutazione plenty of time to set them up to get going. They were sitting ducks.

It was time for my evening stint. I threw a blanket over the viewers. This was one project which, all said and done, was going extremely well!

Enjoy your last hours on Earth, Countess Krak. Shortly you will be out of the way for keeps!

Chapter 5

I peeked into the front room. The next lesbian couple had arrived. The husband—a thin, American Indian girl—was apparently named Chief Malcomb. The wife was a plump high-yellow they were calling Bucket.

Miss Pinch was taking a stylish blanket coat off the husband. She was saying, "You're going to love this, Malcomb. Psychiatric Birth Control is for the (bleeps). It's as big a fraud as psychiatry itself, and that's saying something! You just have NO idea how marvelous natural sex can be!"

Malcomb said, "I'm scared half to death."

That did it! I rushed into the room. I yelled, "I don't want to see any dead, staring eyes! I can't stand it! I can't stand it! I can't STAND IT!"

They looked at me with some alarm. But I was not to be gainsaid!

I knew what I had to do. I made Miss Pinch phone out right then for a rental electrocardiograph. Only when it had arrived and I had it fastened on Malcomb's wrists, with the portable machine positioned beside the bed where I could watch the needle clicking and drawing on the paper the heartbeat of the girl, would I consent to remove my clothes and begin to do my duty.

Even then, I had my attention on that needle to such an extent, making sure that she was not a corpse, that I hardly knew what I was doing.

Miss Pinch, with pursed lips, didn't approve at all.

But the needle swung when the woman screamed and I watched it carefully. Her heart was still beating.

I mopped off my brow, sitting at last on the side of the bed. I felt it had been a near thing. Maybe I should also have one on my wrist: my heart was beating fast enough!

It was even worse with Bucket, the lesbian wife. She was certainly no virgin but, even so, I had to bat the needle several times to make sure it wasn't stuck.

Frightening!

All in all, they must have found it pretty unsatisfactory, even though they admitted afterwards that they had never had anything feel that way before.

After they'd gone, Miss Pinch lectured me about my duties and how I lacked gratitude for the huge pay I had been drawing.

"We almost didn't make it, Inkswitch," she said reprovingly. "You don't understand the critical situation with that Bucket woman. That's twice we're having to change the mind of that poor thing. She used to do it every day with her Great Dane and sex is a big thing for her. You're a soldier in a hard campaign and this is not the time to go soft!"

"With a Great Dane?" I said. "You mean a Danish man."

"No, no. A Great Dane is a dog and dogs have peculiar (bleeps): they swell up huge with a bulb in them and lock in. It's one of the Psychiatric Birth Control methods and it's pretty big competition. You have no idea how that psychiatrist worked on her. He was so solicitous for her plight, he went to the greatest possible lengths. He even gave her the Great Dane out of a government grant from the National Institute of Mental Stealth—they help the needy, you know. And we had an awful time: the

Great Dane bit everybody who came near her and we had to get him run over with a hit car. Then the psychiatrist caught her on the bounce and got her enamored with Malcomb, using a policeman's billy as a dildo. And Malcomb had to do so many weight-lifting tongue exercises to build it up that she sprained her jaw. And your poor performance tonight, that was aimed to get into her with natural sex, might have sent that poor woman to the dogs again. It's a hard campaign, Inkswitch, and you've got to stiffen up and fill the gap!"

I was pretty contrite. But when bedtime came and I insisted Miss Pinch and then Candy wear the machine straps, they kept getting passionate and their writhing around disconnected the straps. This, of course, stopped the electrocardiograph needle, and supposing in horror that I was now doing it to a corpse, I would leap off.

Miss Pinch acidly declared that I had not earned my money that day and refused to pay me. They even made me sleep by myself on a sofa in the back room.

I was lying there wondering what could possibly have gotten into me when the phone rang.

"Torpedo here," he said.

Expecting some marvelous good news, I said, "Are you calling from Hairytown?"

"No. I'm in Harlem."

"WHAT? Listen, you idiot. The target is in a huge land yacht with paper-thin aluminum sides that wouldn't stop a spitball!" And I gave him the license number and description. "It's parked right this minute in Kingsland Point Park, seven-tenths of a mile due west of North Hairytown, overlooking the Hudson. You could walk right in, put the rifle against her head and bango, your job is done. You better get going! For Gods' sakes, what delayed you?"

"I had to get a rifle and I got a beauty. It's a Holland and Holland double-barrelled elephant rifle, .375 H & H Magnum. Blow the side off a barn! It's got a Bausch and Lomb superpower night scope, hit anything up to a thousand yards. It took time to steal them but they work great."

"Work great? How do you know?"

"Well, you wouldn't want me to use an untested gun on a real hit and mess it up, would you? I'm a craftsman. I really lay into my work."

With acid sarcasm, I said, "Well, I hope it tested all right."

"Sure did," he said. "I come up to Harlem after it got dark. There's this alley, see, right next to a joint that's got the world's loudest band. So I waited until a black girl passed and drilled her. Almost blew her spine out. Then I dragged her into the basement and ripped the clothes off the corpse and had her. She sure was juicy. Just laid there staring at me with those sightless eyes, staring at me. I must have done it six times. She cooled down, though, and got too stiff, so I thought I'd better phone in."

"You are being paid to do a job!" I railed at him.

"Of course, of course! I was just practicing. Also, I didn't want to go out on a real job. Up to an hour ago, my hands were still shaking from the shots."

"They ought to shoot you," I said bitterly.

"Oh, hell, yes," he said. "They have to. You see, this prison psychologist had syphilis and he gave it to me in the (bleep) and mouth and told me to spread it around. So I have to have arsenic shots to keep the sores from running. But it was a waste of time on his part because a corpse don't care if you give it syphilis: it just lies there stiff and stares at you and don't say a word."

"SHUT UP!" I screamed at him. "Get on the job!"

"Oh, you bet. I hardly took the edge off at all with that black girl. I know exactly where the target is now. I'll grab a car, go right up, shoot her dead, lay it into the corpse and when it gets too cold to (bleep) I'll phone in again and report. I hope you're having a good time, too!" He hung up.

I tried to get some pleasure out of knowing now that the Countess Krak would shortly be a defiled corpse.

But suddenly I got to worrying. That girl the night before, Butter. She had said that she had had coitus with a goat.

I had read somewhere that the Spaniards, when they came to America, had picked up syphilis and taken it back to the Old World. And modern research had found that the disease had been generated by an American beast known as the llama that was a sort of long-legged goat.

Had that goat given her syphilis?

Did I now have the disease?

I tore into the tattered books on the library shelf. I found a medical text. It said the onset was very mild and the first sign occurred in from ten to thirty days, at which time a small bump appeared and then went away. But skin eruptions then occurred; one went totally to pieces internally and usually went crazy. I searched further in horrified frenzy. Nothing like this existed on Voltar. There probably wasn't a doctor around who could touch it. I had to know all I could about it, realizing that I had ten days at least to wait before I would know. I calmed myself with an effort. I had no real evidence I was in trouble.

Then my eye chanced to light upon a fatal paragraph. The disease was named from a character in a poem: *Syphilus!* The man was a SHEPHERD!

And shepherds tend GOATS!

Oh, believe me, I spent an awful and restless night! I knew I was doomed to break out in sores and go crazy.

The pale horror of dawn spread its contaminating fingers through the window. The phone rang!

I jumped like I was shot.

Maybe it was good news, I told myself, to still the small screams that tried to rise from my diseased body. Maybe Krak was dead.

"Torpedo here," he said. "Look, I got bad news for you. That land yacht wasn't there. I found a lot of package wrappings in the litter bin close by: Newark stores and quite fresh. And one had marked on it 'Land yacht steaks, put in freezer at once' and another with the license number you gave me and 'cook uniform' scribbled on it. So they were there all right just hours ago. They must have been the convoy of a huge motor home followed by a smaller one that I saw waiting at the westbound toll line to cross the Tappan Zee Bridge over the Hudson. That's only a mile or so south of Hairytown. I remember saying to myself, 'Jesus, look at that huge motor home and all the chrome,' when I exited off from the New York State Thruway onto U.S. 9 to enter Hairytown. So I know what it looks like all right. But that ain't the bad news."

Oh, Gods, what now?

"You know that envelope you gave me with the money in it? Well, a few hours ago the message and paper simply evaporated. That wouldn't be so bad because I remembered your phone number. But the money that had been in it evaporated, too! There's nothing left of it but some green powder."

Oh, (bleep)! The timed disintegrator spray had gotten on the money in the envelope!

"So I'm broke."

Oh, that idiot! He had had the land yacht right in view and missed it! I knew at once what I would have to do. He was too dumb to do anything but kill.

Impetuously, I said, "Drive down to Eleventh Avenue and 50th Street. Start now. I will meet you on the northwest corner!"

He said that he would be there.

I stole out into the front room. I found Miss Pinch's purse. It had two thousand dollars in it! I took it.

I wrote a note. I told her I was haggard with worry that I hadn't pleased them last night. I was going to go find a mountaintop and sit on it and work out what was wrong but in a week or less I would be back, ready to go again.

I took my Federal credentials. If I was apprehended with a hit man I could say I was on a government project and had hired him to execute a government contract, "in the national interest," like they had executed on Martin Luther King and President Kennedy and Lincoln and lots more that had gotten in the government's road.

I armed myself.

I took my viewers and some clothes.

I stole out of the flat.

I would make sure, personally, that Torpedo found the right target and that the Countess Krak would die!

Chapter 6

With rifle ready and my hit man's finger itchy on the trigger, I spent the next three days combing the highways for the Countess Krak.

There were only a limited number of routes she could take south, and working back and forth, cross-country, asking service stations and toll bridge people, we patrolled every one of them.

On the very first day, about noon, I caught a glimpse on my viewer. She was standing on what seemed to be a hill crest, gazing at mountains that were shrouded in blue mist. She looked at no signs and shortly afterwards interference came on again. But the clue was unmistakable: she was somewhere inland where the Atlantic coastal plain rises into the Appalachians. That eliminated any roads nearer the coast. I felt we were zeroing in.

I was personally having a very poor time of it and was held to my search only by my sense of duty as an Apparatus officer. I couldn't stand to be near Torpedo Fiaccola.

Not only did the filthy beast stink, he kept whining that I wasn't being fast enough. He wanted to get on his kill and he twisted and agonized about how frustrated he was and how he had to have it. He kept stroking his rifle barrel and unloading the gun and spitting on the cartridges and reloading it, crooning to the slugs to get him his next orgy. My disgust rose like vomit in my throat just to hear him.

On the second day, beside a road we were alertly watching, I took a moment out to get a look at Heller.

He was still in Florida, totally oblivious of the gruesome fate that was stalking his darling.

He was walking toward a ramshackle hotel that stood amongst palms on a sand-spit. A high wind bent and threshed the trees. An alligator scuttled across the road ahead of him.

A contractor, in khaki that was stained black under the armpits with sweat, was saying to him, "Mr. Floyd, how in HELL do you lay out those foundation corners so accurate? Most engineers use a transit. Never seen anybody do it with a watch."

"It's timing," said Heller, his mind obviously on other things.

They entered the hotel. A black bartender saw Heller coming and set out a Seven Up. Heller said to him, "Have there been any phone calls for me?"

The bartender went to yell at somebody. In the mirror I could see construction men strung along the bar. And down at the end, who was that? Raht! Very inconspicuous, dressed in sweaty khaki like the rest, mustache unmistakable: at least he was on the job and obviously undetected by Heller.

A switchboard girl, a Mexican by the looks of her, phones on her head and disconnected jack plug in her hand, walked up to Heller. "*Nada, nada,* Mistaire Floyd," she said. "I try all morning while you gone and they don't answer. The *Norteamericano telefonista operador dice que*—excuse me, I have not been in country long— the operator say they on vacation. They no answer."

"Yes," said Heller, "I know they're on vacation. But look, keep trying." And he gave her a ten-dollar bill.

She grinned and looked him up and down speculatively. But he shooed her away.

For a moment it occurred to me that if I had not disconnected their phone by putting it on "vacation," I might have picked up her whereabouts from Heller's mushy interchanges with his sweetheart. But it was too late to worry about spilled milk. I had every confidence I could find her.

The second day, as we combed the mountains of Pennsylvania, I got another glimpse of her. She was sitting by a lake looking pensively at the reflections of an island in the still water. There were a lot of shrubs about that had white, leathery-looking flowers and others that were budding in purple. I did not know the flowers and it seemed too soon in the year for such display but the weather had been unseasonably warm this very early spring.

We looked for lakes along the route and, with Torpedo whining and drooling and stroking his bullets and pants, inspected three. No land yacht. No Countess Krak.

On the third day, after a fruitless morning between Hagerstown, Maryland, and Winchester, Virginia, covering U.S. 81, I got a clue. I noticed I was entering an area where the same types of shrubs I had earlier seen her looking at were now in bloom. We were getting closer.

And then a break! Just after lunch I eagerly hunched in the back seat of the Ford we had and turned on the viewers. There she was! She was staring into a shallow valley where a small brook ran. All about her were flowering shrubs. What a target if we could just find her!

I ignored Torpedo in the front seat: he was whining his usual whine that he couldn't stand holding off much longer, that he itched and burned to get it into the

fresh-killed target and why couldn't I hurry up before I
drove him mad.

An engine roar sounded behind her. She turned.
Bang-Bang sprang out of a jeep and approached her. It
gave me a new clue: that second motor home must be
pulling a jeep on a tow bar like they often do. Made it
easier to identify.

Bang-Bang seemed excited. "Miss Joy, I called like
you said. And I think I've got a trace of him. After he
got hurt, he retired to a rest home!"

She said, "Great! Then just start calling every rest
home!"

Bang-Bang said, "Beggin' your pardon, ma'am, but
three days' worth of telephones has shot the wad! Since
the mobile phone went dead, we musta spent a thousand
bucks on pay phones."

"Oh. Well, I'll come back with you and draw another
thousand on the credit card."

I ground my teeth. I had forgotten you could draw
cash. My half-million certificate in Squeeza Credit hands
was more and more at risk.

They got into the jeep and Bang-Bang drove with
wild abandon down a bridle path. He burst into a clear-
ing. A sign said:

General Store
Bogg Hollow

It seemed an unpopulated, sylvan place.

The Countess Krak went in and used the credit card
to get her change from a smiling clerk. She also bought
a black, smoked Virginia ham that was hanging in the
rafters and told the clerk to send it to the cook. So she

was in Virginia! I was not wrong. I was also in Virginia and so was the whining, itching Torpedo.

Bang-Bang walked to an outside pay phone and closed the kiosk door. The Countess Krak, (bleep) her, did not follow him and so I could not see the number that would give me the absolute pinpoint for our hit.

She walked down a path and there before her stood the vehicles. The land yacht and the other smaller motor home were parked so as to make an L. They had their awnings out. Very colorful. In the center of the L was a large picnic table that seemed a permanent fixture. The vehicles were hooked up to water lines: this must be some kind of a national park, very groomed and beautiful.

An elderly lady, obviously Italian, in a stewardess uniform, was laying out a lunch at the picnic table. She saw the Countess coming and looked up and smiled. And then the Countess was inside the interference zone and my screen wiped out.

Anxiously I began to tear through my accumulated maps and guidebooks. I found three separate places named Bogg! None of them were called Bogg Hollow. But ALL of them were north of Lynchburg!

I grew very cunning. The only way you could get to Fair Oakes on a main highway was going through Lynchburg. To think was to act.

I instantly pushed the whining, suffering Torpedo aside, started up and drove like mad to Lynchburg. I found a motel just south of town on U.S. 29.

It was a shabby, tattered place but the room I got on the second floor was ideal. It covered the highway with a view of such expanse that I could not miss. And the parking lot on the other side of the room afforded the quickest possible launching pad from which to give chase.

I hated to share the same room with Torpedo. He

was whining worse and worse, getting absolutely frantic. But I had to watch my cash and motels are expensive.

I sat down with my viewers and my highway view. I had only to wait.

Heller's movements interested me. He was running about, pounding stakes with ribbons on them into the sand. Finally he ran out of stakes and walked back toward a mound of them. A man in a pilot's uniform was nearby, making notations in a small book and looking toward the ditches some digging machines were excavating. He saw Heller and came over.

"Mr. Floyd, what's the tonnage in these cooling pipes?" the pilot said.

"Thirteen point two three," said Heller. "Are you still going to pick them up tomorrow?"

"That's the plan," the pilot said. "Two freight choppers leave for the foundry at Scranton, Pennsylvania, tomorrow afternoon."

"Mind if I bum a ride?" said Heller. "Fair Oakes, Virginia, is not too far off your route."

"Never heard of the place," said the pilot. "Probably boxed in by trees. If you don't mind going down a ladder, come ahead."

"They scare me to death," said Heller, telling what I knew for a fact was an outright, vicious lie. He hung by his teeth on safety lines from spaceships just for kicks.

But the pilot saw through the lie. "I'll bet. Glad of company."

"See you tomorrow afternoon," said Heller.

It made me anxious. This was going to be close. I promptly sent Torpedo out, rifle cocked and eyes hot, to visit every Bogg I had located.

Torpedo came back late. He had not connected. He was screaming with frustration.

"You got to get it," Torpedo whined, "to really understand what I've got to do. All day now I've known I have the clap."

"What?" I said, aghast.

"Yeah, that (bleeped) black corpse in Harlem. I wondered at the time why it was so juicy. Now I know. She had the clap. Now I've got it. But I know how to handle it. The prison psychologist always told all us cons the only thing to do with it was spread it around fast. So, God (bleep) it, where is the target? Where, where, where? I got to find her and do it, now that I got the clap. I need a bloodhound!"

It was an unfortunate remark. I suddenly went into alarm. "A bloodhound?" I said. "Is that anything like a Great Dane?"

"Same color. Just a little smaller, that's all."

Oh, Gods, the full implication of this hit me like a club. That woman, Bucket!

If the medical advice was to seek a bloodhound when one had the clap, then this would also include Great Danes!

Had that Great Dane had the clap?

Had Bucket had it?

Did I now have the clap?

I told myself how irrational it was. But I couldn't shake it and I sat there at the window through the night, watching for the land yacht, trying miserably to accept the fact that I probably was not only going to go crazy because of goats but also would cave in and have my bones rot from dog-carried clap. It was an awful thing to have to face. I knew my career was probably coming to an end. But I would be true to duty to the last and, crazy and rotted away though I might be, still an Apparatus officer.

At least I could put a crown on my shining record by ridding the universe of a scourge known as the Countess Krak. But somehow it didn't help. Somewhere in my career, had I gone wrong?

Was there somebody else I had failed to maim or kill? I was being punished for something, I was sure. But it was not because I had not tried to do my Apparatus duty always, like now. I was sure of that. It was just that the Gods are treacherous. They had it in for me.

Chapter 7

In the afternoon of the fatal fourth day, after a ceaseless and worried vigil of the highway, with Torpedo twitching and whining on the bed, I walked over to the viewer and there she was!

She was looking at the same blue-misted mountains she had been gazing at, at noon on the first day!

She had not shifted location in all that time!

And there was Bang-Bang's voice, "Miss Joy! Miss Joy! I found him!"

She turned and I listened intently. This was the clue I needed so crucially to reach her and kill her before Heller arrived.

Bang-Bang was scrambling up the rocky path. He was all out of breath. He sank down on a rock near her, trying to get his wind so he could talk.

"Oh, Bang-Bang!" said the Countess. "This is wonderful news. We can get this done before Jettero arrives. He'll be so proud of us! But come on, tell me."

"Can't get my breath," he wheezed. And then he said, "He wasn't in a rest home or retirement home. No wonder it took five hundred calls. He's in a private hospital owned by a doctor friend. He's sort of hiding out. But we better hurry, 'cause they say he may not have long to live."

He paused to catch his breath and ease a stitch in his side. I gritted my teeth at this delay. It was Krak who didn't have long to live if I could get that address. That was where she'd keep her rendezvous with death.

He fumbled in his pocket for a paper scrap. He read it to her. "He's in Room 13, Altaprice Hospital, Redneck, Virginia. That's only thirty-five miles west of here!"

"Quick," said the Countess. "Race back and tell the crew to pack it up and get the show on the road! We're on our way!"

I grabbed my maps.

I had her!

She was SOUTH of me! Those (bleeped) retired Greyhound bus drivers had cannonballed her down here to her operating area in what must have been eight hours from Hairytown! She must be in the Smith Mountain Lake resort area southeast of Roanoke, Virginia. And she had been phoning, phoning, phoning from there in comfort while I tore all over the Middle Atlantic states! How she must be laughing!

She deserved to be killed and defiled at once!

It would be easy! There was ample time before Heller could arrive. Redneck was only twenty miles south and east of where I was.

I turned to give Torpedo his orders. I would not accompany him on the actual kill. But it was too easy, now.

I opened my mouth to speak.

There was a knock on the door!

140 L. RON HUBBARD

The blanket I was using to hide the viewers had fallen to the floor. I was trying to untangle it.

Torpedo sprang up like a ghoul off the bed and opened the door.

A cop was standing there! He had on a black plastic jacket and white motorcycle helmet. He glared at Torpedo. "That your black Ford out there? It's the same license registered to this room. You left it parked out on the highway verge. It's an offense! Move it before I give you a ticket!"

He turned his back on Torpedo to point to it, stepped toward the balcony rail to do so. It was a fatal action.

Before I could move or call out even if I would have, Torpedo acted!

The hit man snatched a knife out of his belt!

His left arm reached out and grabbed the cop's throat to stifle any cry.

He plunged the knife to its hilt in the cop's back!

He dragged the cop back into the room. He dropped him. He closed the door.

The cop kicked a couple of times and was dead. The knife must have cut his heart in half from behind.

Torpedo turned the body over on its face and, before my horrified gaze, unfastened its belt and began to pull down its pants.

"No, no!" I cried.

Torpedo's hand snaked to the dead cop's holster and I was suddenly confronted with a cocked gun. "You try and stop me!" snarled Torpedo.

I gazed in horror at what he was doing. And then the idiocy of his action hit me.

"You (bleeped) fool!" I screeched at him. "Your target is right south of here. She's in your grasp! Shoot her and do it to her! Get out of here! She'll be arriving at Altaprice Hospital, Redneck, Virginia, in just an hour or two! Get going!"

"I got to test this out," he panted.

He finished what he had begun.

I expected to hear calls outside or sirens.

"Oh, would that prison psychologist love this!" chortled Torpedo. "(Bleeping) a screw! Clap and all!"

"Get out of here!" I screamed.

He got up grinning ghoulishly. "That just whetted my appetite. Now I can go for a real kill!"

He grabbed his rifle case and bullets.

He tore out of there.

A moment later, I heard the Ford starting up. Torpedo was on his way.

I looked at the dead cop on the floor. I didn't want to touch the corpse, disease contaminated as it was.

I was paralyzed with the thought of being caught here with that. I opened the door a crack. There was no one in the parking area. The dead cop's motorcycle was sitting there.

Acting swiftly, I hauled the corpse outside. Masked by the railing and its covering vines, I dragged it down a short flight of stairs and dropped it. I pulled up the pants. I left the knife in the back.

Carefully, I made sure there was no trail of blood, eradicating the few spots that I found. I put my room to rights.

The dead cop lying out there with his sightless eyes made me sort of frantic.

I had no transportation. I could not ride that motorcycle. I was not going to abandon my baggage.

(Bleep)! What a thing to happen in the middle of a hit!

Inspiration! I went out to the motorcycle and picked up its radio. I called the dispatcher.

"This is Inkswitch. I'm a Fed. Someone seems to have killed your motorcycle cop. You better come and get him. This is the Mucky Motel."

Minutes later squad cars were there. They looked at my credentials. "The suspect is a black man," I said.

"We knew it!" said their chief.

"I found this poor fellow lying here," I said. "I saw the black man racing away on the other side of the field. He has this officer's gun. I knew I should call you to form a posse."

"We'll get the (bleepard)," said the chief.

"I'm on a secret Federal case, myself," I said. "So keep me out of it."

They didn't really hear me. They were already tearing off across the field, obliterating the absence of the footprints.

I joined them to make it look good.

After an hour, they took my description of the black man, carefully photographed the corpse and cleaned the area up.

That handled, I went back to the real business of the day: the hit on the Countess Krak.

PART FORTY-SIX

Chapter 1

Heller's viewer was blank. I knew what must be happening. That (bleeped) Raht was shifting the 831 Relayer from Florida to Virginia, which told me that Heller must be on his way.

The viewer of the Countess Krak was totally flared out with interference.

I sat there restively. My nerves were in pretty poor shape after the cop murder and rape. I wondered why these things were having such an effect on me. By psychology theory, there was neither limit nor personal penalty to crime unless it happened to oneself. Nothing had happened to me yet. Why was I reacting? Psychology and psychiatry surely couldn't be wrong. That was unthinkable. Man was just an animal that had no conscience or soul, just a rotten beast, in fact. So, of course it shouldn't affect me, no matter how many rotten things I did.

To take my mind off it, I began to wonder at the possibility that maybe, when he had made the hit, Torpedo might be crazy enough to just go on straight home. You could only depend upon him to kill and rape. He might get the idea cops would come and be waiting for him because of the motorcycle patrolman's death.

I went out and surveyed cars and a getaway route. Yes. There was an old car sitting there that in emergency I might use. They apparently utilized it to haul manure, the way it looked, a sort of passenger car cut into a truck.

I made some other precautionary arrangements.

Feeling more secure, I went back to my viewers.

Krak's was still flared out.

But what was this on Heller's? An electrical disturbance? I watched intently. Yes! It was becoming a flareout. Raht must have come up last night by commercial plane and bus. He must have Heller bugged or watched to know where he was going.

The viewer suddenly went all wavy and then came in very clear. Raht must have turned off the switch of the 831 Relayer.

I was looking at a patch of ground below the skids of a freight helicopter. There was a patch of asphalt surrounded by low trees. It made me dizzy to look down.

A ladder was unreeling below the chopper. The beat of engine and blades came through the door that Heller was holding open.

Heller looked at the sky: although clouds were still bright with sunset glow, dusk was gathering on the ground. The time was about 5:45 in the afternoon. He moved toward the pilot and gave him a pat on the shoulder. "Thanks for the lift!" he yelled.

"Any time, Mr. Floyd," the pilot said.

Heller had closed the door. He edged back to the front of the cargo cable area. He lifted a small musette bag he was carrying and put the strap around his neck. He gave his black engineer gloves a tug at each cuff and looked down.

The swaying ladder dwindled away toward the square of asphalt. The helicopter dropped lower.

Heller didn't bother to put his feet on the rungs. With one hand on the cable which made up one side of the ladder, he swung into space.

Releasing and tightening his grip, he slid about five feet at a time down the ladder. It made me dizzy and feel even sicker than I already was.

He got to the bottom of the swaying ladder. The pilot dropped a few more feet. Heller simply let go and fell lightly the last two yards.

He looked up at the chopper and waved his hand. It spun away into the sky.

Heller looked around. It was dusky dark. Lights suddenly flashed on. Plastic, colored twirlers. Lines of cars around the edges of the asphalt. A big sign:

HARVEY "SMASHER" LEE'S BARGAIN CARS
FOR TRUE VIRGINIANS
MONEY BACK SOMETIMES

Oh, this was good news to me. Heller must have forgotten he was wanted in that town! Or maybe he thought the FBI reports had wiped it out. Or maybe he thought he could trust the friend of the late Mary Schmeck, Harvey Lee.

And that was who came out of the sales office. Big, plumper than ever, Harvey Lee stepped into the lights, ready to say what the hell is going on dropping in by chopper. He didn't say it. He saw Heller. He stared. His flabby face went sort of white. He almost ran back into the office.

"Hello, Harvey," said Heller. "Got any cheap cars?"

That stopped Harvey Lee. Nervously he came closer. "Is . . . is Mary with you?"

"There's nobody with me," said Heller.

"Oh, well," said Harvey Lee. "You want a car?" He was doubtless remembering the way Mary Schmeck had

whittled him down on that Cadillac Brougham Coupe
d'Elegance.

"Something cheap," said Heller, "something I can
just use and throw away."

A look of cunning came into the used-car salesman's
eye. He pointed to a strange-looking car: the top came
up to a point like an idiot's head. It was badly beat up.
"That one there. It's a freak. It's attracting too much
attention. It's a French Karin. You can recognize it a
mile away. Nobody wants it. It runs. You can have it
cheap."

Heller glanced into it. It had a very wide front seat
and a lot of room behind it.

"The French put it out," said Harvey Lee, "as their
dream car. But folks around here think it's more like a
nightmare. But it runs okay. It's just that it looks so odd."

"How much?" said Heller.

"How much you got?" said Harvey Lee with a cunning look.

"Three hundred dollars," said Heller.

"I'll take it," said Harvey Lee promptly. I really
blinked. The French Karin might be a dog—for all
French cars are—but I just couldn't imagine Harvey Lee
letting go of a foreign luxury car for pennies like that.
Then Lee said, "But at such a cheap price I can't throw
in any registration or bill of sale. Paper work costs
money."

"I only need it for a few hours," said Heller.

"Well, then I'll be glad to buy it back, so let's make
it two hundred and seventy-five," said Lee, but there was
a peculiar look in his eye. "No use doing the paper
twice."

"All right," said Heller and handed over three one-
hundred-dollar bills.

Heller got in and examined the oddly placed controls. He started up the car and ran it to the gas island. Harvey Lee filled it up and checked the oil. It needed a quart.

Counting out the forty dollars for the service, Heller said, "Now, where can I find Stonewall Biggs?"

Lee thought a moment. Then he swivelled his eyes sort of sideways. He said, "Stonewall Biggs is at the courthouse."

"Isn't this kind of late for him to be there?" said Heller. "The whole town looks like the sidewalks have been rolled up."

Lee sort of floundered. Then he recovered. He said, "Well, since it burned down, he comes in evenings and tries to do some construction work. It's just a temporary shed now. So he's there all right."

Heller got the car started again after a couple tries and rolled down to Main Street, past the bus depot, and then climbed the hill to the courthouse.

There was very little left—just a gaunt, charred shell. But a temporary building had been put up behind it to house, probably, the vital functions of the county and possibly the town. The dusk was very thick and the temporary building was all dark.

Heller killed the engine, which was already suffering. He got out.

Instantly, from a pile of rubble close behind him, came a loud and deadly voice. "Hands up! One false move and you'ah daid!"

Heller whirled. The only thing in view was a handgun, levelled and cocked, aimed straight at him.

Another voice from in front of the car. "It's him, all raht! Keep him covered, Joe! You'ah undah arrest fo' stealin' a cah f'um Hahvey Lee!"

I chortled in glee. Clever Harvey Lee. He must have phoned ahead and alerted these cops! Now he not only could keep the three hundred but he'd also get his car back! And what an ally for me to suddenly acquire! They'd hold Heller and it would leave the Countess Krak wide-open for Torpedo!

"Lean up against that cah!" said the cop in front, walking into view. "Watch him, Joe!"

"I don't have time for this," said Heller. "Can't we put this off until business hours?"

"So you tryin' ta squirrel outa it! What else have you stole?" The cop in front advanced threateningly.

"I give up," said Heller. "It's all in the back seat!"

The cop made Heller move forward and bend over the hood. Then he pulled the Karin's door wide and leaned into the car.

Heller moved suddenly!

He kicked the open door.

It flew inward, crashed against the cop's legs!

The door recoiled open again.

Heller was behind it.

Joe fired from the rubbish pile!

The bullet hit the door!

The cop with the bruised legs screamed, "Don' shoot, Joe!"

Heller had the cop by the collar.

He threw him at Joe!

There was a crash by the rubbish pile.

Heller was onto them in a single dive. He reached down, grabbed collars and bashed their heads together.

After the dull clunk of skulls, the cops were inert and quiet.

Heller opened the temporary courthouse door. He located a small closet.

He went out and dragged the unconscious cops in. He took their own cuffs and locked them back to back.

He shut the closet door on them. He looked around the dark interior. "Well," he said, "I guess Stonewall isn't here."

He went out and got into the Karin. After fighting with it a bit, he got it started once more.

He drove down the hill, past the bus station and up the state road to Harvey Lee's.

As the Karin entered the lot, due to the funny shape of its windshield, Harvey Lee evidently could not see who was driving it. He sprinted out of the office laughing. He came up to the car, "Well, Joe," he said, bending down, "I see you got the car back. That was quick!"

Heller's hand shot out and grabbed Lee by the shirt collar. "This is quicker," he said.

Harvey Lee was gargling.

Heller opened the door, shifted hands on the throat. "You don't seem to realize I'm not here to play cops and robbers. Where's some wire?"

Dragging Harvey Lee along, he located some ignition jump wires. He wrapped them around Lee's wrists and ankles. He found and threw the switch that shut off the lot's lights. "We'll just close the place," he said, "to prevent further crooked deals." He dragged Lee over to the Karin and dumped him over the front seat and into the back.

"What happened to the cops?" wailed Lee.

"Some urgent business tied them up at the courthouse," said Heller. "Now, earlier this evening, I asked you a civil question: where is Stonewall Biggs?"

Silence.

"If you cooperate, we'll forget about this so-called deal. Pretend you are not a crooked used-car salesman

now, and pretend you are a guide. Start guiding. Where
does Stonewall Biggs live? Or do I get out and put a torch
to these cars?"

Lee started babbling directions.

Heller drove back past the bus station, turned down
a side street and, at instructions, drew up before a house.
The mailbox said Stonewall Biggs.

He parked the car, went through the gate and
knocked upon a white-painted door. An old black woman
peered out cautiously. "Some young whaht mans," she
called over her shoulder into the house interior.

Then the door was thrown wider and Stonewall Biggs
was standing there.

I blinked. I had been sure from what I had overheard that he was retired and in a hospital. And here he
was, though stooped with age, well and strong.

"Well, Junior!" he cried. "Mah, this sho' is a su'-
prise!" And he was pumping Heller's hand and beaming. "C'm in, c'm in and set a spell! Mah, am ah glad
t'see you, boy!"

He led Heller into the kitchen and sat him in a chair
at the table. "We've et. You et? Marcy, git some vittles
on. Some of that friahd po'k 'n greens."

"Ah'm mahty glad t'see you well," said Heller,
unstrapping his musette bag and laying it on a chair.

"Aw, they cain't kill off an ol' coon dog lahk me,"
said Stonewall Biggs. "They thought ah was done fo'
aftah you pulled me aht of that fiah but ah was jus'
singed, jus' singed. Marcy, he do look a bit ga'nt. Hurry
up them vittles so's we c'n talk."

Oh, good, I said. Delay him all you can, Stonewall
Biggs. I don't know who is in Room 13 of that hospital
at Redneck, but the Countess Krak will be there and Torpedo will have his chance.

Marcy delivered and Heller began to eat under the attentive eye of Stonewall Biggs. Always the polite Royal officer, the fool, he said, "Things goin' well with you, Mistah Biggs?"

"Oh, ah cain't complain. Ain't got no cohthouse though. Drafty as all git-out in that temporary buildin'. How goes things with you, Junior?"

"Cain't complain," said Heller.

Seeing his guest had reached his cup of coffee, Stonewall Biggs said, "Is theah anythin' ah c'n do fo' you, Junior?"

"Well, yes theah is. Has a young lady called you?"

Stonewall Biggs shook his head. "No."

I was delighted. The Countess Krak had avoided this trail utterly. She must have another line she was working on. Torpedo would have ample time and chance.

Heller sat there for a bit. He finished his coffee. "Mistah Biggs," he said at last, "tha' naht ah seen you, ah got the impression maybe you knew mo' about the birth than what you sayed."

"Well, tha's raht, Junior. But not much. If'n it maht he'p to ease yo' min', ah'll tahl you. But ah'm afraid it ain't much."

"Be glad t'hear," said Heller.

"Well, one naht abaht fifteen year ago, the doctah, he was purty drunk. He drunk hisself stupid a lotta times so ah got t'wonderin' an', as county clerk, ah figgered ah had a raht to know. So ah pried away and he said, 'Ah done a lotta rotten things in mah tahm, but at leas' ah nevah murdered th' two of them.' Tha's all he said.

"But theah'd been rumors aroun' abaht th' Styles girl bein' up nawth in th' shows an' comin' home married to Delbert John Rockecenter. She was all swole up big an' th' husban' wasn't along. But th' girl disappeahed an' talk died down.

"Ah suppose you'ns is heah 'cause you think yo' grandparents was murdered. But, Junior, you'll nevah prove nothin' at all. Th' chief heah is also county sheriff an' he'd sell his soul fo' a shot a' whaht mule. An' even if it was a funny cah accident, mo' lahk a bomb, y'd nevah get any evidence. So tha's all ah know, Junior." He sat for a while. Then he said, "You mus' be of legal age now. Maybe you c'd he'p rebuil' th' cohthouse. Costs money, labah bein' what it is. Even th' coons git paid these days."

"What was this doctor's name?" said Heller.

"Tremor Graves, M.D. He wuz th' local G.P. heah, had his own hospital. But he drunk too much. He wuz in a rest home fo' a whahl, but ah heah jus' this las' month his rheumatiz got so bad they took him to a hospital."

"Where?" said Heller.

"Some doctah friend of his named Price. Owns a private health hospital, Altaprice, ovah in Redneck. Millionaire kin' of place."

"Mistah Biggs, c'd ah ask you the favah of showin' me the way ovah theah?"

"Why, sho', Junior. It's on'y abaht fifteen mile." He went and got his coat and hat.

Heller thanked Marcy for the meal and she beamed.

They went outside.

Heller stared.

THE CAR WAS GONE!

That clever Harvey Lee had apparently got himself untied and probably with another key had spirited the car away!

Biggs evidently supposed somebody had just dropped

Heller off, for he opened the garage beside the house and unlocked the door of an old vintage Buick.

Heller, with a glance toward the direction of Harvey Lee's lot, possibly thinking of future revenge, got into the Buick. Biggs backed it out and they were on their way.

I thought fast.

There was yet a way to stop Heller and give Torpedo his chance.

I grabbed the phone. Telling the operator it was a Federal emergency, she rapidly connected me with the Fair Oaks chief. He was evidently at home. He sounded rushed.

"This is a Federal agent," I said. "We have just gotten data by satellite that your son, Joe, and another officer are tied up in a closet in the courthouse. Harvey Lee is a witness to a car theft. The man you want is in an old Buick headed for Room 13, Altaprice Hospital, Redneck. If you drive fast you can intercept him on the road!"

"Jesus!" said the chief. "That confirms what Harvey Lee just reported. We're on our way!"

I hung up.

I beamed. Heller would be stopped.

Torpedo would have his chance!

Chapter 2

I thought I had better check up on Krak. I moved her viewer closer to me to get a better look.

She seemed to be just staring down a hall. She

wasn't moving. So I did a fast replay. Maybe I could catch a glimpse of Torpedo.

She had left the land yacht in company with Bang-Bang and walked to the bottom of the hospital steps.

"Now Bang-Bang," she had said, "you go in and tell the doctor you're in pain and somehow get the receptionist to help you to his office. You make him examine you and groan around and keep him there."

Resignedly, Bang-Bang had gone in, attracted the receptionist's attention and had gotten her to inform the doctor he was there. But she had come back and had told him to wait despite his plea that he was sure he would perish any instant. For quite a time he had sat there, rolling about in the chair and groaning. And all that while Krak had been outside. Torpedo, I felt sure, had private plans for when she went inside.

Finally, as Krak had seen through the window from the porch, a tall, blond man in a black coat, who must have been Dr. Price, had come out and, with the help of the receptionist, had gotten the collapsing Bang-Bang into his office.

Krak had slipped in and gotten out of sight at the end of a hall.

Now, as I watched, two nurses sauntered by. Once they were gone, Krak went up the hall, found Room 13 and slipped in.

The room was very plain. A night-black, uncurtained window was in the far wall. White metal tables, chairs and other hospital things stood about.

An old man was groaning on the bed, his face twisted in pain. He focused on the Countess Krak. She was looking at a chart that hung on the bottom of the bed. It said, "Dr. Tremor Graves."

"Do I know you?" said Dr. Graves.

"I am the new therapist," said the Countess Krak.

She reached into her shopping bag. She pulled out a helmet. She slid a recording strip into the slot and pushed a button that said Record. She plonked the helmet onto his head, threw the switch, plugged in the microphone and sat down.

The Countess Krak looked at the black window, glanced at the door, listened for a moment and then got down to business. "Sleep, sleep, pretty sleep."

Graves, who had been threshing about, lay more quietly.

"What do you know about Delbert John Rockecenter's wife and son?" she said into the microphone.

Graves went rigid. From under the helmet came a fearful voice. "Murder. Murder. I will not be blackmailed."

"You had better tell me exactly what happened," said the Countess Krak. "Then you can't be blackmailed."

The old doctor twisted restlessly. "This arthritis is worse than blackmail."

"Pay attention," said the Countess Krak. "Your pains will all go away if you tell me and you will never have them anymore."

Dr. Graves, in a hollow, muffled voice, as though it came from some deep tomb, began to talk.

"I know much of this from the girl and from the woman psychiatrist. And I know full well what happened to them in my own hands." He halted, restless again.

"Tell all," said the Countess Krak. "Begin with who you are."

"I am Dr. Tremor Graves, M.D., retired many years, a victim of my own drink and drugs and folly. I owned my own hospital in Fair Oakes but now even that is gone." He fell silent again.

"Rockecenter and his wife and son," prompted the Countess Krak.

"Delbert John Rockecenter kept his marriage secret. According to the girl it was because his family would be furious if they found out he had married someone so poor. The girl was Mary Styles, the only child of Ben and Charlotte Styles who owned a farm near Fair Oakes. She was stage-struck and went north some nineteen years ago. She got a job in the chorus of the Roxy Theater. That was all known in the local town and nobody much approved.

"Then apparently at a pot party she met Delbert John Rockecenter, then a man of about twenty-five. In a crazy moment they got married in a fast-marriage place. To Rockecenter it was just a joke. To the girl it was her whole life.

"She used to meet him secretly through the back doors of hotels because he was afraid someone, mainly his Aunt Timantha, would find out.

"Then she became pregnant and could no longer hide it. She refused an abortion and in panic he sent her to her parents here. And that's where I came in." He fell silent, twisting about.

"What happened?" prompted the Countess Krak.

"She was only in town a day or two when a psychiatrist showed up, a woman named Agnes P. Morelay, Ph.D., M.D., a newly graduated acid thing. I did not like her.

"This psychiatrist had some men with her. They grabbed the Styles girl and then I found myself talking to Dr. Morelay. This psychiatrist kept the parents quiet—I do not know how. And she wanted me to kill the girl and say it was suicide. But I wouldn't because I was afraid they would be able to blackmail me, then, for murder. Then this Morelay wanted an abortion done to the girl. But she was too far along and I said that would be murder, too.

"So I promised, for money, to hold the girl in a padded cell they hastily built in my hospital and then, for more money, to kill the mother and baby at birth." He fell silent, very agitated.

"Go on," said the Countess Krak.

"Just before the delivery, news came that the parents had been killed in an auto accident. It was a terrible shock to the girl. But it would have made no real difference. It was a breech birth and she bled to death internally. And I didn't want to be blackmailed by the psychiatrist for killing the baby, so I didn't, but I told Dr. Morelay that I had. I have done many evil things in my life," and the voice became a wail, "but I did not kill the two of them!"

"What did you do with the baby?" said the Countess Krak.

"I made it identifiable so I couldn't be blackmailed and would have some blackmail in my turn if I ever needed it. I tattooed a black dollar mark on the sole of the left foot of the boy and put it in the county poor farm under the name of Richard Roe. I told them it had been found on the hospital doorstep. I filed the mother's death certificate and never mentioned the child. I know psychiatry is for the rich to keep the poor in line. But if Morelay ever seeks to keep me in line, I can threaten to produce the child."

"That has been heard," said the Countess Krak. "But I will now tell you the additional thing that happened and you will remember it that way. And then you'll have no more pain. Is that all right?"

"Yes."

"What you have said is all correct except for this: Mary Styles gave birth to twins. They were nonidentical." She consulted a note she drew from her pocket. "The one that was born first, you put a dollar mark on the right foot sole. You sent this boy to a doctor friend in Georgia that professional ethics will not let you name. You told him to replace a stillborn child whose parents were Agnes and Gerald Wister, and name it Jerome Terrance Wister, and record that it was born in the Macon General Hospital, Bibb County, Georgia. And the other doctor agreed and is since dead. And any date disparity is because of the arrangements you had to make. Now, you remember this clearly."

"Yes."

"Now that we have all this clear in your mind, you will feel compelled, when you awake, to ease your soul of guilt, to write this all up as a formal confession. And only if you do that will your pains go away. And you will feel no more pain.

"Now you will forget I put a helmet on you. You will only remember the real incident as I have just told you and feel the compulsion to confess in writing. When I snap my fingers, you will awake."

She took the helmet off, turned it off and put it in the shopping bag.

Bang-Bang slid into the room, making motions.

The Countess Krak snapped her fingers.

Graves opened his eyes and looked around with some anxiety.

Chapter 3

Bang-Bang whispered to the Countess Krak. "That doctor said I couldn't be cured. But he's making his evening rounds. We better split!"

Footsteps sounded. Bang-Bang looked anxiously at the window, apparently to see if it could be dived out of.

More footsteps.

Dr. Price walked in!

He looked very severely at Bang-Bang. "I thought you had left. Maybe I should reexamine you for some other symptom such as snooping. Aha, and what is this young lady doing here?"

"We couldn't find the exit!" wailed Bang-Bang.

Dr. Price went around to the other side of the bed. He gave his black coat a professional twitch. He swept his blond hair out of his eyes. He bent over and took hold of Dr. Graves's wrist. "If you've been disturbing this patient . . ."

The door opened.

Stonewall Biggs walked in!

"What is this?" said Dr. Price. "A camp meeting?"

"Biggs!" cried Dr. Graves, sitting up and freeing his wrist. "Biggs! 'Fore God, get me a pen and some paper! This arthritis is killing me!"

Biggs looked startled. Then he looked at the Countess Krak. "You must be th' young lady . . ."

"Here," said the Countess Krak, pushing a pad and a pen into Biggs's hand.

"I can't allow this patient to be disturbed!" said Dr. Price.

"Give me that paper!" wailed Graves.

Biggs promptly did so. The Countess Krak pushed a bed table into place. Graves bent over it and furiously began to write.

Biggs looked at the first words that Graves put down and then he rushed from the room. A moment later he came back, dragging two of the hospital nurses.

"What is this?" cried Dr. Price, tearing at his blond hair.

"Shut up," said Stonewall Biggs. "It do seem that ol' Tremor heah is busy on a confession. And all of you watch because you'ns is goin' to be signin' it as due, prop-ah an' authentic, done by his own free will an' accord an' without no threat of duress!"

"You can't invade his privacy!" cried Dr. Price.

"He's invadin' it hisself," said Stonewall Biggs. "Confession is awful good fo' th' soul. An' as county clerk, ah c'n invade anythin' ah please. So jus' stan' theah an' watch."

Dr. Graves was writing at a mad rate.

Suddenly I realized that Heller was unaccounted for. His viewer was tipped a bit away from me and I had been too engrossed to watch it for his fate, which, after all, I considered sealed. The view was of the silly French car, the Karin, seen from a distance in the gloom and I supposed they had intercepted him on the road and now had him standing somewhere securely cuffed. I did not have time to play back the strips. I could enjoy that later.

Right now the question was, would the Countess Krak get away with this flagrant violation of all legal rules of evidence? Surely men as clever as Price and Biggs, themselves, would see through this: the eagerness of that racing pen would look strange to them. Graves was practically quivering!

And then I realized something else: the chance Torpedo now had. The Countess Krak was standing across the room from that window. Dr. Price, on the other side of the bed, had his back to it but was not blocking it. All Torpedo had to do was shoot past Dr. Price and he would nail the Countess Krak! No thin windowpane could even deflect a .375 Magnum Holland and Holland elephant slug! Come on, Torpedo!

Dr. Graves was finished. He signed the confession with a huge signature and then sank back. A beautiful smile suffused his aged face. "Oh," he said, "what a relief! No pain!"

Biggs was reading the confession. The Countess Krak was looking over his shoulder. "So!" said Biggs. "Theah *were* two lahk he said!"

The nurses were also trying to get a glimpse of what Graves had written. "No, no," said Biggs. "Th' rest of you don' have t'read it. You'ah jus' heah t'witness that he writ it. So you sign, heah at th' bottom, each one of you."

Dr. Price and the two nurses signed as Biggs thrust it under their noses.

"Now, Tremor," said Biggs, "raise yo' raht han'. Do you solemnly sweah that this is th' truth, th' whole truth and nothin' but th' truth, so he'p you God?"

"Oh, yes," said Dr. Graves. "It's the only decent thing I ever did in my whole life."

"Good," said Biggs. "Now by th' powah invested in me as Notary Public of th' Sovereign State of Virginia, Justice of th' Peace an' County Clerk of Hamden County, ah do pronounce this document valid an' bindin' on all pahties, so he'p me God, Amen!" He got out a stamp

and put a notary form at the document end. He signed
it and dated it. He got out a pocket embossing seal and
crunched it over the signatures. He took out a little book
and recorded the date and number of the paper and then
had everybody sign his little book.

"Now that," said Biggs, handing it to Krak, "is th'
mostes' legal document this county evah see!"

"Thank you, Miss," said Dr. Graves. "I feel so comfortable, now I can die in peace!"

CRASH!

The window shattered!

The boom of a rifle!

Everything went into a blur.

Something hit the Countess Krak!

She was down on the floor!

Bang-Bang let go of her.

He hit another set of legs. "Down! Down!" Bang-
Bang was shouting. "Hit the dirt, you rookies!"

A fusillade of other shots!

More glass flying through the room!

I thought that Torpedo must be firing the dead
motorcycle cop's gun now.

The shots stopped.

"Anybody hit?" shrilled Bang-Bang.

"I'm not hit," said Dr. Price, crawling further under
the bed. "It just went through my coat."

One of the nurses raised up. She screamed!

The other nurse got on her knees and looked. She
cried, "Dr. Graves is hit!"

A flick of movement on Heller's viewer caught my
eye. He had glanced up. A hospital window! He was outside! He was creeping through the brush!

I raged! The dirty sneak had not been caught! He

must have decided to be cautious and had remained outside letting Biggs go in!

A nurse on her knees at the edge of the bed said, "Dr. Graves is dead!"

Biggs on the floor muttered, "Ah hope Junior is all raht."

The Countess Krak—eyes level with the planks—looked at Biggs. "Junior? You mean my darling is out there?"

"He saw some kin' of a French cah in th' bushes an' thought Hahvey Lee maht have come heah," said Biggs. "He sent me in."

The Countess Krak got up to her knees and started toward the door.

Bang-Bang grabbed her, pushed her down. "No you don't, Miss Joy. The terrain out there must be swarming with gooks and you ain't got no helmet."

"Holy smokes," wailed Stonewall Biggs, "aftah all this, ah hope they don' kill Junior! Ah ain't got mah new cohthouse yet!"

Chapter 4

Out of the night, through the shattered window, the blast of a bullhorn blared. "Come out of there with your hands up!"

"Good God," said Stonewall Biggs. "Chief Fawg!" He raised his voice to an outraged shout. "You God (bleeped) fool! Quit shootin'!"

The bullhorn roared, "The place is surrounded.

Throw your guns out the window and come out quietly with your hands up!''

Biggs howled, ''(Bleep) it, Fawg! This is Biggs! Theah ain't nobody in heah! You jus' killed Doctah Graves!''

A nurse screamed, ''He's right!''

I got Heller's viewer turned so I could see it better. He was in the brush. He was looking at the backs of three cops and Harvey Lee! Beyond them was the hospital. Heller had that big, fancy Llama .45 automatic pistol in his hand and it was trained right between the shoulder blades of Chief Fawg!

Biggs inside was yelling, ''What th' hell ah you doin'?''

Chief Fawg shifted the rifle he held. He lifted the bullhorn. ''We're doin' our duty. We're after that criminal that was with you!''

''Theah ain't no criminal in heah!'' shouted Biggs.

''You cain't fool us, Stonewall. We seen him right there with his back to the window!''

''You (bleeped) fool!'' shouted Biggs. ''That was Doctah Price an' you done ruined his coat! Cleah away f'um heah!''

''No you don't, Biggs. You're harboring a criminal an' a fugitive in there. Last year he beat up two cops. Tonight he done it again and he stole another car from Harvey Lee. We got witnesses and you c'd become a accessory! Send him out or we start firing again!''

Heller had been moving forward. I had no way to warn them. He was now within two feet of the back of Harvey Lee who was, himself, to the rear of the chief and two officers.

Suddenly Heller's hand lashed out and seized Lee. With a jerk, he had Lee standing in front of him as cover. The used-car salesman yelped as some pressure point was pressed.

The cops whirled. They raised their guns.

Heller said, "Go ahead and shoot Lee. He's a thief, aren't you, Lee?"

"I'm a thief!" screamed Lee. "Please let go my arm!"

"Go on," said Heller, apparently applying more pressure to the spot he was holding the used-car salesman with.

Lee babbled, "I sold him the car for three hundred dollars and didn't give him a bill of sale."

"Go on," said Heller.

Lee screamed, "I thought I could get the car back and keep the money!"

"Chief," said Heller, his automatic trained on Fawg from under Lee's armpit, "this is a Mexican standoff. Now, do we flip a coin to see whether I shoot you or you shoot Lee?"

Chief Fawg seemed to be shaking with indecision and rage. "You criminal! This won't do you any good! We always get our man!"

Suddenly Biggs was behind the chief. "You leave him alone, you hospital shootah! You know (bleeped) well th' man that done them crimes las' September was repohted daid by the FBI! You nevah got a good look at him. You said so y'self!"

Chief Fawg had turned to meet this new onslaught. Biggs was stamping his foot he was so mad.

Biggs demanded, "Do you know who that boy is?"

Fawg sneered, "God, I suppose."

"Naw, suh!" cried Biggs. "Higher! That boy theah be Delbert John Rockecenter, Junior!"

The chief and the two cops glanced toward where Heller was holding Harvey Lee. Then the chief said to

Biggs, "Stonewall, you better not try foolin' me!"

The Countess Krak was suddenly on the scene. Right out in the open, an easy shot for Torpedo!

She shook her finger under the chief's nose. "Oh, no, he's not fooling you. You come right around here, if you don't believe it!"

The shaking finger turned into a pointing finger, right between the chief's eyes. He suddenly started following her as she led him away.

The rest of the group followed and Heller, still holding Lee, brought up the rear.

The land yacht was sitting there. She darted into it and the viewer flared out. A moment later the viewer stabilized again and she was standing before them once more.

She had a card. She flashed it under the nose of the chief and then the two cops. They stared at it. Then suddenly they turned and went down on their knees before Heller.

The Countess Krak looked at the card and showed it to Biggs and I could see in Heller's viewer that she had a ghoulish grin.

It was the registration card of the land yacht. It said "Delbert John Rockecenter" on the owner line!

Biggs towered over the kneeling chief. "You idiot! You've been shootin' at th' son of th' man who rules th' world!" Biggs turned to Heller. "Junior, what shall we do abaht this murderin' (bleep) that killed po' Doctah Graves?"

"What's customary heahabouts?" said Heller, lowering his gun and releasing Lee.

"Sentence an' lynchin' ever' time," said Biggs. "As Justice of th' Peace, ah have t'write up th' sentence, all legal, an' with yo' he'p, Junior, we'll use that tree ovah theah. But only if you approve, of co'se."

Chief Fawg wailed, "Please, dear God, NO! Please, Mr. Junior."

Joe and the other cop grovelled on their knees. They raised their clasped and pleading hands to Heller. "Mercy!" pleaded one. "I have a wife and children," begged Joe. "Don't lynch me, Mr. Junior!"

Heller said, "Stonewall, my dear friend, let us be merciful. Let's let them contribute all their ill-gotten gains and part-time labor to the building of the new cohthouse."

"All right, Junior," said Biggs. But he pointed to Harvey Lee. "What abaht him?"

"Oh, Jesus God," said Harvey Lee. "I just realized I tried to pull a cheap car deal on the son of the richest man in the world. Shoot me!"

Biggs looked down at the kneeling cops. "Fawg," he said, "git up offen yo' knees an' go home, but jus' remembah, ah got blackmail on you fo' th' rest of yo' days. Po' Doctah Graves."

I realized suddenly that all that shooting must have held Torpedo's hand. He was still around there. There was still a chance. If only now they'd leave the Countess Krak unguarded, Torpedo would still have his kill. This very night!

Chapter 5

"Wheah you goin' now?" said Stonewall Biggs to Heller. " 'Cause ah got something else t'show you tonaht."

Heller moved an indicating hand toward the Countess Krak. "It do look lahk th' ordahs is comin' f'um th' High Command. What do we do now, dear?"

"We're leaving for the county poor farm right this minute," said the Countess Krak.

Biggs said, "Miss Captain, if'n ah c'd intrude, tha's now the County Agricultural Farm an' you won' find it on these back roads onless ah leads th' way."

"Lead on, lead on, doughty Stonewall Biggs," said Krak. "Just so long as we can find the other son."

Stonewall Biggs gave a gallant bow and trotted to his car. Bang-Bang raced up and down telling drivers to get underway.

The Countess Krak pulled Heller toward the land yacht and their viewers flared out. I was quite resigned then to being blind and suddenly I was most amazed to see the reception come back on!

It wasn't very good and it was full of flutters and blurs but it was there. They must be at the extreme back end of the vehicle, a considerable distance away from that generator. As near as I could make out, it was a tiny surgery room.

They had evidently done their kissing and greeting right after they had stepped inside for Krak was all business now.

"Sit right there, dear," she said to Heller, pointing at the tiny operating table against the land yacht's outer skin. "Take off your right boot and sock."

The land yacht was speeding along. The Countess Krak, braced against the sways, was rummaging through the white-faced instrument drawers.

Heller obliged but he was looking at her. "What are you up to now, dear?"

She had what she wanted from the drawers and she

was now opening the Zanco Cellological Equipment and Supply case she had stuffed full at the base. "I am putting a dollar mark on the sole of your right foot. If it's not right, and doesn't compare exactly to the other one, I can remove it."

"What do I want with a dollar mark, dear?" he said.

She thrust the papers at him. "Read this and you'll see."

She got to work on his foot, using cosmetics and other things. Heller, bracing himself against the swaying of the land yacht, read what Dr. Graves had written. Then he sat there, watching her, evidently thinking.

She finished the job and, holding his foot up, admired it. She bent his leg and showed him. "Does that look old enough to you?"

"Dear," he said, "Bury is not an honorable man. He doesn't keep his word. I don't think he would have given me the Wister name and birth certificate. I think you must have gotten Graves to alter this some way."

"Me, Jettero?" she said.

The land yacht was stopped. Bang-Bang's voice, "Beachhead in sight! Hit the nets!"

Their viewers flared out but shortly came on again. They were walking from the vehicles up a flight of steps to an institutional sort of building, its bricks a shabby red in the vehicle lights.

Biggs was pounding on the door. "They go to bed wi' th' chickens heah. But ah c'n roust 'm aht." He pounded some more.

A sleepy man, still buckling his pants, came out. "Biggs? Wha's the fuss? Anothah cohthouse fiah?"

"Sweeney," said Biggs, "min' yo' tongue. You hahborin' a boy name Richard Roe heah?"

"Young Dick?" said Sweeney. "You heah to drag him back to the State Agriculture College? I c'n tell you now, Biggs, he won't go. He gets too lonesome fo' his pigs!"

"Wheah is he?" said Biggs.

"Why, he be down to the pig sheds, of co'se."

"Show th' way," said Biggs.

They went down a winding path to some concrete buildings. Sweeney turned on some floodlights and there were a lot of startled grunts and then complaints from the covered pens.

Sweeney took them up a flight of outside stairs and opened a door. He turned on an inside light. "Dick," he said, "they finally come to drag you back. Ah'm sorry, boy, but ah cain't go up ag'inst the law. It'd be mah job."

Krak peeked in past Sweeney. It was a small room. The walls were plastered with cutout pictures of pigs, all colors and types. On a narrow mattress, fully clothed, except for shoes, a tall, blond boy had been asleep. He was trying to sit up now, defending his eyes against the light. He looked to be about an Earth eighteen. He looked amazingly like Delbert John.

"Ah won' go!" he said. "Ever' tahm ah leave heah, Sweeney, if only fo' one term, ah come back an' fin' mah pigs ahl in neglec' an' pinin' away. You tell them fo'ks to jus' go away."

"They got guns, Dick," said Sweeney.

"Guns!" cried the boy, leaping bolt upright. "Git away f'm heah with guns! You m'aht shoot a pig!"

The Countess Krak moved smoothly in. "I'd better handle this," she said. "Nobody is going to shoot your pigs."

"Whoosh!" said the boy, staring at her round-eyed. "Who be you? A angel or somethin'? Hey, who be this, Sweeney? Wow, she's pretty enough to be a pig!"

"I'm just a friend," said the Countess Krak. She pointed a finger at the boy's forehead. She said gently, "Just sit down on the mattress, please."

The boy sat suddenly, still staring.

The Countess Krak reached down and pulled off his left sock. She upended the foot and looked at the sole.

You couldn't see anything. It was too soiled!

"Bang-Bang," called the Countess Krak. "A bucket of water and a rag, please."

There was a scurrying on the stairs and shortly, with a clatter and slosh, Bang-Bang appeared. The Countess took the bucket of water, set it down and dipped a rag in it. She washed off the sole of the foot. It took a while to cut through the layers. The water in the bucket got black from repeated dips of the rag. The boy watched her in fascination, studying every move.

At length, she was satisfied and held the foot sole up to the light.

A DOLLAR SIGN!

Small and dim, it spread out on the heel.

"Well, theah she is," said Biggs in the door.

The boy sensed they had seen something. He grabbed his foot away from her and, with some contortion, looked at the sole.

"Well, golly be," he said. "I ain't never noticed that afore. It do look lahk a dollah ma'k. Is it some disease? Hoof-rot mebbe? What's it mean? Tell me quick!"

"It means," said the Countess Krak, "that you are not a nameless orphan foundling. It means that you are the son of the richest man in the world, Delbert John Rockecenter, found at long last."

He looked at her round-eyed. He saw that she meant it. And then it hit him. He fainted dead away!

Chapter 6

The Countess beckoned to Heller. "Dear, take off your right boot."

Heller moved past Biggs and I saw where Sweeney had gotten the idea of guns: Heller had that decorated .45 glittering in his belt. I hoped that he would go away and leave an open field to Torpedo.

Heller removed his boot and sock. The Countess took his foot and held it alongside that of the Earth boy. Actually, they weren't a bad match: the real one on Rockecenter's son and the counterfeit dollar mark on Heller's. Residual dirt obscured any difference of the boy's.

Biggs saw them both. "Well, there she be twice. Unidentical twins reunited." He produced a police identopolaroid he must have taken off the chief. He shot a picture of the feet together, then he shot one of Heller and then he shot one of the boy, not bothering with the fact that the youth still lay there unconscious.

"Now that this heah event is full recorded," said Biggs, "you fo'ks come along. Ah got somethin' else to show yuh." He went down the steps beckoning.

The Countess followed to the last two steps and then she stopped. "You go along, dear. I'll stay here. When he comes to, he'll need somebody to hold his hand."

"Wait a minute," said Heller. "I don't like to leave you here."

"Oh, I'll be all right. Now, listen, all of you, Mr. Biggs and Mr. Sweeney. You keep this find quiet, do you

hear? That poor boy is going to need weeks and weeks
of coaching and training to take his proper place in the
world. So no publicity. The papers always get things
wrong."

"Nobody ever believes me anyway," said Sweeney.

"Yes, ma'am," said Biggs.

"Now, Bang-Bang," said the Countess Krak, "you
follow Jettero in the jeep just so he can get back to the
circus wagon over there on the other side of the farm."

"Yes, ma'am," said Bang-Bang. "I'll handle it."

They left her at the foot of the stairs in all that glaring floodlight. She would be all alone in an isolated part
of the farm. And if Torpedo had any sense, he'd kill the
boy, too! A setup if there ever was one! Even quiet
enough for the corpse rape!

The men walked the considerable distance back to
the main building. The drivers had pulled the motor
homes over to the side of the drive. Sweeney went into
the building to finish his sleep. Heller climbed into the
Buick beside Biggs. They drove off and shortly lights
showed up, following behind.

Biggs drove over bumpy roads for quite a while.
Then he turned at a rural mailbox and went much slower,
his lights pointing through an orchard and, as the
entrance road twisted, playing back and forth across
some decrepit farm buildings. He stopped and before
them lay an old-fashioned, two-story, brick farmhouse.

"You probably don' remembah this place, Junior. It's
passed to th' Hodges now through death duties an' taxes.
But it's th' ol' Styles farm, yo' granpappy's on yo'
mothah's side. Early tonaht I got me a hunch, so le's see
if'n she bears fruit."

He got out of the car, walked up the porch steps and
began to bang with an old brass knocker much corroded

with age. It took quite a while but finally a woman in a nightcap and dressing gown turned on the porch light, peeked through a window and opened the door.

"Whut you doin' here at this ungodly hour, Stonewall Biggs?" she said. "Don' you know it's the middle of the naht?"

"Miz Hodges," said Biggs, "ah do apologize. But have you clean yo' attic recently?"

"Biggs, you know danged well theah ain't no Yankee regoolation that anyone has to clean a attic. Don' tell me theah be a county one. Nobody nevah cleans no attic! An' if'n you come here this time of naht to tell me to clean mah attic . . ."

"No, no," said Biggs, with great charm. "Ah sho'ly wouldn' insult th' fines' housekeeper fo' miles aroun' with that! But taxes can be reduced fo' unused space. An' ah jus' wanted t'see if you was ovahtaxed!"

"Oh, well, tha's better."

"So could ah have a look in yo' attic?"

"He'p y'self so long as you let me go back to bed!"

"Chahmed," said Biggs.

Biggs went in and Heller sat down on the porch and waited. At long length, the porch light went off, Biggs came out and closed the door of the house behind him. He was carrying what appeared to be a big hatbox.

They got in the car and drove out. The jeep at the gate backed out of their way. They went down the road and Biggs stopped. He turned on the dome light.

"People," said Biggs, "nevah throw nothin' away. This was stuck cleah back undah th' eaves along with a bundle of election pohstahs fo' Jeff Davis an' a bundle of Confederate notes. They hid it but ah know mah people heah in Hamden. They hold on!" He dropped the hatbox into Heller's lap. The dust geysered up. The strings had already been untied.

Heller sneezed and opened the cover. Lying there were packets of letters, all tied, some loose envelopes and a photo album.

Heller opened the album. The first picture, somewhat yellow, was that of a very beautiful blond girl in a dancing costume.

"That yo' mammy," said Biggs. "She was jus' abaht th' mos' beautiful girl in these pahts. A belle fo' shuah! You take aftah her. Ah knowed it th' firs' moment ah laid eyes on you. Same hair, same eyes."

A yellowed clipping was wedged under the photo. Heller took it out.

LOCAL GIRL
JOINS
ROXY CHORUS
IN NEW YORK

Mary Styles, the only child of Ben and Charlotte Styles of the Styles farm in Hamden, graduate of the Fair Oaks High School and winner of last year's State Beauty Contest, has made good in Yankeeland.

It went on but Heller slid it back in place. He opened more album pages. They were pictures of chorus lines and publicity photos.

Slid loosely into the book were several enlarged nightclub and snapshot photos. The first was Delbert John Rockecenter, a better-looking man in his mid-twenties, sitting at a table with Mary Styles, surrounded by waiters and champagne. Another was the pair of them, arms around each other in a bar. Another was of them semi-dressed at a beach resort sipping from the same Coke with two straws.

"The boy at the farm," said Biggs, "take mo' aftah his fathah, but that w'd be the case with unidenticals, ah guess."

Heller closed the book. He picked up a pack of letters and glanced through them. All were handwritten from "Delie" to "Mary Yum-Yum." They concerned arranging secret rendezvous in resorts and hotels and were heavy with caution about being seen.

Crumpled up over at the side of the box was a pair of half-torn sheets. Heller spread them out. It had an embossed letterhead. The date was over eighteen years ago. It said:

AGNES P. MORELAY, Ph.D., M.D.

Dear Mr. and Mrs. Styles,
It is my sad duty to inform you that your daughter Mary, after a hasty and ill-conceived marriage, could not stand the strain of sudden elevation in the world. She contracted a serious mental disease known as delirium altaphasis. *While she appears sane at times, she can be very dangerous to herself and those around her.*
She is unfortunately pregnant. Until the child is born she cannot be treated professionally as the convulsion therapies would produce

miscarriage which I am sure you do not want.

To announce or even whisper her marriage would subject her to wild mental states in which she might seek to destroy herself.

As soon as the child is born, she can be treated with professional psychiatric care. So please assist us in quietly placing her in the fully competent care of my colleague, Dr. Tremor Graves.

If word of her marriage or condition were to leak out, even if she didn't destroy herself, she would have to be committed to the state insane asylum for life.

Adequate funds for her care, which is extremely expensive, running into the thousands of dollars per month and quite beyond your means, will be given Dr. Graves and your-selves from time to time, but these will be cut off if she becomes formally committed and a charge of the state.

I know you have her welfare at heart and so does her poor, distracted husband and will realize that this is all for the best.

Once the child is born, she can be cured by the most professional possible means and can take her rightful place in the world.

Please do not cost her that chance.

In professional confidence,

AGNES P. MORELAY

"So that's how they kept the parents quiet," said Heller.

"They didn't have to ver' long," said Biggs. "They was kilt in a auto accident. But this, ah think, is what you'ah lookin' fo' an' which ah came to fin'."

He reached in and pulled out an official-looking envelope. He opened it and gave it to Heller.

It declared that DELBERT JOHN ROCKECENTER and MARY CHARLOTTE STYLES had been joined in marriage at Elkton, Maryland, the place of instant marriages, a year before the date of birth. It was an imposing certificate, all stamped and sealed.

Stonewall Biggs said, "So you ain't even a bastard, Junior."

"Valuable," said Heller.

"Now ah got to go back and write that other boy's birth certificate," said Biggs. "We'll jus' call him Delbert John Rockecenter, th' Second, if that all right with you, Junior."

"Fine," said Heller.

"An' whahl ah'm at it, ah'll do a duplicate of yo' mothah's death certificate an' some additional copies of yo' own. You may need them. Ah'll bring them ovah to th' fahm in th' mo'ning if'n you'll still be theah."

"Tha's what the captain said," Heller replied.

"Now, Junior, onto othah things. Ah don' think that chief has got much muscle in him. Do ah get a grant fo' that new cohthouse?"

"Only if you guarantee to build a absoloot ohriginal that George Washington slept in."

"Tha's mah boy!" cried Stonewall Biggs. "Smahtest thing ah evah did was to get th' late Tremor Graves drunk that night!"

Chapter 7

Since Heller now would be going back, I hastily turned to the viewer of the Countess Krak to see if Torpedo had his opportunity and could shoot her in time.

She was sitting in the upper room of the pig building, back to the window, a perfect target for anyone outside.

The young man had come around. He was sitting on the edge of the littered bed, his blond hair in disarray, his eyes dazed. "It's nahce of you t' sit up with me. Ah'm too confused to sleep. Who'd evah thought ah had a real ma and pa jus' like pigs do!"

"Well, listen," said the Countess Krak, "I know it's late at night but if you're to get any sleep, there's something I could do. You know football?"

"Oh, yes, ma'am. Ah played it at the aggie college."

She reached into her shopping bag and pulled out the hypno rig. "This is a new type of football helmet. It teaches you."

"Aw, youah kiddin'."

"Try it on," and she put it on his head and threw the switch.

Torpedo's voice! "GOT YOU!"

I tensely stared at the viewer. Had Krak not heard him? She didn't turn around.

Then suddenly I realized that the voice had not come from the speaker.

IT WAS IN THIS ROOM!

I whirled.

Torpedo was standing in the open door!

His gray, prison-pallor face was contorted with rage! The huge rifle was ready in his hand!

He was frothing! "You set me up, you son of a (bleepch)! You knew the car we had was stolen! You tipped off the cops! They were laying for me at the hospital! You're going to pay for that!

"I had to abandon the car and walk back here all night! You're going to get gut-shot for that!

"But, you (bleepard), you never told me that that was the girl of the man who trapped me at the Brewster and pushed me off the elevated and collected my fee and cost me all my future with Bury. You just sent me there so he could kill me! And for that, after I shoot you, I'm going to rape your corpse and give it syph, clap and all!"

He was raising the gun to shoot!

The arrangements I had earlier made had been needed after all! I closed my hand on the Apparatus radio relay ring I had put on. It activated the vibration speaker I had planted on the balcony rail outside the door.

A scream went off behind him!

He whirled!

He was standing on the door end of the runner rug. I reached down and grabbed my end and yanked.

With a flip he went forwards.

He staggered.

He hit the balcony rail.

With a clatter he went over and fell fifteen feet to the ground!

I wasted no time.

I grabbed up my things and jammed them in a suitcase.

I snatched up my viewers.

I scrabbled around. I couldn't find my gun! The (bleep) must have stolen it or I had dropped it earlier in the day.

No time now to search.

I streaked out of the room.

Running like mad, I got to the manure truck.

I threw my things into it. I jumped under the wheel. I jimmied the ignition. It started.

I tore out of there, horse biscuits flying behind me in the wind!

Had I had my gun, I might have shot him. But I certainly would not have touched anything he touched, so using his rifle was out. In retrospect, as I drove, I thought it might have been smarter to have gone over to him on the pavement and stamped his head in. But again, I hadn't wanted to touch him. Yes, I was doing right. Just get out of there and fast!

I thought I was safe. The motel proprietor would never suspect anyone would steal this manure truck. He probably wouldn't even notice it was gone until much later in the day, for he never seemed to be around. And if the police stopped me I could say it was a Federal commandeer of transport.

So I felt safe as I drove in to an all-night trucker's station to the north of Lynchburg and filled up with gas and oil.

I was just pulling out of the island when I chanced to look back.

Here came Torpedo! Wild-haired and wild-eyed, insane for revenge, he was driving an old Toyota subcompact!

I stepped on it!

With screaming wheels I went tearing up Route 29. I was outdistancing him!

Charlottesville, Culpeper, Warrenton, Arlington. In the dawn I was rocketing around the Capital Beltway of Washington, D.C.

Anxiously stopping again for gas, I looked behind. I thought I had lost him. For the next hour, I drove more sensibly. I was on the John F. Kennedy Memorial Highway and just passing Elkton, Maryland, when—*BLAM! SCREEYOW!*—an elephant slug hit the car top and went ricocheting away!

Oh, after that I drove!

The prospect of not only being dead but raped and not only being raped but infected totally gave me a very heavy foot upon the throttle.

The New Jersey Turnpike is usually fast but it was too slow for me that awful day.

I had almost come abreast of Staten Island when the horrible realization came to me that I had no place to go!

Torpedo knew my phone number at Miss Pinch's. And furthermore my welcome at that apartment would be very violent.

Driving in that stinking truck, my head spun in a quandary. Then Apparatus training took over. Go to the least expected place. Go to the place where one might get protection.

HIS MOTHER!

She would defend me, that was for sure! She hated her son.

The Goethals Bridge lay just ahead. I turned off the New Jersey Turnpike onto it. I went down the Staten Island Expressway like a fired cannonball. I got across the dizzy heights of the Verrazano Narrows Bridge and was shortly speeding up the Queens Expressway.

Rounding corners on two wheels, I rocketed toward safety. I slammed on the brakes before the house and leaped out of the steaming car. I raced up the steps and pounded on the door.

The hulking monster of a woman recognized me. I crowded past her into the hall. In a voice I was carefully keeping from sounding hysterical, I told her that her son was after me with intent to kill.

She nodded, seeming to understand. She went up the stairs and was gone a bit. Then she leaned over the banister and beckoned. I went up.

Apparently the room at the top of the stairs had once been Torpedo's. He had painted bars on the window-pane. The bedstead was cold iron. A portrait, a photo-graph, hung on the wall. The man in it had a crooked, leering face. It was autographed:

> To Torpedo,
> my best con,
> J. Q. Cortikul, Ph.D.

His prison psychologist!

Mrs. Fiaccola pointed to the closet and indicated I should enter it.

A POUNDING OF FEET ON THE STAIRS! TORPEDO!

"Where is the son of a (bleepch)?" he was screaming and I realized he had seen the car.

"Torpedo!" she said. "You want a kill. You're going to get one!"

His mother was beckoning him up to the room. Her right hand was obscured in the folds of her skirt.

He was snarling and agitated. But he was obeying.

Firmly, she pushed him into the room and made him sit down on the bed.

She made a shushing signal with her left hand and

then used it to gesture at the closet. "He's in there," she said. My hair stood on end!

His mother lifted her right hand. She was holding his leopard, the sawed-off shotgun!

She pushed it vertical at his chest as though to force him to take it.

He reached out to grab the breach.

With a quick movement, his mother lowered it so that the barrel was against his chin from below.

SHE PULLED BOTH TRIGGERS!

The noise was deafening!

The whole of Torpedo's jaw and head hit the ceiling!

His mother wiped off the triggers with the hem of her skirt. She curled his dying fingers around the guard.

She then opened a drawer and got out some gun cleaning materials and put them on the bed.

Then she stood back. "Ever since you been out of the Federal pen," she said to the dead body, "you talk psychology, psychology, psychology. So I read up. Now you got some psychology, you no-good, filthy, rotten philanderer of corpses! I hope the devil makes you read psychology the rest of infinity!"

She turned to me and beckoned me out of the closet. "You witnessed it. He was cleaning his gun and it went off, wasn't he?"

I nodded numbly.

"So that's the end of my no-good, carrion-(bleeping) (bleep) of a son. And a pleasure it is to see him lying there dead even without the twenty-five thousand insurance I now get."

Only then, at that very moment, was the brutal truth borne in upon me.

Torpedo had failed.

I personally would now have to handle the whole situation.

The fate of Earth, of Rockecenter, of Lombar and the entire Voltar Confederacy depended upon one haggard and worn frail reed, Apparatus Officer Soltan Gris.

And it was more vital than ever to remove the vicious Countess Krak.

As I went out into the night, I shook my fist at the sky. "By all the stars, by all the Gods and Demons of the firmament," I cried. "In spite of what you are doing to me, I must prevail! Do what thou wilt, I shall still terminate that awful woman!"

A deadly oath.

I meant it!

PART
FORTY-SEVEN

Chapter 1

I did not have too much money. I could not go back to Miss Pinch's and endure those women.

I drove to midtown Manhattan and abandoned the manure truck on a side street. Lugging my bag and viewers, I made my way to a hotel I had noticed at times in the past. It was a wino hangout, shabby and dirty, the lobby littered with collapsed human wrecks. The very place to hide out, for here they didn't even bother to sort the living from the dead.

I got a room with a cracked window, cracked washbasin and cracked floor. Cockroaches swarmed, thriving on the remains of a soiled carpet.

I should have been exhausted, but I was not. I had too much to do.

Despite the lateness of the hour, I got out pad and pen and sat down at the rickety table. One must be orderly, one must do things by the textbook. I must be careful and precise, for only in that way was I ever going to bring about the demise of the Countess Krak.

I wrote down the Apparatus fundamental musts:

1. PREPARE A BASE BEFORE YOU ATTACK
2. HANDLE YOUR TROOPS BEFORE YOU ATTACK
3. PLAN BEFORE YOU ATTACK

4. GATHER WEAPONS BEFORE YOU ATTACK
5. PINPOINT OBJECTIVES BEFORE YOU
   ATTACK
6. TIME EVERYTHING

I knew you had to do these things in exact order. Geniuses, long since, have worked these things out. If an organization such as the Apparatus has the prime duty of undermining a civilization, it must be thorough. One must make the maximum amount of trouble for the maximum number of people for the minimum number of reasons. That rule holds good for governments, for governmental organizations and for government officers and agents. Even on Earth, which is primitive about such things, the FBI and others adhere to these maxims totally. So I knew I was being wise.

So I took up number five first. That was the easy one. The primary objective was the Countess Krak. I knew that very well from long and bitter experience.

As to number one, I had my base in this hotel room.

As to number six, I looked at my watch and carefully noted the hour, minute and second and put them down.

Suddenly, I realized that I was not taking these in perfect order. I got a grip on myself. I should be working on number two, handling the troops.

The only troops was me. I fully realized that now. Bury and Torpedo and even Madison had failed me. I was entirely on my own.

What was the matter with the troops?

Venereal disease. What with goats and dogs and Torpedo, this was obviously the case. While there was no sign of it, in every text you read on military matters it is a problem. Good.

Determined to do things right this time, I let first things be first. Even when they were second on the list.

To handle the troops required rest. I carefully noted the time as required in number six and went to bed.

Bright and early I got up, brushed the cockroaches off my clothes and dressed.

Marching with bitter determination, I made my way to a phone kiosk in the lobby and looked up VD clinics. There was one close by. I made an appointment and was promptly there.

I was the first in and I got quick service. I laboriously filled out a card. A young doctor, without looking at it, sat down in the interview room where I had been placed. He said, "All this is in confidence. You can talk freely. What symptoms have you noticed?"

"None," I said. "It is simply inevitable."

"What have your contacts . . . you know . . . been?"

And here I could give him real information. "I have been in contact with a horrible blond woman, a fiend in human form, that treats life as if it were chaff. It is all her fault. She is five feet nine and a half inches tall. She hypnotizes everybody!"

"How long have these contacts continued?" he said solicitously.

I counted it up rapidly, using my fingers. The first time I had collided with the Countess Krak was in Spiteos about half a year before Heller came along. She had murdered an agent who sought to grab at her sexually. "Thirteen months," I said.

"How do you know you got it from her?" he asked.

"She forced me into it," I said. "If it weren't for her I would never have had any association with dogs or goats or llamas from Peru."

He was shocked, as well he might be. He held up his hand. "Oh, I think we had better not even waste time on examinations. This sounds pretty desperate. Nurse! Bring the big tray quick!"

And thus began a treatment course which lasted the better part of ten days.

I endured it because it just showed all I had suffered at her hands.

First there were the antibiotic shots, seven kinds. Every one of them was agony. I hate needles!

Then I stoically endured a harrowing experience in which my body temperature was raised to 106 degrees while under medication.

Next, when I was able to get around again, I got neoarsphenamine-606. The doctor told me that it killed one in every ten thousand and I half expected to be the one. It would show people what she had put me through.

Finally, a bright day came. I had hardly any money left. I had lost many pounds. The doctor was reviewing the last series of tests.

"Null," he said. "You now do not have the faintest sign of anything. So the whole course has been very successful. You have been very lucky, really, since there are strains about today which do not respond to any cure at all. Now let me give you one solid piece of advice: Do not ever have any physical contact with that woman ever again. And terminate any association with her as soon as possible!"

I promised him earnestly to adhere to his advice. I would get on with my termination of the Countess Krak now, as soon as I was able to complete my program.

Gods, what that woman had put me through!

Chapter 2

The next part of the campaign was "3. PLAN BEFORE YOU ATTACK."

Accurate planning requires data. Accordingly, I brushed the cockroaches off my viewers to see what the most horrible monster in the universe was up to now.

They were still in Virginia!

Heller and the two retired Greyhound bus drivers were sitting in the spring sunlight. Heller was in shorts, getting a suntan in a deck chair. The two drivers, with their collars open and caps on the backs of their heads, were drinking what looked like mint juleps and playing cards under an awning nearby. Loafing at my expense!

The land yacht and other motor home were parked in an L in a grassy field with their awnings out. The blue-misted mountains were plain in Heller's sight.

The roar of an approaching motor caused Heller to look up a forest road. It was the jeep, leaping all over the place with Bang-Bang at the wheel. The Countess Krak was in the front seat.

Suddenly I realized her viewer was blank. (Bleep)! That was because I had her activator-receiver and 831 Relayer here and I was probably four hundred miles or more away!

The jeep skidded to a halt. Heller rose and went over. He helped the Countess Krak out. She seemed tired. He led her over to a reclining deck chair. A stewardess came running up with a tray and cold drink.

The Countess Krak patted at her moist face with a

handkerchief and took the drink gratefully.

Heller sat down. "And how goes the training on young Rockecenter?"

"Well," she said, "I *am* making progress. I've got him so he'll bathe in water instead of mud. He's stopped making grunting noises and scratching his back against posts."

"Well, that's something anyway," said Heller. "But aren't you using a hypnohelmet? I should think you could do it with that pretty fast."

"I'm trying to train him so he doesn't become a robot," said the Countess. "So I have to preserve his basic personality. But so far, he won't do anything a pig won't do. He just plain won't sit at a table and let any other diner have anything to eat—he keeps pushing them away with his nose. At first I just thought it was early behavior environmental influence, but now I'm afraid I'm up against heredity—a family trait."

"Well, you're making progress. We could leave soon."

The Countess Krak frowned. "That's the trouble, really. He won't abandon his pigs."

"Oh, is that all?" said Heller. "Bang-Bang, come over here." Bang-Bang came over and hunkered down on the grass, nursing a tall Scotch and ice the stewardess must have given him. "Now, why don't I just have Bang-Bang here call Izzy and tell him to rent half a dozen pig trucks?"

"I'm afraid they're county pigs," said the Countess.

"Well, we could have Bang-Bang tell Izzy to just buy them. And we could also have Izzy buy a pig farm up near New York, maybe across the river in New Jersey. I smell pigs every time I go by there."

The Countess said, "Dear, that's a beautiful solution. But let's not bother poor Izzy: he gets so upset

FREE

Send in this card and with any order you will receive a FREE POSTER while supplies last. No order required for this special offer! Mail in your card today!
- ❑ Please send me a FREE poster!
- ❑ Please send me information about other books by L. Ron Hubbard.

ORDERS SHIPPED WITHIN 24 HRS OF RECEIPT

___ L. RON HUBBARD PRESENTS WRITERS OF THE FUTURE® volumes: (paperbacks)

❑ vol I $7.99	❑ vol II $7.99	❑ vol III $7.99
❑ vol IV $7.99	❑ vol V $7.99	❑ vol VI $7.99
❑ vol VII $7.99	❑ vol VIII $7.99	❑ vol IX $7.99
❑ vol X $7.99	❑ vol XI $7.99	❑ vol XII $7.99
❑ vol XIII $7.99	❑ vol XIV $7.99	❑ vol XV $7.99
❑ vol XVI $7.99	❑ vol XVII $7.99	❑ vol XVIII $7.99
❑ vol XIX $7.99		

___ L. RON HUBBARD PRESENTS THE BEST OF WRITERS OF THE FUTURE:
(trade paperback) $14.95   _____

OTHER BOOKS BY L. RON HUBBARD

MASTER STORYTELLER: AN ILLUSTRATED TOUR OF THE FICTION OF
L. RON HUBBARD hardcover coffee table book $49.95   _____

THE KINGSLAYER AUDIO BOOK
Audio 3, CDs $25.00   _____   Audio 2 cassettes $20.00   _____

MISSION EARTH® series (10 volumes paperback) $6.99 ea   _____

- ___ Vol 1 The Invaders Plan
- ___ Vol 2 Black Genesis
- ___ Vol 3 The Enemy Within
- ___ Vol 4 An Alien Affair
- ___ Vol 5 Fortune of Fear
- ___ Vol 6 Death Quest
- ___ Vol 7 Voyage of Vengeance
- ___ Vol 8 Disaster
- ___ Vol 9 Villainy Victorious
- ___ Vol 10 The Doomed Planet

All ten volumes	$69.90	_____
Audio cassette, 3 hours each volume	$15.95 each	_____
specify volumes:_____		
All ten volumes	$159.50	

___ BATTLEFIELD EARTH® paperback $7.99_____ Audio $29.95 _____
___ Final Blackout paperback $6.99_____ Audio $15.95 _____
___ Fear paperback $6.99_____ Audio $15.95 _____

SHIPPING RATES US: $2.00 for one book. Add an additional **TAX*:**   _____
$.50 per book when ordering more than one.
SHIPPING RATES CANADA: $3.50 for one book. Add an **Shipping**   _____
additional $2.00 per book when ordering more than one. **TOTAL:**   _____

CHECK AS APPLICABLE:

- ❑ Check/Money Order enclosed. (Please use an envelope.)
- ❑ American Express ❑ Visa ❑ MasterCard ❑ Discover
★ California residents add 8.25% sales tax.

Card#:_____

Exp. Date:_____Signature:_____

Credit Card Billing Address Zip Code:_____

NAME:_____

ADDRESS:_____

CITY:_____ STATE:_____ ZIP:_____

PHONE #:_____

Call toll free: 1-877-8GALAXY or visit www.galaxypress.com

BUSINESS REPLY MAIL

FIRST-CLASS MAIL   PERMIT NO. 75738   LOS ANGELES, CA

POSTAGE WILL BE PAID BY ADDRESSEE

GALAXY PRESS
7051 HOLLYWOOD BLVD
HOLLYWOOD CA 90028-9771

when he can't get things exactly like you want them. The phone is working again so why can't Bang-Bang just make the calls right from here?"

"Well, okay," said Heller. "You're the captain on this voyage. But if we short-circuit Izzy, how do we pay?"

"Why," said the Countess Krak, brightly, "just put the pig trucks and the pigs and the farm on my Squeeza credit card, of course."

Bang-Bang leaped up. "It's wonderful to have that card. What would we do without it? I'll get on the phone at once."

Angrily, I thrust the viewer away. That woman! That fiend! Mudur Zengin would get down to the last pennies of the cash left in his hands and then that half-million-dollar Swiss certificate would be forfeit. Maybe it had already happened!

She was just doing it to ruin me.

They would be coming north now.

I must get on with the next item of my program without delay!

PLAN BEFORE YOU ATTACK.

I must have steel jaws open and ready to snap. And those jaws must have teeth!

Chapter 3

I went over my basic outline. Apparently I was a little bit out of sequence. If one is going to attack, one must have something to attack *with*. It is no good, I discovered, to do a plan to use a tank and then have no

tank to gather. So I had better pay some attention to
"4. GATHER WEAPONS BEFORE YOU ATTACK."

All right, what weapons could I gather? I looked
around. I didn't have a tank. This was going to require
real brains.

My eye happened to land on an old, decayed scrap of
newspaper some cockroaches were towing possessively
across the floor. I took it away from them. It said "... 'S
MORALITY IN QUESTION."

It was an omen.

MORALITY!

I well knew Voltar customs were different. The tremendous life expectancy there meant that one had to be
pretty sure who he or she was marrying before taking the
plunge: otherwise one could be stuck with an unsuitable
partner for a century and a half. So it was quite usual
for a man and woman to live together for anything up
to two years before tying the final knot. The only way
you could get a "divorce" in the Confederacy was by finding the other partner guilty of bigamy or adultery and getting him executed, as the penalty for these was death. So
marriage was a totally fatal step.

But Earth customs, I knew, were quite different. One
was expected to take the plunge without any data at all
on the other person. They frowned heavily at loose living, no matter how much they practiced it.

It was a weapon.

Instantly, I shook the cockroaches out of my clothes,
dressed and rushed to 42 Mess Street.

Madison was sitting at his desk. His sincere and earnest face was somewhat overcast with cloud. I realized I
had arrived in the nick of time.

"How is it going?" I said.

"Smith," said Madison gloomily, "we're not getting

front page the way we should. The Whiz Kid went into hiding in Kansas. It was a mistake."

"What's this fixation on Kansas?" I said.

"That's Jesse James country. We're still following the Jesse James image pattern, of course."

"What's the state of morality in Kansas?" I said.

"Morality? That is the Bible Belt. Bunch of hypocrites. Very hot on morality."

"Good," I said. "Now open your ears, Madison. The Whiz Kid is leading an immoral life. He is living with a woman to whom he is not married!"

Madison looked at me and blinked. Then he cupped his chin upon a palm and thought. Suddenly he smiled like the sun coming through the clouds on a stormy day. "I think you may have an idea there, Smith. Not very pro. Not polished, of course. But it is definitely a germ."

I didn't want to hear any more about germs. I left quickly.

I went back to the wino hotel. I am sure any self-respecting spider gloats when he has spun a web to trap flies coming his way. I turned my viewers on.

For some time I only got a flare on Heller's screen. Then suddenly it went off. He had alighted from the land yacht.

They were heading north!

The view I had was of the very service station where the gawky country boy had taught Heller all about cars on his original trip to Washington.

And there was the gawky country boy himself, staring wide-eyed at the huge land yacht.

Then suddenly the gawky country boy came forward and looked closer at Heller. "YOU!" he cried and stood standing there with his jaw dropped.

"Hello," said Heller. "How's business?"

"Good golly! Whereja get this big motor home? That's the flashiest vehicle I ever see!"

Heller said, "I think my girl stole it."

"Gosh!" said the gawky country boy in awe. "You look like you made it real good!" Then he looked behind the land yacht, his eye sweeping down the long length of the convoy which had now pulled off the highway and stood waiting their turns, evidently, at the pump. "Who are all these other people?"

"Call them my mob," said Heller.

"Holy smokes! You mean you're a big-time gangster now with a mob and everything?"

Heller said, "You got diesel for all these trucks?"

"You said it."

"And some water for the pigs?"

"PIGS?" cried the gawky country boy, staring at the convoy.

"Sure," said Heller. "We're taking them for a ride. They're squealers."

Bang-Bang's voice as he approached: "What's this about gangsters?"

Heller said to the boy, "Let me introduce Bang-Bang Rimbombo, the most notorious car bomber in New York."

"Gosh!" said the boy, pumping Bang-Bang's hand. But the rental trucks down the line were honking their horns. The boy hastily began to refuel the land yacht. Bang-Bang gave him a hand. In a voice that barely reached Heller, Bang-Bang said, to the boy, "When did you meet the boss?"

"Years ago," the boy said. "I'm the one who gave him his start. And look at him now!"

The Countess Krak came into Heller's view. She was rummaging in her purse. I realized in horror what

she was about to take out: to pay for all these hundreds
of gallons of diesel fuel, she would use my Squeeza credit
card!

I turned the viewers off hastily.

But never mind, flies. The web is spread and you
are flying straight into it.

The attack might be slow but I was sure it would be
deadly. I knew Madison. I had seen the gleam in his eye.
This would be a kill!

Chapter 4

Sure enough, the very next morning, Madison had
front page:

WHIZ KID SURRENDERS
TO KANSAS POLICE

EXTRADITION
PROCEEDINGS
WAIVED

WHIZ KID TO BE
ARRAIGNED
IN NEW JERSEY

After hectic weeks of hiding from the clutches
of the law, Wister today surrendered . . .

I knew that Madison was just setting his stage. While I was not quite sure what he meant to do, I had a return of confidence.

Both Heller's and Krak's viewers were functional, now that they were within a two-hundred-mile range.

They were walking around a farm, apparently in New Jersey since the country was very flat. Yes! Krak looked across a stretch of water and there was the skyline of New York City!

Rockecenter's son, Delbert John II, was racing about the rental trucks, shouting "Hello," and "You're here," and "Look at your new home" to the pigs inside. Then he sped excitedly to some concrete buildings, raced in, raced out. He cupped his hands against his mouth and made a sort of squealing noise and gave a signal to the trucks.

Apparently the drivers dropped gangways, for here came an absolute torrent of pigs!

Like a traffic cop, the boy was shunting them into the pens. Finally, he closed some gates, waved to the pigs inside and came beaming over to Heller and the Countess Krak.

"Oh," said Delbert Second, "Ah'm goin' to love it here. Jus' smell that breeze from the othah fahms. What a beeootiful aroma of pigs!"

"Hey, Bang-Bang," said Heller, looking around to where Bang-Bang was leaning on a post. "I don't see any house."

"That's how come we could get the place," said Bang-Bang. "It burned down. I took it up with Twoey and he said it didn't matter. He'd sleep in the pens."

"No," said Heller. "That won't do."

"It's just fahn with me," said the boy. "These yere

two men that come with the place and me will make out great."

Heller looked at two very dirty men who stood nearby, evidently Armenians. They were nodding brightly.

"Dear," said the Countess in a low voice, "I think we had better leave them the land yacht."

"They'd ruin it," said Heller.

"No," said the Countess. "I will have to be coming back and forth to continue his training and I can't work in a pigsty: trying to do that has been the trouble. Now, this has been a good crew: unemployment is high and they'd just be out of work. So we will just leave the drivers and mechanic and stewardesses here to look after the vehicles and the boy. It isn't costing anything, as I can just have Bang-Bang call Mike Mutazione and have him continue their wages and any farm expenses on my Squeeza credit card. We can simply take the jeep back to the office."

"Well, all right," said Heller. "But they'll need the jeep to operate this place."

The Countess looked at him and then smiled brightly. She beckoned to Bang-Bang and they went inside the land yacht.

The rental trucks, job finished, had departed. Heller made some arm signals and presently had the two retired Greyhound bus drivers, the mechanic and the two aged stewardesses around him.

I watched bitterly. As a Fleet officer he didn't have any idea at all of firing people the way you are supposed to do in business.

"You've done a great job," said Heller.

They all smiled.

"Would you like to stay on and take care of the vehicles and the boy?"

They cheered.

"I'll also see that you get a voyage bonus of a thousand apiece," said Heller.

They cheered louder.

I wondered if I could stand any more of this.

The Countess Krak came out of the land yacht with Bang-Bang. "Guess what," she cried. "We're in luck! Just today Mike Mutazione got in an almost brand-new Rolls Royce Silver Spirit. And he's got a real English chauffeur that used to work for a lord. I can use it to commute back and forth to finish the training. We're only a few miles from Newark and he's sending it over this evening. A bargain, too, only fifty thousand dollars. But that doesn't matter, as it goes on my credit card."

I knew I had left the viewer on too long!

I paced back and forth. Mudur Zengin would be in a frenzy with all these bills coming in. My security deposit must be going up in smoke.

Oh, I had to get this handled for more reasons than one!

The trap I had laid absolutely HAD to work!

Chapter 5

Because it had been late, they stayed the night at the farm, settling the boy in.

Madison had his front page:

WHIZ KID REFORMS

JOINS WASP
PURITY LEAGUE

"No more crime," was the startling statement of the notorious outlaw, Wister, as he deplaned, handcuffed, in Trenton, New Jersey. (See photos page 8.)

"While hiding out," he said, "I was a paragon of virtue. I realized crime did not pay. And when I was approached by an officer of the WASP Purity League on the plane, I instantly signed the pledge."

Judges in both Kansas and New Jersey breathed a sigh of relief. Judge Hanger of the Supreme Court stated, "When an outlaw such as Wister can stand forth pure and noble and vow such a vow, there is new hope for American youth."

Wister, the only man in four centuries to steal an American city . . .

I was not quite sure which direction this was going to go. But I knew Madison by now. He was on the trail of something hot.

I vigilantly watched the viewers, hoping that Heller or Krak would pick up a paper or someone would call it to their attention.

They rode that morning to the Empire State Building in the Rolls Royce Silver Spirit. A solemn English chauffeur courteously opened the door and said, in cultured accents, he would send their baggage up.

Heller and Krak ascended and walked down the halls. He opened the door with the jet plane on it and for an instant I thought somebody must have been in ambush and that they were being attacked.

Of all the peculiar, screeching noises!

It was the cat!

It sprang, yowling, into Heller's arms, sprang off, sprang into Krak's arms, leaped into the center of the room and ran in circles, making wild noises the whole time! What a fuss! It took him minutes to finally consent to be held by Krak and petted. What peculiar conduct for a cat: they are so aloof and disdainful. Could he have missed them?

But I had no time to ponder that. Here came Izzy! I have seldom seen him so wild with excitement.

With no preamble, no hello, Izzy cried, "Have I got news for you!" He was waving legal documents like banners. "Sit down. You won't be able to stand this standing up."

They sat down. Izzy pranced before them. "Mamie Boomp has sold Atlantic City! She unloaded it on the Crown Prince of Saudi Yemen! He has been slavering to get a chance to get his hands on Miss Americas. Now he can have his pick of them year after year. Oh, what a businesswoman Mamie Boomp turned out to be! She sold it for cash with plenty of operating expenses available and some other properties the Crown Prince already had. He's honoring the staff contracts and has retained Mamie Boomp as president and general manager."

"Oh, that's great!" said Heller.

"Mamie Boomp is a smart woman," said Krak.

"No, no, that isn't the good news. Come with me!"

He went tearing out. They followed him. Heller managed to steer him into the Silver Spirit instead of a cab and they went roaring uptown at Izzy's excited directions.

They were on Central Park West. Izzy pointed to an underground entrance and they drove into a spacious garage. He got out, still beckoning. He pushed them into an elevator.

When the elevator stopped, Izzy did not open the door. He said, "Now, you will remember when I said that Miss Joy was far too beautiful to live in an office. Well, that's oh, so true. Part of the price the Crown Prince paid was eight posh apartment houses in Manhattan. Now LOOK!"

He threw open the elevator door.

They were gazing at a roof garden. A vast expanse of cultivated paths and plants with areas glassed in.

Izzy took them over to the edge and threw out his arms. And there before them, many stories below, lay Central Park.

He didn't give them any time to look. He was rattling a ring of keys. He rushed to a tall glass door and unlocked it.

Before them spread a pillared interior. The columns were light tan and around them coiled designs in glittering stones, edged and banded in gold. The floor was colored marble squares. The furniture was scrolled and curving. A very posh place. Like a palace!

"Fifteen rooms!" said Izzy. "Surrounded by so much roof garden it takes three gardeners to keep it up. And the whole next floor below for servants and storage. Do you like it?"

"Beautiful!" said the Countess Krak.

"It's your home," said Izzy.

Chapter 6

The following day, I brushed the cockroaches off the table and put down the stack of papers. Madison had front page again:

NEW JERSEY GOVERNOR PETITIONED BY PURITY LEAGUE

WHIZ KID CASE BEFORE GOVERNOR

With mass demonstrations (see photos page 12) and avalanches of telegrams, the governor of New Jersey was pleaded with today to have clemency in the case of the notorious outlaw, Wister, known as the Whiz Kid.

Different variations of the story appeared in all the papers. It was national press.

I knew it would be on TV and radio. The WASP Purity League has real clout.

I watched the viewers to get a reaction from Heller and Krak.

They were very busy moving into their garden penthouse. The Porsche had been put in the garage and under the charge of the chauffeur and Heller was trying to explain to him how come this Porsche didn't burn "petrol" but blocks of asphalt and didn't need refuelling more often than once a month. The chauffeur was being doubtful but if the master said so about the Porsche, that was fine, as it was German and who could tell about *them*. But when Heller suggested changing the Silver Spirit, that was different: it was an English car and a proposed change of its motor in any way would have to be passed upon by the Archbishop of Canterbury before it was done. And did the master know that the first Rolls automobiles had locks on their bonnets and only the company had a key? No? Well, he thought Heller might not know, being an American. So the Rolls would do better to just go on being a Rolls, and guzzling gas or not, tradition was tradition, right? Not to be flouted.

The Countess Krak was having better luck. Izzy had caught her with a broom in her hand and, a bit reverently, had taken it away from her and steered her into the "Etruscan Salon" where she was faced with a horde of domestics from which to choose her staff. Izzy explained the need of three gardeners, a butler, a chef, a second cook, two housemen, a chambermaid, two security men and, last but not least, a lady's maid for herself. He apologized that he could not presume to choose her staff.

So she was involved with picking them out, only to find that they had already been screened, that there were just exactly twelve people who just exactly fitted the posts named. So she "chose" them and Izzy instantly handed the broom over to a houseman and they all promptly went to work under the eagle eye of the butler.

I still watched to see if they would pick up a paper.

The Countess was driven over to New Jersey to do some training of the son.

Heller was trying to put his "study," or den, to rights and stow his things.

The only other thing that happened was that his tailor arrived to measure him for his uniforms. It appeared that there would be a regimental ball in a couple of days and Heller, though an ROTC member, seemed to have neglected to get any uniforms.

Bang-Bang was on the scene, giving the tailor some tips. It seemed that an officer of the ROTC—Wister was a second lieutenant, being a senior—and an officer of the U.S. Army wore the same uniforms except for a shoulder patch which was green with a red bar, a gold torch and had ARMY ROTC letters on it in white.

"I haven't rubbed my brains raw and marched my legs to nubs to have you coming out looking like an Army bum," Bang-Bang explained, and proceeded to give the tailor the subtle tips that somehow converted the uniform, without changing its colors, slightly in the direction of a "self-respecting Marines officer."

Well, I thought, they are busy today. Maybe they will look at the papers tomorrow.

Tomorrow came. Sure enough, Madison had more headlines.

WHIZ KID PARDONED

GOVERNOR ANSWERS NATION'S PRAYERS

It was announced tonight to cheering throngs that Wister, the Whiz Kid, has been pardoned unconditionally by the governor of New Jersey.

The glad news was celebrated by torchlight parades. (See photos, center spread.)

"It is not that I yielded solely to the pressures

of the WASP Purity League,'' the governor said.
''It is obvious that the young man has reformed
and is, in his own way, a saint. Besides, Atlantic
City was not given to Nevada but has been
returned to the territorial jurisdiction of New Jersey by its new owner, the Crown Prince of Saudi
Yemen, in a special treaty agreeing to let New Jersey tax collectors in, providing they also promise
to use their bribes in gambling.''

Actually, I didn't much care for the story. A lot of
the papers sort of went overboard on how the Whiz Kid
was merely the victim of environmental underprivilege-
ment and was at heart a sterling example of moral prob-
ity. Several mentioned the redeeming factor that not a single shadow of sexual immorality blotted his past.

I watched the viewers anxiously to see if there was
any reaction to this. I even sat up the whole evening,
glued to the screens, hoping that in some unguarded
moment somebody would mention that Heller had been
pardoned.

They were at the regimental ball. It was a very colorful affair, held beneath the draping flags of the New York
Regiment Armory. A military band was trying to play
hot pop.

Heller was resplendent in his uniform. Nobody
seemed to know him, which was not strange as this was
the first contact he had ever had personally with the
ROTC. They probably thought he was some ROTC second lieutenant from Boston, as one officer asked him
how things were, up that way.

The Countess Krak was resplendent in a white silvery evening gown that must have cost me ten thousand bucks, (bleep) her. The men she was dancing with seemed absolutely overwhelmed, gazing at her, the idiots. The women were more sensible: they had daggers in their eyes.

Colonel Tanc, whom I eagerly hoped would instantly arrest her or do something else to bring her down, merely bowed, his face quite red, a model of proper decorum.

I was quite put out by the affair. Those uniformed popinjays and the empty-headed belles that swarmed around the regimental ballroom, including their senior officers, were just too plain stupid to realize they had a pair of extraterrestrials dancing in their midst. How were things going in Boston, indeed! How were things going on Voltar was more like it. Had Lombar asserted Grand Council control as yet? Did I have my orders to kill them?

They didn't mention a single word about the pardon!

The next morning Madison again had his front page. He was really batting high!

WHIZ KID HONORED
BY WASP PURITY LEAGUE

HIGH APPOINTMENT
GIVEN AT PARDON
CELEBRATION BANQUET

At a fund-raising dinner last night, the age-old tradition of the WASP Purity League was broken unanimously.

An outlaw, Wister, the Whiz Kid, guest of honor, was appointed to high-official rank.

In the appointment speech, the President of the WASP Purity League, Agatha Prim, said, "It is my privilege to appoint Gerry Wister VICE-President in Charge of Intolerance. We have examined this from every side and can find no slightest hint of real misconduct in his past. He is an unstained knight who has never stooped to gratify gross sexual appetites. His theft of Atlantic City can be looked upon as a gesture of protest against vice and gambling and evil."

The dinner, attended by everyone that mattered in the Four Hundred, raised funds for the Campaign for Suppression of Puerto Ricans, whose sexual licentiousness has long been a target of the League.

The Whiz Kid, in accepting the appointment, said, "I have never raised so much as a finger in lust in my whole life. I shall immediately use my influence to prohibit the Simmons Mattress Company from making double beds."

I held my breath. While Heller and the Countess had been carousing at the regimental ball, did they at all suspect what was going on in the real world of the media?

I clamped on to the viewers. The Countess and Heller were having a leisurely breakfast in the spring sun on the garden terrace of the penthouse. The butler appeared to serve Heller more Bavarian Mocha Mint. There was a newspaper on the tray!

The Countess sighed. "I have to go over to New Jersey again today. I have to wash my hair every time I go over there to get the smell of pigs out."

"How's it going?" said Heller, sipping his mocha.

"Well, one thing worries me a bit. Most of the time Twoey is all right but there's some kind of viciousness hidden in his makeup that I can only suppose must be hereditary."

"Such as?"

"When people get in his way, he begins to mutter that human beings ought to be sent to the slaughter pens."

"Hey, that's too like the Rockecenter family," said Heller. "It might be dangerous to leave him in charge of the planet."

"Well, there's one saving grace, darling. He thinks the sun rises and sets on his brother, Jet. He'll do anything you say."

"Wait," Heller said. "I know he seems to like me but I didn't think it went that far."

"Oh, yes. You're very charming, you know. And also, strangely enough, ever since he met Izzy, Twoey is absolutely terrified of doing something that Izzy does not like."

"Whoa," said Heller. "Much as I admire him, this is the first time I ever heard of anything being terrified of Izzy Epstein."

Very primly, the Countess said, "Well, it's a fact!"

Heller looked at her suspiciously. "Dear, are you sure you aren't tampering with Twoey's basic personality?"

"Me, Jettero?" she said.

Oh, she might fool Heller. She might blind the rest of the world with her innocent face and extreme beauty. But she didn't fool me. I saw through her plot at once!

She was preparing a puppet emperor for Earth just so she could go home and get married! Women will stoop to anything to gain their foul and despicable ends. She was even putting up with pig aroma just to eventually get her own way!

The newspaper lay neglected when they left the table. I knew Madison. It was really just as well that they did not suspect the trap he must be baiting.

The very next day, I could not buy all the papers. My money was running out. And it was a shame not to have every single front page, New York and across the world. For that sterling, priceless Madison, doing anything to retain his front page, as I knew he eventually would, sprung his trap.

The story was absolutely gorgeous!

Headlines! Big ones! Glaring!

WHIZ KID NAMED
IN PATERNITY SUIT

FARMER'S DAUGHTER
SUES FOR $2 BILLION!

Attorneys Dingaling, Chase and Ambo today filed a two-billion-dollar suit against Wister, the Whiz Kid, on behalf of Maizie Spread of Cornhole, Kansas, stating paternity out of wedlock had been malfeased.

Alleging that the notorious outlaw continuously rolled her in the hay while hiding out on her father's farm, to which he came a year ago, the innocent girl said, sobbing, in a press conference attended by all media, "I could not resist his wiles. In my innocence I did not understand that he was not really trying to protect my milk-white complexion from the sun by lying on me. I didn't get knocked up for five months but now, much to my embarrassment, I'm all swole up with child."

The Whiz Kid could not be reached for comment. His attorneys, Boggle, Gouge and Hound, said that they were not available for comment.

Rumor is rife that the Whiz Kid has fled to Canada, a fact regarded by legal experts as tacit acknowledgment of guilt.

Oh, what a story! And the other papers, particularly the sexier ones, went into wild orgies of description of what had happened. One even pictured the Whiz Kid as dancing in the moonlight with rabbits all around and shouting to them, "Come, come! Let me protect you from the sun! With fifty strokes!"

SCANDAL!

The trap was sprung!

Chapter 7

Eagerly I hung on to my viewers to witness the inevitable blowup. The Countess Krak was prone to jealousy. One glimpse of that paternity story would blow the lid off. She might simply leave him!

I watched while they breakfasted. I watched while the butler laid the paper on the table. I watched while they got up and were helped into their coats. I saw them leave their penthouse condo without ever a backward glance toward that paper.

Oh, well. Sometimes the radio was played in the Rolls Royce Silver Spirit. And this morning, news bulletins about the suit were coming on every fifteen minutes: Madison was doing a masterly job of coverage.

But this morning, the Countess Krak told Bang-Bang, who was riding in the front seat while she and Heller rode in back, to put "a good tape cassette on" and he, of course, left to his own choice, put on the Italian opera *Rigoletto*, where everybody kills everybody and even drowns them in a sack still singing. It wasn't the kind of blood I wanted.

At the office, Heller sat down at his big white desk and put in a call to Florida. Right in front of him, folded, lay the morning papers.

The Countess Krak sat down on the arm of an interview chair, watching him patiently. Right in her line of view were those fatal newspapers, folded up but available.

Heller apparently had a lease line to Ochokeechokee and he went into a lot of chatter about some regulation they'd come up against down there about the allowable heights of stacks in swamps. It seemed that a "propulsion stack" had to be at least five hundred feet high to get "impulsion."

"They've got to blow rings," he said. "Big green rings of spores. If they are not propelled high enough, they won't reach the stratospheric winds. One goes every minute and if the stacks are any shorter, the perfection of the ring will foul and the resultant tumble will impede successive firings. They *have* to be five hundred feet tall."

The contractor at the other end was very unhappy with Florida regulations but said that was what they said.

"They sell sunshine down there," said Heller. "With all the soot and gases in the atmosphere, it's getting pretty dim. Put some pressure on them. Make them see that it's good sense to clean up the world's air."

"Good sense has nothing to do with it," said the contractor. "It's just what's written in the little books the Florida State Inspectors carry. But I'll tell you what I will do: I'll send a lawyer to Tallahassee to talk to the governor. Maybe we can get a waiver on the regulation."

Heller had to be satisfied with that. He clicked off and looked up. He saw the Countess was still sitting there. He said, "Isn't your class ready?"

"Yes, dear," she said. "All fifty of them, some of them the country's best electronic engineers. You didn't give me the notes you made last night."

"Oh, I'm sorry," said Heller. He reached right across the newspapers to an attaché case, opened it and brought out a sheaf of notes. He handed them to her.

She glanced at them and then gave him a kiss and walked out the door.

She went down the hall and halted at a sign which said:

Power, Power, Power, Inc.

She straightened her jacket, opened the door and walked in.

The large office had been converted to a temporary classroom. It was filled with men of various ages, ranged in school chairs. They all rose respectfully. The Countess Krak walked to the platform and blackboard.

An elderly man had been addressing them. But now he surrendered the platform, saying to the group, "I will now turn the class over to Miss Krackle."

The men all applauded politely.

The Countess put down the sheaf of notes on a table. "Gentlemen," she said, "you have been employed as engineers for Power, Power, Power, Incorporated. I am privileged to be able to address some of the top electronic and power engineers of the planet. Some of you have been selected for your abilities in foreign languages as well.

"Far be it from me to tell you, who are experts in the field, how to do your jobs. I am solely here to relay to you certain technology, that with which you will work."

She looked at her notes. "The beaming of power from central collection stations to distribution units and then to consumption absorbers by microwave accumulators and reflectors may be, in some respects, new to you."

She turned to the board, chalk in hand. "If we regard power as a stream of water which yet can be beamed and focused, we can see that a central collection station in a country may receive the power from a source and then deflect and focus it to subreceivers which, in turn, can focus it upon consumption units." She began to draw a pattern upon the blackboard, giving flow lines.

It came to me with a shock that she, using Heller's notes, was laying out a standard planetary power-collection-and-distribution system using microwaves.

That the Countess Krak would be lecturing so learnedly was not much of a surprise for she was simply relaying material.

What got to me was that here was a whole new insidious plot I had not even been aware of. I did not ask myself what they were going to use as a power source, although that was a mystery. All I knew was that if she was genning experts in on microwave-relay technology of power, Rockecenter's empire might well be in the soup! Some of his billions depended upon burning fossil fuel—oil and coal—locally and inefficiently to furnish power expensively and profitably to industries and homes. So what if, as the environmentalists said, Rockecenter practices were wrecking the atmosphere? The environmentalists were missing the whole point! The action was PROFITABLE and that was everything!

The Countess Krak was furthering an insidious plot to destroy Octopus! And that plot was very far advanced, even to the point of hiring and training engineers to build and install equipment!

That wasn't chalk she was holding as she copied Heller's drawings on the blackboard. That was a dagger aimed straight at the heart of Rockecenter and, through him, at Lombar Hisst! If Rockecenter's grip on the planet relaxed, we might no longer be able to export drug ammunition to Voltar!

(Bleep) her!

This had to be stopped!

I looked back at Heller's viewer. He was just sitting at his desk drawing up more notes, translating Voltar technology into Earth terms.

There lay the newspapers with the fatal story, completely neglected!

After half an hour, the Countess Krak came back into his office. I was willing her, straining my neck muscles, to get her to pick up that newspaper.

Heller looked up. "Did it go well?"

"Of course, dear," she said. "Your notes covered all their questions. I've turned the class over to Professor Gen. I think it will take them a month or two of class-work to review all their own texts and reconcile the systems. They have to shed some preconceptions, but they'll make it."

"Well, I'm sure you can take care of that," said Heller. "It's just a matter of their shedding a few prejudices about energy."

The Countess reached across the desk to the newspaper! She picked it up! I really held my breath.

She went over to the bar and got a can. She put it in an opener.

She spread the newspaper on the bar. She dumped the contents of the can on it.

The cat jumped up and said "Meow" and began to eat.

The Countess Krak picked up her purse. "I'm going over to New Jersey now."

She gave him a kiss on the cheek and walked out!

The only one reading that newspaper was the cat!

I ground my teeth!

Then I knew what it was. It was a policy they must have. A conspiracy! You could only be happy on the planet if you never read newspapers or listened to the news. And while this was perfectly true, it gave them no license to gang up on me.

That beautiful story was failing!

She was going right on helping Heller to undermine everything worthwhile: MONEY!

Between the two of them they were going to salvage life on this planet! Oh, the villainy of it!

I knew I would have to act!

Chapter 8

After considerable pacing, I went back and read the story again.

INSPIRATION!

No sooner conceived than acted upon. I must attack!

I brushed the better part of the cockroaches off my coat and with determined stride made my way to the subway.

Fifteen minutes later, I stood before a shabby building. It had a porno store on the first floor. It had a massage parlor on the second. The local chapter of the National Association of Mental Stealth was on the third floor. It was the fourth which I wanted.

I went up the stairs.

I set my jaw grimly.

I strode into the offices of Dingaling, Chase and Ambo.

I was about to unleash the most terrible weapon ever devised: the American legal system!

There was no receptionist. I walked right through the empty waiting room and into the second office.

A baldheaded man with foxy, shifting eyes looked up from a scarred desk. He rubbed his hands. He said, "You been run over? You slip on somebody's floor? We're the very people you want to see." He raised his voice, "Chase! Ambo! We've got a customer!"

Two other doors opened. Two other baldheaded men with foxy, shifting eyes rushed in.

"I'm here on the Wister case," I said.

They looked very alert. Chase then approached and patted me over to make sure I wasn't carrying a tape recorder or gun.

"For or against?" said Dingaling, the first man.

"Against," I said firmly.

They promptly got me a chair and all three helped me sit down.

"You're from . . . ?"

"I am sure," I said firmly, "that Madison must have retained you on behalf of Maizie Spread."

They looked wary.

"I am Madison's boss," I said. "My name is Smith. You can check with him but do not tell him I am here."

Chase vanished. I heard him phoning. He came back and nodded to the other two.

"There's a real suit here," I said.

"Oh, come, come," said Dingaling. "It's just a publicity retainer, Mr. Smith. A maximum harassment in the media. The usual thing. An attorney firm like ours does it all the time."

"There's money to be made," I said.

"Oh, come, come, Mr. Smith," said Ambo. "You know full well that this Wister has no money."

"There is something Madison neglected to tell you," I said. "There is a real Jerome Terrance Wister."

They frowned, perplexed.

"He has millions, even billions available," I said.

They stiffened and stared.

"The man Madison put you on to is a double. The REAL Wister lives in a ten-million-dollar penthouse on Central Park West, has a domestic staff of twelve and is driven to his posh office in the Empire State Building in a Rolls Royce Silver Spirit."

They were absolutely flabbergasted. They plied me with questions and I answered.

They began to mutter, "A real case!" "A defenseless millionaire!"

"If you serve your suit subpoena on the real Jerome Terrance Wister at his penthouse at five o'clock this afternoon as he comes home, you're on the way to making a fortune!"

I gave them further details.

When I left, they had made a ring and were dancing round and round in the office, shouting in hysterical joy.

Chapter 9

Five o'clock found me glued to the viewers.

The Countess Krak in the Silver Spirit had picked up Heller at the office.

They drove into the garage.

They ascended in the elevator.

Heller unlocked the door at the top and stepped into the small hall. The Countess Krak was right behind him.

A shabby man in a shabby overcoat with a shabby hat pulled over his eyes stepped out from behind a potted plant.

"Jerome Terrance Wister?" he said.

Heller stopped.

The man shoved a court summons into his hand. "You are duly served in the matter of *Spread vs. Wister*," he said and then bolted down the fire escape.

"What is it, dear?" said the Countess Krak.

"I don't know," said Heller, "but he almost got himself shot." He started to toss the paper aside.

The Countess Krak took it from him.

She read a short distance into it.

She went white.

Then suddenly she marched into the salon, across it, to her room and slammed the door!

I had connected!

Heller stood there, rooted.

Then he went to her door. It was locked.

"Dear," he said through the closed portal, "could you tell me what this is all about?"

She was lying on the bed face down with the legal paper crumpled in her hand. She was crying!

"Dear," he called. "Is there something wrong?"

He kept at it and half an hour passed before she ceased to cry.

"Go away," she called at last.

For quite some time, Heller walked around the condo and the garden. He tried several more times to get her to talk to him and each time he failed.

At length she replied through the closed door. "Go away! You lied to me. You had a woman after all!" And then she wailed, "You got her pregnant!"

After that she would say no more.

Oh, I really writhed in glee. What a hit! This would finish everything.

All my confidence in myself came flooding back. I had saved the day! Rockecenter could go right on polluting to his heart's content. Earth could properly go to Hells, heat up and flood. Oh, I was really jubilant.

In a sudden surge of optimism, I decided that if I was successful here, I might now soar to higher successes.

I was out of money. Come morning they would boot me out of the wino hotel for failing to pay the rent.

I decided to chance it. If my luck held this good, I could go back to Miss Pinch and Candy without getting my brains beat in.

No sooner said than done. I packed up. Burdened, I sneaked down to the lobby. The clerk was not at the desk. I threw down my key and walked out into the street.

It was not too much of a hike, from where I had stayed, uptown and east of Miss Pinch's.

Laden, I went down the basement steps and rang the bell. The area light came on. Miss Pinch opened the door.

She just stood there, looking at me, no expression on her face at all.

Shortly Candy, curious, came up behind her. She stared at me, too.

Over her shoulder to Candy, Miss Pinch said, "Get the insect spray. The deadly kind."

I flinched. I thought she meant to kill me. She was staring, staring, staring.

Candy brought the spray can.

To me, Miss Pinch said, "Stand right there and take off all your clothes."

I looked down. It was just a couple cockroaches crawling on my chest.

I stripped. They put my clothes in a garbage bag, spray flying all the while.

They made me take my hardware and papers out. They put everything else in a garbage bag.

They sprayed me from head to foot.

They sprayed all my papers and hardware.

Dead cockroaches were lying all over the place.

They swatted a couple that had tried to run for it into the house.

They took all the clothes I had taken with me and my grip and carried them to the incinerator in the garden, doused them with lighter fluid and touched a match.

They pushed me into a shower with disinfectant soap.

At length I came out, red-eyed but deloused.

I opened the closet and got a bathrobe from the ample wardrobe I had left behind.

It suddenly struck me that neither one of them had said a word to me!

Maybe this wasn't over with yet.

The door to the front room was closed. I heard them whispering to each other. Were they planning to do something vicious to me?

I sat there in the back room, worrying.

Miss Pinch and Candy came in. They had on night-gowns and bathrobes. I flinched.

"I don't really feel up to it," I said.

"Just as well," said Miss Pinch. "We wouldn't let you do it anyway."

Oh, Gods, maybe they thought I had a disease. I had better not tell them I was clean. But I had to know how come this strange shift? "Why?" I said.

"We might miscarry," said Miss Pinch.

"Miscarry?" I said, blinking.

"Yes, we're both pregnant," said Miss Pinch.

Cold terror gripped me by the throat!

The whole room spun around me! I was totally disoriented! I wanted to tell them, no, no, you're all mixed up. It was Heller who got girls pregnant.

"I've never been in Kansas!" I wailed.

But they were both gone. And all that night, I lay in the dark, spinning.

Now and then I would say to the walls, "I am Officer Gris. I am not a combat engineer. My name is not Heller. I am Officer Gris. Miss Pinch is not Maizie Spread. This is New York. My name is not Heller. . . ."

It was a very terrible and eerie experience.

Chapter 10

Apparently, once the media had gotten its teeth into sex and scandal, Madison could just sit back and loaf.

I stole enough quarters out of Pinch's purse to buy the morning papers.

WHIZ KID EXPELLED FROM PURITY LEAGUE

PUBLICLY DENOUNCED

From her padded cell in her psychiatrist's office, Agatha Prim today announced that the Whiz Kid, Wister, had been fired as VICE-President in Charge of Intolerance and expelled from the WASP Purity League.

"Unlicensed lust can be tolerated only by professional psychiatrists," she said.

It went on. It was in other papers. On TV news shots, clips were shown of the Whiz Kid's nomination to post, the demonstrations which caused his pardon, and other bric-a-brac, ending finally with Agatha Prim being wheeled off for her next electric shock.

Radio spot ads were running every hour inviting the public to a mass meeting at the League headquarters to form a lynch mob.

A famous parson was also spot ad-ing to invite people to his sermon, "Low How the Sinners Fall."

The government said that it was investigating to see if the Whiz Kid owed income tax.

The United Kingdom caused a total furor in the afternoon press by announcing it was debarring the Whiz Kid entry to England on moral grounds. This included Canada. That he had never been there, they said, was beside the point!

I turned on my viewers to see how Krak and Heller were taking this.

Krak's I couldn't tell much about. The viewer had a watery tinge. She was evidently still in her room and her eyes were wet from crying.

Heller was something else.

He was just entering the office of Multinational. Izzy rose from his desk and shooed other people out and closed the door. Heller sat down. He spread out the crumpled suit paper on Izzy's desk: Heller must have recovered it from a trash bin, the way it looked.

"What the blast is this?" said Heller.

Izzy read it. "It's a civil suit," he said. "They evidently got service on you."

"*What*," said Heller, "is a civil suit? It sounds awful uncivil to me."

"It means you have to appear and go to a jury trial," said Izzy.

"But it's a pack of lies!" said Heller. "I never even

heard of any Maizie Spread. I don't even know where
Cornhole, Kansas, is."

Izzy opened up one of the stack of newspapers he
had on his desk. It contained a full-page photo of Maizie
Spread lying in a haystack with her legs apart. Izzy
turned the page so Heller could see it closely. The girl
was fat and homely. "You've never seen her before?"

"Absolutely not," said Heller.

"Well," said Izzy, "that just means the legal system
is up to its usual tricks. Anybody can sue anybody for
anything in this country and usually does. There's a
whole segment of the population that makes its living
just suing anybody for anything they can dream up. It's
pretty brutal. Way back, one millionaire named Howard
Hughes—a very famous flier—ended his days in hiding
just because people kept suing him. There's thousands of
people out there who don't dare walk around in public
because people they never heard of are trying to sue
them and make them spend their whole lives and fortune
sitting in courtrooms. And, of course, the press always
backs it all up because it's full of lies and such and
makes good copy."

"Look," said Heller, "I want this cleaned up fast."

"Oh, heavens. That is the one thing that won't happen. This suit will go on for years and years. That's the
legal system."

"It sounds *il*legal to me," said Heller.

"You have to understand how it is," said Izzy. "The
lawyers want all trials as slow as possible. That way they
can make millions out of them."

"An honest lawyer could end this," said Heller.

Izzy laughed hollowly. "You just don't understand
this legal system. The operative word is MONEY. The
only way a lawyer can make a fortune is to sue people

for millions and split the court award with his client. The courts award those millions, too. Now, the defense attorney of such a suit can only make money by dragging it out and bleeding his client white for fees."

"Any honest government would stop such nonsense in a minute," said Heller.

"Listen. The legislators and congressmen are mostly lawyers. They are the ones who make the laws that regulate the conduct of courts. So of course they will pass no real legislation that will cut the awards and fees to their colleagues: when they finish office, these same legislators will be right back there practicing law again and would be unable to become millionaires overnight with insane suits and crazy fees. No, you've fallen into the legal soup, Mr. Jet. Like quicksand or the New York sewage system. They've got service on you. You have to appear. And meanwhile the press wrecks your reputation and even if you win, it will be years from now and you will be out millions, maybe bankrupt."

"Hey!" said Heller. "Nobody can live in a society like that!"

"Listen, Mr. Jet, only the bums win in a society like this. A spectacular, competent fellow like you hasn't got a chance."

"In another place I know," said Heller, "anybody who tried a swindle like this suit would be sent to prison and the attorneys right along with her."

"Well, that's not here, Mr. Jet. And that's why I never let you connect your name to any of these corporations. You're a good guy. That's why, when all this first began, I bought you a ticket for Brazil and told you about the place where they only have ants: not a lawyer in the lot. But now we're into a legal mess and we have to have a lawyer."

"We've got to do something," said Heller.

"I'll give this paper to Philup Bleedum of Bleedum, Bleedum and Drayne, one of the corporation attorneys," said Izzy. "He can file an appearance and torts and writs and stuff. I won't let you talk to him as I don't want you any more depressed than you are. I'll be sure to operate the device that can see the future on the market like mad because we will need millions just to defend this. And maybe five or six years from now, it will be over."

"I can't wait that long."

"Oh, it probably really won't be that long," said Izzy. "Usually in such a suit, especially when it is false, vexatious and harassing, the defendant has to file personal bankruptcy long before it is over, as he cannot possibly pay his own attorney fees."

"Izzy," said Heller, "are you just being your usual pessimistic self?"

"Oy, Mr. Jet! I'm talking about the legal system. Knowing what I do about the ruination it is built around, I thought I was being optimistic! I didn't mention possibly going to jail for contempt and losing the whole thing for not appearing in court."

"This could wreck my whole mission," said Heller despondently.

"That's all the legal system is designed to do," said Izzy. "Enrich the lawyers and bums and ruin everybody else. But cheer up. An atomic war might intervene and settle everything."

"With a legal system as insane as that, they deserve it," said Heller and left.

That alarmed me a little bit. And then I realized that he hadn't packed any atomic bombs I knew of in his suitcase.

But this interview had gotten me thinking.

Yes, I knew anybody on this planet could sue anybody for anything and often did.

Supposing Miss Pinch and Candy took it into their heads to sue me over their pregnancies? *Double* jeopardy.

I could see myself on the run, hiding out in wino hotels for years trying to avoid service of suits, sitting in musty courtrooms for months being worked over by attorneys like Dingaling, Chase and Ambo.

I was guilty as Hells. That made me cheer up a little bit. If I was really culpable, they would find me innocent, of course. Only the innocent were ever found guilty.

Then I saw that the Countess Krak was still in her room, crying as though her heart would break.

It cheered me enormously.

Little did I know the next horror coming my way. I was about to get the anvil's view of the hammer.

PART
FORTY-EIGHT

Chapter 1

For three days Madison let the paternity suit boil along. The sex-and-outlaw theme really got its play. The farmer's daughter, Maizie Spread, was on prime-time national TV, giving diagrams of where and how and about how many times and even offering to demonstrate. It was POPULAR!

Heller was walking around distractedly. The Countess Krak stayed in her room. Mission Earth had been brought to a HALT!

But there was a danger that activity on their part might start up again. I phoned Madison.

"We've got a hit," said Madison. "When that suit gets into the courts, it can run for years. The climax will come when she claims he got other members of his gang to rape all the livestock, but that won't be for weeks yet."

"I noticed one of the papers let it drop to page three today," I said.

"Yes, I know," said Madison, "we're using the Rockecenter lines to have the editor fired."

"But what if the other papers start putting it on page three?" I said. I was learning to talk to Madison.

"We'll fire the lot," he said.

"But wait, you can't fire all the editors in the country."

"Yes, I can!" he said.

"No, you can't," I said.

"Yes, I can!" he said.

"Look," I said. "If you did, you might not have any papers."

"Yes, there's that," he said.

"So why don't you deliver some mortal blow?" I said.

"Mortal blow? I resent that, Smith. All we're doing is trying to help the fellow out: make him *im*mortal. We want nothing to do with MORTAL blows! When we get through, he will be the most famous outlaw of all time. He will live forever in song and story. So don't talk to me about anything *mortal!*" He was quite cross.

"You had an editor drop it to page three," I said.

"Yes, there's that," he said. "But Smith, you're not a pro, worse luck. Did you think I wasn't going to climax it?"

"From the number of rolls in the hay I've seen described in press and on TV, I should have thought you were almost out of climaxes."

"Oh, pish, pish, and tush, tush, Smith. I see that you are not only no pro at this business, you also don't know the depths to which it can be pushed in this legal system. I thought you were here at this morning's conference. I didn't notice that you weren't. So now I see why you're wasting my time with phone calls that could be going to important people. I'm not going to go over the briefing again. Just look at tomorrow's press. Goodbye."

Nobody answered the phone when I rang back. He was probably just sitting there glaring at it and letting it ring. Or he was phoning some judge to tell him what to decide on some case.

I was wrong on both counts. When the next morning came, it was very obvious that Madison was, indeed, climaxing it. Banner headlines! The layouts made the paternity suit look like a notice for a church social. The story:

WHIZ KID SUED
BY DESERTED WIFE!

ADULTERY ALLEGED!

SEIZURE OF WHIZ KID
ASSETS ORDERED

Dingaling, Chase and Ambo this morning are filing suit against Whiz Kid Wister on behalf of Mrs. Toots Wister, nee Switch, alleging the grounds of adultery with Maizie Spread.

Under community property laws of Kansas and New York, Dingaling, Chase and Ambo are ordering all the Whiz Kid's assets frozen pending divorce settlement.

To a hushed assembly of all media, the tearful Mrs. Wister, in widow's weeds, sobbed out her pitiful tale. "He abandoned me," she said. "For a whole year I did not even know where he was. And now I find he was rolling in the hay with that Maizie Spread."

I was so delighted I cried out aloud and went prancing around the apartment. I was sure that this would do it.

I watched the viewers. Krak was still in her room.

Heller was walking disconsolately in Central Park. Neither one of them showed any signs of having read the story or seen the blasting coverage this was getting on radio and TV.

Afternoon came. And Madison had not waited for another day. He was striking hot iron with hot iron. The editions carried full photo stories of the background of the marriage.

The girl, Toots Switch, had been a conductor's niece. She was on a train with her uncle. The Whiz Kid and his outlaw gang had robbed the train. But in passing through the cars, looking for rich men to rob so he could give it to the poor Kansas farmers, the eye of the Whiz Kid had lighted on Toots Switch. No sooner seen than desired. Warned by the girl's uncle that he would be violating the Mann Act if he raped the poor girl while they were crossing a state line, the Whiz Kid had flourished his drawn Colt revolvers and demanded a clergyman be found. One was located in the bar and then and there, under the levelled rifles of the gang, the marriage had been performed. The sexy details of its consummation while passing over the Missouri border would be released on the morrow.

Indeed, it was a masterstroke.

But Madison had probably neglected one thing: the real Whiz Kid!

Still seeing no sign that either Krak or Heller—who had now gone to his office—were aware of this new development, I rang up Dingaling, Chase and Ambo.

"Have you served the real Wister?" I demanded.

It was Dingaling himself. He said, "Our process server got cold feet. The last time he served Wister he saw the fellow carried a gun and almost drew it. So we are waiting to collect a backup team from Police Inspector 'Bulldog' Grafferty."

"Listen," I said, "I thought service could just be done by mail or something."

"There are many ways," said Dingaling. "The most common is to serve a member of the household. This is perfectly legal and sometimes the member of the household forgets to give the paper to the defendant and you win by default. But the place seems all locked up, the butler isn't opening the door, and so we were going to get Grafferty to help."

"You don't need Grafferty," I said. And I gave Dingaling some terse and precise directions.

Pinned to the viewers, I watched avidly.

About an hour later, there was a knock on the door of the Countess Krak's room.

She lifted her tearful face off the bedspread. She said, "Go away."

"It is I, ma'am," came the butler's voice. "There is a man at the door who says that he must see you personally."

"Tell him to go away," said the Countess Krak.

The butler's voice, "I told him that through the intercom, ma'am, but he claims that you will see him. He said his name was Hisst."

The Countess Krak sat up like she'd been shot.

"Lombar Hisst?" she said.

"I think that was what he said his name was," came the butler's voice. "Shall I let him in, ma'am?"

"Good Heavens," said the Countess Krak, and Lords know what must have been swirling through her head. Then she said faintly, as I knew she would, "You better let him in."

An interlude. Then an authoritative rap on the door. The Countess Krak opened it.

Standing there was the shabby man in the shabby coat with the shabby hat pulled over his eyes. He thrust a paper at the Countess Krak.

"You're not Hisst," she said.

"Madam, as a member of the household of Wister, I give you this. He has been served." He jammed the paper into her hands and fled.

Confused already by the false announcement, she opened the paper.

And there before her gaze was the Toots Wister nee Switch suit and all its gory details legally phrased.

She took a grip on the side of the door. The paper began to shake.

A wounded cry escaped her lips.

She read the paper again.

She had trouble walking back into her room.

She just stood there for a while, her head hanging down, a posture of betrayal and blighted hopes.

She let the paper fall to the floor.

She walked toward her bathroom and then stood there, propped against the door, a hand across her eyes.

Then she turned and stumbled to her telephone. She pushed the buttons. She got them wrong and pushed them again.

"President Mamie Boomp here," came the voice.

"Mamie," said the Countess brokenly, "he was already married."

"Oh, my God!" said Mamie. "Oh, you poor dear thing! Well, Jesus Christ, that's the way with sailors."

"Mamie, what can I do?"

"Do?" said Mamie. "Well, honey, you don't want to be messed up in that. They lie. You pack your bags, honey, and you come down here where your friend Mamie can look after you. The place is knee-deep in millionaires. Arab princes, too. You just come down and cry on Mamie's shoulder and I'll get you through it some way."

"All right," wept the Countess Krak.

She hung up. A young woman in a maid's dress had entered the room. "Did you call, ma'am?"

Other staff were at the door.

"No," said the Countess. "Yes. Pack my clothes."

She stared a long time at the phone.

Oh, it was a mortal blow all right. I was beside myself with glee. I knew she was debating whether or not to call Heller at his office and tell him good-bye.

She must have decided against it. Listlessly, she pushed a button that opened up a phone number book. She pressed an automatic dialling letter.

"Bonbucks Teller Central Customer Purchasing," a voice said.

The Countess Krak dully gave the number of the Squeeza credit card. Then she said, "I have to go to Atlantic City."

"Quickly or in a leisurely fashion?"

"It doesn't matter."

"Will you be staying long? Is it a round trip?"

"It doesn't matter."

"Would you like to go by bus? By train? By limousine? By helicopter?"

In an introverted, weeping voice, she said, "If I only had my own ship I could go home."

"Well, madam, I've just checked your credit rating here and it's unlimited as always. I had a note here just this morning ... Yes, here it is. The Morgan yacht has just come on the market. It is two hundred feet, twin screw, fully found and ready to go to sea. She has roll and pitch stabilizers, five salons, two swimming pools and gold fittings in the owner's cabin. At Atlantic City she could lie in the Gardner's Basin Maritime Park quite close to the casinos or cruise about to other anchorages in the numerous bays. It would save you the fatigue of having to live in one of those casino hotels. The captain and crew were protesting being paid off. My clerk here on the other phone says the *Golden Sunset*—that's her name—could be standing by off the Hudson Harbor, 79th Street Boat Basin, in about an hour if that's suitable."

"It doesn't matter," said the Countess Krak.

"Well, very good, ma'am. I'll give the orders for the sale transfers and all that to be drawn up in our legal department and assign an adequate allowance from your credit card to care for her expenses and she will be standing by for you. It is a pleasure to be of service, ma'am. And I hope the nice sea voyage will relieve your tedium." He hung up.

I was on the verge of fainting. How much did a yacht cost? And hadn't I heard that Morgan had once said that if you had to wonder about how much the upkeep of such a vessel was, you didn't have any business owning one?

I was certain that I had just seen my half-million credit card guarantee, that had been held by Squeeza, go up in a puff of funnel smoke.

I was torn between the glee of seeing the Countess Krak crushed and the horror of knowing that Mudur Zengin was quite likely to do anything villainous he could think of now!

I watched the viewer but there was nothing much to see. The Countess Krak was just sitting there, staring at the floor. Only in her peripheral vision could I detect her lady's maid packing up her clothes and the fatal legal paper lying, walked upon occasionally, in the center of the rug.

But fate was not through playing with me that day. Stamping on me would be a better term. Fate was getting ready, as the hours passed, to do a ghoulish dance step.

The Countess Krak's baggage had been shifted to the 79th Street Boat Basin by cabs. The white expensive length of the resplendent yacht was standing by in the river, and two flag-streaming speedboats were curving ashore from her, throwing fans of spray, ready to pick up the Countess, her baggage and her maid and carry them away.

It suddenly occurred to me that she could shortly be out of range of the activator-receiver. She would be on a yacht and might take it into her mind to go anywhere, and I had no way to keep tabs on her. Well, never mind. Maybe the yacht would blow up and sink. I had to look on the brighter side of things.

Just as the grizzled old captain in all his gold braid was gallantly assisting the listless Countess to step into the speedboat, I heard the front door of the apartment open.

I covered up the viewers. I did not go out.

A certain amount of fear had been with me since my return to the apartment. Miss Pinch and Candy were not talking to me but their whispers to each other, I was certain, boded no good.

And I was right.

Miss Pinch and Candy had not taken off their coats. They came in. Miss Pinch was taking off her gloves.

They both sat down.

"Listen, you," said Miss Pinch, severely, "we have to talk."

"What about?" I said in fright.

"The children when they are born," she said.

"No, wait," I said. "Rockecenter sends anyone who gets pregnant to his abortion clinic. There's no reason both of you can't go. You'll get fired if you don't."

"That's just it," said Miss Pinch. "Psychiatric Birth Control is for the (bleeps). So all they say of childbirth must be as well. We are determined to experience the joys of motherhood. There is only one way we can't be fired."

The hair began to rise on the back of my neck. It always did when she fixed her eyes on me like that.

"Candy and I are agreed," said Miss Pinch. "There is no other way."

"Than?" I pleaded, expecting the worst.

I got the worst.

"You have to marry us," said Miss Pinch.

Chapter 2

When Miss Pinch brought me to by throwing a glass of water in my face, I sat there transfixed, eyes staring sightlessly.

I tried to speak. I tried to tell myself my name was not Heller. I tried to tell Miss Pinch that her name was not the Countess Krak.

Apparently, I wasn't making any sounds at all.

Candy said to Miss Pinch, "He seems to be stricken dumb, Pinchy. Let's have a bite of supper and let him recover a bit and then you can tell him the rest of it."

They went off.

I sat there.

After about half an hour, Miss Pinch came in. They had apparently finished supper but she still had a fork in her hand. She used it to prod me into the living room. Defensively, I sat down on the sofa. My legs wouldn't hold me up very long. I knew more was coming.

Candy said, "Let's put him in the mood." She went to the clamshell stereo and put a platter on the turntable. "I'm sure you remember this song," she said. "You played it the first time you raped us."

The song started up, very emotional crooning:

> *Sweet little woman,*
> *Please marry me,*
> *Man and wife together,*
> *How happy we will be.*
> *And then we'll have some kiddies,*
> *Maybe two or three,*
> *So here's the ring and there's the church!*
> *Oh, come, my honey be!*

I found my voice. "Turn it off!" I begged. I felt I knew what this was, now. A sadistic and evil revenge for all the favors I had done for them.

She turned off the record but in doing so turned on an FM radio station. It was pumping electronic pop music. You couldn't understand the words, so that was better.

"You must think," said Pinch, "that we're trying to

do you in, Inkswitch. This is not the case. It is a simple arrangement. You marry us and then we won't get fired if we have these babies. We can show that we are actually married. Be reasonable, Inkswitch."

I sat there, still stricken.

"I'll tell you what we will do," said Miss Pinch. "You have signed quite a few blank invoices. So the original money of yours is almost intact in that safe." She pointed to where it stood, covered now so as to look like a rock wreathed in sea foam. "You're always bleating around about money."

I flinched at this reference to goats.

Miss Pinch smiled thinly. "If you give us your word to go through with this without giving us any trouble at all, no matter what, I'll give you the combination to that safe, and also you can draw whatever you want from petty cash thereafter. I will simply bring it right home to you and drop it in your lap. That's around sixty-five thousand from the safe and unlimited drawing thereafter. How can you lose, Inkswitch?"

Inkswitch! It was not my real Earth name. I clutched at a straw and also at the funds necessary to make it possible for me to flee at the earliest opportunity. Still, marriage? I shuddered to the depths of my soul. I unclutched.

She saw my hesitation. She said, "We don't want to use the alternative of suing you," she said.

The horror of Izzy's description of the legal system reclutched at my throat.

Words stuck in my voice pipe. I forced them out anyway. "All right."

"What?" said Miss Pinch.

I realized I had spoken in Voltarian and with a Fleet

accent, too! I choked and finally made it in English. "All right."

She smiled grimly. Candy clapped her hands.

The only trouble was, Candy did the hand clapping in rhythm to the song that had just come on. It was one of those rare modern songs where one could understand the lyrics. It said:

> *I'm dying,*
> *I'm dying,*
> *I'm dying!*
> *I'm rolling all over the ground.*
> *I'm dying,*
> *I'm dying,*
> *I'm dying!*
> *A poor devil that you've downed.*
> *I'm dying,*
> *I'm dying,*
> *I'm dying!*
> *You've got me up a tree!*
> *I'm dying,*
> *I'm dying,*
> *I'm dying!*
> *And never more will be!*

Ill and spinning, I got out of the front room and back to the rear. I closed the door to shut out the awful electronic music. But the drumbeats kept coming through like thuds of doom.

Chapter 3

It was more by chance than design that I saw what happened at the condo. Heller's voice, "Dear?" The blanket had slipped off the viewer and I, sitting there, staring with dilated pupils, noticed that Heller was looking into Krak's room.

Boxes were thrown about but the place was otherwise cleaned out.

The butler was in the door, looking very unhappy.

"Where did she say she was going?" demanded Heller.

"She didn't say, sir. Her maid packed for her and went with her. But she did not take the car. She called a fleet of cabs and they loaded her baggage and left."

"Didn't she leave any note?" said Heller.

"No, sir. She wasn't talking to anyone, sir. The maid even called the cabs."

"What cab company?"

"I don't know, sir. I'm terribly sorry, sir. She did make a phone call and at the time I thought it must be to you. Otherwise I would have phoned you myself. She seemed very crushed, sir. I thought perhaps there had been a death in the family."

"She made a call," said Heller. Then he snapped his fingers. "Mamie Boomp!"

He grabbed the phone. He punched the automatic button.

"President Mamie Boomp here," said the voice.

"This is Wister. I must contact Joy. She's gone."

Mamie's voice was sniffish. "I shouldn't be surprised."

"Look," pleaded Heller. "Please tell me where she is or where she will be. I am very worried."

"Young man, I get pretty tired of you good-time Charlies. You can push it on the short stretch but never on the long haul. I think you've horsed that poor girl around enough. Now go find yourself a floozy that's low enough for the likes of you and leave good women alone!"

"I don't know what you're talking about," said Heller.

"They never do," said Mamie. "All take and no give. Have you ever even handed over a diamond?"

"No," said Heller. "Miss B——"

"I thought not," said Mamie. "Thought the promise of the little gold ring was enough. Even when you knew you couldn't hitch up to run double and knew it God (bleeped) well. The old story!"

"Miss Boomp," said Heller, "if you know where she is, for Gods' sakes, tell me. I'm out of my mind with worry."

"You were out of your mind to think you could pull a raw stunt like that and get away with it, sailor. She's better off without you. And just to keep you from runnin' up the phone bill—since it's no pleasure at all to talk to a lying, two-timing cheat—I do not know where she is except that she has left you. And that is final. Don't call me again, you would-be bigamist!" She hung up.

Heller stood there. He turned to the butler. "This doesn't make any sense. No slightest idea what cab company?"

"No, sir. I didn't think it was important. Actually,

the staff thought she was going to her family somewhere. She has been crying lately. We thought someone was dying."

Heller turned to the phone. He called Central Airline reservations. He demanded to know if any reservation had been made on any airline for Miss Heavenly Joy Krackle. The answer was negative. He called charter aircraft clearance. No such name on any charter.

He called Twoey in New Jersey. No, Twoey knew nothing except she hadn't turned up for lessons lately so he could teach her more about pigs.

Heller called Izzy. Negative. He had Izzy ask Bang-Bang. Negative.

He said to the butler, "She wouldn't touch a train as she hates them and with all that baggage she couldn't take a bus. She must have gone to a hotel somewhere in this very city. Now, listen, think hard. Did anything happen just before she left?"

"Well, yes. A man came and insisted that he see her. And then the man ran away. Isn't that the paper there, sir? Under that box?"

The butler picked it up and Heller grabbed it.

He stared at the legal paper. He read it. He stared at it again. Then he crumpled it up with a savage closure of his hand.

"Blast them! I understand now," he said. He slumped down on the bottom of the bed. Then he said, "The poor kid. The people who keep this rotten legal system going should be killed. Oh, the poor kid." And he was crying.

Chapter 4

After a horrible night, I awoke to more horror.

I had had constant nightmares in which I was Heller being sued by Meeley, my old landlady on Voltar, for counterfeiting a marriage to the dead mistress of the colonel of the Death Battalion who had been strangled by Torpedo.

Miss Pinch was standing there. She was dressed, most unlike her, in an organdy dress. She had laid out a black suit, the kind they bury people in on this planet. The old Jew must have been a storekeeper with foresight for including the outfit in my wardrobe.

Like an automaton, I got dressed. Somewhere far off I heard a crackle: it sounded like gunfire in volley, just like the final grave salute. Miss Pinch said it was just Candy opening and closing the fridge. I didn't believe her.

We went outside. A rental car, a Datsun, stood at the curb. Miss Pinch got behind the wheel. Candy came out wearing a black cape. I hadn't seen Miss Pinch put it on but she was wearing a black cape, too.

"Oh, we're all too solemn for a wedding day," said Candy and turned on the car radio. It was playing that dying song again.

Miss Pinch drove with expertise and speed. She seemed to know exactly where she was going and apparently had been there before. We tooled along on expressways and soon were out of all skyscrapers and cluttered streets and on the Merritt Parkway.

I had the distinct impression I was being taken for a ride. But a Datsun isn't a long, black limousine: it bobs and buckets about. I was reassured, as the jolting kept me informed that I was still alive.

"Where are we going?" I said timidly from the back seat.

They didn't answer.

An hour and a half out of New York, we were looking for a parking spot. The signs said we were in

Hartford
Connecticut
Population 819,432 ½
The Home of Colt
Patent Firearms

Now I knew why we had come there. I was going to be shot.

In no time at all we were marching into the city hall, following signs which said Danger Ahead and Marriage. It was no solace to be told the Danger Ahead signs referred to the traffic department. I knew what they referred to. A bunch of frightened men and gleeful women were standing in a queue.

In a quiet, deadly voice, Miss Pinch said, "All arrangements were done beforehand by a private detective."

"I thought private detectives came after marriage," I said.

"Be quiet. All papers are in order. All you have to do is say yes."

"Yes," I said.

"Not here, you dummy. When we get in front of the clerk."

The line of couples sped forward at an alarming rate.

Candy and Miss Pinch took off their black cloaks. Candy was dressed in a wedding gown! Miss Pinch was dressed as a bridesmaid.

With the suddenness of a natural cataclysm we were at the counter. A gray-headed clerk did not look up. Miss Pinch shoved the papers under his nose.

I looked for a direction to run.

There was none.

The clerk said, "DoyouCandyLicoricetakethismanto-beyourawfulweddedhusband?"

"Yes," Candy said.

"DoyouSultanBeytakethiswomantobeyourawfulwed-dedwife?"

A sharp instrument in the hands of Pinch prodded me. "Ow!" I said.

The clerk raised a gavel and brought it down on the desk with a sharp rap. He said in his rapid slur of a voice, "BythepowersinvestedinmebytheStateofConnecti-cutIherebysentenceyoutomarriage. Signthebook. Paythe-cashier."

Candy signed. Miss Pinch had my wrist clutched. Everything looked faint and faraway. I scribbled something.

Two witnesses who seemed to be on regular duty signed the book. Stamping machines banged. Copy machines roared.

Miss Pinch snapped her pocketbook shut.

We were out on the street.

They got in the Datsun.

"Turn your back," said Candy.

"And don't try to run away," said Pinch.

There was a scrambling in the Datsun.

"Get in," said Miss Pinch.

I turned around. The girls, right there in the parking lot with everybody looking except me, had swapped dresses.

Miss Pinch, now in the wedding gown, drove grimly north.

Something was bothering me. I could not pinpoint what it was. There had been something just a bit odd about that ceremony.

We drove for thirty-five miles. A sign said we were in

Springfield
Massachusetts
Population 167,500 ⅔

Another one said:

United States Armory
Small Arms
Home of the
Springfield and Garand Rifles

Now I was very certain I would be shot.

Shortly we were standing before a counter in the city hall. My vision was kind of blurred but I could have sworn it was the same man that had been in Hartford and I wondered how he could have made the trip faster than we did. But Datsuns are not very fast cars.

Miss Pinch in her wedding dress, although holding a bouquet, yet had a lock on my arm.

The clerk said, "DoyouAdoraPinchtakethismanto-beyourawfulweddedhusband? DoyouSultanBeytakethis-womantobeyourawfulweddedwife? Signthebook. Paythe-cashier. Next."

Somebody was pushing my hand to sign. All of a sudden I saw what I was writing:

Sultan Bey!

I was not writing "Inkswitch"! I was writing the name I really bore on Earth!

"Wait!" I screamed.

How could this be? Pinch didn't know that name. She thought my name was Inkswitch.

The clerk and everybody was looking.

"That's the wrong name!" I screamed.

They stared at me.

"He thought he was in Boston," said Pinch.

They all laughed.

With the sharp ends of the bouquet wires penetrating the flesh of my side, I was gotten back on the street.

"I thought I would be married in the name of Inkswitch!" I wailed.

"You've got a crooked streak in you," said Pinch. "If you wanted us to think your Fed cover name was your real name, you shouldn't babble some outlandish tongue that could be Turkish in your sleep and you shouldn't leave your most-used passport and birth certificate around. For convenience, we will continue to call you Inkswitch. But don't try to pull something like that again! You're very legally married, Sultan Bey."

Something inside me snapped. I began to babble. I heard myself saying, "My real name is Jettero Heller."

"Nonsense," said Candy, laughing. "Next you'll be telling us you're that other name you scream in your sleep, 'Officer Gris.'"

"No, Sultan Bey," said Mrs. Bey nee Pinch. "Make up your mind to it. You are our lawfully wedded husband, for better or for worse, and even though you aren't much, we'll have to get used to it and so will you. Become accustomed to the fact that you are now probably the most married man on the entire eastern seaboard. The knots are irrevocably tied. Let's have some hamburgers and go home."

Chapter 5

In the early dusk of spring, we drew up at last before the apartment which I had left, only that dawn, a free man.

We went inside. A new surprise had been readied. Already shocked, I had not been prepared to behold anything else new.

The whole place was garlanded. The symbols of Aphrodite—doves, swans, myrtle, pomegranate, clamshells and sea foam—had had added to them arches of orange blossoms.

And there were two new people there: a girl named Curly with brown eyes and brown hair, a not bad-looking thirty in a combat jacket; the other a very pale willowy thing with a pretty face and soft lips named Sippy, dressed in absolutely transparent gauze.

They had "The Wedding March" going on the record player and they showered us with rice and did a rather mincing dance and kissed everybody, crying, "Happy weddings to you!"

It was disconcerting. What were they doing there?

I was tired after the long drive and showing signs of

strain. I edged over to Mrs. Bey nee Pinch. "Give me my money now," I said.

"Oh my, dear husband," Mrs. Bey nee Pinch said. "There's cake and other things."

"Here," said Sippy, holding out a glass, "try some of this champagne."

Ex-Pinch and the late Miss Licorice, now Mrs. Candy Bey, had their capes off. Curly rolled out a wedding cake on a tea trolley. With elaborate gestures quite like a sexual approach, she gesticulated with a knife.

She put my hand on the hilt. She put Candy's on mine. She put Mrs. Bey nee Pinch's fingers gripping ours and all three of us cut the wedding cake. It had TWO brides on it! The man, at the very first thrust of the knife, fell over. An omen?

Then they played some pop music and everybody ate cake and danced with one another. I was thirsty and drank quite a bit of champagne. The cake kept sticking in my throat and I kept having to wash it down.

Inevitably, they broke out the marijuana. The joints circulated. Blue smoke began to haze the air. It didn't help my throat a bit.

They were getting quite drunk and stoned. Curly did an impersonation of Rockecenter at his last personnel inspection, making sure that Sippy was still a virgin and when Curly produced a limp dishrag, for some reason it sent them all rolling on the floor with glee, holding their sides.

I took another drag on the joint I was smoking and frowned. I didn't get it. But then, I philosophized, drunks will guffaw at anything, especially when they're high on pot.

Gaily laughing, quite giddy, Candy rummaged in the record cabinet, told Curly and Sippy the joke and

then played "Sweet Little Woman, Please Marry Me." It
was torture to listen to.

I pulled Mrs. Bey nee Pinch to the side. I said,
"Miss Pinch, give me my money now."

"Adora," she said, drunkenly. "You must learn to
call me Adora now, dear husband. I am no longer *Miss*
Pinch."

"Whatever your name is," I said. "Give me my
money now."

"Oh, dear husband," she said. "A marriage isn't
legal unless it is consummated. Don't you want to con-
summate the marriage?"

"No," I said.

"Aha!" cried Mrs. Bey nee Pinch, and I saw she had
become more than a little tipsy. "Trying to give yourself
a legal out, are you?" She thrust her face into mine. "You
know very well that a marriage that isn't consummated
can be annulled." She turned, "Hey, you girls, listen to
this (bleep)! He's trying to give himself legal grounds
to cancel out his marriages!"

Four faces, close to, glared at me.

"No, no!" I cried, quite frightened. "You told me
that if you had sex you might miscarry!"

"You think I didn't think of that?" snarled Mrs. Bey
nee Pinch. "I *knew* you'd try to weasel out! We've got
two virgins here, just for the purpose of consummation!"

"Wait a minute," I begged, "this is crazy!"

"Now he's trying to annul it by accusing us of insanity!" shouted Mrs. Bey nee Pinch.

Candy shook her head. "The courts won't uphold
that, dear husband," she hiccupped.

"This guy doesn't know his law," said Curly.

"No, no," I cried, distractedly. "I'm not trying to
get out of anything. I just want my money."

"Oh," said Sippy, in blear-eyed shock. "Did he just marry you girls for your money?"

"And how will THAT look in the newspapers?" cried Mrs. Bey nee Pinch.

"He trifled with their affections," slurred Curly. "A monster!"

A vision of Crobe's cellological freaks went spinning around my head. "I've had enough of monsters!" I shouted.

"Call us monsters, will you?" shouted Mrs. Bey nee Pinch. "You CREEP!" And she threw a glass of champagne in my face.

"No, no," I cried, spluttering. "This is all a misunderstanding!"

"Oh, yeah?" said Mrs. Bey nee Pinch, "Well, do you admit you're married or don't you?"

She looked so ferocious, reeling there, that I got down on my knees, clasped my hands before my face and said, "Please, please. Please believe me. I admit, so help me Gods and hope to die, that I am married!"

"Good," said Mrs. Bey nee Pinch. "You heard him, girls. He knows now he is thoroughly married. Drink up so we can get on with this 'consummation'!"

The champagne gurgled into mugs, overspilling.

The four of them stood and raised their drinks which clinked together in an apex of arms.

"To a happy married life!" cried Mrs. Bey nee Pinch.

They guzzled down the whole of their mugs, glug, glug, glug, glug!

They threw their glasses at me!

I ducked amidst the splintering crash.

When I dared to look up from the floor where I had been protecting my head, I was hit by Curly's combat jacket.

A pair of pants went sailing past my hair.

A shoe hit me.

I crawled under the sofa for better protection.

Another version of the wedding march was booming out:

> *Here comes the bride,*
> *Fit to be tied.*
> *To how many boyfriends,*
> *Has this chick spread wide?*
> *Here comes the groom,*
> *A relic from a tomb,*
> *All the guests are laughing*
> *As he meets his doom.*

I dared to peek out.

I could see the bottom of the bed.

Feet were twisting and turning, four pairs.

"Oh, you darling!" came Candy's voice.

"What's going on?" I pleaded, staring. "*I'm* the husband!"

"Beat it, buster," came the drunken voice of Mrs. Bey nee Pinch. "This ish OUR conshummation, not yoursh!"

A champagne bottle exploded in a cascade of fizz.

I stared at the bed. A voice floated to me, "Kiss me, kiss me, KISS ME!"

Another champagne bottle exploded all by itself.

The foam flooded across the ravaged cake. The fallen bridegroom twisted over on his side and then sank from view in the froth, feet first.

It dimly occurred to me that something, I could not figure what, had pushed these girls back toward lesbianism. Possibly it was a hangover of psychiatric conditioning. I knew I hadn't had anything to do with it.

Something was troubling me. I somehow didn't feel that my marriages had been consummated. I felt more like a fifth wheel.

I went to my lonely room and fell into a sleep raped with nightmares in which I was Heller pretending to be that clerk in the city halls who travelled about so miraculously marrying everybody. Soltan Gris was in the coffin that Heller the clerk kept using for a marriage ceremony desk. The Manco Devil even got married to Lombar Hisst while Rockecenter, in gales of laughter, stood in as best man.

But what really woke me up sweating was when a Manco Devil stepped out of the coffin and pointed a finger at the middle of my forehead. He—or was it a she?—said, "Ask yourself. Is this all happening to you because you did it to Heller?"

I knew right then, as I stared into the spinning darkness, that things were going to get WORSE!

Chapter 6

Never drink alcohol and take dope at the same time.

The result can be near fatal, as I found out when I awoke to another terrible day.

I heard Mrs. Pinch Bey and Mrs. Candy Bey preparing to go to work. I crawled out just in time to catch Adora before she went out the door.

"The money," I croaked.

Her eyes, as she glanced at me, told me how awful I must look standing there with the cold air on my naked flesh. "We can't be late for work after playing hooky yesterday," she said. "There's no time to go into it now." She dived a hand into her purse and drew out a few dollar bills. She tossed them on the floor. "Just so you don't go robbing banks. We'll take the other up this evening." She was gone.

Nervously, I stared after her. Then I picked the seven dollars off the floor and went back to my room.

A cold shower did not do the least good. I found some aspirin. I took it. It made me feel fuzzy. Then I began to feel drunk all over again: they say champagne does that when you drink water the morning after. I shouldn't have taken the aspirin with water.

I couldn't lie down. I was too spinny and jittery.

I turned on the viewers. Crobe was puttering around a laboratory, doing something with a snake. The Countess Krak's was blank: that was good news for me, it meant she wasn't within two hundred miles. Heller was sitting looking at an untouched breakfast: at least I had him worried sick.

The butler's voice. "Some men, sir. I think they're from the court."

"Well, kick them out," said Heller.

"I can't, sir. There's police with them and they've got guns."

The shabby man in the shabby coat with the shabby hat pulled down over his eyes, unable to look at anybody straight, had followed the butler in. He placed an order in Heller's hand.

"He's served!" called the shabby man toward the door. "You can go ahead."

Heller read the paper. It said:

SUPERIOR COURT
Wister vs. Wister
SEIZURE ORDER:

To protect all property, rights and assets of the PLAINTIFF, Toots Wister, and to prevent actual assets from being hidden under the mask of false or fabricated identity or titles, under the community property laws of this state, said assets shall be frozen by the order of this court until actual titles can be established.

The DEFENDANT shall hereafter and whereas and at once surrender up all bank accounts, assets, possessions real and personal and everything he uses and claims he does not own.

Superior Court
Hammer Twist
Judge
Dingaling, Chase and Ambo

"What the blast is this?" said Heller.

A heavy voice said, "It's a court order and I come along to be sure it's fulfilled without trouble. You pulled a gun on the process server the other day." It was Police Inspector Grafferty!

Men were filing into the condo, picking up things and making lists.

"And what happens if I throw you crazies out?" said Heller.

"You get ninety days for contempt of court," said Grafferty. "Say, haven't I seen you someplace before? I never forget a face."

"What shall I do?" said the butler.

"Follow them around and make sure they don't steal anything," said Heller. "But first tell the chauffeur to get out a car."

"You can't use any cars," said Grafferty. "And you can't live here, either. We're padlocking the place."

"What happens to the staff?" said Heller.

"They get padlocked, too," said Grafferty. "Are you sure we ain't met before?"

Heller picked up his hat.

Two policemen stopped him, removed his wallet and took the money out of it.

Heller took back the empty wallet. He went into his room to get some clothes.

"Can't touch those," a court marshal said. "You're lucky we don't strip you of them you got on. The only thing that stops us is indecent exposure laws."

Heller walked out. Just before he got in the elevator, he bumped into the police inspector. Grafferty said, "I know where it was. Police lineup for sexual offenders three years ago. You got off then, but you won't the next time. I'll see to it personally."

Heller exited from the front door of the condo. The doorman didn't salute. Heller walked over to him. "I've got to make a phone call. Can you lend me a quarter?"

"I'm sorry, sir," the doorman said. "But them was bailiffs that just walked in. I don't know what the trouble is, but nobody ever gets out of a court alive. Even a dime would be at risk. Have a good day, sir."

Heller started downtown on foot. He had most of the length of Central Park to go.

He covered it and entered Columbus Circle. He went down Broadway, all the way from 59th Street through Times Square and on down to 34th Street. Then he went the final part of a long block toward Fifth Avenue and was in the shadow of the Empire State Building.

He stopped. He took out a piece of paper and, glancing around, put it up against the building and wrote a note. He wrote so fast I could not follow it.

He watched the entrance to the building. He stood there for some time. A young man came running out, probably a broker's runner. Heller paced him. At the corner, where the young man was waiting for a light, Heller stepped close to him and pushed the paper into his hand.

"Don't look at me," said Heller. "Turn around and get this to Izzy right away."

The young man must have been from Izzy's own office. He waited for the light. Heller crossed. He glanced back. The young man hadn't followed him. He was gone.

Heller went up the street to the Sukiyaki Bar and Grill. He went in.

A Japanese came over.

"Give me a glass of water," said Heller.

"You no order food? You no order drink?"

"Give me a glass of water," said Heller.

"I'm most sorry, we don't serve water. If you broke, go to Salvation Army soup kitchen."

"You like this place?" said Heller.

"Yes."

"You don't want this place wrecked?"

"NO, sir!"

"Then bring me a glass of water."

"I can't, sir. You can sit there. But no money, no water."

Heller waited half an hour. Other Japanese staff passed by, frowning at him. New York is no place to be without money. I heard somebody say once that the place was as hard as a whore's heart. True, by my experience.

I was beginning to taste some satisfaction in this plight of Heller's. Oh, there was no doubt he was finished. It was even curing my headache. Krak gone. Cars gone. Condos gone. Disaster all around him. I began to smile. This was worth everything I had been put through lately.

Izzy suddenly slid into the seat opposite him. He was pretty flustered, his hair untidy, his horn-rimmed glasses askew, his beak of a nose rubbed red.

Heller handed him the court order. "I didn't want to chance anyone following me to the office. They might not know of its existence. I've noticed it before: people seem to know where I am and where I go."

Izzy nodded. He was reading the court order.

"That can't be very legal," said Heller.

"Well, legal is whatever the lawyers say it is. They try anything, Mr. Jet. And usually get away with it. I'll give this to Philup Bleedum: it will take months for him to untangle it and years to settle the case and he's one of the fastest lawyers in town."

"Now to something important," said Heller. "What did the detective agency say?"

"Well, they've covered all the hotels. No one of that name or description registered. They've covered the hospitals and morgue. No sign of her anywhere."

"Blast!" said Heller. "The poor kid must be really hiding. And from nothing! These suits are just a pack of lies."

"Most suits are," said Izzy. "The total design of the legal system is wrecking people's lives so the lawyers can get rich. The trouble is, this fake Toots Switch doesn't have a dime. The lawyers just take such cases to get 50 percent of any court award. You can't recover damages from such people for all the wreckage they cause. By the way, they've already been to the office this morning."

"What?"

"Yes. A court order to attach your salary. But as you don't get any, it doesn't have any force. They try anything. They don't even have a judgment yet. But you were very wise not to come in. As I was en route here, I picked this up. Have you seen it?"

He handed Heller a paper. The front-page story said:

WHIZ KID BIGAMIST
SECOND WIFE SUES
FOR DIVORCE

Dingaling, Chase and Ambo today filed suit in Superior Court on behalf of one Dolores Wister nee Pubiano de Cópula.

Alleging marriage by a village priest to the notorious outlaw Wister, otherwise known as the Whiz Kid, while he was on the run in Mexico, the delicate Mexican flower bared her tale of woe to the assembled media. It was a very pretty tale.

Posing as a revolutionist, the Whiz Kid, according to the suit, stole into the village and her bed in the depths of a romantic Mexican night and (bleeped) her thoroughly.

Due to the braying of her jealous burro in the

next room, the village priest discovered them and
married them immediately as they lay wallowing
in their sin.

Having searched in vain for her outlaw lover/
husband for two desperate, lonely and heartbroken
years, and finding now that he had since married another woman in Kansas, the pitiful, grief-
withered beauty has decided to sue for divorce.

Property settlements may run into billions.

Heller threw the paper back across the table. "Any
way to put her in jail?"

"With this legal system?" said Izzy. "The truth is,
the cops who came to your apartment couldn't have
received the warrant yet. But one or another of these
girls before the day is out is going to swear out an arrest
order on you for bigamy. It's a criminal offense. I'd keep
out of sight."

"Look," said Heller, "I don't give a blast about these
people. I'm only interested in where the Countess is! I've
got to find her!"

Izzy fumbled in his coat. He brought out a roll of
bills inches thick. He slid it across the table to Heller.

Instantly, the Japanese waiter arrived with two
glasses of water. He went away.

Heller was counting the money.

"I'm sorry," said Izzy. "All I ever keep in my personal box is thousand-dollar bills. I hope it doesn't embar-
rass you changing them. I wouldn't go into any banks,
if I were you. Dingaling, Chase and Ambo will have
everything covered. Here is something else." He slid Heller an envelope.

Heller looked in. It was one of his phony CIA passports and a ticket.

"I still think you ought to go to Brazil," said Izzy. "That's where the ticket is for. I'll get detectives looking even harder for Miss Joy and send her to you."

"She wouldn't come unless I spoke to her."

Izzy looked like he was going to cry. "Oh, Mr. Jet, you don't realize what you're into! They've got you totally enmeshed in the legal system now. The Devil himself couldn't ever escape from it. And he's still in it. No man once grabbed by it has ever gotten free of it. Please go, Mr. Jet."

"I've got to find my girl," said Heller.

Izzy shook his head. He got up and sadly left.

The Japanese came over. "You order now?"

"I'm going to order somebody vaporized before this is through," said Heller. He walked out. He was looking up and down the street, as though by that he could locate the Countess Krak.

I was jolted. I had never heard him sound so cross before. Did he mean me?

Nervously, I threw the blanket over the viewer. Irrationally, I thought he might look back through it and see me.

My head was aching again.

Miserably, I tried to get some sleep. I couldn't. I felt things were not going well. I should be very happy. I was sure that he was thoroughly on the skids and so was the Countess Krak.

Something kept nagging at me.

It was a bad day.

The ex–Miss Pinch, now Mrs. Bey, came home about five. She walked in, took off her gloves.

"You wanted to talk to me?" she said.

"Yes," I said. "You promised you would open the safe."

"That's right," said Adora. She seemed to be waiting for something. Shortly the front door opened and Candy was home. "We're in here," Adora yelled.

Candy came in bringing Adora a beer. She had one for herself. She didn't give me one. She sat down attentively.

"Now that we're all assembled," said Adora, "I'd better lay out the facts of life."

"I've had too many lays already," I said. "All I want is my money."

"Well, you shall get your money," said Adora with a beady eye. "But there is something you should know first."

Candy laughed. I didn't like that laugh.

Adora smiled. I didn't like that smile.

"I don't want to know anything," I said. "Just give me my money."

They both burst out laughing. I surely didn't like that.

"It won't do you any good," said Adora.

"Give him the money, Pinchy. Then tell him. I still love it when he screams."

"All right," said Adora. She went into the front room. She opened the safe. She pulled out pack after pack of my money and put them in a garbage sack.

"Give him the blank invoices, too," said Candy, laughing.

Adora pulled out a sheaf of them. "Go ahead and sign to your heart's content."

I thought they were kidding me. My eyes were on the sack, swinging in her hand.

I thought I would test it. I wrote a petty cash invoice for $40,000! I signed it *George Washington*.

She took it. She said, "You'll have it tomorrow."

She tossed the bag of money into my lap. I dived into it. Beautiful bills! There must be $65,000 here or more!

"Tell him, Pinchy," said Candy.

I stopped my counting uncertainly. I did not like the way Adora looked.

"You wanted the money so you could run, didn't you?" said the ex–Miss Pinch, Mrs. Bey. "You've been planning to light out the moment you had your hands on that dough. Oh, yes you did. But dough, my dear husband, won't do you a (bleeped) bit of good."

She leaned forward and her eyes were cold. "You see, you son of a (bleepch), you have just committed the crime of BIGAMY!"

The room started to spin. Dancing before my eyes was the news story I had just seen, "Whiz Kid Bigamist." THAT was what had been nagging at me!

"If either wife," said the ex–Miss Pinch, Mrs. Bey, "cares to prefer charges, you can be sent to prison for the rest of your life. Extradition amongst the states is automatic. You can be run down anywhere you go, brought back and thrown in the tombs." She flashed the marriage certificates from her purse. "We have these. So go ahead, you (bleepard). Try to run. That money won't help you at all. The legal system will bring you home and throw you in the pen. Either one of us will pretend the other did not know. So spend your dough, bigamist. You ain't goin' nowhere but right here."

They suddenly burst out laughing again. I must have looked very deflated.

The ex–Miss Pinch, Mrs. Bey, got up. "Now that that's settled, dear husband, take a shower."

"Why?" I pleaded. I had had enough horror today.

"Why?" she mimicked. Then her eyes narrowed and she poked her face very close to mine, for all the world like Lombar. Her voice became very deadly indeed. "You can stop your underhanded, chauvinistic machinations right now! By plying us with champagne and pot on our wedding night and then refusing to do your duty, you thought you could throw us back into lesbianism. You tried to make me break my sacred vow to crush Psychiatric Birth Control forever! Well, buster, you did NOT succeed!"

She slapped at my side just like Lombar. "It was NO good! You only confirmed my determination! Two lesbians will arrive in the next half hour and they'll be two ex-lesbians when we're through. And no more tricks to wreck the program! No more whining about them being dead!"

She stood back and surveyed me. "Learn to toe the line, dear husband, or we'll blow the whistle on you. Clean yourself up and get ready!"

They walked out. At the door, Adora looked back. "Bigamist," she said.

Defeated utterly, I began to crawl out of my clothes. I felt terribly confused. I kept thinking I did not want to have sex with Dolores Wister nee Pubiano de Cópula's burro. But there was nothing I could do about it.

Belatedly, I started screaming. I hate burros!

PART
FORTY-NINE

Chapter 1

The following morning, worn and weary, both from overexercise and a sleep that wasn't sleep but a parade of nightmares, I took a review of myself in the bathroom mirror.

I had a scratched face.

One of the candidates for sexual reeducation last night had been a thin thing, mostly bones. In addition to an immature body, her breasts had not yet developed fully. I speculated on her age: she must have been fourteen or fifteen at the most. Someday she would be good-looking, maybe, but right now her eyes were too big and round and her oversized mouth was far too large for her face. She wore her light brown hair in a ponytail. She chewed bubble gum with very loud satisfaction.

Her name was Teenie and her job was licking stamps in Rockecenter's Medical Association Control Department. I had gathered that she had not been on the job very long, had come straight out of some psychology sex-education group in grade school and had not been wholly converted to Psychiatric Birth Control yet. So, according to Adora, it was important that pains be taken with her: my pains of course!

Last night Teenie had certainly expressed her enthusiasm for reeducation! But "enthusiasm" is too mild a word for it. She had been all over the place and me!

ACTIVE! And the others had just smiled indulgently and wouldn't pull her off!

It wouldn't have been so bad, perhaps, except that she had expressed her passion with fingernails, time after time!

But she made me realize that my own education was deficient. I didn't have a clue what "Ride 'em, cowboy!" meant. We don't have any cows on Voltar and if we did, we wouldn't keep hitting them with a hat! Or scratching them! Inhuman!

Yes, all in all, that very active Teenie had been a wearing experience. I hoped there would not be too many more like that! Too draining!

I put some patches on my face to hide the scratch marks. I hoped I would not be permanently scarred.

I thought I would cheer myself up by examining and counting and fondling the money. It was on the top shelf of my closet. I got it down. And then I just sat there staring at it. Was it worth it?

The thought had no more than begun when I sat up with alarm. Was something costing me my love of money? What if I went into a state of hypernegation?

Look at the state that Heller and the Countess Krak were bringing me to!

New alarm filled me. Heller might suspect me. And the Countess Krak, now that she had disappeared, might be looking for me. Supposing she took it into her head to turn Crobe loose on me when I went crazy!

I had not looked at Crobe's viewer much. Was she in contact with him?

Anxiously I turned Crobe's viewer on. He could make it very hard to watch due to his one penetrative x-ray eye. But today it was quite clear.

Crobe was standing in front of a group of evident psychiatrists. It was probably the operating amphitheater at Bellevue. The audience was very intent.

Before him there was a patient strapped in a chair. I gasped: Crobe was up to his old grafting tricks.

A reptile was rearing out of the patient's skull! The deadly snake head was moving about to right and left.

Crobe's voice boomed out: "Dis broofs de t'eory dot man iss running on de reptile brain. By zimply feeding de batient Drug 32, de reptile gortex 'as been restimulated do grow! Und it 'as grow and grow. Und vinally 'ere iss de broof!"

The assembled psychiatrists were taking notes anxiously. A medical photographer was shooting flash shots.

The fraud! He was always monkeying around with grafts. That was how he made freaks and this is why he had been condemned to death before Lombar got him and put him to work in Spiteos. Here he was corrupting the sacredness of psychiatric science!

"Zo!" cried Crobe with a flourish, "you dgentmens iss zo right! Dere iss a reptile brain. Man runs on de reptile brain. It iss the zource which makes man zo evil! Zychiatric zience iss right!"

There was applause from the assembled learned men. Some cheers as well.

A spokesman stood up. "Dr. Crobe. I wish to announce to this gathering, now that we have seen it with our own eyes, that you are being proposed for the award of Psychiatric Genius of the Year."

"No, no," cried Crobe impatiently. "Zit down! I 'ave not vinished! Dere iss more broof!"

The hall went into a hush.

"Zis patient coom here zuffering from inanity. By

feeding Drug 32, I 'ave brought de cause to light. Now, right beefoor yer eyes, I vill CURE de patient!"

The emotional-scale letters on the viewer said:

GLEE

The hall hushed. Crobe took a huge knife from the table. He flourished it. It whistled through the air.
THUNK!
It severed the snake from the skull!
Blood spurted all over the place!
The patient went into death seizures.
He died.
The letters on Crobe's viewer flashed:

PLEASURE

Crobe's voice rang out in triumph. "You zee? De end broduct uf psychiatry 'as been attained. ZE PATIENT ISS QUIET!"

Thunderous applause broke out. The psychiatrists were on their feet in a standing ovation!

Suddenly out of the cheering throng rushed a clot of media men. Foremost amongst them was a reporter with a *Slime Magazine* press card in his hatband. His voice could hardly be heard above the din. "Dr. Crobe! We want you on the cover of the magazine! Scientist of the Year!" A TV crew was pushing him aside. "We got it all but we gotta have close shots."

Psychiatrists were pushing the newsmen back, trying to shake Crobe's hand.

What a turmoil!

I averted my eyes and shut off the viewer.

I sat there. Psychology and psychiatry were stimulating Crobe. It was Heller's fault for making it necessary to send Crobe to Earth.

A sullen rage began to grip me. Was there some way I could use this? Maybe even now I could steer Heller or the Countess Krak Crobe's way. Courts sent felons to Bellevue. Better: the courts sent people there just to be examined. An examination by Crobe would be fatal!

I cheered up.

I thought I had better keep track of Heller. Down as he was, an opportunity might arise to get him sent to Bellevue by court order for examination. Somehow, I felt, I could overcome Krak's influence. If Crobe didn't see Heller's face he wouldn't run. Yes, I had better watch Heller and see if he found the Countess Krak. Then I could work something out. I had all the resources in the world. Rockecenter's influence permeated everything and it was at my fingertips whenever I cared to use it.

I would strike back!

Chapter 2

I phoned Dingaling, Chase and Ambo. I got Ambo. "This is Smith," I said. "How is everything going?"

"Wonderful," said Ambo. "We've got his possessions tied in a knot. He's still on the sidewalks but he won't be long."

"How's that?"

"We've got a warrant now for bigamy. It's moved from civil to criminal. Once we have him held in jail on

this criminal charge we can beat him down and milk
him for everything he has and then grab everything he
ever will have. A wonderful case. He hasn't got a chance."

"You may have trouble arresting him."

"Oh, I think not," said Ambo. "We have connections in the police and we will now have every airport
and bus station and train depot watched. They try to run
when they get hit this hard. So we'll pick him up, throw
him in the can and then make him squirm. Standard
legal procedure. The old routine shakedown. Sue them
civilly, trump up something criminal and then bleed
them to death. Routine."

"There's something else you can do," I said.

"What?" he said eagerly. "We're always open to inno-
vations that make people even more miserable."

"I want you to write a court order and put it on file
that when he is arrested, he is to be sent for mental examination to Bellevue."

"Oh, wonderful! That implies that, committing bigamy, he is irresponsible and of unsound mind and we
can be appointed executors of his estate, split it up
amongst ourselves and be rich! This is wonderful."

"In the order," I said, "specify that as his face is too
attractive, it might pervert nurses and so it is to be blackened."

"Nothing easier. You can write anything in a court
order. Then all you have to do is get the judge to sign
it and he never reads what he signs. An absolutely novel
idea. Will make good press, too. Gives the whole thing
a sinister ring. You can't win these things, you know,
unless you try them first in the press."

"There's another order you can write," I said. "He
has a gun moll. Her name is Heavenly Joy Krackle.

She has been known to help him. What can you do about her?"

"Oh, nothing easier. You just allege conspiracy and undue influence prejudicial to the interests of our clients, issue a restraining order which puts her in prison if she violates it, issue another order to have her picked up as a material witness and imprisoned until she sees it our way. You know, the usual things. Do you have a description of her?"

"Five feet nine and a half inches tall, blond hair, gray-blue eyes. An absolute fiend in appearance. Goes into rages. Uses an electric whip. Hands like claws. Stamps men to death with scarlet heels caked with dried blood."

"Oh, my God," said Ambo. "That *is* a menace to the case. Yes, I'll get out the orders immediately! Oh, I'm certainly glad you told us about this!"

"Be sure you specify the woman is sent to Bellevue masked as well. Her face has been known to turn men to stone!"

"That I will!" said Ambo. "It's a relief to know that the courts and police always do their duty. This Wister and this Krackle should be locked up!"

"In Bellevue," I repeated.

"Oh, there's no trouble with that. Any citizen can be picked up and sent to Bellevue under existing laws. I'll get a doctor's commitment signature presigned to the order."

I had a momentary qualm. Supposing they were sent to Bellevue and despite all these precautions, Crobe still recognized them. That would undo the whole plot. Wasn't ordinary psychiatry enough? That would incapacitate them thoroughly forever.

"Specify in the order," I said, "that Dr. Phetus P.

Crobe, a leading psychiatrist there, is specifically forbidden to examine them. Get another psychiatrist to sign the order. After all, it is just a routine legal matter."

"As you say," said Ambo. "Just a routine order. My goodness, Mr. Smith, it's wonderful to have your help. You think just like a lawyer, nicely circuitous. You have greatly assisted this case." He rang off.

I glowed with the compliment. How unlike Madison's sneers. My genius was appreciated.

I sat back, feeling really great. Then I began to giggle. Even if Crobe spotted them, he would not recognize them. He did not know the names Wister or Krackle. They would probably be delivered drugged, placed in electric-shock machines and ruined for the rest of their lives. Ordinary psychiatry was quite good enough for them.

The courts and the law and psychiatry were a priceless team. Why had I bothered to hire a hit man when I had *them* at my beck and call?

How could I miss? If Heller was not caught at once, he might find Krak and if he found Krak he might bring her straight into this morass the lawyers had made so they could become rich. It was a bottomless pit and would swallow them both! With a grinning gulp! Bless the Earth legal-psychiatric liaison! It might be totally insane but, good Gods, was it useful to the power elite!

Chapter 3

When I turned my attention to Heller, he was standing at the water's edge, watching a parade of ships en route to sea. The water before him was tinged with the blue of cloud-flecked sky, almost innocent of smog. It was a bright morning of a spring day. There was no wind; when he looked to his right, the grass was fresh and green. Then his eye shifted to a monument.

The Battery! Heller was standing near the statue of Verrazano, discoverer of Manhattan, who had landed, the sign said, near this very spot, the southern tip of the island, in 1524.

In Voltarian, he said to the statue, "Did the natives try to raise the mischief with you, too?" Then he read a recently erected plaque that was more extensive. It said that four years later, Verrazano had been eaten by cannibals. "I'm not at all surprised." It seemed to make him restless and he scanned the walks of the park. "Where are you, Izzy?"

I acted!

Now that I knew for certain a warrant was out for him, I knew, too, that Police Inspector Grafferty, that glory hound, would be anxious to be in on the kill.

I got through to Grafferty's office. I said, "Give me the Inspector quick. I have his quarry in sight!"

"The Inspector is out on a case," his office man said.

"I'm sure it's the Wister case," I snapped. "You tell him that the man he wants is right down in Battery Park by the statue of Verrazano. He's waiting for a contact. PICK HIM UP!"

"Very good, sir." He rang off.

Heller drifted north up a curving path, the towering skyscrapers of the financial district visible past the stern, red sandstone walls of Castle Clinton. He was looking up at a gunport when a voice spoke behind him.

"Mr. Jet." It was Izzy.

"Have you found her?" said Heller, his voice anxious.

"No, Mr. Jet. We have three private detectives out. No word."

"Blast!" said Heller.

"Mr. Jet, you look awful," said Izzy. "You must have slept in the park. Oh, I can't tell you how sorry I am that you're being put through the wringer of this awful legal system. It's the law that's criminal, Mr. Jet."

"Did you get the things I asked you for?"

Izzy handed him a bulky sack. "It's the last thing I can get out. About a minute after I finished collecting these, they'd padlocked your office. Two patrolmen are waiting in the hall in case you show up. There's a warrant out, Mr. Jet. Criminal charges. Bigamy. Look, Mr. Jet, Bang-Bang says they'll be watching all the airports and bus and train terminals but he can steal a helicopter and pick you up anyplace you say. We can land you on a freighter for Brazil. You should go, Mr. Jet. I can't stand the thought of you being in jail for years on some phony charge!"

"I've got to find my girl," said Heller.

Izzy sighed deeply. "Then take this," said Izzy, and pushed another thick roll of thousand-dollar bills in his hand. "Please don't shoot anybody. It's cheaper to buy them in the long run."

"Thank you," said Heller. "You're a true friend, Izzy."

"It's really your money," said Izzy. "I made that wad just this morning with the future device machine. Cotton went up. I wish I could help more."

"Keep the projects going," said Heller. "We'll come out of this."

"Oy, I wish I had your confidence. This legal system was designed only for bad-intentioned men so I'm afraid

we haven't got a chance. Please take care of yourself,
Mr. Jet."

Izzy walked swiftly away.

Heller walked toward the financial district. Shortly
he was into the crowds. He began to go quite fast.

He drew up before a very ratty-looking bar, the
Stockbroker. He went in. The place was papered with
old issues of shares and the cash register was a ticker-tape-
looking thing. He sat down at the bar. Big signs said:

Crash Pick-Me-Up
for Those Dow-Jones Blues
Suicide Special:
Why Throw Yourself Out of Windows
When Our Potion Can Do It Quicker?

His reflection in the mirror looked awful: hollow-eyed.

"Give me a Seven Up," said Heller.

"The market is down this morning, sir," said the
barkeep. "More like a Suicide Special."

"Can you change a thousand-dollar bill?"

"Seven Up it is, sir; you must be selling them
short."

"Somebody will wish he'd been sold short when I
get through with him," said Heller. "Can I use your
washroom?"

"Help yourself, sir. Anybody with a thousand-
dollar bill could buy the place."

Heller went into the washroom. It was a dingy lava-
tory. Not even scraps remained of the mirrors. Heller
hung his coat up on a hook. He opened the big sack
Izzy had given him. I couldn't tell what was in it.

Heller muttered, "Blast, what's this?" He was holding up a triple-blade razor that Izzy must have bought.

Then he looked into the sack again and apparently decided he would have to use the thing in lieu of his own spin razor.

He tried to shave. He cut himself. He tried again and cut himself again. He finished somehow.

He found a small Voltar vial of lotion. He put it on his face. Then he got out a little light that I had seen used in cellology. He beamed that at his face. Then he got out some bandages and put them on his face.

He spinbrushed his teeth.

But I had seen enough.

I phoned Grafferty's office again.

"The man he wants is at the Stockbroker Bar!" and I gave him the number on Church Street.

"I relayed the data to Grafferty," his office man said. "He is on a case but he is taking care of it. Public cooperation is always appreciated in criminal matters, sir."

I rang off, satisfied. New York's finest was on the job.

Heller folded up his coat, put it in the bag and then took out a dark blue, engineer's coverall suit, like a workman's. He put it on. Then he put on a plain blue workman's cap. He looked deeper in the bag. "Blast!" he said in Voltarian. "No engineer gloves. Only these cotton things." But he put them on. Then he found a redstar engineer rag and put it dangling out of his hip pocket.

He tidied up and went back out into the bar.

The place was still deserted except for the barman, and that worthy had put the Seven Up at a side table with a sandwich. "That Seven Up is awful stuff," said the barman. "No alcohol in it. So I give you a pastrami cushion. What else can I do for you?"

"You can show me where the phone is."

The barman dragged a long-corded phone over to the table. "I see you got some sort of a system for sneaking up on the market. Going to make another thousand?"

"I've got an idea I can hit the jackpot," said Heller.

"Yes, SIR! I promise not to listen much."

Heller dialled a number. The other end said, "Really Red Cab Company."

"Listen," said Heller. "Is Mortie Massacurovitch back on the job yet?"

"Oh, I wouldn't advise it, sir. The doctor said . . ."

"I know all about his eye infection," said Heller. "I've been told about nothing else for two days! Can you connect me?"

"Not directly. But he is back on duty."

"You tell him to dump any fare he has and get down to the Stockbroker Bar on Church Street. Tell him Clyde Barrow needs him bad and right now!"

The dispatcher said he would and rang off.

Clyde Barrow? He was a notorious gangster of the thirties! Then I recalled that that was the name Mortie Massacurovitch knew him by.

"I get it," said the barkeep. "You're going to do a bag job on some broker's office for the insider information. Smart."

"Yeah," said Heller. "I'm going to make a killing."

I chilled. That was three times now he had threatened vengeance. It was not like him to be that way. I knew pretty well what I had felt all along. Heller was going to go gunning for ME!

Hurry up, Grafferty!

Heller drank his Seven Up and ate his pastrami.

The door burst open and Mortie Massacurovitch came in, hit a table, bounced off, hit the bar.

"Over here," said Heller.

Mortie had bandages over his eyes, just looking through a slit. "Hello, kid," he said, looking in another direction.

Heller got his change and gave the barkeep twenty bucks for his trouble. He steered Mortie outside. The cab was parked with two wheels on the sidewalk. Heller got him into the passenger side of the front seat.

"Mortie, I'm in trouble," said Heller, settling himself under the wheel.

"Ain't we all," said Mortie. "I'm going broke. A dumb spick hit me in the face with a load of mace and I been off for a week."

"I know. I been trying to reach you for two days."

"They disconnected my phone for nonpayment," said Mortie. "The (bleeped) company wouldn't even let me have a cab this morning until I gave the dispatcher a black eye. I ain't never blind enough not to be able to hit what I aim at! So who you driving for now, kid?"

"Right now, you," said Heller. He shot the red cab away from the curb. I cursed. He had not looked at the number and the city swarmed with red cabs. I listened closely to pick up their destination.

Heller stopped. All I could see was poles and cobblestones. Where the Hells was he?

"Now, Mortie," said Heller. "A string of cabs was ordered." And he gave him the exact time and place they were ordered from. "I've *got* to locate what company and where those cabs went."

"Oh, hell, kid, that's easy." Mortie began to fumble around under the panel. "I always bring this little device. I hook it into the company radio. I can get every dispatcher of every cab company in New York. Helps to pick up the juicy, long-run fares before their own cabs can get there."

He started talking to dispatchers, giving fictitious cab numbers of their own fleets. The story was the same, "I got an old-lady fare here that was so pleased with some service that she wants regular service. She's forgotten the company. Was it ours?" And he would give the time and departure point and the dispatchers would look on their logs.

Suddenly, on his fifth call, Mortie stiffened and nodded at Heller. "Thank YOU!" he said and clicked off. To Heller, he said, "Smeller Cabs. Whole bunch of baggage. Took five cabs. They went to the 79th Street Boat Basin, Hudson Harbor."

"Hudson Harbor?" said Heller. "Nothing leaves from there. Not even a ferry."

"Beats me," said Mortie.

"Well, we're on our way," said Heller. And he shot the red cab into motion up onto the recently completed West Side Elevated Highway, and was shortly speeding north at a high rate.

I had my destination.

I phoned Grafferty's office. "Your man is heading north to the 79th Street Boat Basin!"

"Well, I sure as hell hope you're right. Grafferty just this minute got through chewing my (bleep) out. He wasn't at that statue place, he wasn't in the Stockbroker Bar and the (bleeped) bartender wouldn't even give him the time of day. You sure this is on the level this time?"

"Tall blond man, blue eyes. You tell Grafferty you got this tip from a Fed and tell him to get a move on!

You're dealing with Federal satellite surveillance, buster!"

"That's different," said the office man. "Yes, sir. Right away! But what's the Federal interest? He'll want to know."

"Secret Federal New York Grand Jury indictment," I lied. "We want Grafferty to make the public pinch so we don't show our hand."

"Ah, a standard Federal operation! Get the man for anything at any cost. And Grafferty gets the credit?"

"Tell him TO GET MOVING!" I half screamed. I hung up. I turned anxiously to the viewer. Heller must not be left to get away, the criminal. He was the cause of all my troubles after all! And he must pay for it!

Chapter 4

The 79th Street Boat Basin was in the throes of spring. The long lines of small pleasure craft, winter-landed on the dock in chocks, lay like a forest of leafless trees. Other assorted yachts bobbed around the landing stages. Many workmen swarmed around, apparently readying these millionaire toys for the joys of a boating summer.

This was the view that met Heller as he slid the red cab along the ranks at low speed, avoiding piles of this and that and people.

A sign said Dockmaster and Heller stopped. He went in the hut. A small, round man looked up from a desk.

Heller gave the probable time and date. "Five Smeller cabs," he concluded. "Did you see them?"

"Matey," said the dockmaster, "they come and go and I don't pay much attention."

"It's quite important," said Heller. "I have to find out where they went from here."

"Wait a minute," said the dockmaster. "The looker! Would the woman have been a real tomato?"

"I suppose you could say so."

The dockmaster looked at his log. "Yeah, I remember now. They rented a service boat to take out the baggage. Too much for their speedboats. They used a Squeeza credit card, Sultan Bey and Concubine. I remember the boys saying, 'Jesus, look at that God (bleeped) concubine, those foreign (bleepards) sure are taking over.' What a looker! She sure was sad, though, but I guess anybody would be sad being sold off to some God (bleeped) Turk."

He got up from the desk and walked outside and looked out at the river. Then he yelled over the side of the dock to a man working with some rope on the deck of a miniature tug. "Remember that looker the other day? What yacht was that you took the baggage to?"

"The Morgan yacht," the man called back. "The *Golden Sunset*."

"Oh, well, that figgers," said the dockmaster. "She's got too much draft to come in here. Too big."

"How do you find out where yachts go?" said Heller.

"Oh, I dunno," said the dockmaster. "Nobody keeps much track of documented yachts. They don't have to clear in and out unless they've been foreign. You could try Boyd's of London, the insurance people. They keep track of ships."

"Thank you," said Heller.

"Glad to be of help. That sure was some sad tomato."

A far-off wail of police screamers was audible, getting louder. Aha! "Bulldog" Grafferty was on the trail!

Heller went to a phone kiosk near the dockmaster office. He called to Mortie, sitting in the red cab, "I think we've got it."

He ruffled through the book and got the number. He got a British hello. Heller said, "I want to know where the Morgan yacht, the *Golden Sunset*, is."

"Put you onto Shipping Intelligence, old boy."

Another came on and Heller repeated his question.

"The Morgan yacht?" Shipping Intelligence said. "We have only one *Golden Sunset* in the American Yacht Registry but it's crossed out. Oh, yes. It was the Morgan yacht but I'm afraid, old boy, that she is no more."

"You mean it's been LOST?"

"Let me check with legal, old fellow. Just hold on."

Police screamers penetrated the glass of the phone kiosk. Heller glanced down the dock. Three police cars were racing up, full blast, toward the dockmaster office. I hugged myself in glee.

"Are you there?" said the British voice. "I'm afraid you caught us with the panties half off, old boy. The yacht fell between registries. She should now be in the Foreign Yacht Registry. Been bought by some barbarian Turk and transferred to the Turkish flag. We simply hadn't reentered it."

"Could you tell me where she is now?" begged Heller.

"Oh, really. We can't possibly give out information like that. Confidential, doncha know."

"I'm trying to collect something," said Heller.

"Oh, a bill collector. That's different. Half a mo'. I'll see if we have it on the board."

Heller looked out. Half a dozen cops had off-loaded and were racing around grabbing people, demanding answers.

Cops raced by the phone kiosk.

I blinked! They hadn't looked into the kiosk!

Heller cracked the door slightly. A cop had the dockmaster at bay. "We're looking for the Whiz Kid! If you've seen him, you better (bleep) well report it or we'll run you in as an accomplice!"

The dockmaster was shaking his head. The cop gave him a shove and went off to grab somebody else.

"Are you there? Yes, we have the *Golden Sunset*. She's at anchor off Gardner's Basin, Atlantic City."

Heller thanked him and hung up. And then I blinked!

Heller walked out of the kiosk and up to the dockmaster. He indicated the rows of dry-landed vessels in their chocks. "Are any of those for sale?"

"Usually," said the dockmaster. "With the price of fuel, the amount of use is cut down. It's spring, though, and a lot of owners think that's the time to get a high price. You know boats?"

"Well, not too well," said Heller, "though I was in the Fleet."

"Yeah, well, then you don't want no sailboat. Get you in trouble if you're not experienced." He started to walk down the line of small craft. "There's a trawler type there I know for a fact is for sale. Diesel. Good sea boat. Patterned after the fishermen." They were looking up at a forty-foot cabin cruiser.

"Is it fast?" said Heller.

"Oh, hell no," said the dockmaster. "Who wants a fast boat? Reason you buy them is to get away from things. But you don't look like you're a yacht buyer. You interested for somebody else?"

"A company," said Heller.

"Oh, well. Why fast?"

A cop rushed by.

"Let's just say I like to get away from things fast," said Heller. "What's that one?"

"Why that's a Sea Skiff."

"Skiff?" said Heller. "I thought a 'skiff' was just a little rowboat."

"Oh, well, hell, I don't know why Chriscraft called them that. Most speedboats, you see, do all right on lakes and smooth water. But that one is an oceangoing speedboat. It's thirty-six feet, heavy built to take the pounding of the waves. But look at it. No cabin, just an open cockpit. The bunks, if you can call them that, are up under the foredeck."

"Is it fast?" said Heller.

"Oh, hell, yes. Does forty knots in heavy ocean waves if you can stand the pounding. But your company wouldn't want that."

Heller was looking up at the dry-landed craft. It was heavily tarpaulined but you could see the sleek, almost vicious, lines of it. "Why not?" said Heller, as a cop raced by in front of him.

"Why not? Listen, she's powered with gasoline engines, that's why not. Two Chryster Crowns, huge things. They make her just stand up on her rudders and rocket. Costs a fortune to run."

"I think my company would be interested," said Heller.

"One is born every minute," said the dockmaster. "Hey, Barney! Is this Sea Skiff for sale?"

A rugged-looking sea dog came over. "That Sea Skiff? Hell, yes, it's for sale. The Faustino mob has been trying to offload it since last year. The Corleones sort of drove them off the sea, you know. They used to use it to race out beyond the continental shelf and pick up dope cargos off freighters in it. Has radar, autopilot and even radio controls."

A cop was looking under tarpaulins and into the cockpits of the beached craft.

"How much?" said Heller.

"Oh, Jesus. I don't know," said Barney. "They carry it on their books for twenty thousand, they said. But I think five would take it."

"Could you get it in the water and get it gassed up and running?"

"You *buying* it?" said Barney, incredulous.

Heller was peeling off thousand-dollar bills.

"Jesus," said Barney. He turned and yelled at a workman, "Hey, Fitz! Run the travelift over here and get this Sea Skiff in the water before this guy changes his mind!"

Heller handed five thousand-dollar bills to Barney with another thousand for service, gas and water.

In a casual way, Heller walked over to the phone kiosk. He dialled a number. A girl answered. Heller said, "Tell Izzy she's in Atlantic City aboard the yacht *Golden Sunset*. I'm handling." He hung up. He was about to leave the kiosk when he stopped, door partly open. He put his hand back on the phone.

A cop was walking up to the red cab. He glared at Mortie in the front seat. "We're looking for Wister," snarled the cop, "and you're a lead! You tell me who

your fare up here was or I'll have your hack license
with one short call to city hall! You told us nobody. It
must have been somebody!"

"All right, all right," said Mortie. "That kid over
there is driving for me today. He brought us up here
hoping for a fare. Known him for years. Taught him
how to hack, in fact."

"What's his name?" snarled the cop, glancing
toward the kiosk.

"Clyde Barrow."

The cop took quick steps to a cop car and made a
call. He came back. "He used to be on the most-wanted
list but you're lucky there's no outstanding warrants.
Now you listen to me carefully: we're after Wister. You
keep your eyes open. You see anything of him, you
report it!"

"You mean the Whiz Kid?" said Mortie. "Jesus,
what's he done now?"

"Bigamy, that's what!" said the cop. "Stealin'
cities, robbin' trains. But now he's really done it. Married TWO women!"

"Jesus," said Mortie. "That IS asking for trouble.
That Whiz Kid don't care WHAT he takes on!"

"Shows he's crazy," said the cop. "We also got a
commitment order. So you keep your eyes open!"

Grafferty came up. "You and Sloan," he said to the
cop, "stay here in case he shows up. We coulda been
ahead of him." He walked off and got in his car.

I was the one who thought he was crazy. What
were all these cops doing practically WALKING on
Heller?

I phoned Grafferty's office. "You God (bleeped)
fools!" I said. "He's right there in the phone kiosk!"

The office man hung up on me.

In an agony of suspense, I stuck to the viewer.

Heller was watching the launch of the Sea Skiff. The travelift was a big contraption on wheels that lifted the large craft up into its belly and then rolled over to the dock edge and lowered the vessel into the water.

Workmen swarmed down into the oceangoing speedboat. They opened its engine covers and did things. They lowered in some new batteries. They got the engines going and checked to see if the cooling water was pumping. Then they ran it over to the Octopus Marine fuel float and gave it gas and oil and water.

Heller walked over to Mortie. "How much do you owe in bills?"

"Two G's. I'll never be able to pay off."

"Here's two G's," said Heller, "and another big one for your help today."

"Jesus! You been robbing banks?"

"They think so," said Heller. "Now, take some time off and get your eyes well. So long."

"Wait a minute. I can see well enough to know they put a man-killing boat in the water for you. You're not going out in that, are you?"

"I think so," said Heller.

"Jesus," said Mortie. "You wait right here!" He drove away at a mad rate.

Barney came over. "I checked the safety gear. If the Coast Guard stops you, you got the right foghorns and all that."

Heller said, "You got some charts?"

"Oh, there's a lot of old charts in the forward bunk space, up and down the coast. How far you goin'?"

"Just cruisin' around," said Heller.

"Well, if you're goin' further than a hundred miles,

I better yell over to the float and tell 'em to put extra gas aboard.''

"You do that," said Heller.

A cop walked over, eyeing Heller, the same cop who had talked to Mortie. "Come over here," he said, gesturing.

Heller walked over to him.

"Did you know there was a reward out for the Whiz Kid?" said the cop. "Ten big ones."

"That's not very much," said Heller.

"Well, I agree," said the cop, "considering that he's a notorious outlaw, but it is money. Now look, these (bleepards) around here are playing it dumb. Level with me. You was here when we arrived. Did you see anybody arrive or leave?"

"Not a soul," said Heller.

The cop shook his head in bafflement and looked up and down the dock.

Mortie screeched his cab to a halt in front of the dockmaster office. Heller went over.

"Here," said Mortie. "From me to you. Ten pastrami sandwiches and a special submarine with lots of garlic. And a six-pack of nonalcoholic beer. But that ain't what I went for. Man, will you need this!" He shoved a package into Heller's hands. "Dramamine. Seasick pills, kid. You're a hacker and you don't know what you're getting into. Let me tell you, that sea is dangerous! Waves as tall as the Empire State Building!"

"Gee, thanks," said Heller.

"So long, kid. But get back to something healthy like hacking." Mortie sped away, caroming off a cop car.

Barney was there again. "Who do we make the bill of sale to? The Coast Guard will want to see it."

"Close Shaves, Incorporated," said Heller.

I was going absolutely crazy! These dumb cops had him right in their hands! The whole situation was insane!

Heller was shoving papers in his pocket and climbing down into the oceangoing speedboat, which bobbed as he boarded it. He studied out the controls. A dockhand cast him off.

Heller was standing behind the windshield, sun blazing down upon the chrome controls. One hand was on the wheel. With the other he waved at Barney and the dockmaster and they waved back.

Heller fed some throttle and the Sea Skiff leaped like it was spurred.

Throwing two gigantic plumes of spray, it sped out into the Hudson and banked as it curved away to the south!

The mighty roar of pounding engines lifted the vessel high in the water. It was picking up speed, planing.

HE WAS GETTING AWAY!

Chapter 5

The Coast Guard!

They had mentioned it twice.

Ah, yes! I had the exact way to stop him now. But I needed just a little more data.

Viewed from the speeding craft, seen through a white fan of spray, the skyscrapers were going by like a picket fence.

There was no wind this bright spring day aside

from an occasional cat's paw. The clouds were actually reflected in the blue Hudson!

Heller was fiddling with a control attached by cord to a gyrocompass. He was evidently figuring out what it was and how it worked. It did not take him long.

He put his eye on a centerline behind the wind-shield, sighted past the chock on the foredeck and spotted the Statue of Liberty several miles ahead. He pressed a switch on the autopilot control and, utterly ignoring the crowds of traffic on the river, opened the companionway door that led down under the foredeck.

There were two narrow bunks, a toilet and a minuscule stove and water tap, an area so small you could not stand up in it. He opened a drawer and found a stack of charts. He sorted quickly through them, took two that he wanted and came back to the cockpit.

He checked the autopilot. The Sea Skiff was streaking straight toward the Statue of Liberty, still miles away. He went close under the stern of a big container ship without a second glance.

Typically Heller, he perched himself sideways on the edge of the pilot seat, hooked a foot under a rung and without the least concern for the absolutely jammed traffic on the river, sat comfortably in the warm sun and began to examine the chart.

He was giving me the data I needed.

His finger went close to the Jersey shore, past the Verrazano Narrows Bridge, changed course to Fort Hancock and Sandy Hook, followed the dots of the Intracoastal Waterway as they went through the expanse, wide open to the Atlantic, found the point where it entered sheltered waters at Manasquan Inlet, went down past Silver Bay, traced south through the wide, long waters of Barnegat Bay, past Barnegat

Light, then the rest of the wide inland waterway past
Beach Haven Inlet and then, curving round, to Atlantic
City.

"Well, well," he said. "There we go. About a hundred and eight nautical miles, give or take a few. Right
to Gardner's Basin. And lady love, like it or not, here
I come!"

And here you don't! I said grimly. I had everything
I needed to know. On that chart I had seen—right
across from the Statue of Liberty—Fort Jay, the Coast
Guard station! He would be going close to it!

I called the United States Coast Guard. To the
reception telephonist who answered, I snarled, "Give
me the man who polices New York Harbor, fast!"

Switches clicked. Then a cheerful voice, "Harbor
Traffic Control Tower, Fort Jay. Seaman Second Class
Dicey Bergsom, U.S.C.G., on watch. And what can we
do for you today?"

"You can apprehend a criminal!" I snapped,
offended by his cheery tone. "You see that speedboat
coming down the Hudson?"

"I'll take a look. Oh, yes. I've got it now. It just
changed course a bit, went under the bow of a cruise
liner. Yes, I see the one you mean. Let me get a telescope on it.... Petey, you got a speedboat out there,
about two-eight-four true on your radar. Clock it....
I'm trying to read its numbers, mister. She's moving so
fast she's hard to keep in my field.... Got it! *Sea Skiff
329-478A?* Is that the one, mister?"

"(Bleep) it, yes!"

"Jesus, is that right, Petey? Mister, Petey says
she's clocking 42.3 knots. Man, look at her go!... Hey,
wait a minute. That number is familiar. Petey, ain't
that the old Faustino Sea Skiff?... Yeah, I thought so.

Man, look at her GO! Petey, git your nose out of that radar and eyeball this. . . . You ever see a prettier sight?"

Another voice, "Yowee! Man, would I like to be in that on a beautiful day like this, huh, Dicey?"

"(Bleep) it!" I screamed. "DO something!"

Seaman Second Class Dicey said, "I'm sorry, mister. That's just some guy from the Narcotici mob going out to pick up a load of dope from some foreign freighter off Sandy Hook. Why would the Coast Guard be interested?"

"Arrest him!" I howled.

"There's no speed limit where he is now. He can't be arrested unless he doesn't have a foghorn and I didn't see him throw anything overboard to litter the harbor."

I glared glassy-eyed at my viewer. Heller was going by the Statue of Liberty with a roar. He raised his hand to it just as if he were returning the salute of a raised torch. He was sighting in on the Verrazano Bridge several miles ahead and getting ready to shave the westernmost point of Brooklyn to pass through the Narrows.

I had an inspiration. "It's a stolen boat!"

"Hold on, please," said the guardian of New York Harbor Traffic.

Heller reset his autopilot. He glanced to his left toward the very point I was talking to, Fort Jay.

Seaman Second Class Dicey was back on the phone. "I'm sorry, sir. I just called the Hudson Harbor dockmaster and he said they just sold it to Close Shaves, Incorporated. So it ain't stolen, sir."

"(Bleep) it!" I screamed. "Let me talk to your commanding officer!"

There were a bunch of clicks on the line. Then a very gruff, old voice. "What's all this?"

I said in a deadly voice, "A desperate criminal is escaping in *Sea Skiff 329-478A*."

"Is this Federal?"

"YES!"

"Who am I talking to?"

It was time to take the gloves off, time to roll up the carronades and give them a broadside. I had become wise. And deadly. "Swindle and Crouch, the Rockecenter attorneys," I said.

"Jesus!" Ah, what a satisfactorily shocked voice! "What was that number again?"

"*Sea Skiff 329-478A*. He's heading for Atlantic City via the Intracoastal Waterway!"

"And you want him arrested?"

"Put in leg irons," I said, "and delivered to the New York City Police!"

"Well, it would do no good to send a chopper after him. They don't carry irons."

"Are you going to act," I snarled, "or do I get you court-martialled?"

"Oh, yes, sir, yes sir, we'll act. Just a minute. Hold on!" There was a pause. Then, "The fast patrol craft *81* happens to be patrolling down off Barnegat Light. It can speed north and intercept him. Should be able to make contact well before he can enter Manasquan Inlet. He'll still be in the broad Atlantic and not yet in protected inland waters."

"Is that patrol craft armed?"

"Oh, yes, sir. They carry a forward gun that could blow that Sea Skiff to bits. And the *81* can go a bit faster than the fugitive vessel. I'm sure it can do the job."

"You make (bleeped) sure it does!" I grated.

"Oh, yes, sir! You can depend on the Coast Guard where Rockecenter interests are involved. My name is

Grumper. Captain George C. Grumper, U.S.C.G...."

"Issue the orders!"

"Oh, yes, sir. I'm writing the message right now! 'Sea Skiff 329-478A on southerly course from New York, travelling at 42.3 knots. Intercept before it can enter protected waters at Manasquan Inlet. Arrest the man in it. Put in irons. Deliver to the New York Police. Succeed at any cost. Do not fail.' I am sending this to the 81 with highest operational priority instantly. Will that be all right?"

"Yes," I said. "But you better deliver, Captain Grumper!"

I rang off.

Only then did I permit myself a smile, a very Apparatus smile. Heller was just passing under the Verrazano Narrows Bridge, white spray, blue water and bright, spring sun. Little did he know the trap that had been laid.

He had gotten past or around the police some way I could not fathom.

But I had not mentioned any name of identity to the Coast Guard. They would grab anybody in that boat! And I would make sure, through Dingaling, Chase and Ambo, that that was a grab that would be made to stick!

Heller, admire the gulls as you streak by. This is NOT the day you will see your lady love!

Chapter 6

About an hour later, Heller was well past Sandy Hook and was flashing down the coast of New Jersey with the broad Atlantic to his left. The glassy swells were slight, the scattered white clouds reflected in them. As the sea was on his beam, all it did was make the Sea Skiff rise and fall a bit, rhythmically, as it planed. It did indeed seem to be riding with only its propellers and rudders in the water.

It was on autopilot and Heller had the long-cabled remote control in his pocket. He was walking about the cockpit drinking a nonalcoholic beer and eating a pastrami sandwich, admiring the distant shore and evidently enjoying the sun.

How typically Heller, I thought. I would have been as seasick as a dog and it made me feel queasy just watching him enjoy the day and his lunch.

I began to wonder what had happened to the Coast Guard. And then Heller, looking forward, caught sight of a speck several miles away, dead ahead.

There had been other ships, big freighters and tankers, parallelling the coast. He seemed to detect a difference in this item. I couldn't distinguish it on my screen but evidently he could with his naked eye.

He finished his beer and threw the can into a trash bucket. He stepped up on top of the instrument ledge and over the windshield, standing up on the foredeck, to raise himself a few more feet. He leaned against the wind of passage. He looked intently.

"Hello, hello," he said. "You look like a military craft. And travelling at high speed."

He stepped back over the windshield and dropped to the cockpit. He perched on the edge of the pilot chair. "And now we'll see, Mr. Military Craft, if you have any interest in me."

He hit his autopilot remote and banked the ocean speedboat due east, away from the shore and more than right angles to his former course.

He watched the speck.

"Aha," he said. "An intercept!"

Baffled, I wondered how he knew and then I realized that the Coast Guarder had promptly changed course when Heller turned.

"Now, how fast are you?" said Heller. He watched it intently. Then, having somehow worked it out, he said, "Doing about 3 percent more speed than I am. That's bad."

He shifted his course a bit more southerly. The speck became a mast and bridge that even I could see. The vessel had a single large gun in the bow. It was manned!

"Well, nothing like finding out," said Heller.

He banked the speedboat in a steep turn of flying white spray. He sighted across his bow chock and began to close the distance!

He reached down through the companionway hatch and threw the switches of his radio on. He spun a dial.

"*Sea Skiff 329-478A!*" the radio crackled above the engine roar, "lie to! We will come alongside!" The message was repeating over and over.

The interval between the ships was closing at blinding speed.

Heller hit the remote. The Sea Skiff banked into a foam-flying 180-degree turn. He brought it on its new course, going straight away from the Coast Guarder.

A flash from the bow!

A GEYSER OF SALT WATER DEAD AHEAD OF HELLER!

BLAM!

The sound of the shot reverberated like a single beat of a bass drum.

The Sea Skiff tore through the geyser made by the projectile.

"That's all I wanted to know," said Heller.

He hit the throttles a clip, closing them. The Sea Skiff sagged out of its plane.

Heller was diving into the bag that Izzy had brought. He came up with a Voltar handgun!

His thumb spun its control dial.

I thought, my Gods, I didn't know he was armed!

His eye was trained across the handgun sights. A finger was spinning another dial.

The Coast Guarder was about two hundred yards away. It killed its speed. The gunsights passed over the bridge, then centered on the black, round hole of the forward deck gun muzzle. At the instant that circle passed the sight, Heller hit another button. The handgun swung back.

BAM!

Heller had fired!

For an instant I thought hopefully he must have missed. Nothing flew apart on the Coast Guarder. It didn't blow up. It swerved to the south as it slowed.

Then suddenly the two-man gun crew leaped away from their naval piece, screaming!

THEIR GUN BREACH WAS MELTING!

Heller had fired a heat shot, centered by handgun computer, down the barrel of the thing!

"Now that the odds are more equal," said Heller, "we can get back at it." And he slammed his throttles wide open!

He sent the Sea Skiff toward the shore, glancing back to see what the Coast Guarder would do.

His radio was still on. It began to crackle. The Coast Guarder was calling his base.

"Can't have that," said Heller.

He raised and centered the handgun. He twirled a knob.

BAM!

The handgun fired.

The big whip aerials of the patrol craft shimmered and melted!

Heller aimed the handgun at the patrol-craft bridge. The Coast Guarder was getting underway in pursuit.

"Blast," said Heller. "I don't want to kill you guys. You're Fleet."

It was the kind of insane gallantry you could count upon from Heller. I felt now that we still had a chance to get him.

He shoved the handgun into his belt. He grabbed the sack Izzy had given him and got something out of it. Then he reached under the foredeck and grabbed an Aldis signal lamp.

The Coast Guarder was streaming after him. Heller raised the Aldis lamp. He centered it on the *81*'s bridge. He began to send a single letter over and over.

A dot and a dash. Ah, International Code. That letter must mean something like "You're running into danger."

The Coast Guarder did not slacken its chase. White fans of spray flying, it was roaring after Heller. But through the Aldis sights, the men on its bridge could be seen coming out and training glasses on Heller, peering. Then a couple of men with rifles raced up to its bow. One of them fired!

Heller spelled out audibly, "Y-O-U-R E-N-G-I-N-E-S A-R-E A-B-O-U-T T-O B-L-O-W U-P."

Sudden racings about on the other ship!

Three men sprang up out of an afterhatch and raced forward.

"Now that you're all in sight..." muttered Heller. And he put a small box device on top of the Aldis lamp and pressed its trigger.

There was no sound. There was no flash.

ALL THE MEN ON THE COAST GUARDER DECK COLLAPSED!

He had said he wasn't going to kill them and then it appeared that he had!

Heller glanced at his device as he shut it off. Suddenly I knew it: a radio nerve-paralysis beam!

He looked forward.

The shore of New Jersey was dead ahead and coming up fast!

"Oh, you blasted fools!" he muttered. "You left your engines running! You're going to have a marine disaster!"

He threw down the Aldis lamp.

He was grabbing some twine out of his pocket. He wrapped it around his throttles.

Both ships were tearing straight at the beach!

Moving fast, Heller flipped some fenders that were tied along the coaming so that they fell outside. He grabbed the throttle strings he had fixed.

He worked the autopilot. The speedboat banked in a wide curve.

The Coast Guarder was streaking straight at the beach at forty knots!

Heller timed it. He was just ahead of the fast patrol craft and to its port. It overtook him.

He swerved the Sea Skiff slightly.

The suction that occurs between two ships brought them together side-by-side with a crunch.

Heller leaped up and grabbed the patrol-craft rail. He hit the autopilot switch and yanked the strings.

The Sea Skiff swerved away, engines suddenly silent.

Heller sprang over the rail. He jumped across the reclining bodies.

He stared ahead.

The beach was almost there!

He leaped into the pilothouse. He looked at the controls. He yanked a pair of levers back.

There was a racing whine and then a crunch.

He spun the wheel.

He had reversed the propellers at full speed!

Forward way had carried them into light green water.

Sand was boiling up.

There was a thump and scrape.

And then the Coast Guarder was backing into darker, deeper sea.

He looked out on the deck where a man with a lot of chevrons on his jacket was lying draped over a bitt.

Peevishly, Heller said, "You're supposed to SAVE people, not GET saved."

Chapter 7

I wondered what he would do now. The Apparatus would never have acted this way so I was totally adrift. He should have left the *81* to explode itself to bits against the beach and gone happily on his way. There is no understanding these Fleet people!

My next guess was that he would take her out into deeper water and sink her with all hands. Maybe he thought that would destroy the evidence. There were houses along the Jersey shore here. Maybe he didn't want witnesses.

As soon as I found out what he was going to do, I could call Captain Grumper and let him organize other effective steps to handle.

Heller got the *81* well clear and then, at slow speed, went back to the drifting Sea Skiff. He coasted the patrol craft alongside. He got a line and fastened it on the foredeck chock of the Sea Skiff and then passed it aft on the Coast Guarder and made it fast to the towing bitts.

Then he came back to the *81* forward deck.

One by one, he dragged the unconscious crew into the salon. He went back and collected the rifles and a couple of caps and then threw them in.

He looked at the gun breach. It surely was melted.

It was still hot and smoking. He found a CO_2 extinguisher and sprayed it, probably to cool it off. Then he picked up its canvas cover and lashed it in place, probably to obscure the odd damage.

Next he looked at what was left of the aerials: just puddles of melted metal. Methodically he scraped up the silvery blobs and threw them overboard.

He got his sack and took out a pair of cutters and neated up the aerial stubs so they looked sheared, not melted.

That done, he affixed a short piece of wire to one of the stubs and left it dangling.

He went into a ship office and started going through bookcases. He found a manual which gave the uniforms and ship complements of the Coast Guard.

He went back up to the salon and gazed at the recumbent bodies which lay upon the floor.

Apparently satisfied, he went below and started going through quarters and lockers. He located the uniforms of the most senior man aboard and changed his clothes.

He went back up to the bridge.

He eased the throttles forward and soon, towing the Sea Skiff, had the *81* going down the coast at a leisurely pace. He put it on autopilot.

He went to the radio and turned its volume high. Sure enough, there was a constant chatter, rather faint due to the lack of much aerial, calling for the *81* to come in.

Heller picked up the mike. He acknowledged.

A voice from the speaker, "What's wrong? We couldn't raise you!"

"We had a little mishap," said Heller.

"You're coming in only Signal Three here. I can barely hear you."

Heller yelled into the mike, spacing his words distinctly. "We had a little mishap to radio and engines. Nothing serious. Everybody is a bit flaked out. The capture was successful. We are proceeding down the coast at reduced speed." He began to imitate a fade-out with his voice. "Radio is packing up. See you tomorrow afternoon. . . ."

"Repeat last sentence, please."

Heller put down the mike and went back to gaze at the beautiful day.

It was probably his attitude, probably the way he propped his elbow on a radar and cupped his chin in his palm. Heller can drive anybody absolutely insane with things like that!

I went crazy. I phoned Captain Grumper.

"What's wrong now?" he said.

It was on the tip of my tongue to scream that an extraterrestrial had just seized his fast patrol craft. I checked myself in time. It would sound odd.

"The man," I said, "that you were supposed to capture has TAKEN OVER THE *81!*"

"Oh, I think not," said Grumper. "We've just had a message here that after a brave sea battle, fully commensurate with the exacting standards of the Coast Guard, the capture was made."

"You haven't got the full story!" I snarled.

"Well, they did have some trouble. Engines and radio. But it's all handled."

"You're not in communication with that craft!"

"Well, as I said, they had radio trouble."

"Why is he heading south instead of north?"

"Oh, is he?" said Grumper. Then, after a moment, "But his base is to the south."

"Listen, Grumper, if you value your commission, you had better send out ships and planes and recover your craft!"

"Yes, sir! At once, sir!"

I rang off. I had jarred them out of their complacency. What riffraff! Letting an extraterrestrial Royal officer walk right in and grab off one of their ships!

It made me pretty angry, I can tell you, having to sit there and watch Heller's view.

He seemed to find the sea gulls interesting.

Then he YAWNED!

He finally got busy. He checked the chart and some landmarks. He was going right on by Manasquan Inlet. He wasn't going to go into the Intracoastal Waterway where it went inland! He was just continuing on down the coast in the broad Atlantic! He was even edging further and further from the shore. You couldn't make out the houses now.

He got interested in the radio log. He found the message directing them to intercept him.

"Hmm," he said. "Strong language."

He looked over the ship's log, noting the time they had first sighted him and then the sketchy entries of the chase. These ceased abruptly with the notation of his Aldis lamp message to them about their engines.

Heller got his sack and looked through it. He took out a small vial. With great care he eradicated all the entries from the moment of first sighting on.

He got a scrap of paper and practiced calligraphy from earlier entries.

Then, instead of "Sighted *Sea Skiff 329-478A*," he wrote, "Sighted appalling sea monster—orange wings, purple horns, flaming breath, 300 feet in length. Speaks Scandinavian."

He made the next entry, "Giving chase. Sea monster travelling at 48 knots."

Then he wrote, "Sea monster has turned on ship. Demanding coffee." Then, with appropriate times, "Has now boarded over bow." "Is melting cannon with flaming breath." "Ate antennas." "Crew fainted, all except me. Good-bye, cruel world."

A roar of engines sounded in the sky.

Heller glanced out.

Three choppers were swiftly overtaking the slow-moving patrol craft.

One in the lead dived close.

Heller put his arm out of the pilothouse and waved.

THE THREE CHOPPERS WENT AWAY!

Raging, I got on to Grumper. "You're being hood-winked!" I screamed. "That patrol craft is in enemy hands!"

"Oh, come now," said Grumper. "It's as I said. We have the Sea Skiff in tow. And one of the pilots even recognized the chief petty officer that is captain of the craft. Chief Jive, one of the most able blacks we have in service. Please, Mr. Swindle and Crouch, can't you let us get back to our normal duties? The Coast Guard's work is efficient beyond reproach."

The phone dropped out of my hand.

I sat there, stricken.

At first I had thought that the cops hadn't recognized Heller at Hudson Harbor because they had all seen the Whiz Kid on TV and thought they were looking for buckteeth and glasses. And now the truth dawned. He'd done it in the Stockbroker's Bar!

(Bleep) Spurk! With this rig, you couldn't see the

man's own face! Heller had used the same trick he had played in Connecticut! As he was wearing black cotton gloves, I hadn't seen his hands and neither had anyone else.

I watched with great care. And I confirmed it in the pilothouse window reflection at last. Heller was black-faced! And blacks all look alike to whites. No wonder the day had looked so beautifully hazeless! He was wearing tan contact lenses!

(Bleep) Heller! How can you keep up with such a man!

I did the only thing I could do, then. I phoned the harbor master at Atlantic City. I told him, "I am a Fed. I have to advise you that an attempt will be made to board and blow up the *Golden Sunset* sometime later today or tonight."

"Good Christ!" he said. "Blowing up a ship that size would make a harbor obstruction!" He was horrified.

"Precisely," I said. "So alert the ship and put her under arms. Don't let any vessels approach her, particularly the Coast Guard."

"Coast Guard?" he said. "Why not?"

"They're not all they're cracked up to be," I said. "They lose ships right and left and won't listen. But here is the important part: the saboteur is a black man, the most evil and deceptive (bleepard) anyone ever saw. If you catch a glimpse of him, don't even challenge. Just shoot on sight."

He promised faithfully he would.

PART FIFTY

Chapter 1

The afternoon was waning and I could see, as Heller looked at a chart and spotted his position, that he must be doing only ten knots or less and that it would be hours before he came abreast of Atlantic City.

It was just as well. The girls were home as I could hear. Quite a hubbub. They were not alone.

Presently Pinchy or Adora or Mrs. Sultan Bey—or whatever the Hells her name was now—came to my door and peered in. "You can watch TV later," she said. "Come on, you (bleepard), and do your husbandly duties!"

Very mindful they could have me arrested for bigamy and thrown in the clink if I did not please, I put on a robe, patted my face plaster so the edges would not lift, and went out.

Two lesbians were there. Mike, a somewhat sallow woman of thirty-five, dressed in very mannish clothes, was smoking a joint in a long holder and swinging her leg as she sat on the arm of a chair. She was not bad-looking really, though awfully tall. Mildred, the other one, might have been twenty-five: she had a rosy complexion, was soft and round and quite pretty. She was eyeing me with a speculative smile. Neither one of them looked like they were going to perish during the reeducation into sex and I started to feel better.

And then I saw the other one! She was standing back of Candy in a corner. TEENIE! What the Hells was she doing back here?

I said to Adora, "WHAT THE HELLS IS SHE DOING BACK HERE?"

"Oh, pish, pish and tush, tush," said Adora. "She felt she didn't have it right. As an adult, dear husband, one has certain responsibilities, as you should learn. These consist of making sure the young are properly educated. How would you feel if you let her grow up to womanhood with totally wrong conceptions and conditionings in the field of sex?"

"I'd feel great!" I said, eyeing this bony, scrawny specimen with her proclivity for sinking nails in faces at the slightest (bleep).

"Well, that may be, dear husband," said Adora, "but Teenie is an opportunity. During her slack time in licking stamps for Rockecenter's office, who knows? He might proposition her and (bleep) her on his desk when Miss Peace isn't looking. And if Teenie knew her business and Rockie had a real (bleep), it might cure him of this God (bleeped) determination to push Psychiatric Birth Control. So it is of vital necessity that we educate the young, whatever you may think. Besides, she's just here to watch and take pictures so she can develop the knack."

"Ignore me," said Teenie, her huge hazel eyes entreating. "I promise to be very quiet and very good. I love spectator sports but I won't even cheer. I promise."

There was no arguing with five women. I opened my robe and Mike, the tall one, went kind of white. "Jesus!" she said.

Right away the others saw she was going to pull a last minute sales rejection and say she did not want the item after all. They grabbed her. They pulled off her oxfords. They turned her upside down and shucked her out of her pants. Her shirt went flying through the air, followed by her very masculine BVDs. Her breast compressor hit the wastebasket. "After tonight," Adora told her, "you won't want that again, ever."

Adora got behind me and gave a mighty shove. "Have at her, dear husband."

The clamshell top of the bed vibrated and Candy hastily grabbed it as it shook, preventing it from falling down.

Mike's face, close under me, showed wonder as she said, "Oh, it isn't a falsie after all! Oh, you're wonderful!"

Here was appreciation! She was . . .

FLASH!

For an instant I thought we had been hit with spaceship landing-preparation blueflash and got all ready to go unconscious. I didn't. I stared around.

Teenie! That Gods (bleeped) kid had a flash camera! She had just taken a picture.

To Hells with her. With determination I got back at it.

Adora was smiling indulgently as Mike crooned, "Oh, you honey baby!"

Mildred was bobbing her head in expectant rhythm as Mike cried, voice throbbing with passion, "I have never, never, never felt anything so wonderful. A real MAN!"

I grinned with the compliment and concentrated as she moaned.

FLASH!

There it was again! Gods (bleep) it, it took my mind off it utterly!

I gritted my teeth. I got going again.

Teenie was struggling with her camera.

I kept one eye on her. I must beat her to the draw!

The whole bed quaked and the clamshell top tried to come down but Candy grabbed and held it.

I rested for a moment, panting, and then gave Teenie a sneer. I'd beaten her!

Adora was in there with her usual pitch as soon as Mike had come around. And Mike said, yes, oh, yes indeed! Emphatically! That was the end of biting and scratching. And using Polish sausages for dildos.

Now it was Mildred's turn. But frankly, I felt sort of under a strain. Nerves.

Candy was very nice. She took me into the shower and turned it on and it did help a little. A few minutes later I came back. Mildred was lying on the bed, sheet held up under her chin, looking at me speculatively.

Teenie was having trouble with her camera. Adora was fixing it for her. My restored ardor deflated.

"No more of that!" I said angrily. "Send her home and right now, at once!"

"But her education," said Adora.

"I don't give a (bleep) if she's a dropout," I said. "Get her out of here!"

"Oh, pish, pish and tush, tush," said Adora. "You have no feeling for the young."

But I was having trouble. Adora got a joint. She shoved it into my mouth and lit it. I took a puff. She hit me in the stomach and I exhaled violently. She jammed the joint into my mouth and when I pulled my breath back in, a whole city of smog came with it. I coughed but the stuff was in my lungs. The walls began to recede and draw near.

Adora sat me down and got me to smoking quietly.

Mike stumbled over and sat down beside me. Her

eyes were filled with wonder as she petted my shoulder. It did marvelous things for my morale and I began to take confidence.

Adora gave me a persuasive pull toward the bed.

Mildred watched me approach, expectantly.

Candy made sure the bed-top shell was hooked more solidly to the wall but it had already begun to move. She looked down at the bed appreciatively.

Mike smiled as she watched in dreamy knowingness as the moans started up.

FLASH!

I came straight off the bed!

It took me a moment to see again that it was not a spaceship landing.

Teenie's oversize lips were smiling sweetly. "That was a good one," she said. "She looked just like she was dying!"

"Kill this kid," I said bitterly to Adora.

"Oh, why should you be upset with a little thing like that? After all, it was only the artistry in the girl. Education and art go hand in hand. She saw something she wanted and she took it."

"I'm going to kill her," I said.

Adora got me back on the sofa. She lit another joint. Candy found some champagne. I drank it between puffs and started to calm down.

Mildred was threshing around, moaning on the bed.

"Not one more picture!" I said.

"I won't do it again," said Teenie.

Soothingly, Adora led me back toward the bed.

Candy was steadying the top of the clamshell as it began to move once more.

Mike, still in dreamy appreciation, began to bob her head in rhythm as she watched.

I was gritting my teeth with effort.

Candy hastily grabbed the top of the bed as a seeming earthquake threatened to collapse it.

I sat up triumphantly with a sneer at Teenie. In spite of her I had made it!

When Mildred came around, Adora was in there with her sales pitch. There was no sales resistance. "Men, men, men," whispered Mildred. "Give me *men* every time!" It was a pretty good testimonial. She was lying there dreamy-eyed and purring like a cat.

Candy gave me another glass of champagne and I raised it as a toast to myself. I was swallowing the bubbly brew and had half a glass to go when I heard a voice.

"Now Teenie wants some more pictures."

When I was through coughing and wheezing and trying to get the champagne out of my lungs, I hoarsed, "Where did you put the duelling pistols? I am going to kill that kid!"

Adora said, "Look at that poor child! You have frightened her half to death!" And then she put her face close to my ear and said in a deadly voice, "You're going to do what you're told, bigamist."

I said weakly, "But there's nothing else to take pictures of! The two girls are satisfied."

"I need demonstration shots," said Teenie. "How can I do my homework without accurate and detailed examples? If I have nothing to study, I won't make it at all!"

"You hear?" said Adora to me. "Just tell us what you want, Teenie."

"Well, ice skaters have to have pictures of themselves to perfect their technique. You said so yourself, Pinchy. I don't have those pictures yet."

"Of course," said Adora indulgently.

"Could you operate the camera?" said Teenie, parking her bubble gum on the head of an Aphrodite statuette.

"Of course," said Adora. And she accepted it. "Now what do you want exactly?"

Instantly, Teenie's dress flew through the air.

I was still sitting on the sofa.

She came over and stood in front of me. She looked down critically at me and shook her head. "This will never do," she said.

Teenie turned to Adora.

"What we need is some music," said Teenie. "I have just bought the latest Neo Punk Rock record by the Naughty Boys. It's right here in my purse. Do you mind if I play it?"

She would have put the 45 straight onto the stereo but I took it from her hand. Anything to do with Teenie was pretty deadly stuff. One had to be cautious. The label said:

NEO PUNK ROCK
MORAL
For Grade-school Kiddies
International Psychological
Association Approved
Educational Ditty
The Naughty Boys:
Biffer, Poker, Slider and Wowie.

Oh, well, Hells, it was just some childish gibberish and if the psychologists approved it, it must be quite all right. "Go ahead," I said.

She expertly set the stereo on 45 rpm and fixed it so the record would repeat over and over. She turned the volume high and around it went. The needle came down.

Six crashing tom-tom beats followed by three thundering tympani strokes. *POW, POW, POW, POW, POW, POW! BOOM, BOOM, BOOM!* And then it repeated. And then it kept right on repeating! Forceful, compelling, savage, primitive!

All the people in the room began to jerk in rhythm to those drums. Teenie was wide-eyed, beating time with her hips and heels.

Then the whine and moan of electronic instruments. Then a chorale like a tribal chant:

> *Freddie was a jumper!*
> *Jump, jump, jump!*
> *Freddie was a jumper!*
> *Pump, pump, pump!*
> *Freddie jumped his teacher!*
> *Pump, pump, pump!*
> *Freddie jumped his sister!*
> *Pump, pump, pump!*
> *Freddie jumped his brother!*
> *Pump, pump, pump!*
> *Freddie jumped his papa!*
> *Pump, pump, pump!*
> *Freddie jumped his mama!*
> *Pump, pump, pump!*
> *Freddie jumped a ROBOT!*
> *Oh, my God!*
> *Poor, poor Freddie,*
> *Hasn't got a rod!*

And then in a perfectly normal voice at the end it said: *So that's the moral, little kiddies. Don't never (bleep) robots!*

The women in the room had almost had (bleeps)

from the rhythm. I thought I had read the label wrong.
I leaped up and snatched it from the turntable before it
could repeat. Yes, it was approved by the International
Psychological Association and its title was "Moral."

Teenie snatched it out of my hands. She put it back
on the turntable. It started up again, *POW, POW, POW,
POW, POW, POW! BOOM, BOOM, BOOM!*

She got into the rhythm of it. "Ain't it dreamy?" she
said with a beatific smile that made her oversize mouth
look like a hungry cavern. She looked to see if Adora was
ready. Then she turned to me, "Come on, cowboy, let's
get into the first pose!"

She reached out and yanked me to my feet so fast my
robe flew out behind me.

She bent back and looked at me with an astonished
expression on her face. She snapped her fingernails.

FLASH!

Adora had the picture.

Teenie made a grab for me.

I hastily tried to bat her hands away and disengage.

FLASH!

It was strange: stamped on my retina was a look of
awe upon her face.

But right now, there was anything but awe in Teenie. She was stamping her heels to the music. I was reassured because I thought it was distracting her.

But no!

She suddenly grabbed the lapels of my robe, making
it fly wide.

I tried to seize her wrists to get her off me. But she
had the flat of her hands against my chest and was pushing ME away.

FLASH!

A look of horror was stamped on my retina. But it wasn't there now.

The music was going and pounding. Her body writhed against mine, bruising me. The marijuana and music were spinning in my head.

Teenie suddenly dropped to her knees.

I hastily grabbed at her shoulders to make her stand up.

FLASH!

She then stood up but was I surprised!

She slapped me.

Right in the face!

A deadly insult! An invitation to a duel!

Oh, that was too much to take from this teen-age kid! I wanted to kill her!

She tried to escape me but the back of her knees hit the bed.

FLASH!

The look of fear that was momentarily branded on my retina was not put on—of that I was very sure.

Killing her would be a pleasure!

She whirled around and tried to escape by climbing on the bed.

I seized her ponytail.

She backed up! Against me!

FLASH!

I made my hand flat to give her behind a powerful swat. "I'll teach you to insult me!" I snarled.

But Teenie was laughing!

Teenie turned over on her back and began to hold her sides with mirth.

Adora was laughing.

Candy was laughing.

Mike and Mildred were laughing.

I could not for the life of me figure out what they were laughing at.

I stamped off to my room and slammed the door.

I went to bed and glowered into the dark.

Blasted teen-age monstrosity!

To HELLS with her education!

I could still hear them guffawing in the other room.

Oh, I said, as I gnawed my pillow, when Lombar was finally through with this planet and needed it no more, what a pleasure it would be to blow it up. Especially with Teenie in the middle of the cataclysm. It couldn't be too soon!

Chapter 2

Exhausted by my evening's work and rage, assisted by the marijuana and champagne, I fell into a restless nap, only to be awakened by a nightmare in which, no matter how hard I tried, I couldn't get the fuse lit that would explode Earth.

Trying to look at my watch told me two things: I had a terrible pain in my skull and it was 8:00 P.M.

There were no sounds coming from the front room. They had obviously gone out to dinner and a show as they often did.

I took a cold shower, trying to get rid of the headache. It didn't work. But it suddenly brought me alert enough to realize I was neglecting the real reason I had to endure all this travail: Heller!

Cursing the man for now even sicking teen-agers on

me, I towelled off quickly and uncovered the viewers. Krak's was still blank, Crobe's was no interest. But Heller's was another thing. It was dim but unmistakable: he was still at sea.

I blew out a sigh of relief. I was in time to watch him being blown to bits as he tried to land at Atlantic City. And what a joy THAT would be after all the trouble he had caused me!

The night was a flat calm. There was a glow against the sky which must be Atlantic City. The patrol craft was dead in the water. He was preparing to go in!

Oh, I knew I could count on the harbor master: they don't like blown-up ships clogging their channels. Heller, I said, you are going to catch it good this time and I hope to the Gods that Lombar has removed your Grand Council contact, for tonight, now, you could get your head blown off. And a pleasure it will be to see it done!

He verified that the running lights of the patrol craft were burning bright. Then he went to a chart table and laid out a chart that showed the East Coast of the U.S. and the Atlantic past Bermuda. He looked into a Coast Pilot and found the Devil's Triangle. It said it was an area south of Bermuda where ships had been known to disappear from causes never established. He then spotted this area with a pencil point on the chart and drew a line to it and read the course from where he was, off Atlantic City, to the Devil's Triangle. He couldn't get it very exact, apparently, for he drew in a bunch of question marks on the chart.

He then went to the pilothouse controls and put the engines back in gear, slow ahead. With the wheel, he brought the craft to the course he had just found and then locked the autopilot in.

Heller turned to the log and, imitating the calligraphy, wrote, "2012 hrs. Sea Monster has told us where to solve mystery in the Devil's Triangle. Following him at his standard cruising speed, Course 152° T. Will report revelations after he has had coffee."

He then went into the salon, checked each of the crew lying there and arranged the unconscious bodies so they were comfortable.

Heller said to them in general, "When you boys wake up and find yourselves where you will be, I hope, amongst you, you can also find a great way to explain your whereabouts to your Coast Guard superiors. I've left you one and, who knows, after the spot they put you in, they might even buy it. I'm leaving now. Don't bother to pipe the side." He turned out the light and closed the door.

He went to the rail, climbed over it and dropped into the Sea Skiff which was towing alongside. He started its engines, checked the water pumps for cooling and then, with the slash of a knife, cut the taut towline and was almost at once bobbing back in the patrol craft's wake.

He looked toward the lights of Atlantic City, a hazy dome of dim whitish blue in the blackness. He said, "Now we'll try to land once more on this hostile coast and see what the natives have cooked up this time. No cannibals, I hope."

I blinked. Had he guessed the trap that had been laid for him? Then I relaxed. Typically Heller. He was referring to the Verrazano plaque he had read that morning. You could never tell when he was joking. It was a disconcerting trait, typical of the villain. Threw you off. He had owned the place once: he knew very well that,

aside from Federal tax collectors, there were no cannibals in Atlantic City.

He fed throttle to the Sea Skiff, heading for a point
to the north of the glow in the night. As he picked up
speed and the Sea Skiff planed, the fans of spray cast a
glow of their own—phosphorescence.

I grabbed a map. Judging from the position of Atlantic City's lights off his port bow, he was not heading for
the harbor entrance, Absecon Inlet. He must be going
for Little Egg Inlet, ten miles to the north. Then I realized that he was not taking a frontal approach to the
harbor. He was going to join the Intracoastal Waterway,
go down Little Bay and Reed's Bay back of Brigantine
Beach! He was going to enter Absecon Bay by the back
door!

Sneaky! Oh, you could never trust Heller! (Bleep)
him! With what bitterness I recalled all he had put me
through when I had had to leave Istanbul by sea.

I phoned the harbor master at Atlantic City. "This
is the Fed. Your man is in a Sea Skiff, travelling at 42.3
knots. He will be coming down the Intracoastal Waterway and will approach through Absecon Bay."

"Aha!" said the harbor master. "That means he'll
come down Absecon Channel to get to the yacht! We'll
muster at Farley State Marina."

"Be sure to get him!" I said. "He's a very desperate
black terrorist, trained by the PLO."

"Have no fear," said the harbor master. "We've sup-
plemented the regular force with a squad from the New
Jersey National Guard. We'll let him have it with machine guns!"

"Have you alerted the yacht?"

"Got her surrounded by collision floats in case this
(bleep) tries a kamikaze."

"Good thinking," I said. "I estimate he'll be amongst you in half an hour."

"In half an hour," said the harbor master, "your man will be blown to bits!"

"Knew I could count on you," I said. "The national interest must be served." I rang off.

Heller was streaming along over the black, glassy water. There was a little radarscope back of the gyrocompass and he was apparently steering by that. The shapes of land were very clear on it and he was rocketing straight into a black gap. Tricky navigation at very high speed: those inland channels looked complex.

He was doing something else! I couldn't quite make it out in the dim glow around him. Was he holding a bomb? I watched.

A can of beer!

He was drinking a can of beer!

Oho, I thought. You don't suspect. Far too sure of yourself, Heller, much too relaxed.

I watched him as he banked into a constricted channel, speeding south. There were some marker lights. He didn't seem to be paying much attention to them. Then I realized that that Sea Skiff, with only its propellers and rudders in the water, probably did not much care about the depth of the channel. He was taking short cuts! Running by land masses, not buoys! He had me lost!

I studied my map anxiously. I wished I could read a radarscope. I saw a restricted place ahead of him. He was roaring toward it. I relaxed: it could only be the opening which carried him into Absecon Channel—the islands to the right and left were so long that he could not detour around them. In only a mile or so now he would reach Brigantine Bridge. There were its lights ahead! Right where they invisibly waited for him with machine guns!

He was doing something else now. He was propping something up in the pilot seat.

"Now you just sit there," he said, "and keep your eye on things."

A shape. A form! Good Gods, had he taken one of those luckless Coast Guardsmen prisoner? And making him run the boat?

Then Heller put the arms on the wheel and tied them with a flip of cord. The arms were too limp to be human.

A dummy! A work suit stuffed with pillows that had a pillow face.

Heller walked to the back of the Sea Skiff. He picked up a big sack.

He pulled something down over his face.

He rolled off the stern!

Right into the churning wake!

SPLASH!

He bobbed up.

He had something in his hand, hard to tell, silhouetted against the lights of the distant town. It was wrapped in plastic.

He pressed it.

The Sea Skiff banked!

He pressed it again, watching the spray of the roaring craft.

The Sea Skiff banked the other way!

A radio control! (Bleep) him! He had rigged the autopilot to the craft's radio the moment I had my back turned. He was holding some sort of trigger in his hand!

The Sea Skiff was closing the distance to the bridge very quickly now. He made it zigzag.

A CHATTERING BURST OF MACHINE-GUN FIRE!

"I thought so," muttered Heller.

He pressed the control. The Sea Skiff banked into a steep turn.

Rifles were going now!

A ricochet came skipping over the water and made a vicious whine past his head.

The Sea Skiff headed to his right.

"I'm sorry," said Heller. "You were a good boat."

The Sea Skiff turned again. It passed under the bridge and was racing toward a nearby marina entrance.

The sharp staccato hammer of machine guns above the roar of engines.

The crash of a shattered windshield!

The vicious multiple whines of ricochets!

A heavier burst of fire!

Still surging toward the marina docks, the Sea Skiff seemed to stagger. Then it went lancing on!

A gout of flame!

The blue-white flash of exploding gasoline!

All the extra fuel cans must have gone up as one!

BLOWIE!

The remains of the rocketing speedboat hit the end of a pier!

CRRRRASHHHHH!

Wood and bits of metal flew into the flame-rent air!

What seemed to be a body was visible for an instant and then was gone!

Flaming bits of debris were spattering all around, hissing as they hit.

The end of a dock was burning and lighting up the scene.

A searchlight came on and raked the water.

Heller dived.

I was instantly on the phone. I demanded the harbor master. There was a wait. He came on the line.

"You missed him!" I shouted. "He escaped off the back of the boat before you fired!"

"Nonsense," said the harbor master. "The boat was under control and seeking to avoid us."

"He had a radio control!" I yelled. "He's still out there in the harbor."

"You bet he is," the harbor master said. "In bits and pieces. I saw him fly through the air myself and explode to nothing!"

"That was a dummy!"

"I know a live man when I see one that is dead!" said the harbor master. "We got him! Are you Feds trying to take away the credit?"

"No, no! The credit is all yours! But mind what I say. He's still alive. He will still try. You search that harbor and if you find him, kill him. It's a Federal order!"

"All right," he said and rang off.

I was fuming. How could Heller have known? Then I recalled that he had read the message sent by Captain Grumper of the Coast Guard and might have suspected it had gone to all points.

(Bleep) Heller! Him and his can of beer!

Chapter 3

Haggardly, I watched to see what would happen next.

All I got for two solid hours was an occasional slop of water and a bubble's-eye view of the harbor.

They had a workboat under searchlights recovering debris. But that was not important. They also had a patrol launch cruising around, sweeping the water with long beam fingers.

I couldn't really make out where Heller was. At length when he lifted his arm, I saw that he was wearing a wet suit. I cursed. He had had a whole afternoon and all the resources he could loot from the Coast Guard ship to prepare his entrance. He was operating in a practiced role, that of the Fleet combat engineer, an officer with a fifty-volunteer star. But he was in very hostile waters and I doubted if ever before he had had as accurate a spy device on him as I had placed: this very viewer system.

I called the harbor master twice more, telling him I knew for sure the man was in the water and would be making for the yacht. He said he was taking every precaution.

Then suddenly I got a clear view of the ship. The *Golden Sunset* was lying to anchor, well away from everything else. My, she looked big—like a liner.

Floating stages were all around her, secured to her by cables. On her starboard side, her own landing ladder and white side were bathed in her own floodlights.

The view vanished and I had only blackness.

Then suddenly another view: her bow loomed up like a knife. Then it was gone.

If I could just determine exactly where he would be, I could alert them!

Another view. The ship seemed far away. She was broadside on and the landing stage and floodlights were glaring beyond the black expanse.

Excitedly, I called the harbor master. "He's about a hundred yards abeam of the ship on her starboard side!"

"Got it!" he said and slammed the receiver down.

And he certainly did! I heard the approaching pulse of engines almost immediately. The harbor master, bless him, must be in radio contact with his patrol launch.

A brief view of the launch, coming head on at speed, directly toward Heller!

Then blackness in the viewer.

I waited, breathless. A minute, two minutes, three minutes . . .

Another view! He was directly astern! About fifty yards from the yacht! The scroll, *Golden Sunset, New York*, was plain in the shimmery harbor lights.

I got the harbor master again. "He's fifty yards astern of the yacht! GET HIM!"

"Right!" barked the harbor master.

The view was gone. But engines began to churn in the audio, getting louder.

A water-washed glimpse of the patrol launch showed. It was coming straight at him!

Blackness. One minute, two minutes, three minutes. I was holding my breath. Four minutes, five minutes . . . What the Hells was going on?

Dizzy and lightheaded from not breathing, I shook my head to clear it. My viewer was just staying black!

Scuba gear! He must be using scuba, taken from the *81!* Yes, there was the hollow, rhythmical sound I had ignored. But where was he?

Time passed.

Then I thought I saw something. I could not be sure. It was just blackness against black.

I turned up the viewer gain all I could. Yes! An underwater piling! Heller was underneath a dock!

A view!

He was looking at a gas/diesel supply float with a huge sign on it. The Marina!

I grabbed the phone. "Now you've got him!" I shouted. "What's the dock directly across from your floating fuel stage?"

"That's my office!" said the harbor master.

"He's in the water under it!" I said. "SHOOT HIM!"

The phone went back on the hook hurriedly.

Voices! I heard voices in my audio.

"That God (bleeped) Fed on the phone says he's right under this dock!" It was the harbor master's voice!

"How the (bleep) would he know?"

"The hell with that! Get down on that fuel stage with rifles, fast. You, Hyper, get down that ladder and start shooting under there!"

Blackness.

The funky thud and moan a bullet makes going under water! Another shot. Another!

The churn of the launch engine.

A view!

It was from mid-channel, looking back at the dock.

BEROOOOOOM!

Flame geysering into the sky!

Concussion in the water!

The whole office went in slow motion up into the sky, turned over and fell apart in flaming chunks.

BEROOM!

The patrol launch disintegrated in a flash of fire.

BEROOOOOOOOOOOOOM!

The whole fuel depot went up! A roaring mushroom of churning fire blossomed in the sky.

Fragments struck with a thunk and hiss close by.

At water level, a sweep of the scene.

It was just fires now, burning bright.

"Well, it wasn't underwater detection gear, anyway,"

muttered Heller. Then his eye fastened on a distant floating body. He said, "I'm sorry, you guys. May your Lord Jesus Christ have mercy on your souls." He sounded very sad.

I was cursing. I didn't have anybody I could call.

But hope was not dead. The yacht had been alerted and he still had that gauntlet to run. That lighted landing stage could not be approached. Possibly they'd get Heller yet!

Chapter 4

About ten minutes later I got another view. It was of a wire cable, lighter black against the darker black of night.

He looked up. He was on the dark side of the yacht. He was holding on to the edge of the rigged collision stage which lay against its side. From where he was, the wire that secured the stage went up twenty or more feet to the lowest visible deck.

There were two more decks visible above and a man was visible against the stars and faintly luminescent sky. A guard. With a rifle. He was looking aft and across the water to where the explosions had recently occurred. The light of a renewed burst of flame flicked against his white uniform.

Heller reached up and took hold of the wire cable. With his other hand he made sure that the semi-floating sack was secure to his scuba-tank straps.

Then, hand over hand, he began to lift himself up the cable.

"Ouch!" he said in a whisper. He was looking at his right hand while he held on with the other. He had apparently snagged his palm on a wire cable fray.

It made me feel better, with all the trouble he was causing me! He didn't have engineer gloves and wire cable always has loose strands like needles broken in it and sticking out. Served him right, getting in my way!

But it didn't stop him. With a glance at the guard above, Heller began to climb again, hand over hand, up the wire.

I couldn't understand why the guard couldn't see him! All he had to do was look down!

Heller stopped twice more. The cable was biting his palms, tearing the cheap cotton gloves to bits!

Hand over hand he went. He glanced one final time at the guard above and went over the rail onto the deck.

Why hadn't that idiot seen him! Then I realized belatedly that the guard, glancing now and then at the fire on shore, was keeping himself night blind, the stupid fool! He couldn't see something black against black water.

Heller found a deck locker, probably life jackets. He opened it. He crushed aside whatever it held and then got out of his scuba tanks, mask, weight belt and flippers and put them in.

He picked up his sack and went to a deck door. With ear against it, he listened. Then he opened it and stepped into a passageway. The lights were on but they were dimmed for night.

He looked around, orienting himself.

Footsteps clattering down a ladder.

Heller opened a door and stepped in, closed it

behind him. He fumbled for a switch and turned the lights on.

A crewman was asleep in the bunk!

He was in the crew area of the ship!

A cook's hat was on a peg.

Heller shut the light off.

The cook turned over with a grunt.

Heller opened the door and listened. Only some machinery running.

He went out, located some steps and went up a deck. Suddenly he found what he could use: a posted emergency-drill plan of the ship. It was set in a brass frame upon a walnut-panelled wall. It gave an outline of the ship, deck by deck, with all lifeboats, fire hydrants and compartments plainly marked.

I had not realized how extensive this yacht was! But two hundred feet of vessel with lots of beam must make her at least two thousand tons. Music salon. Nightclub. Theater. Steam baths. Breakfast dining room. Luncheon dining room. Banquet hall. Gymnasium. Inside swimming pool. Sun swimming pool. Squash court. Race track ... race track? Yes, there it was marked, and beside it, Miniature car garage.

Cabins, cabins, cabins. The ship must have room for fifty guests or more. In suites, yet! What a yacht! More like a liner! And apparently fairly new, judging by the modernness of the decor. It must have cost a fortune to build and was costing another one to keep up.

He found what he thought he wanted: Owner's Master Suite. He traced out the ways to get to it from where he was.

He went up another deck. He halted, listening, before he went into a passageway. He looked around carefully.

Polished walnut and mahogany and brass with colorful tiled decks.

In a rush he went to another cross passage, stopped and listened. Footsteps on the deck above. He froze. They receded.

He got something out of his sack. I held my breath. Was he going to shoot up this ship? Blow it up?

He moved into the passageway again. There was a big, impressive, brass-bound door ahead of him. Owner's Master Suite, Drawing Room. He passed it by. Next door, Owner's Master Suite, Bathroom. He passed it by. Next door, Owner's Master Suite, Dressing Room. He went by it. Then, Owner's Master Suite, Bedchamber. He halted.

He didn't try the knob. He went silently to work with a picklock.

Chapter 5

He went in through the door so quickly and shut it so silently behind him that the surprise was absolute. The Countess Krak was propped up in bed, wearing a blue negligee. A silken cover was over her bent knees against which she was holding a neglected magazine. She was looking out through a square, brass-bound port toward fires on the beach. But her posture showed no interest.

Something must have made her aware that someone else was in the room.

She whipped her head sideways. She went white!

"THE BLACK!" she cried.

With all her might she hurled the magazine across the room!

It struck him with a thud in the chest.

"No, no," he said. "It's me. I'm sorry I frightened you!"

She peered at him, up on her knees now, on the bed. Then, "Jettero, get away from me! Your sins have blackened your face."

"Dear," he said, "you've got to listen."

"There is nothing to listen to!" she flamed. "You lied to me about other women! You married some cheap harlot! And then you married another one! You have blasted all my hopes and dreams! Get out! I never want to see you again!"

"Dear, are you going to listen to me or do I sit on you!"

"Don't you touch me, you philandering, unprincipled beast!" Her hands had been grasping about. She seized a bottle of sun lotion and hurled it at him with all her might!

It grazed his head and crashed against the wall behind him!

She leaped off the bed, grabbed for a chair to throw at him. It raised my hopes. She could kill men!

Heller suddenly dived. He hit her legs just above the knee.

She went down with a thump against the Persian carpet.

Instantly she was back at him, scratching, trying to bite.

He caught her arms and then quickly shifted to grip both her wrists with one hand. He sat down on her and with one of his thighs, pinned her kicking legs to the floor.

"You brute!" she screamed.

She tried to bite the hand which held her wrists. He moved it and her wrists up above her head and held them against the floor.

"You," he said, "are going to do some listening!"

"I won't!"

With his free hand he was snaking his sack toward him. He fumbled inside it, brought out a stack of papers and laid them on the floor.

She struggled valiantly to get loose. Then she lay back, breathing hard, her eyes flaming. "Now I suppose you are going to rape me like you did those other women!"

Heller had taken a piece of paper off the stack. He opened it and shoved it in front of her face. "Look at this."

"I won't!" She turned her head away from it.

Remorselessly, using the elbow of the arm that held her wrists, he forced her head over the other way toward the paper he held. She closed her eyes, tightly and violently.

Heller said, "LOOK AT THAT PAPER! What is it?"

"You can prove nothing to me!" she said.

"Answer me. What is that paper?"

"You're hurting me. Ouch." She looked. Her eyes flamed. "It's that nasty suit by that awful Mexican (bleepch)!" She struggled to get free.

He shifted the paper in his hand and pushed it at her face. "Read that paragraph! What is the date in it?"

She was hissing and snarling. Then, "Ouch. You're breaking my arms! ALL RIGHT! It says you married her twenty-six months ago!"

He threw that aside and took another paper. She tried wildly to get loose.

"Look at this paper! What is it?"

"You're bruising my neck. It's that suit from that whore, Toots Switch!"

He shifted the paper. "Read that paragraph! What's the alleged date?"

"It says you married her fourteen months ago! Why are you torturing me? I hate them. I hate them! I hate them!"

Heller had the front page of a newspaper. "Look at this news story. What is it?"

"You're breaking my legs! It's that awful Maizie Spread."

"What does that line say?"

"That you came to her father's farm a year ago. And oh, you brute, I bet you had fun! I hate her!"

He now picked up a booklet. "Now look at THIS. What is it?"

She tried to get away from him again. She closed her eyes. He applied pressure. "It's your Fleet combat engineer log!" she snapped.

He opened it. "Look at this. Look at these pages. Do you see Planet Earth? Blito-P3?"

She struggled but she scanned the pages. "No!"

"Now look at this last page."

Suddenly she freed her wrists and grabbed the log. He must have relaxed his grip for now she was able to sit up. She did so, eyes riveted on the log.

She turned it over to verify it was actually the log. Then she tore through the pages again. Then she stared at him. She said, "You never even saw this planet until a year ago! And you never even landed then!" Her eyes were wide with astonishment.

Suddenly she began to cry. She reached out and put her arms around his neck, clutching him convulsively, sobbing.

There was a rap on the door. A gruff voice said, "Ma'am, are you all right in there? A sentry reported something breaking somewhere this end of the ship."

She raised her head, swallowed hard and made a determined effort to speak.

"No, nothing is broken now!" she cried. "Thank Gods it's just been mended!"

The footsteps went away.

Chapter 6

After a while, the Countess Krak stood up and began to pace, barefooted, in her negligee, back and forth across the yacht bedchamber. She seemed very agitated.

Heller, sitting in the middle of the Persian rug, still in his black underwater suit, watched her and I watched his viewer. Hers was still off.

She stopped suddenly, wringing her hands. "Oh, how I have wronged you!" she said with a wail.

"No, no," said Heller. "We'll just forget about it and start over as though it never happened."

"NO! I refused to accept your word. I didn't trust you. I told you to your face that you were a liar. Oh, how AWFUL! I even sullied the honorable word of a Royal officer of the Fleet! You will never forgive me!"

"But I do forgive you."

"Oh, no! It is too horrible!" She got down on her

knees beside him. "I can never make it right! It's an absolutely unforgivable thing I did!" She sprang up again and began to pace. "Oh, dear! Oh, dear! How can I ever make it up to you!"

"By just being your beautiful self," said Heller.

"Oh, no," she said, shaking her head. "I believed those false suits. I believed the newspapers. I believed what those fiends said but I didn't believe my darling Jettero!"

She dropped down on her knees beside him once more. "I was absolutely HORRIBLE!" She was staring at his face. "Oh, Heavens! I even slashed your face to ribbons with that bottle I threw!"

Heller touched his face, looked at his fingers to see if there was any blood. Then he touched a bandage. "Oh, you mean these. Those are just razor cuts. Nothing."

She had a hand tentatively touching his chest. "Is there anything broken here? A rib? Oh, dear," she wailed, "I smashed your chest with that magazine!"

"Magazine?" said Heller. "Oh, that. It didn't seem worth ducking."

She was touching his head and shoulders anxiously. Then she looked down and let out a shriek. "Your hands! They're cut to bits!"

She had his palms lifted and was staring at the torn gloves. There were some tiny spots of blood.

"It's nothing," said Heller. "I just got them climbing up a wire rope."

"OH!" she wailed. "You're just trying to spare my feelings and make me think I didn't cause these AWFUL injuries. But I did!" She suddenly put his head against her breast. "I've hurt my darling Jettero! Oh, I should be whipped!" She pushed him back and looked anxiously at his face. "Are they paining you terribly?"

Then she shook her head. "You wouldn't say if they were. Here, I'll be as gentle as possible. Can you stand?"

"Of course I can stand!" said Heller, getting to his feet.

"Here, lean on me, I'll get you over to the couch." She eased him down on it. "Sit there," she said anxiously. "I'll get a basin of water and soak your hands so we can get those blood-caked gloves off of you."

She rushed off and came back with a basin of water. She put his hands in it. She was working to get the cotton off them. Bending over the basin, her tears were splashing into the water. "I've hurt my darling Jettero. And all the time he was innocent!"

"Listen," he said. "That's all over now."

She looked up at him. "No, it isn't. For the next hundred and fifty years, every time you look at me, some little part of you will say, She didn't believe me and she attacked me and all because of her I got maimed and crippled."

"Oh, no," said Heller. "I wouldn't do that."

"Oh, yes. But worse, I would know it myself." She got up suddenly and walked back and forth, wringing her own hands. "I have to make this right! I have to do something to make amends for it. I can't live with myself unless I do!" Then she wailed. "I even deserted you when you needed me!" She stopped and knelt before him pleadingly. "Tell me you forgive me!"

"I forgive you utterly," he said.

She got back up. "No. That isn't enough. I can't permit you to forgive me. It is too awful!" Then she suddenly stood up very straight. She said in a firm voice, "I have no right to inflict my upset on you when you're in so much pain. You don't need an emotional female on your hands. So stop worrying. I will be efficient and effective."

She got down on her knees again and peeled off his gloves. She rinsed his hands in the basin and set it aside. She peeled him out of his wet suit. At his direction, she got the light out of his sack and played it on his face, evidently turning it back to its natural color.

She went and got the Zanco medical kit she had assembled. And with far, far too much instant-heal and with far, far too many cups and bandages, took care of his very superficial injuries.

Then she went over to the phone by the bed, made a call, and after a bit, when a tray was delivered, brought it in. She made him get into bed, propped up, put the tray of broth and crackers on his lap and began to dip crackers into the broth and put them in his mouth.

That done, she made sure he was very comfortable, lying back on the pillows. "Do you feel up to talking?" she said.

"Listen," said Heller. "I'm not sick. I'm okay."

"Please stop pretending," she said. "I can face up to what I have done and it is absolutely disgustingly AWFUL. So don't try to spare my feelings. Just tell me now everything that has been going on and don't gloss over any details."

So he told her about the race and the publicity and the suits and the Sea Skiff and the Coast Guard and, under her questions, anything else he could recall, including the fact that there were arrest warrants out for him.

She thanked him and sat back. "It's the women," she said. "They caused the trouble. And because my Jettero is so handsome and so darling, I was a jealous fool. Yes. It was the women."

"Izzy says——" began Heller.

"No, no. Izzy is a man. He wouldn't understand these things," said the Countess. "A woman—any woman—would move Heavens and planet to get her hands on my Jettero. I understand that completely. It all makes sense."

"I think there is more to it than . . ."

But she was not listening. She got up and went to another room. She was gone for a while and there were some goings and comings and the murmur of voices.

She came back. She had a glass of water and two capsules. "Now, you're in pain and you have been under a strain. The captain told me that if I had any trouble sleeping, to tell him. So I have just done so. These are called Nembutal. You will be able to sleep. You are quite safe. Nobody knows you are here. So take them and get some rest."

"I don't think I need——"

"Take them," she said and put them in his mouth. She gave him some water to wash them down.

"Now just lie back and relax," she said. "Everything is going to be all right." She reached over and gave him a gentle kiss amongst the overdone mass of bandages. She turned off the light.

My viewer went black. The audio carried the faint hum of ship machinery. And then the gentle breathing of Heller.

I set the viewer alarm for when he would awake. Obviously, it would not be for some time.

At least I knew exactly where he was. And no threat to me at the moment. Or so I thought.

I, too, went to bed.

Fool that I was, I had no clairvoyance whatever of the blazing storm of disaster which was about to be turned loose! With me in the eye of the worst series of catastrophes Hells had ever unleashed.

Stupid with shock, champagne and marijuana, I had no inkling that my last days on Earth were about to pounce.

Looking back on that moment, I am incredulous that I could have been so unalert and calm.

Dark, devilish disaster was on its devastating way.

PART FIFTY-ONE

Chapter 1

When I arose the next morning it was nearly noon.
I could not think. The combination of marijuana and
alcohol was giving me a far worse hangover than the one
before. I decided it had been that awful experience with
Teenie and her (bleeped) flashgun. Somebody ought to
kill that kid, I decided, but my wits were so thick and
thinking was so painful that I could not even dwell on
that pleasant prospect.

Limping around, wishing Prahd was there to grow
me a new head, I wandered into the back garden. It was
a beautiful spring day for some people but not for me.
The warm sun, however, seemed to relax my nerves and
I stretched out, hopeful of an undisturbed hour.

Not so. A buzzer was going somewhere. I finally recognized it as coming from my room. It was the viewer.
I sat down thickly to watch it.

Heller was awake. He was sitting up in bed. The curtains of the sleeping cabin were all drawn shut. He was
staring at a little sign, suspended with a blue ribbon
from a pipe. It said:

Please push Bell S

I was so stupid after last night, not even a sixth sense
warned me of the catastrophe this was to begin.

He looked around. There was a button panel. One said S and had a small drawing of a steward beside it. He pushed it.

Instantly, like a magic genie, a gaunt-faced man dressed in a white short jacket and black pants came in. He bowed. "Madam gave me strict instructions, sir, for when you rose."

"And where is the lady?" said Heller.

"You are to go to the breakfast room when you are quite ready, sir. There is no hurry." He was holding out a small bottle. "I trust your injuries are not paining you too much, sir. If they are, you are to take one of these aspirins."

"I'm fine!" said Heller, waving the bottle aside. "I feel great."

"That's very brave of you, sir, after the extensive wounds madam described to us." He was holding a white robe. "If you can manage holding out your arms, sir, I can get this on you."

Heller took it away from him and put it on.

The steward was bowing him into the bathroom. A small seat was in the middle of the tiled floor and the steward got Heller to sit down. The steward was picking up a straight razor and can of lather. "I'll do the best I can, sir, shaving around your injured face."

Heller apparently resigned himself to it. There appeared to be extensive bandages.

"Frightful row on the beach last night, sir. In all the upset, I am afraid I did not see you come aboard."

"It was pretty dark," Heller said. And in the mirror I could see that a smile was twitching at the areas of his face the bandages left exposed.

The steward finished shaving him. "Now, if you will just get into the tub, sir, I can wash your back. You don't have to get your hands wet. I promise to be very careful of the chest injuries."

Heller endured the bath. When finished and dried, the steward bowed him back into the bedchamber, a towel wrapped around him.

There in the splendid room stood an older man, also in a white short jacket, but with gold epaulets and *Chief Steward* above the pocket.

"I've laid out your clothing, sir. I am afraid they are not tailored but they were the best quality madam's maid could find in the stores. I do hope they serve."

There was quite an array of clothing and shoes laid out, all more or less seafaring except for a white silk dinner jacket.

"I took the liberty of laying out something casual," the Chief Steward said, pointing to an outfit displayed upon the chair. It was a nautical jersey, white with horizontal red stripes, white pants, a red sash, deck shoes and a yachting cap. "Now, if it does not give you too much pain to sit down, we can help you into them. Unless, of course, you would rather go back to bed."

Heller sighed. He got into the clothes.

They escorted him with no little ceremony down a broad stairway and into a cheerful breakfast salon with murals of sailing craft blending in color with nautical designs on the tiled floor. A resplendent table was set in the middle. It had snowy white linen, silver dishes and plates and a single huge red rose in a tall white vase made a centerpiece. There was an engraved menu on the plate.

The Chief Steward, the steward and a waiter seated Heller. He looked at the other side of the table. There was neither chair nor place set.

"Wait a minute!" said Heller with some alarm. "Where is the lady?"

The Chief Steward bowed and pointed. "I had very strict instructions to make certain you received this, sir."

An envelope was propped against the white vase. On it was the single word *Dear*.

Heller opened it with some alarm. He read:

Dearest,

This was all my fault for not believing in you.

The only way I can earn your pardon is to clear this matter up.

If you went back, they would arrest you.

These are just women and women are best handled by a woman. It shouldn't take long.

I will send you a radio when it is all settled.

Love, love, love!
K

PS: I told them your name was H. Hider Haggarty, as that is on your CIA passport.

PPS: I took all your money so you can't bribe the crew.

"Where are we?" cried Heller, leaping up.

He rushed out to a foyer and burst out upon an open deck.

Apparently the captain had already anticipated just this. He was standing right there. He was a grizzled man with a very craggy face. He was dressed in whites. He saluted.

"I am Captain Bitts, sir. Good morning to you. I have specific orders from the owner's concubine to treat you extremely well but in no case to permit you to go ashore until further orders have been received from her personally."

Heller stared at him, then looked about, saw another ladder and rushed up it. He came out on a flat deck topside, open all around.

He stared in a circle. It was a beautiful spring day with fleecy clouds and blue water. There was no land! Not even another ship in sight!

Captain Bitts had come up.

"WHERE ARE WE?" cried Heller.

"Sir, I would suggest you go back and finish your breakfast. I believe they have English kippers waiting for you. After that, as madam arranged, you can commence the physical therapy program the sports director planned so that you can begin to recover your strength after your extensive injuries."

"You've got to put me ashore!" cried Heller.

"I'm sorry, Mr. Haggarty. It has been carefully explained to me by the owner's concubine that elements in the United States, hostile to the national interests of Turkey, were on your trail."

"Turkey?" said Heller.

"Why, yes. We're under the Turkish flag now and the owner's interests are our interests and the owner's country our country, of course. Events of last night certainly proved that somebody was on your trail, that is for certain. So you'd best just batten down, all snug and shipshape aboard. We'll do all we can to make your cruise a happy one. BUT I have specific orders to stay outside

the continental limits of the United States and under no
circumstances to go near land or other ships or let you
ashore or obey any other orders from any other source
until that radio comes." He saluted and walked away.

Heller took hold of a funnel stay. He glanced at the
letter he still held and then looked all around at the very
empty sea.

"Well, I'll be blasted!" he said. "I'm a prisoner!"

Chapter 2

It was totally and completely the fault of the mixture
of drugs and champagne. I am ashamed to confess that
the import of what I had just seen and heard did not register on me at all. I freely confess that it was the greatest
omission of my entire career. That shows what drugs and
alcohol can do to one: People should beware and little
children should be warned. The fates of nations and
empires were hanging in the balance that very moment
and all I was thinking about was my AWFUL headache.

The doorbell rang and the second catastrophe of the
day began, with all its sinister implications, and once
more I did not grasp it.

Woodenly, thinking it was one of those (bleeped)
paper boys who want you to subscribe to a paper you are
already subscribing to, so they can get an all-expense-
paid tour to reform school, I wrapped my bathrobe
around me and, barefooted, went to the front door and
opened it.

TEENIE!

I slammed the door hurriedly. I put on the burglar chains. I shot the heaviest bolts in place. I went into the front room and slammed the shutters shut and put the forged-iron fasteners on. That done, I leaned against a closed shutter, panting. I went back to the front door and checked it. It was locked tight.

My Gods, what was Teenie doing coming here during business hours, especially when I was alone in the house. Let me tell you, my headache had surged up to a point where I could hardly see.

I tottered to the fridge and got some ice. I held it against my brow. That was better but not much better.

Staggering a bit with the aftermath of shock, I groped my way to my back room.

I stopped dead.

I thought I was having hallucinations. They say marijuana can give you those.

Plain as day, I saw a wraith that looked just like Teenie come over the top of the garden fence, step down off a trellis, walk in through the back door, remove her coat and sit down in an easy chair.

I could not believe my eyes. I was SEEING things!

She was sitting right there with her knees apart. She wore no underpants. Then my knowledge of psychology restored the reality of the world. I was dealing with a sexhibitionist. If she matured—which I doubted, from the way she enraged me—she would probably become a model for nonexistent women's clothes. No. A female flasher! Yes, a sexhibitionist all right, unfortunately real and no hallucination. Bless psychology!

She looked at me with her oversized eyes. She wiped the back of her hand across her too-big lips.

"I've GOT to complete my education," she said appealingly.

My Gods, didn't she realize that we were alone in the house? That there was nobody around to defend me or protect me from her nails?

"NO!" I cried. "What are you doing here during work hours?"

"I've been fired. And all because I am not educated enough."

"They can't fire you because of that."

"Oh, yes, he did. And Pinchy's plans for me are blasted totally. And all because I am instruction deficient."

"That's not possible."

"Oh, yes, it is. I ran out of stamps to lick and I walked into Rockecenter's office. And there he was down on his knees in front of an elevator boy, going after it like mad. And I said, 'No, no! That's not the right way to do it!' And I got on the desk and pulled up my skirt and reached for the elevator boy to show them what I'd learned here."

She gave an audible sniff and brushed away a tear. "But I couldn't have possibly had it correct because Rockecenter screamed at me that I was a stupid brat and had the security men throw me out of the building. See? My elbow is skinned and I lost my hat. They wouldn't even give me back my underpants. So I came to you to ask... You're not listening to me!"

"I HAVE A TERRIBLE HEADACHE AND I DON'T NEED ANOTHER ONE FROM YOU!"

"Oh, the marijuana. I wondered if you wouldn't get one when I saw you drinking champagne with it. You have to be streetwise about these things. Is your throat raw?"

"I can hardly talk."

"There. You see what lack of education can do? It

does happen that I know about marijuana, like any other school kid. Sit right there."

I wasn't going anyplace. My head felt like it was about to burst whenever I even blinked my eyes. It was her fault. Both last night and appearing so suddenly today.

She was bustling around in the front room. Suddenly she came back. "Music is what you have to have with marijuana. They go together. So I put a new Neo Punk Rock record on. You'll feel better shortly."

The massive stereo speakers in the front room clicked as a needle dropped. Drums began to boom. Every stroke of the stick was tearing my eyeballs out! Guitars screamed and a chorus brayed:

> *Subliminal, subliminal.*
> *A toy car,*
> *And a toy girl,*
> *Ran up a tree!*
> SMASH!
> *A toy house,*
> *And a toy boy,*
> *Fell out of the tree!*
> SMASH!
> *The toy car*
> *And the toy baby,*
> *Dropped the tree!*
> SMASH!
> *Where was NASA?*
> *Where was NASA?*
> *Where was NASA?*
> SMASH!

"Now, don't you feel better?" said Teenie.

"Oh, Jesus, no!" I cried.

"Aha!" said Teenie. "You have to get it balanced. Too much music, not enough marijuana. Just sit right there."

I could hear her rummaging around in the cupboards in the front room. Then another "Aha!" and she came back with something that looked like a museum sculpture. She was cramming green leaves and buds into the top of it. It had a tube. "This," she said, learnedly, "is called a bhong, or carburetor. Because the smoke goes through water first, it doesn't irritate the throat." She lighted it and got it going. "Adults can sometimes be pretty ignorant," she said, "and they should not be ashamed to ask those who know. I AM educated in some things. My trouble is that I am NOT educated in vital matters. Now take this mouthpiece and take a long, slow pull on it. Hold the smoke in your lungs as long as you can and then exhale."

I tried to avoid the mouthpiece but it hurt too much to turn my head. I let her put it in my mouth. I could not get any worse so I did what she said.

"Now again," she instructed.

I did it again.

"Now again," she repeated.

I did. A soft haze began to gather around me. I felt like I was floating.

"Now is your headache better?"

Gingerly, I found I could move it a bit without agony.

"There," she said. "You see the benefit of being educated about some things." She took a couple puffs and then put the pipe aside. "We don't want you stoned," she said, "as I have to talk to you."

"I don't want to seem ungrateful," I said, feeling oddly disconnected, "but you better leave." I was sure the relief was temporary and the headache maybe even would come back aggravated.

"No. I do not know enough," she said.

"It seems you know too (bleeped) much for your age," I said.

"Well," said Teenie, "I'm not like other teen-agers you know. I'm different. I have a mental problem."

"I'll bet you do," I said.

"You see," she said, "I lost my parents when I was eight. They were sent to the electric chair for murdering my grandparents so they wouldn't have to pay the rest home fees. I became a charge of the court and they appointed a wino as my guardian and he used to beat me and lock me in a closet when I couldn't find enough in garbage cans for us to eat. But that wasn't what my mental problem was."

"For Gods' sakes," I said, "then what WAS your mental problem?"

"Hyperactivity. You see, I was very fond of sports and took them all up. I was on every school team I could get on and I even won a championship skateboarding. The school psychiatrist noticed it one day and he was very alarmed. He diagnosed it very quickly and in the nick of time. Hyperactivity. And he said I needed lots of sex to keep me calm. He told them I couldn't continue in school unless I got competent professional care. He even gave me the first treatment himself. He showed me how to go down on him and I did."

"Wait a minute," I said. "That's interfering with a minor. That's punishable by law."

"Oh, no. You don't understand. My guardian—he drank himself to death three years ago and they never appointed another, due to the usual legal delays—told the judge the treatment was making me so tired I couldn't

look in garbage cans. I was there. The judge explained
that psychiatrists and psychologists are professionals and
they are not bound by ordinary law: they can even
murder people and nothing is done about it because they
actually work with the government and courts and, like
them, are above the law. They can do anything they
want with anyone placed in their care. Even murder
them. I was surprised when my guardian questioned it
because we were always taught in school that psychiatrists and psychologists are kind of sacred. But that's just
a bunch of horse (bleep). I know that now."

"Hey, whoa," I said. "You're too young to know
what you're talking about!"

"I am not! It's just like Pinchy says. They're a bunch
of chauvinistic pigs. They lie!"

"About what?" I said with a superior air. The idea
of this teen-ager talking about my most sacred subjects
made my blood seethe, marijuana or no marijuana. "They
are the very epitome of truth! You don't understand: they
deal with SCIENCE! They never lie."

"The hell they don't!" said Teenie. "Listen to this:
That psychiatrist turned me over to the school psychologist to carry on the treatment and the psychiatrist repeated the same thing—he'd told me every time since the
first, I was not to swallow it or I would get pregnant. But
I couldn't help it sometimes. And then the school psychologist, when he treated me, would say the same thing
but I couldn't help swallowing. And I didn't get pregnant."

"Now listen," I said sternly, oblivious of the fact it
was probably the marijuana talking, "such men usually
are sterile. They've been operated on so as not to embar-
rass husbands whose wives they treat. So you've just
proved nothing!"

"Oh, yeah?" she said, in her turn very superior. "So try this on for size, buster. The school psychologist had a lot of very mentally sick boys in the school. They were classified as oversexed. And he used to line them up in his office and go down on them to cool them off. And every day or two he'd get an overload of cases and he'd send and get me excused from class so I could come in and help. He'd stand and watch. There were so many of those boys sometimes that I could hardly get my breath from one before another had to be done. It was a fast clinical line, let me tell you. And some of those boys were fifteen and sixteen and pretty foamy. You just couldn't help swallowing! And I never got pregnant once, so there!"

I dazedly seemed to realize that she had a point.

"But that wasn't what I had against that (bleeped) psychologist," she said. "Oh, yes, when I was through he would kiss me and tell me what a good girl I was and give me my own treatment, which was doing it to him. BUT, never one God (bleeped) time did he offer the least word of criticism, coaching or anything. He'd just stand there watching and holding himself. So I never got real top-grade education. A thing like that requires coaching. . . . You're not listening to me again."

The marijuana had not worked. Or if it had, this rattly (bleep) was making it worse. "I feel terrible," I said. "Please leave."

"Hey," she said, "there's other things which make you feel good. I may never have had proper education in it but experience counts for something."

Before I realized what was happening she had come over, knelt in front of me and was peeling back my robe. She looked at me with her oversized eyes and said, "This therapy will help."

I looked down at her, not realizing at first what she was actually doing.

Then suddenly I had an awful thought. "Utanc!" I cried. "I must not betray you!"

I leaped out of my chair as though I were shot from a catapult.

Teenie was thrown backward on her (bleep) with an awful jolt.

She looked at me woundedly. "You see," she said, "I'm not even well enough trained to do that!"

"GET OUT OF HERE!" I bellowed at her.

She just sat there, staring at me.

I was baffled, and frightened, too. There was no telling what this teen-age female monster might do next.

I backed up. I tripped over a footstool and landed flat on my spine.

She was up off the floor like a leaping panther.

She sprang astraddle of me!

I gave her a tremendous shove!

She flew across the room, hit the wall and sat down at the bottom of it with a crash.

She got up. She walked around in a very fidgety way. She looked at me a little crossly and then she went into the front room and put on another record.

The drums were booming hard enough to lift my aching hair half an inch each stroke!

A whiny, high-pitched voice came on. A man? A woman? Who could tell? Amongst the whang and wow of guitars and the echoes of a chorale, the song went:

> *Don't stop me (bleeping)!*
> *Don't clog my plumbing*
> *With too much chumming.*
> *Keep that thing thrumming!*

Keep your hips drumming!
I know I am bumming,
And it ain't becoming.
But it is so numbing
When you stop my (bleeping)!

The piece ended with a pistol shot and the thud of a body falling. And a spoken, hoarse voice said, *"It served 'em right!"* After the mangling effect the drums had had on my brain, I felt like the shot had gone straight through my tortured skull.

Teenie came back in, switching her ponytail. "Now, how is that? Is your headache all gone now?"

I was too much in pain to get off the floor and find a gun and shoot her. "God (bleep) you," I grated in a deadly voice. "Get the Hells out of here and now, now, now!"

"Well, I like that!" she said indignantly. "I'm only trying to help you!" Her eyes got deadly. She stamped her foot. "The trouble with you, you (bleepard), is pretty plain! You're a JERK! I try to give you a hand and what do you do? You spit on me! You don't know what decency is! Where the hell are your manners? Listen, you (bleepard), you've got the finest sex equipment I've ever seen in my life and believe me, I'm an expert! And do you know what to do with it? NO! You're cruel, obscene, selfish, rotten, mean, perverted, depraved, sadistic, vicious and STUPID!" She stopped. She had run out of adjectives. Her large eyes glared like a panther's. "And besides that," she finished, "you're no gentleman!"

I tried to find something to say. Every word had gone into my skull like a sledgehammer. I wanted to strangle her. But the room was spinning.

"So you haven't got a thing to say," she said. "Well,

that's good, because I have! I came over here today, thinking that in my plight, you could help. You're rich. I haven't even got a job now. I got no job because I'm uneducated. I came over here thinking that out of decency you would give me enough money to go to school. But you're so rotten, you don't have the slightest God (bleeped) idea of anything but wrecking people's nerves. So there's only one thing I can do."

I was horrified that she might put on another record. What came was far worse!

"And you know what I'm going to do?" she demanded. "I am going to stay right here and reform the hell out of you until you are decent enough to at least associate with mangy dogs! I'm going to nag, nag, nag you until you decide there is somebody else in the world besides yourself. I'm going to——"

"Wait," I pleaded, for I could stand it no more. "What would it take to get you to leave and never come back and never see you again, ever?"

"Five thousand dollars," she said. "I got to finish my education. I live in an attic by myself so living don't cost much, but tuition does. There's a Hong Kong whore that runs a special school that teaches all the ins and outs of sex. I can buy a crash course. Then I'll know what I'm doing! I've got to unlearn everything the psychiatrist and psychologist taught me and everything in the grammar-school sex textbook. And I got to get me some real education! I'm a fast learner: you got to learn fast if you live on the streets of New York and want to stay alive. So I'm quick. She'll take me as a pupil, despite my age. But I need five thousand dollars. Then I can find some satisfaction and succeed in life. I can grow up and amount to something. I can make people happy and . . ."

Her voice had been literally smashing what was left

of my brain cells into ragged, mangled pulp. I said, "If I do that, will you promise faithfully, swear, attest, affirm that I will never in all my life, ever, ever, lay eyes on you again?"

"Cross my heart and hope to die!" she said.

Oh, Gods, it was worth it. I crept to my money hoard. I counted out five thousand dollars.

She took it. She counted it. Then she put it in the pocket of her cloth coat and pinned it there with a safety pin.

Before I could stop her, she gave me a moist kiss. She pulled back. She smiled happily. "I'm sorry I had to tell you the truth about yourself," she said. "But sometimes the truth pays. Are you sure I can't do anything else for you? Fix you another bhong? Play you some more records? Go down on you so you will have a calm afternoon?"

"Get out of here," I wept.

"Well," she said. "I'm not as ungrateful as you are. If you ever change your mind about seeing me, I live in the garret of one of the old houses in Tudor City." And she gave me the exact number. "All you have to do is climb the fire escape and slide in the window. It's permanently stuck open. Tudor City, you know, is just south of the United Nations and you get there over a bridge from 42nd Street. The buildings used to be kept up and they had little parks of their own and private footpaths, but the last couple of years they've gone to hell and the parks are used to grow marijuana, mostly. At least that's what I use them for. Now, please remember the number." And she gave it again twice. "If you don't mind climbing a fire escape and if you don't mind dust and old trunks, we can just lie there and do it for hours and hours the right way, or if your back gets tired I can use my mouth on you while you rest up. I'm used to that, you see, and I don't mind a bit, really. And then when your back gets rested, we can do it the right way again. And then you can rest while I——"

"Get OUT of here!" I wailed.

"I'm going," she said. "I keep my bargains. But don't forget the number." And she gave it to me again. "In case you change your mind. Good-bye, now, although it is a shame with us alone in the house not to use the rest of the afternoon . . ."

I got my hands over my ears.

She picked up her coat and put it on. She went out the back door and climbed the garden fence. She waved from the top. And at last I was left to my fuddled misery.

How often in life does one go through the first tremors of a catastrophe and never realize that they were but the unheeded warning? Ah, but if only one could change the fleeting moments of a yesteryear. How different would life be. I should have killed her when I had the chance!

Chapter 3

The following morning, I had twice the head I had had the day before.

The reason was not hard to isolate. Preparing me for the proper execution of my duties, Adora had unfortunately heeded my plea that I must have something to drink. My throat had been dry as dust itself. She had found the bhong set up.

"You've been at the Acapulco Gold," she said. "That is what is making you so thirsty." She had come in with a full tumbler of beautifully cold liquid. It looked like water. I had drunk it gratefully, gulp, gulp, gulp.

VODKA!

The effect was almost instant. I not only had no headache, I had no head. It had blown off!

Consequently, I have no slightest recollection of what had gone on that evening. If there were two lesbians who had then become ex-lesbians, I could not tell you to this day. Since, when I woke, I had no bruises on me nor daggers sticking in me and no one was arresting me for bigamy, I could only assume that I had performed.

I felt so bad that even my loss of memory did not disturb me.

I pottered about in the midmorning empty apartment. I got an aspirin. I went out into the garden and gazed with distaste at the sunlit day. I went back in and glanced at the viewers.

Crobe was busy giving electric shocks and the emotion digitals in his viewer kept flashing

SATISFACTION

every time a patient was carted away, sheet over his face, en route to the morgue. Normal Earth psychiatric duties. One never would have suspected that he was an extraterrestrial. Not very educational. I turned it off after a while.

Krak's viewer was completely blank, so I was not disturbed at all. This evidence showed to me she must be miles and miles away, even the North Pole, perhaps.

Heller's was a view of the sea. He was leaning on a

rail, puffing. "Wow," he said, "the lady was right. I've gotten out of condition."

"Oh, I wouldn't say that, Mr. Haggarty. Anyone who can run up to the top of the mainmast and down ten times without stopping can't be said to be in serious shape." It was a gravelly voice and Heller looked sideways. The man had a broken nose and the words *Sports Director* were on his T-shirt. "I think you've achieved a remarkably fast recovery from those multiple injuries. CIA agents are seldom so resilient."

Heller swept a hand toward the sea. "Where are we, anyway?"

"See those high, towering clouds? Shaped like castles? Now look at the water. See the little scraps of seaweed? And look at its color: indigo blue. We're in the Gulf Stream. That's what makes the weather feel so balmy."

"How long a swim to get ashore?" said Heller.

The sports director laughed. "You'd have to swim awfully fast to beat the tropical sharks. You're not going anywhere, Mr. Haggarty. The next item on your schedule today is a hundred laps in the sun pool. It's just been refilled with warm Gulf Stream water. So let's go."

I pondered this. The Gulf Stream. The yacht must be somewhere in the Caribbean. How did it get down there so quickly? No yacht is that fast. The problem made my head ache worse.

Totally oblivious that I had all the evidence of absolute catastrophe around me, I went back to bed.

Some hours later, I was apparently having a nightmare. There was a mighty roll of drums and then a rhythmic beat. The whine and yowl of electric guitars shrieked and dripped with sex. A chorale beat at me:

Do it in the morning.
Do it in the night.
Do it to me, baby
And do it right.
Do it in the water.
Do it in the clouds.
Do it long and tenderly
And make me proud.
Do it, do it, do it!
And do it once again.
Write a day of ecstasy
With your lovely pen.
Do it, do it, do it!
Don't be shy!
Do it, do it, do it!
And gaze up at the sky.
For this must be heaven,
You can hear the angels cry,
"Do it, do it, do it!"
So open up your fly!

What strange music for a nightmare! It must be a nightmare, for everything was black. But it was accompanied by a moist, delightful sensation. I lay there. The music had stopped but the sensation continued. Then the same piece started up again and the sensation mounted. Was the music the sensation?

Suddenly I realized there was something on me. It was moving to the beat of the music!

Hey, this was too real for a nightmare even if everything WAS black.

I ripped at my eyes. There was something on my eyes! I tore it off.

TEENIE!

She was sitting astride me!

She stopped rocking back and forth and looked at me with her big eyes. "Now you've spoiled it," she said.

"Spoiled what?" I raved, trying to get her off of me.

She sat there, not budging an inch. "I was keeping our bargain. You said you never wanted to see me again, so I covered up your eyes. Now you've taken it off and broken our agreement."

"How did you get in here?" I raved.

"You left the back door open," she said. "And don't scold. I am NOT playing hooky. I went straight out yesterday and enrolled in the Hong Kong whore's school. I'm doing it night school and days. I got A plus on my first lessons and now I am doing my homework."

"Get off me and get out of here!" I grated.

She clung firmly astride. "I learned some nice things. I never knew you could do so many things with muscles inside and outside. And I knew you would be fascinated at the rapid progress your protégé was making. Feel this."

She sat perfectly still, apparently, but inside her there was a gentle stroking feeling.

"That's just one internal muscle moving," she said. "It's the yummy-yum muscle. All the muscles have names. If I set another one opposite it going, you would (bleepulate) and we don't want that so quick. So, pretty good for a street urchin, huh? I can see that you liked it. Right now I'm holding you in the 'whoa-boy' position that prevents a 'too-soon.' Oh, I feel I'm getting somewhere, now. Even my parents will be proud of me."

"Hey, I thought your parents were dead."

"Oh, no. They are doing life in a maximum-security Federal pen. They engineered a presidential-assassination attempt that failed and when they went to prison I was made a ward of the court. But the judge wouldn't appoint a guardian: he kept me in his chambers so I could handle him with oral testimony and relax him in the middle of difficult cases."

I stared at her. This was an entirely different story of her life than she had told me yesterday. What was I dealing with in this female monster?

"You get out of here," I said, "you broke your bargain!"

"No. You broke it. You're the one who took the cover off your eyes. Don't blame others for your own misdeeds."

"Teenie," I said, "you get off of me, put your clothes back on and get the Hells out of here. And take your (bleeped) Chinese positions and muscles with you!"

"This one, too?" she said.

My hand clutched the side of the bed. Then it began to relax. My fingers straightened out stiffly, quivering.

An errant bee wandered in from the garden, buzzed in circles round and round at the window.

A potted plant began to spin.

The buzz of the bee went up and down in volume.

"This is 'rickshaw boy, chop, chop,'" said Teenie in a strained voice.

The potted plant swung faster. "Now I'll let you!" Teenie cried.

The potted plant exploded.

The bee soared off into the sky but it wasn't its buzz I was hearing. It was the expiring croon of Teenie. She raised her eyes to me triumphantly. "Oh, boy," she said, "now I think even you will agree that I will amount to something when I'm fully educated."

I didn't push her off. I felt too weak.

After a little, she said, "Now kiss me." As her mouth

was on mine, I couldn't avoid it. She raised her head a bit. "No, not like that! Here's a proper kiss. Open your mouth slightly, put it in the Q position. Now take your tongue . . ."

I groaned as a second potted plant began to spin. Then a third one started to turn. Then a fourth one began to rotate.

The second exploded. The third exploded. The fourth exploded.

I conked out, unconscious.

A long time later, a voice said, "For God's sake! It's five o'clock! And you're still in bed!" It was Adora.

I looked around wildly. The effort made my head feel like it was being hit with an axe. No Teenie. I was all alone in bed.

"Where is she?" I babbled.

"She's in the other room," said Adora. "Both of them are. One is a blonde, the other a brunette, and they're hot as a forest fire to find out what real sex is. This is no time for you to be having wet dreams when the quarry is in the front room. So tallyho. Let's get after the tail!"

"I can't," I said. "I'm totally exhausted and my head is killing me."

"Oh, that again!" said Adora. She went to a table, stuffed and lit the bhong. I searched in vain within me to find energy to object. She came back and put the stem in my mouth. "You want to fool with a bhong, then stop fooling with it. By the numbers, six big inhales. One . . . hold it, hold it, hold it. Exhale. Two . . ."

We got through the six. Everything had gone gray and soft. I was floating. Memory was starting to fade. So was the instinct to survive.

"You seem to have developed a taste for music," said

Adora. "Good sign. I'll go out and play the record you left on the stereo."

Presently here it came, booming through the room—
Do it, do it, do it!

Adora was there again. She had a pill and a glass. She put the pill in my mouth. I could not object, given the deadly and determined look on her face. "That's Benzedrine," she said. "An ordinary upper. Well, don't just lie there holding it in your mouth, you idiot. The capsule will melt and the stuff is bitter. Chase it down with this."

The pill *was* bitter. I gulped the liquid convulsively. GIN!

A tumbler full of raw gin! And I had it down before I found out!

I was gasping painfully from the assault on my throat. Then flame exploded in my stomach.

Adora's eyes held that deadly gleam. She said, "Now get out of that bed and go into the front room. And do it, do it, do it!"

I have no memory at all of that evening. She had said they were a blonde and brunette but they might as well have been horses for all I knew of it.

About 3:00 A.M., it must have been, I heard a deadly voice. "For Christ's sake, stop screaming!" It was Adora. She was standing beside the couch where I now slept in the back room. She was a bit tousled from having been asleep.

"They're after me," I told her.

"Who's after you now?"

"The Fates," I babbled. "They're standing all around the corners of the room with pills and bhongs in their hands."

"Oh, you're just seeing multiple. It's me, standing

here, trying to give you a sleeping pill. Quit spouting nonsense and take it."

I took it but Adora Bey nee Pinch was wrong. The Fates *were* after me, as I shortly was going to find out! With shock!

That very afternoon, I had missed my second opportunity to kill Teenie. And the horror of it is, I didn't even realize it until much later—fatally MUCH later.

And right then, had I had my wits about me, I might have seen another Fate face grinning at me ghoulishly.

I didn't even think of Freud and his unerring analysis of dreams. Frankly, I will be candid, that omission was the only mistake I ever made in my entire professional career. Oh, I could weep tears of blood as I recall it now. One should never desert his Gods as I deserted Freud that night. Even two minutes spent on dream analysis would have told me of horrors to come that even now I have difficulty facing.

Chapter 4

Adora awakened me by the simple expedient of kicking me in the stomach. It was morning. I evidently had fallen out of bed. She was standing there, dressed for work.

"Listen, you (bleep)," she said, "you're sleeping too much. Get up and around and stir yourself. Go for a walk. Get some air. A hell of a looking husband you are. You're developing prison pallor. Are you listening?"

"Yes," I said apprehensively, watching her feet at the

level of my face. My head felt like a balloon and I was afraid she'd kick it and burst it.

"I woke you up to give you some good news," she said. "A compulsory attendance staff meeting has been called at Octopus. It's a lecture on abortion with a live demonstration by some new star of the psychiatric world, Dr. Crobe. He's just another (bleeping) quack like they all are, but I know it will go on half the night with Rockecenter drooling. Did you know the (bleepard) fired poor Teenie?"

I was watching her feet carefully.

"The rotten ape was giving a personal staff inspection the way he does every month and he spotted she was full of semen. He had her kicked clear down the stairs."

Something was awry. "That isn't what she said."

"Has Teenie been here?"

"She was on the phone," I lied quickly. There might be something wrong with telling the truth and it's always safer to prevaricate in such moments.

"Well, the Chief of Security was my source and he was right there. He may be a (bleep) but he doesn't lie. The poor kid is so uneducated she didn't even know enough to take a douche after she was here. So there went my plans. But never mind, I'll find other uses for her. Anyway, that's beside the point. One of the girls last night said you looked like a warmed-over corpse. So get out and around and get some air. Then maybe tomorrow night you can put on a better show."

She left and I was very glad to no longer have feet with a kick impulse in them near my head. Belatedly, the corpse remark struck me. Was somebody intending to make me into a corpse?

I was sort of confused. Maybe I had better look at the viewers.

Crobe was busy preparing lecture notes and knives. Heller was just then taking a look all around the horizon from some high place. Nothing in sight—not even a ship. Lords, he must be a long way away.

Krak's was blank.

I felt sort of fixated on the viewers. There was something wrong here. It eluded me. I concentrated very hard. If Heller was far away and still on the viewer and Krak wasn't on the viewer, then Krak had to be further away. . . . I sort of gave it up. Something was odd.

A bright voice almost made me jump out of my wits. "Those morning programs don't have any good rock groups on them. And you have to get the soap operas in the afternoon to get good sex. So why are you watching TV at this time of day? God, do YOU need education!"

Teenie.

"How the Hells did you get in here?"

"I took your key yesterday. I had it copied. Here's yours back. I'm on my way to school. I can't stay long."

"Good! You wore the hell out of me yesterday."

"Really trained, hey?" she said, grinning like a ghoul. "Shows you what education can do. I'm so glad you liked it. But the reason I stopped by was to tell you I can't be here this afternoon."

"Wonderful. I hope you're leaving for China for a ten-year postgraduate course!"

"No, no. The crash course is not that long. It's only a couple weeks. That's why I have to put in extra time this afternoon. I have an appointment for a special rundown on hygiene and disease control. Special demonstrations."

I flinched. "Disease?" I had specters of suddenly coming down with all kinds of oriental germs. "Look," I said anxiously, "yesterday, before you were here, you hadn't just done it with a bunch of Chinese men, had you?"

She gave her ponytail a sad tug. "*That* is what is so frustrating. It's not the *old* Chinese method. It's the new, *scientific* Chinese system. They use probes and meters. They set a probe to register just one muscle and put it in you. It's hooked up to a big scope and you watch the scope. Then you have to learn to locate that muscle yourself and when you do, it shows up on the scope. It's like learning to wiggle your ears. Once you find the muscle yourself, you can move it. You get so you can locate and independently move each muscle at will." She sighed. "But there are absolutely dozens of different muscles. It's pretty tedious, sorting them all out with nothing in you but a probe. But look."

Before I could stop her, she opened her coat and pulled her skirt up above her flat, thin belly. She had a single muscle in her stomach moving. "I had a (bleep) of a time finding that one." She sat down and fanned her legs apart and pointed to the inside of her thigh. "But the nerve-impulse exercises are the worst. See the tape mark? They put an electrode on you, one place at a time. It's joined up to a big scope, too. And you learn to send an energy impulse at that exact point and if you master it, it shows up on the scope. You have to get so you can send energy surges through about fifty different places and THEN learn how to block them. After that, it gets a bit more interesting. You have to be able to do it yourself on *another* body."

"Cover yourself up," I said. "I feel terrible."

"What interests me, though," she said as though I had not spoken, "is the daily hour of sexual choreography. Watch!" She leaped up, pulled her coat and skirt up under her armpits and her hips went into a very fast rotating grind. "That's the *siva-siva*. The Chinese say they taught it to the Tahitians long ago. Isn't it wild? I can just stand here relaxed and rotate like this for hours. It sort of feels good, too. And there's dozens of these." She gave a leap and came down grinding against a chair in a new way.

The bounce and sudden movements to which she was prone made my eyes and head hurt, just watching. "Please leave," I pleaded. "I feel utterly awful!"

She stopped. "Jesus Christ, Inky. Haven't you got any appreciation for art either?" She came over and looked at me, her big eyes a lot too close. She put her hand on my forehead. "Hey, Inky. Have you got a headache?"

"You got the idea," I said.

"And after all that good therapy I gave you, too," she said. "Have you been eating something or drinking something?"

"Gin," I said with a shudder.

"GIN? With *pot?* Oh, Jesus Christ, Inky, you need some time on the streets. You NEVER mix alcohol with drugs, you dumb (bleep)! You could kill yourself. And yesterday. Maybe the night before. Did you drink anything?"

"Vodka."

"Well, Jesus Christ, Inky. No wonder the good old grass didn't work yesterday. Honest to Pete, Inky, you need a nursemaid."

"Not you," I flinched.

"And I thought all the time something must be wrong with the Acapulco Gold. Jesus, Inky. You listen to me. You lay off that alcohol. It's the killer. Stick with pot every time."

She ran off and rummaged around in the bathroom

and came back with two bottles and a glass of liquid.
"Vitamin B$_1$. And aspirin." I was trying to push the
glass away. "It's just water," she said. "Now be a good
boy and open your mouth." She literally poured the
bottle of B$_1$ into my mouth and made me wash it
down. Then she gave me two aspirin and made me wash
them down. She looked at her watch: it was a new one,
Mickey Mouse's hands pointing the time. "Jesus Christ,
I'm going to be late for school if I don't run the whole
way. When I'm gone, fix yourself some strong coffee.
And next time, don't go running down pot! Alcohol!
You're too stupid to live!"

I gave her as hard a scowl as I could manage.
"(Bleep)!" I said.

She picked up her purse and went to the door. She
stopped. She said, "It's too bad you're such a no-good,
unappreciative jerk, Inky. You need your diapers changed
constantly but who'd bother."

"Get the Hells out of here!" I screamed. I had
missed my third opportunity to kill her! And that would
be the last one. I would look back on it with longing
from that day on.

Chapter 5

I awoke in the late afternoon.

Amazing! Unless I shook it violently, my head didn't
ache. Incredible as it might seem, that (bleeped) kid had
been right about something: it must have been the alcohol!

I got myself some strong coffee and, wonder of wonders, I could think. And thinking brought my attention to the viewers. I uncovered them and turned them on.

Captain Bitts was teaching Heller some card game. They seemed to be in the main salon of the yacht, a room decorated in amber and beige carpets and brass. Poker. Bitts was explaining what hand beat what and Heller was being very attentive. I thought, you better watch it, Captain Bitts, that sneaky Heller will probably take you for a year's pay if my experience with him held true. But who cared what happened to Captain Bitts?

Crobe was en route to his lecture.

The Countess Krak's was blank.

I looked back at Heller's. Through an open door, he could see an empty expanse of sea. I thought to myself, you know, that Raht must really have reformed: there that yacht was, clear down in the Caribbean, and yet Heller was still on the screen. So Raht must be down in the Caribbean, too. And he could tell me exactly where that yacht was in case I wanted to do anything to it.

I got the two-way response radio and buzzed it.

"Yes?" Raht's voice.

"Where are you?"

"New York office," he said.

Ah, he had planted the activator-receiver someplace. "When did you get back?"

"I haven't been gone," said Raht.

"Wait a minute," I said. "Didn't you follow that Royal officer (bleepard) down to Atlantic City?"

"Oh, did he go there?" said Raht.

I began to get confused. "He's out on a yacht. Didn't you even follow him to Atlantic City? You must be tagging him around. His screen is still live."

"The 831 Relayer is still off," said Raht. "Actually, it's still on the TV antenna of the Empire State Building."

Unease began to run through me with icy feet. "Look, I had him on the screen clear to Atlantic City so you MUST have been following him. I think you've gotten tangled up some way. Maybe a more-than-unusual attack of terminal inefficiency."

"Well," said Raht, "*I'm* not tangled up but I won't say nobody else is. According to you, the gadget is good for two-hundred-mile range. Atlantic City, straight line, is only about a hundred miles. So he still must be within two hundred miles of you."

"He is further than that. He's in the Gulf Stream and that's clear down in the Caribbean."

"I beg your pardon, Officer Gris. The Gulf Stream runs between Cuba and Florida, comes all the way up the U.S. coast, runs quite near New Jersey, goes past New York and then crosses the Atlantic to England and goes on back to the Caribbean. So he's within two hundred miles of New York or he wouldn't be on your screen."

"Wait a minute," I said. "There's something wrong. Your figures must be all out. The woman got on the yacht and went to Atlantic City and went off my screen."

"Well, you've got her electronic box, Officer Gris. I haven't. Did you drop it or something?"

"Are you inferring I mishandle equipment?"

"Well, if the Royal officer was still on the screen in Atlantic City, then wouldn't you say the woman should have been? You better check her boxes, Officer Gris. They weren't mishandled by me when I had charge of them."

I had had quite enough of his impertinence. I clicked off.

I sat back, rather incensed at his accusations. Then it occurred to me that maybe the activator-receiver of the Countess Krak might have become inoperative. Spurk was not infallible. Maybe if I shook it or kicked it, it would turn on again.

I tried to remember where I had put it. I went around searching. Dimly I recalled lifting a pillow and putting the box under it. But it wasn't on the sofa and hadn't fallen behind it. Then, with a surge of memory I recalled putting it on the top shelf of the closet.

There was a pillow up there. I gave a jump and grabbed its corner. The unit flew off the shelf and hit the floor with a crash.

I picked it up and, by plan, shook it. Nothing rattled. I turned it over.

It had a pressure switch on the back. It was off. Idly, I punched at it. Maybe putting the pillow on it or the gathering weight of the pillow had pushed it.

Movement caught my eye. The viewer was sitting over there. It lit up.

The full import of this took several seconds to sink in. And then a freezing horror began to chill my bones. THE COUNTESS KRAK WAS WITHIN RANGE OF ME!

For days she had not been observed!

She might this very moment be picking the lock of the front door to come in and kill me!

Something worse than terror gripped my throat.

I raced to the front door and looked. No. She wasn't there.

I sped back to the garden and looked around.

No. She wasn't there.

I wrung my hands in extreme agitation.

WHERE WAS THE COUNTESS KRAK?

Chapter 6

Shocks of that character are very hard on one. They shorten the life span. And in this case, I felt with certainty I might only have seconds to live.

It was Teenie's fault for distracting me. It was Adora's fault as well. Were they in league with the Countess Krak? Was the Countess Krak paying them to keep my attention elsewhere while she sneaked up to do me in?

I made myself stand very still in the middle of the floor. Aloud, I said, "Steady. Be calm. Your heart is still beating. There is hope yet. Steady. Be calm."

THE VIEWER!

If I looked at the viewer I could tell where she was.

Half expecting to see my own face in it, I stared at the screen.

A shabby building was on the viewer. Then she turned. She was looking at cars going by. She must be standing on a corner. Rush-hour traffic was heavy. People were going home.

Another view of the shabby building. The ground floor had a porno store. The second floor had a massage parlor. The third floor had the offices of the National Association of Mental Stealth. She looked back at the traffic.

My wits began to work. Didn't I know that building?

Krak turned and looked at it again. This time her eyes went to the fourth floor. Yes!

THE LAW OFFICES OF DINGALING, CHASE AND AMBO!

The Countess had it under surveillance!

There was a movement at the door which led to the upper floors.

Three girls came out. Did I know them? They looked familiar! One of them had an enormous belly. Maizie Spread!

The other two were Toots Switch and Dolores Pubiano de Cópula, the alleged Mrs. Wisters! Their pictures had been in the papers often enough for me to be absolutely positive. They were giggling and talking amongst themselves. They walked along up the street.

The Countess Krak, obscured by the rush-hour traffic from these poor, unsuspecting, innocent young ladies, BEGAN TO FOLLOW THEM!

I knew at once what was going to happen. The Countess Krak was going to rush up to them and stamp them into the pavement. I was watching a murder about to happen.

Oh, thank Gods, I had been in time after all. I grabbed the phone. I rang Dingaling, Chase and Ambo.

"Did you get the injunction order and the commitment papers on that female fiend?" I screamed into the phone.

"Oh, yes, certainly. The process server is right here this minute! This is Dingaling. Are you Smith? This sounds like hysteria!"

"It is hysteria! That demon is following your three clients! Get her served! Get her committed fast! LOOK OUT YOUR WINDOW!"

"Instantly!" said Dingaling.

I rang off.

I clutched the viewer with both hands.

Oh, thank Gods, I had not been too late after all.

The Countess was following the three girls. She was not twenty feet behind them. You could even hear their giggles and laughter above the traffic roar.

The dark Dolores seemed to be in particularly high spirits. She said something especially gay and then gave Maizie Spread a hard punch in the swollen abdomen. Toots Switch laughed uproariously, like a train whistle.

Oh, the poor dears. All too soon would their gay and innocent laughter be stilled! Come on, process server!

THERE HE WAS!

The shabby man in the shabby coat, his shabby hat hiding his alert eyes. He knew the Countess. He had seen her personally in the condo. He was walking right abreast of her. I expected him to whip around and present his paper.

He was looking back. Maybe he was waiting for the police to assist or the Bellevue wagon to arrive.

He must be very cunning. A process server would have to be. He was now a yard ahead of the Countess.

He turned!

He went racing back down the street, looking at everyone he passed.

The process server raced by the Countess Krak again. He raced by the girls.

He turned and came speeding back. He passed the Countess.

With a shock, I realized that she seemed to be invisible to him. He hardly glanced at her. What crazy magic was this?

The girls walked three blocks.

They turned to some steps and walked down into a restaurant and bar, still laughing loudly.

The Countess Krak remained on the street. She

walked over to the curb. She looked up and down.

Then she turned and walked into the restaurant.

The three girls had taken a table over to the side. Toots Switch was calling out, "Where's the (bleeping) proprietor of this crummy joint?"

"Bartender!" yelled Maizie Spread. "Move your (bleep) and bring three shots of rye over here!"

The Countess Krak walked straight over to them. "Flowers? Flowers?" she was saying in a quavery voice I did not recall ever having heard before.

She reached down into a bucket she was carrying and picked up three corsages of violets. She leaned over the table and, one, two, three, pinned them on the coats of the girls.

The process server brushed the Countess aside and leaned toward the three girls. "Have you seen a huge woman? A fiend?"

They laughed at him, the poor innocent dears. "You flipped your wig, Shover?" said Dolores. Oh, Gods, what courage in the face of death!

"You!" said the process server, whirling around to the Countess. "You see any foul fiend in here?"

The Countess put a red carnation in the buttonhole of his overcoat. "That will be one dollar please," she said.

The poor man. He looked so frustrated. He ripped the flower out of his buttonhole. He threw it on the floor. He stamped on it with violence. "I've missed!" he shrieked. He rushed away, looking everywhere.

The Countess reached over and picked up the purse of Toots Switch. She had it open. "That's five dollars for your corsage," she said.

Toots let out a screech. She snatched the purse back. "Get away from us, you old bag!" she yelled.

The Countess picked up Maizie's purse and opened

it and fished inside. "That's five dollars for yours," she said.

"Well, (bleep) you!" howled Maizie, and grabbed her purse back.

Dolores was more alert. She had her purse up in the air, removing it from reach. The Countess reached right across. She grabbed it and opened it.

A gruff voice sounded. "What's this row?"

Krak turned. It was the proprietor. She said, "They won't pay me for the flowers they bought."

The proprietor snarled, "Get out of here, you old (bleep)!" And he grabbed at the purse to recover it.

The purse spun on its strap.

It collided with the top of the proprietor's head.

He went down like a building had fallen on him.

The Countess Krak walked out.

A guy on the street stopped. He said, "I'll take one of those, mother." And he bought a bunch of carnations from her for five bucks!

With a shock, I realized that the Countess, with all her stage experience, had disguised herself as a flower seller! No wonder the process server couldn't recognize her! They were common as soot along that avenue! They stood along the street or on corners and sold them to drivers.

Oh, I could handle that!

I reached for the phone to make the call that would get her picked up and sent to Bellevue.

But wait. What was the Countess doing? She had stepped into an alley. There was a rear entrance light dimly above her.

She was reading three cards! Oh, (bleep) her, she had taken something from each purse!

ADDRESSES!

She had the addresses of those poor, defenseless innocents.

All three were the same! The girls lived together!

It was an apartment way up in the Bronx, miles and miles from where I was.

Oh, Gods, this was HORRIBLE!

I grabbed the phone.

"Chase here."

"The woman you're trying to get served and committed is disguised as a flower seller!" I screamed. "She's plotting to slaughter your three clients with smashing brass heels! ACT! ACT! ACT!"

"Do you know anything else, Smith?"

"Isn't that enough?" Why wouldn't they listen?

"I mean," said Chase, "do you know where the murders will be done?"

"YES! YES! YES! In their apartment! She has the address!"

"But that's impossible. Not even the press knows about it. And that's pretty extreme security for us when we have been letting reporters sleep with them to get good stories. I think you must have..."

"My information is correct! I have undercover men on it. Informers! GET THE POLICE!"

"No, no!" said Chase. "Business like ours is far too touchy to cut the police in on it. We don't do it that way. We have a tough security company we use. Real man-killers. We'll put them around the apartment at once with orders to shoot on sight and at long-range. We'll also go through the formality of serving the commitment paper if the person is only wounded. Have no fears, Smith. We do these things well and legally, always. Anyone who tries to reach them won't have a chance. Thank you for your timely warning."

I rang off. I was much relieved.

Thank Gods, Dingaling, Chase and Ambo and I were on the job.

The trap was laid.

The Countess Krak didn't stand a chance.

Is this the end of
the Countess Krak?

Read

Read

MISSION EARTH

Volume 7

VOYAGE OF

VENGEANCE

About the Author
L. Ron Hubbard

L. Ron Hubbard's remarkable writing career spanned more than half-a-century of intense literary achievement and creative influence.

And though he was first and foremost a writer, his life experiences and travels in all corners of the globe were wide and diverse. His insatiable curiosity and personal belief that one should live life as a professional led to a lifetime of extraordinary accomplishment. He was also an explorer, ethnologist, mariner and pilot, filmmaker and photographer, philosopher and educator, composer and musician.

Growing up in the still-rugged frontier country of Montana, he broke his first bronc and became the blood brother of a Blackfeet Indian medicine man by age six. In 1927, when he was 16, he traveled to a still remote Asia. The following year, to further satisfy his thirst for adventure and augment his growing knowledge of other cultures, he left school and returned to the Orient. On this trip, he worked as a supercargo and helmsman aboard a coastal trader which plied the seas between Japan and Java. He came to know old Shanghai, Beijing and the Western Hills at a time when few Westerners could enter China. He traveled more than a quarter of a million miles by sea and land while still a teenager and before the advent of commercial aviation as we know it.

He returned to the United States in the autumn of 1929 to complete his formal education. He entered George Washington University in Washington, D.C., where he studied engineering and took one of the earliest courses in atomic and molecular physics. In addition to his studies, he was the president of the Engineering Society and Flying Club, and wrote articles, stories and plays for the university newspaper. During the same period he also barnstormed across the American mid-West and was a national correspondent and photographer for the *Sportsman Pilot* magazine, the most distinguished aviation publication of its day.

Returning to his classroom of the world in 1932, he led two separate expeditions, the Caribbean Motion Picture Expedition; sailing on one of the last of America's four-masted commercial ships, and the second, a mineralogical survey of Puerto Rico. His exploits earned him membership in the renowned Explorers Club and he subsequently carried their coveted flag on two more voyages of exploration and discovery. As a master mariner licensed to operate ships in any ocean, his lifelong love of the sea was reflected in the many ships he captained and the skill of the crews he trained. He also served with distinction as a U.S. naval officer during the Second World War.

All of this—and much more—found its way into his writing and gave his stories a compelling sense of authenticity that has appealed to readers throughout the world. It started in 1934 with the publication of "The Green God" in *Thrilling Adventure* magazine, a story about an American naval intelligence officer caught up in the mystery and intrigues of pre-communist China. With his extensive knowledge of the world and its people and his ability to write in any style and genre, he rapidly achieved prominence as a writer of action adventure, western, mystery and suspense. Such was the respect of his fellow writers that he was only 25 when elected president of the New York Chapter of the American Fiction Guild.

In addition to his career as a leading writer of fiction, he worked as a successful screenwriter in Hollywood where he wrote the original story and script for Columbia's 1937 hit serial, "The Secret of Treasure Island." His work on numerous films for Columbia, Universal and other major studios involved writing, providing story lines and serving as a script consultant.

In 1938, he was approached by the venerable New York publishing house of Street and Smith, the publishers of *Astounding Science Fiction.* Wanting to capitalize on the proven reader appeal of the L. Ron Hubbard byline to capture more readers for this emerging genre, they essentially offered to buy all the science fiction he wrote. When he protested that he did not write about machines and machinery but that he wrote about people, they told him that was exactly what was wanted. The rest is history.

The impact and influence that his novels and stories had on the fields of science fiction, fantasy and horror virtually amounted to the changing of a genre. It is the compelling human element that he originally brought to this new genre that remains today the basis of its growing international popularity.

L. Ron Hubbard consistently enabled readers to peer into the minds and emotions of characters in a way that sharply heightened the reading experience without slowing the pace of the story, a level of writing rarely achieved.

Among the most celebrated examples of this are three stories he published in a single, phenomenally creative year (1940)—FINAL BLACKOUT and its grimly possible future world of unremitting war and ultimate courage which Robert Heinlein called "as perfect a piece of science fiction as has ever been written"; the ingenious fantasy-adventure, TYPEWRITER IN THE SKY described by Clive Cussler as "written in the great style adventure should be written in"; and the prototype novel of clutching psychological suspense and horror in the midst of ordinary, everyday life, FEAR, studied by writers from Stephen King to Ray Bradbury.

It was Mr. Hubbard's trendsetting work in the speculative fiction field from 1938 to 1950, particularly, that not only helped to expand the scope and imaginative boundaries of science fiction and fantasy but indelibly established him as one of the founders of what continues to be regarded as the genre's Golden Age.

Widely honored—recipient of Italy's Tetradramma D'Oro Award and a special Gutenberg Award, among other significant literary honors—BATTLEFIELD EARTH has sold nearly 7,000,000 copies in 26 languages and is the biggest single-volume science fiction novel in the history of the genre at 1050 pages. It was ranked in the top three of the 100 best English language novels of the twentieth century in the Random House Modern Library Reader's Poll. Additionally, this *New York Times* and international bestseller was voted the #1 science fiction novel of the twentieth century by the American Book Readers Association.

The *MISSION EARTH®* dekalogy has been equally acclaimed, winning the Cosmos 2000 Award from French readers and the coveted Nova-Science Fiction Award from Italy's National Committee for Science Fiction and Fantasy. The dekalogy has sold more than seven million copies in 13 languages, and each of its 10 volumes became *New York Times* and international bestsellers as they were released.

The first of L. Ron Hubbard's original screenplays AI! PEDRITO!—WHEN INTELLIGENCE GOES WRONG, novelized by author Kevin J. Anderson, was released in 1998 and immediately appeared as a *New York Times* bestseller. This was followed in 1999 with the publication of A VERY STRANGE TRIP, an original L. Ron Hubbard story of time-traveling adventure, novelized by Dave Wolverton, that also became a *New York Times* bestseller directly following its release.

His literary output ultimately encompassed more than 250 published novels, novelettes, short stories and screenplays in every major genre.

For more information on L. Ron Hubbard and his many acclaimed works of fiction visit the L. Ron Hubbard literary Internet sites at: www.galaxy-press.com, www.authorservicesinc.com and www.battlefieldearth.com.

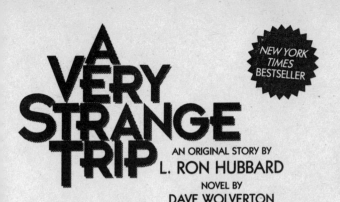

A VERY STRANGE TRIP

AN ORIGINAL STORY BY
L. RON HUBBARD

NOVEL BY
DAVE WOLVERTON

"*A WILD, HIGH-TECH RIDE!*"

— Brian Herbert, co-author,
Dune: House Atreides

While transporting a contraband Russian time machine and developmental weaponry, Private Everett Dumphee finds himself cast into new settings when the device suddenly activates. What follows are fantastic high-tech experiences that might be called the *ultimate off-road adventure.*

For the determined Dumphee—narrowly escaping with his life and three beautiful women—it is not necessarily a matter of will he make his destination, but when. These four vivid characters trek through this fun and fast moving journey like there's no tomorrow. Wherever that may be.

New York Times bestselling authors L. Ron Hubbard (*Battlefield Earth* and *Mission Earth®*) and Dave Wolverton (*Star Wars: The Courtship of Princess Leia*) deliver a highly absorbing and entertaining story with more than one interesting twist.